See Me
as I am

Cheryl Wanner

IMMORTAL WORKS
SALT LAKE CITY

Immortal Works LLC
1505 Glenrose Drive
Salt Lake City, Utah 84104
Tel: (385) 202-0116

Cover Art by Ashley Literski
http://strangedevotion.wixsite.com/strangedesigns

ISBN 978-1-953491-54-1 (Paperback)
ASIN B0C2MCGV31 (Kindle)

For my husband, Ed.
You're the inspiration!

Chapter 1

You know that killer awesome thing you can't imagine happening to you? Like, never in a million years happen? And then, impossibly, it does?

Well—it did.

And I'm on adrenaline overload, standing at the foot of the stage (waiting, actually) in Portland's Moda Center, fifteen minutes after my favorite band of all time—O'Shannon, direct to the U.S. from Cork, Ireland—cleaned up the most epic live performance ever.

Seventeen-thousand-plus people crowd from the arena, seats thudding, everyone talking, gear getting dragged over the stage floor above my head, and my best friend Morgan Townsend standing so close her body heat radiates into mine.

"Okay, this should be her now," Morgan hollers, over-the-mob-loud to be heard.

My Moda Center contact. The one I can't hear coming till she stops dead in front of me.

"Jenny Ryan?" Her voice has a southern flavor.

Not Oregon-born.

I blow out the breath I didn't know I was holding. "Yeah, hi." I reach out because it's less awkward for everyone if I make the first move. "I'm Jenny."

"Carrie Wallace, Guest Services." She takes my hand, shakes it. "I'll need to see your photo ID."

"Sure." I reach into the purse slung over my shoulder. Pull out my wallet, pop it open, flip it to face her.

My ID is always slotted first.

"Okay, thanks. Here's your pass." She places the laminated card in my hand. It hits the waistband of my jeans when I slip the lanyard over my head. "I'll take you in and bring you out. No idea who they've lined you up with, but you'll only have twenty minutes, so I'd make the most of it."

"Okay." The nerves I shoved down earlier jangle again in my stomach.

"Any chance I can come, too?" Morgan cuts in.

"I'm sorry," Carrie says. "Some acts are more flexible than others, but for this one, I'm only authorized to take Jenny."

"I do a great guide dog impersonation," says Morgan. "I got her down from our seats way up there." She's pointing, obviously.

I loop my arm through hers. "Seriously, she's good."

Hint, hint.

"I'd say yes if I could." Carrie's voice lifts with that extra bit of cheeriness you don't get from someone with a straight face. She slides in beside me. "You can take my arm if you like."

I have my cane folded inside my jacket pocket, but jarring as it is in here, I'm going to need an assist from somebody with working eyes.

Most of the time, that's Alexis. I actually *do* have a guide dog. But working her isn't always practical, like in tight-quartered stadium seating for brutally loud rock concerts.

"Sorry, Morgs." I detach myself from her arm.

She sighs massively, so no one misses the point. "No biggie."

Of course, it's a mega deal to her. She's totally into Kyle Finnegan (aka Kyle Finn), O'Shannon's lead guitarist, and she spent days going over what she was going to say if, by some unthinkable miracle—like the one staring me in the face—she got a shot at meeting him.

Carrie pulls my hand through her elbow, clearly trained on what to do. She's in a long-sleeved shirt, cotton fabric, and smells faintly of lavender.

"We'll be at the south exit in half an hour," she says over the top of my five-foot-flat.

"Sure." To me, Morgan says, "If you meet Kyle—"

I hold up the printed ticket she handed off for autographing. "Consider it done."

"Thanks. Good luck. Have fun." Her voice leaks so much I-wish-it-was-me I wince at leaving her behind. "Tell him hi for me."

If I get to meet him.

I'd rather meet Liam.

Kyle's phenomenal, don't get me wrong. But Liam is, well, to put it bluntly—earth-shattering.

And I've been a huge fan since he took over as frontman from his older brother, Michael O'Shannon. The band's been around five years, but nobody—unless they live in Ireland, the UK, or continental Europe—had heard of them till Liam ratcheted up their sound with his razor-edged vocals and raw lyrics that nail you with every word.

Carrie hauls me off, leaving Morgan behind.

"How was everything tonight?" she asks.

"*In*-credible."

Liam in the house, not filtered through my earbuds on Spotify. All that heavy guitar work and synthy strings at blistering decibel levels. The heat of on-stage pyro searing me halfway up the grandstand. And don't get Morgan started on the light show. She said it was more spectacular than the Fourth of July.

"I heard tickets sold out within forty-five minutes," Carrie says. "You're lucky to have grabbed seats."

"The VIP packages were gone before we could log in," I say. "We'd have *so* loved a pair of those."

Even if a meet-and-greet wasn't included.

"I had no idea they were so popular."

Working for the Moda Center doesn't necessarily mean she knows or likes her assigned events.

"They've gained a lot of ground since the release of *Tear at the Walls*," I say. "And this is their first North American tour."

"A sellout's a good start."

Carrie takes me through a curtained exit, thick fabric trailing over my shoulder, and into a corridor. Walls close in, echoes compress, and up ahead another corridor runs crossways full of voices and feet falling on cement. She stops several strides in, opens a door, and pulls me through.

Small room, mostly empty.

Trust me, I can tell.

"How'd you land a private meet-and-greet?" she asks.

"I wrote to O'Shannon Productions and asked if there was any chance of interviewing somebody for a write-up I'm doing for my school newspaper."

"And they said *yes?*" Clearly, she's amazed.

"They did."

Though it's doubtful anyone from the band actually saw my letter. Some office guru emailed me back with *we appreciate you writing to us,* and *we're sorry we can't accommodate your request* before tag lining *we hope you enjoy the show.*

Pretty much what I'd expected.

Then halfway through September, *this* landed in my inbox:

Dear Jenny Ryan,

Someone forwarded your email to me, and I've read it with interest. I've also looked at your blog site—you're talented and have well-defined goals—and I've talked this over with the band's manager, Michael O'Shannon. He authorized me to grant you limited backstage privileges, including a brief interview with one of our people at the Portland show in October. I will make all the necessary arrangements with the venue, and someone will contact you prior to the event.

Wishing you all the best,
Jameson Conway
O'Shannon Productions

Just like that, I was in.

And now that I literally *am* in, I can barely breathe. Because if

Liam walks through that door and says hi to me in his to-die-for Cork brogue—

"There's a chair if you'd like to sit." Carrie's voice shifts away as though she's forgetting herself and pointing it out to me. She's totally at ease, but I'm all sweaty palms and knotted-up stomach.

"I'm fine," I say.

Breathe, I tell myself. *Just...breathe...*

A woman's heels clip up the corridor, rebounding from the walls. She stops at the open door, knocks on the frame, then walks in without waiting for an invitation, bringing in the scent of mocha latte and rosy perfume.

"Hey, girl." The words, light and cheerful, target me.

Carrie steps over to meet her. "Thanks so much for doing this."

"Delighted to," the girl says. Bracelets jingle on her wrists. Her voice turns back to me, Cork Irish accent rising and falling like the notes of a song. "Would you be Jenny, like?"

"Yes," I say, all breathless.

"Hi. I'm Leslie. O'Shannon."

My feet freeze to the floor.

I recognize her now that she's given me a name to connect to the voice. Though, she sounds less polished, more everyday girl without the sound boost and whatever audio enhancements they used on her in the arena.

Leslie is Liam's younger sister. She's eighteen, a year older than me, and she opened the show with a forty-five-minute set from her pop/techno/dubstep debut, *Dance in the Rain*.

"Hi," I squeak out.

Great. I sound like a hyperventilating mouse.

"Happy to meet you, girl."

"Um, you, too." Hardly the professional first impression I'd hoped to make, but my brain's gone total freeze-up on me. I manage to offer my hand.

Her fingers are warm, long and slender. "We say *girl* and *boy* to everyone in Cork, don'tcha know. And *like*, too. Like, a lot."

I laugh a bit. "Same here. And you were fantastic out there tonight. Everything, all of it, was really great."

"Thanks," she says. "So one of our people linked your email to me. Not sure why they did, but you wrote a grand letter, to be sure, and I'd love to interview with you."

"Thank you so much."

For being Plan B, she's perfect!

"Happy to do it," she says. "Will I be gettin' you something to drink, like? We had Starbucks brought in if you want a latte or a cappuccino or anything."

"No, I'm fine. But thanks."

Not even the mocha-whatever in her hand, steaming into the air between us, sounds good right now.

"I'll be back in twenty minutes," Carrie says, and then out the door she goes, leaving me here with Leslie O'Shannon like she's just anyone I might happen to meet.

"Shall we sit?" says Leslie. "There's a chair, em...here." She takes my arm and tugs me four steps right and two steps forward, putting my hand on a metal chair back.

"Thanks."

I don't tell her I knew it was there.

Not a chair, exactly. Just...something.

It's hard to explain, but I hear things because they *are* there. More accurately, I pick up sound waves bouncing off them.

Her, for instance. She's taller than me (who isn't?) and model slim. Okay, that last part I got from Morgan. I'm not *that* good. But I'm more aware than most people give me credit for.

"I read your blog, so." Leslie drags up another chair, slides in opposite me. "And it's quite good. It's cool how you get on so well with everything." Her nails scrape the to-go cup in her hand. "And girl, I love your Irish name."

"Somebody on my dad's side came from somewhere over there." I slip my purse off my shoulder and onto the floor. "A long time ago, I think."

"Have you ever been?"

"No." I shrug out of my jacket and twist around to hang it on the back of my chair. Underneath, I'm wearing the *Tear At The Walls* t-shirt—the black one with the tour title and the band's name embossed in metallic green—I bought from the O'Shannon gear vendors on the concourse outside the arena.

"You should come," says Leslie.

"Someday, maybe."

"You'll love it," she says. "And I'm ready, like."

"Is it okay if I record this?"

"Sure, I don't mind."

I pull my Victor Reader Stream from my jacket pocket. It's an electronic device, smaller than my phone, with a face like a calculator. I use it to download books, articles, or podcasts and have them read back to me. It's also an audio recorder and easier to use as such than my phone.

I press and bookmark the record button.

My questions are few, and I've already adjusted them for her.

"Okay, um"—I suck in a breath—"did you always want to sing?"

"I wanted to be a fashion designer," says Leslie. "I didn't even know I *could* sing till maybe...two years ago. Didn't think I was that good, either."

"How'd you discover you had talent?"

"Liam heard me doing karaoke with my phone. He'd just moved up front with the band and said I should try being mic-ed with him. 'Sure, why not?' I said. 'Might be fun.' Next thing I knew, I was in the studio, cuttin' an album and then going on tour with 'em."

"Do you write your own songs?"

"Some of 'em. I didn't know I could do that, either. Liam writes some. Michael, too, of course. And Michael produced it, so he did."

"Is there a second album in the works?" I ask.

"I'm writing some stuff now, so I think there'll be another, like. *Dance in the Rain* seems to be doin' fierce well."

Her single *Where Can I Find You?* has already cracked the top twenty on the American pop charts.

"And what are your long-range goals?"

"I still want to be a fashion designer," she says. "This, the music, is just for now, for fun. I want to use the money to fund a fashion studio someday. In Cork City. Or Dublin, maybe."

"Do you design your stage outfits?"

"Sure, y'know," says Leslie. "Best part of the job."

"And your favorite thing about touring?"

"Seein' the world and meeting so many incredible people. Interacting with the audience. Watchin' them get into the music and up for the show is such grand craic."

"Crack?"

"Em, fun?" She shifts, her chair creaking beneath her.

"What's it like, getting up in front of so many people?"

"Deadly terrifying." She laughs again. "But once I get out there and into the music, I forget everything else and just have fun."

"And living/traveling/working with Liam? What's that like?"

"He's more intense on the road, to be sure, than he is at home. But we talk and tease each other a lot. Play cards and video games on the bus. He's just my brother, after all. And a great friend, too."

"So what's *he* like?" Totally grabbing this chance while I've got it. "Outside the publicity stuff, I mean."

"I grew up with him, so it's hard to think of him as anything but my brother. I guess I'd say he's a regular lad who got this powerful lucky break." Her voice drops as she bends over. Bracelets clink. Her cup settles onto the floor. She straightens again, and her voice smiles at me. "Will I ring him for ya?"

I stop breathing.

Seriously???

"Yes!" I fire off, all professionalism chucked aside. "Sorry, huge fan."

"I can see that, so. Right, then. Ringin' him now."

My settled-down nerves spike straight off the charts. I don't think

I take in air the whole time I sit waiting for him to pick up on the other end.

Please answer, please answer, haven't got a clue what I'm gonna say, but please answer—

"Hey, boy, it's me," Leslie says after a bit. "Ring me back."

Okay. Not answering.

My breath slides out. My heart plummets to earth.

"Sorry," she says. "He does that a lot—lets it go to voicemail. Somebody's always wantin' him for something."

"It's okay," I say like it's not the most epic non-moment of the night. "Thanks for trying."

"I'll make him sign something for you," she says. "Will you be wantin' another shirt, like?"

"That'd be perfect, thanks."

"Any particular style?"

"I was deciding between the one I'm wearing," I say, "and the breaking-down-walls design."

"I'll grab that one. Make 'em all sign, and put it in the post to you. Sorry, don't have time to track 'em down now. But I'll fetch you one of mine. Preference on that?"

"Whatever you choose," I say. "And it's okay to mail it."

"I'll only be a minute, girl." Leslie's already up and headed for the door. She stops, then turns back to me. "Use an iPhone?"

"Yes." My voice lifts at the end of the word.

She steps closer, shoves hers into my fingers. "When he rings you," she says, "answer him."

Then she's out into the corridor in her clippity heels, leaving me alone in this room with the power to talk to Liam O'Shannon in my hands.

Chapter 2

A door sighs open.

Not the one Leslie walked through and closed behind her, but one on the opposite wall.

I'm out of the chair so fast I dump my Reader from my lap. It skitters across the floor, off to my left somewhere. I drop to my knees, slapping Leslie's phone onto the seat behind me, then search, hands open, fingers spread, full-on blind girl mode.

Someone strides into the room—flat-soled shoes, guy steps, the door clicking behind him—and hunkers beside me.

"Oh—so sorry," he says in this straight from the BBC accent. "Let me get that for you." He puts the Reader into my hands. "Looks okay. Nothing broken, I don't think."

Everything feels okay.

And his voice is amazing. Moderately pitched and slightly husky, it's got that high-class London edge I hear from some of the Brit actors I watch (yes, I say *watch*, not *listen to*) on Netflix. It's a quiet voice but in a good way. Like he's naturally soft-spoken.

"Thanks." I switch off my Reader before it records any more of this.

"Jenny Ryan?" he says.

My mouth drops.

Seriously, how many people in this place know who I am?

"Um, yes?"

"Jameson Conway. Though I don't expect you to remember the name."

I do, actually.

We're still crouched on the floor together. Well, I'm kneeling. I'm not exactly sure what he's doing, just that he's down here with me, and he smells of spicy aftershave, wet hair, and something apple-scented. Shampoo, maybe?

"I made your arrangements for tonight?" he says like it's a question.

"Your name was at the bottom of my letter," I remind him.

"Right." He straightens or stands, whichever, then reaches down and touches my arm.

I flinch.

If I can't see it coming, expect a reaction. It's for me what something pouncing out of the dark is for you.

"Sorry," he says. "Didn't mean to startle you."

"No worries," I say.

"Shall I help you up?"

"I'm fine." I get to my feet, shoving the Reader into my jeans pocket.

"I see you've got the same mobile cover Leslie does," he says.

Say, what?

Oh, right. Her phone's lying on my chair.

"Um...it *is* Leslie's. She went to grab me one of her shirts and left her phone with me because—" Really, do I want to say the rest and look all groupie in front of this guy? "Anyway, she's coming right back, and—"

"I wouldn't count on it," he says.

"What?"

"She derails at the slightest thing. Somebody says hi, and she stands talking twenty minutes before she remembers she left you stranded somewhere."

"I don't have twenty minutes."

"I'll see she gets her mobile. And that you get your shirt. Might have to post it to you, but we have your address on record, so consider it done."

"Thank you." I hand over the phone.

It still hasn't rung.

"So, how'd it go with her?" he asks.

"It was—you knew I was interviewing her?"

"She asked me to set her up with you."

"Oh, wow," I say. "She was perfect, thanks."

"And the show?" he asks.

"Killer good."

"In Ireland, we say deadly. Deadly this, deadly that. Or fierce. Everything's fierce, especially if it's the weather. No matter what the weather may be."

I like his voice—how he says *ahhh* instead of *aaah* and the way he stretches out his vowels in *show* and *fierce,* giving them two syllables instead of one. Very posh, as they say over there. And slightly familiar. Like I've heard someone like him in a BBC series or a movie somewhere.

"You don't sound Irish," I say.

The country, I've read, has loads of accents, and only one is the classic Cork brogue most Americans expect when someone from the Emerald Isle opens their mouth.

"I'm, um...from London," he says. "Though I do spend a bit of time in Cork City."

"And you do what for O'Shannon Productions?"

"I'm..." He stops again. Like he's forgotten what he does. "An assistant publicist."

"You work with the media, then."

"Public relations stuff, yes."

"Which is why Leslie came to you with my letter."

"She was intrigued you'd taken the initiative to ask and thought it'd be fun to interview with an American girl her age."

"It was super cool," I say. "Thanks *so* much."

"Happy to have arranged it for you."

We're still where we were when we stood up, not that far apart.

I've scrambled together a rough sense of him. He's a head taller than me, give or take, and he's wearing jeans. Because jeans sound like, well, *jeans*. And the angle of his voice hits me roughly the same as my Dad's five-foot-ten.

"Your letter said you're from Sandy," he says. "Is that close by?"

"Twenty-five miles," I say. "Maybe...forty kilometers?"

"We still use miles in the UK."

"Okay, yeah. Forgot that."

"Did someone drive you? You took the bus?"

"I came with a friend. We drove to Gresham from Sandy, then took the MAX—the light rail—in from there."

"You have someone waiting, then."

"On the concourse. They wouldn't let her backstage with me."

"I should have authorized two passes."

"I won't tell her," I say. "She's still trying to get over not meeting Kyle Finn."

"Kyle's not meeting anyone tonight," says Jameson Conway. "He came off stage ill. Got sick all over the floor."

"Seriously?"

"Probably something he ate. Anyway, I liked your blog, especially your entries on blindness. They were, forgive me, eye-opening."

I crack a smile. "Thanks."

"You said you want to study journalism. Would that be newspaper journalism? Or writing for magazines?"

"Hm...not sure yet. Though I do lean toward covering arts and entertainment."

"Tonight was a good fit for you, then."

"Yes, absolutely," I say.

"Do you have a school in mind?"

"I'm applying to the University of Oregon for next fall. They've got a great journalism program."

"Good luck getting accepted," he says. "From what I read, you'll do well, whichever angle you choose."

"Thanks," I say again.

A text dings at me from my phone.

I ignore it, take a breath, offer another smile. "So would you, um... tell Liam I really liked his show? And that he—all of them—were just amazing?"

"I'd be happy to."

"And if it wouldn't be too much trouble"—I pull the tickets from my purse—"I'd love to get these signed for my friend and me. Her name's Morgan, and she's a huge fan of Kyle. Guess I said that already."

He takes the folded printouts from my hand. "See what I can do."

"Thanks *so* much."

Another text hits my inbox.

Yeah, already, Morgs.

"I should go," he says.

"Thanks again, Mr. Conway. For everything. I can't tell you how much I appreciate this, all of it."

"It's Jamie. And it was my pleasure." Still, he stands here, unmoving, like he's not ready to leave.

The moment stretches into awkwardness.

And I can think of nothing more to say.

Finally, he steps toward the outer door, stops, and says across the room. "Best wishes and safe travels wherever life may take you." And out he goes, taking my last chance of talking to Liam O'Shannon with him.

I sigh and pull my iPhone from my hip pocket, double-tapping the screen with two fingers. To navigate, I use VoiceOver, a built-in screen reader that speaks aloud whatever's under my fingertips and utilizes tap gestures to open apps or find what I'm searching for online. I ask Siri to bring up my messages.

Both are from Morgan.

Where are you?

Followed by—

Are you coming yet?

I've set the speed rate fairly high, so her words (in an Aussie guy accent) blitz past me like those rapid-fire disclaimers you hear at the end of some commercials.

"Coming soon," I send back.

Did you meet Kyle? (smiley emoji).

"I met Leslie O'Shannon. And Jameson Conway—the guy who got me back here in the first place? That's all."

Not Kyle? Or Liam, either?

What part of *all* did she miss?

"Sorry, no," I say. " Kyle's sick. Like, upchucking sick."

Poor baby. Does he need someone to take care of him? (grinning emoji).

"In your dreams," I say. "Be there soon."

Hurry, already. I'm starving, and everything's closed up here.

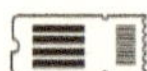

CARRIE ARRIVES MINUTES LATER, apologetic over whatever hung her up, and now she's on a mission to get me off her hands and out the door. I grab my purse, shrug on my jacket, pull out my cane, and flick its interlocking segments into place. We go out the way we came in, back into the arena, then up the grandstand stairs, and through an entrance onto the main concourse.

Footsteps pound over yards of empty cement at me.

"Took you, like, forever," Morgan grouses. "While you're off hanging with the rich and famous, I'm dying up here in nothing's-going-on-ville."

"I wouldn't classify Leslie O'Shannon as famous, not yet," I say. "And whoever heard of Jameson Conway?"

"Yeah, *you* get to meet a guy."

Carrie hands me off. "South exit straight ahead," she says. "You need to go now."

"Thanks for everything," I tell her, then turn to Morgan. "It's not like that. He's an assistant publicist. He was just making sure everything worked out for me."

"Still. A guy."

"Doing his assistant publicist job."

We reach the exits, and Morgan shoves open the door. A gust of wet-scented wind sweeps in, and we step out into the dripping October night.

"Hey, I'm sorry you couldn't go backstage with me," I say. "Seriously, I didn't think I had a chance at anyone from the band. Or even Leslie. I figured I'd get some public relations guy—"

"You did." Said like she's a tad jealous.

"Yeah, but I got her, too. And she's exactly what she projects on stage. Like she wants nothing more than to be your best friend."

"She does sound amazing. You took a selfie with her, I hope?"

"I was going to." And I launch into how my chat with Leslie derailed into a near-miss with Liam and a full-on meet/greet with Jameson Conway, and now I've got two autographed shirts coming in the mail along with our tickets, hopefully, signed.

"Wow, cool," Morgan says as we haul down the wheelchair ramp (quicker for me than taking the steps). "And thanks for handing off my ticket."

"I told him you adore Kyle. He said he'd see what he could do."

"Seriously, thanks."

The pavement levels out beneath my Nikes. Up ahead, a crosswalk announces itself with the word *wait* and the audible click of passing seconds.

"So did Leslie tell you everything you ever wanted to know about her brother?"

"Not even close," I say.

"Give you his number?"

As if.

"No, but I asked Jamie to give him a message from me."

"Wait—he's *Jamie* now?"

"He asked me to call him Jamie."

"Did *he* give you a number?"

"Seriously, Morgan."

We hit the intersection. I stand listening to cars crossing in front of me, the tip of my cane poised at the bottom of the curb, so I know how far to step down. Traffic switches up, the automated voice says *walk*, and Morgan tugs me into the street.

"So, what are you writing up?" she asks. "Don't say rock concert and pop artist interview. What else? Like is *Jamie* getting into it somewhere?"

"It's about the band, okay? And their show tonight. And what somebody from the band—okay, not the band, but close enough—says about her life and what she does." Water hisses beneath tires off to my right. Voices chatter on our heels. "Wanna give me a hand with the visual stuff? Like, what they were doing on stage and the light show and all that?"

"Love to." She stops me on the far side, and I find the curb with my cane. "But I don't think a hot publicist would hurt anything."

"He's not with the band. Not an opening artist, either." I step up. "And I'm hardly one to comment on his hotness. Or lack thereof."

We're almost to the Rose Quarter Transit Center, where the MAX dropped us off five-plus hours ago. Traffic runs behind us now, and voices rise and fall, people walking on all sides, gathering where three rail lines converge into one stop.

"You're gonna Google him, right?" Morgan says as we stand, waiting, on the sidewalk.

"What?"

"*Jamie* Conway. He's gotta be out there somewhere, linked to O'Shannon. Not on the official website, of course, but another one, maybe."

"Why should I want to?"

"Because he sounds intriguing," says Morgan. "And because I think you should."

Blindsight
"The World Through My Eyes"

By Jenny Ryan

People often ask me what it's like being blind, living in the dark, and am I always thinking about not being able to see?

First off, it's not dark for me. It's shadowy, and I can usually tell if it's daytime or if lights are on and what direction they're coming from. But no, I don't actually see anything in the sense that I can tell what it is I'm "seeing."

So what IS it like?

Well, close your eyes. Not just for a few seconds, but longer—say five or ten minutes. It's blank, right? Not black (unless, of course, it's nighttime). Just blank. Try it in the shower. Try finding your shampoo and conditioner, your body wash, and your razor (without cutting yourself), and see if you can do all that without looking. Not too hard. But try going outside somewhere, and you might want somebody's arm to hang onto.

Or how about this—listen to your friends talk without looking at them. How do their voices change when they move their heads? Yeah, you can tell when they're looking at you and when they're not. Or what kind of mood they're in. Or if they're standing or sitting. Though you might miss it if they walk off and leave you behind—unless, of course, you're paying enough attention to hear them do it.

Secondly, do I think about being blind all the time?

Not really.

I think about what's going on in my life at the moment, same as you do. Will I get a party invite this weekend? What should I wear to the Homecoming dance? How about for Halloween? Can my horse and I shave half a second off our best barrel time? Will I get into U of O's journalism program? And, hey, Christmas is coming in eight weeks. Should I be thinking of what to buy?

At first, the blind thing was all-consuming.

But now, it's just a piece of who I am. Like my dark hair and dark eyes. Or the smattering of freckles over my cheekbones. Or the scar on my ankle where I smacked a rock tubing down the Sandy River.

And not even an important piece, not really.

It's just...there.

Chapter 3

Morning hits me like a train wreck. Like I haven't slept at all, though there's this dreamless gap in my head that says I have. A sleep-deprived headache bangs behind one eye, and my brain is so shut down I have to think for a minute about where I am and why.

In bed. At home.

And I saw O'Shannon last night.

My gosh—O'Shannon!!!

Met and interviewed Leslie O'Shannon. Came within—well, I don't know what, but something close-ish, maybe—of voice-meeting Liam O'Shannon. Talked to junior publicist Jameson Conway who set the whole thing up and promised to put two autographed t-shirts in the mail to me.

And I managed to sleep after all that?

I roll over and bang into Alexis.

She has a bed, but she's climbed into mine, and now she's up, yawning with a doggy whine, rattling her tags and sniffing about, then squirreling her nose into my neck. I push her off, but she paws at my shoulder, noses my cheek, whines in my ear.

Get up, let me out, feed me, play with me, take me somewhere, let's go, go, go!

I roll the other way, fumbling one hand over my headboard, and punch the voice button on my clock radio.

Seven-oh-five, a woman says, American accent.

I groan and shove myself up, sitting here all fuzzy-brained, my face in my hands.

I didn't get in till after one last night or to bed before two. And I'm not likely to go back to sleep now, not with Alexis (all sixty-five yellow Lab pounds of her) crawling into my lap.

We've been together since the summer between my sophomore and junior years. You have to be sixteen to go to Guide Dogs for the Blind, and I'd been waiting since I was thirteen, which is when I finally accepted I wasn't going to see again and might as well make the best of myself as I am.

Most kids can't wait to get their license and buy a car.

Me? I wanted a dog.

Training with a guide dog means spending two weeks at the school. They've got a location three miles northwest of here in Boring.

Seriously, that's the name.

They started me out the first morning with an empty harness and an imaginary dog. That afternoon, they brought Alexis to my room and gave me some treats to help us bond. They match you up—personality, walking gait, lifestyle—with the right guide, and you spend the rest of your time there working together, becoming a team.

Alexis is the best thing that's happened to me since that awful day my world fell into shadow. She's my BFF, my eyes, my companion, and yes, my pet, too. Walking with her is way better than caning. Like I'm flying free, not blind at all (except for the not seeing part).

I shove her down, swing my legs over the bed, and pull on my U of O Ducks slippers (yes, with Duck heads on them). Grab my phone off the nightstand and let Alexis out of the room. She pads down the hall ahead of me, jangling her tags toward the stairs.

I've mentally mapped every step in this place. I know exactly how many it takes to get from here to there, where to turn, or how high to reach for whatever I want or need. Mom and my younger sister, Kaitlin, are good about keeping things where they belong, so I don't trip over Kait's Skechers or her gym bag or paw through the linen closet for something Mom relocated elsewhere.

I go down without touching the banister and flop my Duck heads through the dining room and into the kitchen.

Eggs pop on the stove. Bacon sizzles and spits. Coffee and grease scents mingle with traces of the Pad Thai Mom made last night for herself and Kaitlin.

She cooks actual breakfast on the weekends, but not usually this early. Clearly, she has plans for the day.

"Didn't expect to see you up so early," she says.

"Couldn't get back to sleep." I rake a hand through my flatter-than-flat hair, cut just below my shoulders with bangs and a bunch of wispy layers.

"So, how *was* it, Jenn?" Kaitlin's at the table in the squeaky chair that gripes every time she shifts her weight.

Finding her up at this ungodly hour has to be even more shocking than seeing me. Especially since she had a volleyball game last night, followed by the inevitable hang time with teammates and friends.

"To *die* for," I say.

"Who'd you interview?"

"Leslie O'Shannon."

"Wow!" Kaitlin's a total pop girl, and Leslie is exactly who she'd want to meet. "What'd she have to say?"

"In a minute." I tip my chin toward Alexis, nail-clicking over the mud room floor like she can't hold it in much longer.

I take her out on leash, so I know where she's squatting and can find and dispose of what needs picking up. She's trained to go on command. I say, "Do it," and she does.

Back inside, I fill her water bowl, one finger poked over the edge to tell me when to turn off the faucet. Despite her hopeful expectations, feeding time is only in the late afternoon or early evening because I don't want to deal with the doggy bag thing between classes at school.

I'm clearing the kitchen doorway, all set to drop the deets on last night, when Mom says from over by the sink,

"I'm planning a family meeting for tonight."

She says it deliberately like she's put a lot of thought into it. So this is not a let's-plan-for-your-birthday-Kait or what-would-you-girls-think-of-going-to-your-grandparents-for-Thanksgiving kind of meeting.

"Just the three of us?" I find my pumpkin spice capsule, labeled with a Braille sticker, and pop it into the Nespresso. Take a mug from the tree, slide it onto the drip grid, and press the button.

"Well..." she starts.

"Sorry, got plans for tonight," says Kaitlin. "Going to Natasha's for a movie with Malia and Hannah."

"You didn't clear it with me ahead of time," says Mom. "You're not going."

"Wait, what?" Kaitlin's phone slaps onto the table. "Mom, we've been planning this for two weeks now. We can't just—"

"Bryan's free this evening, but not tomorrow," Mom says. "And then we're into weekday schedules. I need you and Jenny tonight, or we'll be looking at next weekend."

And there you have it.

Bryan McKenzie is Mom's boyfriend. She's been seeing him for eight months, and it's a pretty solid relationship, best I can tell. I mean, he's the first guy she's brought home overnight in the three years since she and Dad split up, so I guess that says something right there.

And as boyfriends for my mom go, Bryan's first-rate. He treats her like a queen and takes us shopping and bowling, hiking in the Columbia River Gorge, skiing on Mt. Hood, crabbing on the north Oregon Coast, and whitewater rafting out of Maupin.

He won Kaitlin over in nothing flat.

He's still working on me.

Because Dad's still in love with Mom, though he tries not to be obvious about it. And I'm little-girl romantic (or naïve) enough to believe the prince wins the princess, the Ugly Duckling wears the crown, and Humpty Dumpty gets put back together again.

But the way Mom and Bryan have stepped up their relationship, I guess it's past time to ditch the fairytales and get on with real life. I just can't see it being so final—my folks staying separate the rest of their lives and me caught somewhere in the middle.

Kaitlin huffs, slides her phone off the table, and taps at the screen. "Fine," she grouses. "Whatever."

"So, where are we doing this?" I ask.

"Not sure yet." Mom scrapes the eggs from the skillet. The grease has stopped spattering, so the bacon's off the burner. "I'm going to Clackamas Town Center this morning if you girls want to come."

"Not me." I grab my mug from the drip grid. "I want to update my blog and start on my article."

And I'm hoping Morgan can come over later so we can download our concert pics and videos (I shoot my own) and choose the best ones for my write-up and for posting on Instagram and Facebook. Then we'll move on to the English essay she needs help with.

"Can you drop me at Hannah's on the way?" Kaitlin asks. "We're trying to scramble together a movie plan for tomorrow night."

"I'm leaving here at nine-thirty," says Mom. "I'll pick you up at four, and you"— her voice angles toward me—"after that. Plan for dinner at six. Somewhere out."

Yeah, big announcement on deck.

One I'm not ready to hear.

M e going blind at age twelve had nothing to do with Mom and Dad splitting up and getting divorced a year later.

Or so I've been told.

All I can say is they got along pretty well before my accident, and then everything took a giant U-turn and went due south. Mom left and hauled Kaitlin and me with her, and when the final papers were signed, she got custody, and Dad ended up with visiting rights.

He never wanted a divorce in the first place.

My accident was such a fluke it's hard to believe it actually happened. I was riding some old service road in Forest Park with my best friend, Tiffany Whitman, both of us up bareback (no helmets, of course), when her horse flushed a wild turkey and side-jumped into mine. And off we went in a tangle of arms and legs and hooves that managed not to trample us.

Tiffany walked away, banged up and bruised, but otherwise fine.

I spent ten days at OHSU in west Portland undergoing CT scans, MRIs, surgery (removing and reassembling pieces of my skull, some embedded in my optic nerve), ICU recovery, and all sorts of assessments. I suffered vicious headaches (still do sometimes) and skewed balance, and I could barely put a cohesive sentence together.

That, and I was blind.

Vision loss due to traumatic brain injury is usually partial and temporary. As a result of optic nerve damage, more likely permanent.

My options were:

1. Optic decompression surgery (a dicey procedure)
2. Steroid treatments (of questionable effectiveness)
3. Surgery *and* steroids
4. Leaving well enough alone.

I had the surgery. I took the steroids. My brain recovered. My vision did not. It was and still is this fuzzy mesh of gray, shifting blurs that add up to...nothing.

What was I to do now?

How could I be *blind?*

What do blind people do, anyway? How do they even live?

I folded into myself and refused to come out. Wouldn't eat, wouldn't talk anymore than I had to, wouldn't lift a finger to do anything, wouldn't even get out of bed some days.

Tiffany came to visit for a while.

My mom shunned her. I ignored her. Eventually, she dropped out of my life and never came back.

I missed most of seventh grade, catching up on my studies with a private tutor. I had to do physical therapy, speech therapy, counseling, and orientation and mobility training for the blind. Insurance covered a good share of the costs, and most blind services are free.

Even so, my parents fought about money. They fought over who was to blame. They fought over what to do with me.

"She's got to learn to do for herself, Karen." Dad's voice from the top of the stairs.

"She can do nothing for herself!" Mom's voice from beyond my doorway.

"Because you do it all for her."

"Then you handle it, Ethan! Because I can't take much more!"

I kick the door shut only to trip over the jacket I've thrown down and sprawl onto the hardwood floor, tears pouring from my useless eyes, silent screams rising to the heavens.

God, why'd you do this to me???

My OMS (Orientation and Mobility Specialist) gave me her best shot.

Her job was to make a successful blind person out of me. That meant learning to navigate my house, get up and down the stairs, make my bed, hang my clothes, pour my own milk, fry my own eggs, and a million other things everyone does every day and thinks nothing of. It meant caning down sidewalks and knowing when to cross streets and when to stand waiting for the light to change (not all intersections have talking sensors). It meant labeling my clothes, folding my money in different ways, and putting on makeup without leaving smears. It meant holding my head up and aiming my face at whoever's talking and learning to hear the world around me, to know what was where, and how to recover myself when I misjudged and made mistakes.

Six weeks into it, this gal, Trisha Parks, said she'd had it up to here (wherever that was) with my attitude, and if I wanted to sulk around, hating my life, fine. But she was done wasting hers on me.

"You've got three days," she said and stalked out, banging the door behind her.

I got the memo.

Things would never get better unless *I* made them better, and some stuff I was stuck with no matter what. Did I seriously want to spend my days rotting away in a corner, crying my eyes out one minute, ripping everyone to shreds the next? If life sucked enough with Trisha Parks in it, how unlivable would it be if I chose to flounder through on my own?

It took time, but I worked at turning things around, and little by little, my world shifted into place. Mom relaxed her stranglehold and let me do as much as I was ready for. Eventually, I stopped thinking about being blind twenty-four-seven. And some days, I didn't think about it at all.

By then, she and Dad were long over.

She moved Kaitlin and me to Sandy while Dad stayed in northwest Portland in the only place that had ever been home to me.

Mom established herself as a real estate agent in a new market, and her share of the divorce settlement took us from the two-bedroom apartment she'd rented to the three-bedroom house she's now buying.

She met Bryan last year through this commercial deal she was handling. He was the developer of the project, so of course, they spent time together.

"Just a business dinner, not a date."

"We're getting together to discuss the terms of the contract."

"Strictly a business meeting"—who was she kidding?—*"I promise you."*

Next thing we knew, she was bringing him home for dinner on the weekends, and he was taking us on day trips, trying to convince us he belonged in the family.

And maybe he does.

I mean, he half lives here already.

And I like him fine. He's just...*not* my dad.

So I roll with it, play along. Like I'm not seeing all those second chances I tried to give Dad crumble forever.

"Okay," I say to Mom's heads up about the evening. I lift my voice on the last syllable and smile like it's all good.

She knows where I stand.

We're on to breakfast now, and I'm giving Kaitlin the blow-by-blow of O'Shannon on stage and my interview with Leslie. Kait is suitably wowed and cranks out the questions. But I'm thinking again of what Morgan said about looking Jamie up online.

I *am* curious, never mind how I blew her off last night.

Upstairs in my room, I open my laptop.

For computer stuff, I use JAWS (Job Access With Speech), an internet browser that reads text to me. The various keyboard commands let me navigate web pages or buy stuff online or whatever else I want to do. JAWS is also a screen reader, talking as I type, giving me every letter I put down and reading back each word I've written.

I bring up O'Shannon's official website to look for any possible mention of Jamie Conway.

Nothing, of course. He's not part of the band and only indirectly involved in their career, so *nobody* as far as the public is concerned. The only non-band member profiled is Michael O'Shannon as founder, former frontman, and current manager and producer.

Inputting O'Shannon lead publicist Richard Vaughn's name gets me a few links but very little info. Certainly nothing about anyone working under him.

Jamie isn't listed on Wikipedia or fan-based sites or under any search combinations like *O'Shannon Productions Personnel, O'Shannon Band Publicity/Public Relations,* or *O'Shannon Band Jameson Conway.* And there's nothing under his name alone.

Oh, there are Jameson Conways—the name's not *that* unique— but none with any connection to O'Shannon Productions. Online White Pages for London aren't specific enough. Facebook, Twitter, and Instagram profiles don't fit the bill, and a profile pic is meaningless because JAWS only says *person smiling* or whatever, and that could be anybody—even if I knew what Jamie looks like, and I don't. And I'm not ready to throw the question out to the O'Shannon fan groups and fan pages I follow like I'm some kind of stalker.

I shut down my computer.

Water goes off in the shower. Kaitlin's finally done, so now it's my turn. I'm out in nothing flat, pulling on a pair of soft, worn jeans and the gray sweatshirt I wear for camping, fishing, or lounging around the house.

All my clothes, whether in drawers or on hangers, are arranged by color—black to the left, purple next, then blue, red, and on through the lighter end of the spectrum. If in doubt, I have a phone app for color identification. I've also attached little Braille tags inside collars or waistbands that give the brand name or logo or some other distinguishing mark, and I make and insert them myself with my Braille labeler.

The house is stone quiet; Mom and Kaitlin are already gone for the day. What's left of the rain drips from the eaves, and I have horse chores to do before I even think about getting to my article.

I shoot Morgan a text—"Call me when you're up"—then trot downstairs behind Alexis and pull on my dirty job boots and a ratty jacket before heading outside.

Alexis dashes off the deck and into the yard. We take the path covered in wood shavings down toward Cedar Creek, rattling over rocks and big enough for the fall salmon to come struggling up from the Sandy River. The wind, damp and crisp, smells of decaying leaves and cedar and Douglas fir trees, a trace of wood smoke on the air.

I turn onto the barn path without thinking about it, same as I don't think where to stop and reach for the sliding door.

Tanner whickers as I come through and bangs his head over the gate, hooves sucking at the mix of straw and manure I get to muck out this morning.

"Hey, there, boy." I reach out, and he whuffles my hand, lips at my fingers. I slide them up his face and scrub the swirled hairs beneath his forelock.

My eyes burn.

Mom cozying up to Dad beside the campfire, her hand on his knee, his arm around her shoulders. Me staring into the flames while Kaitlin blackens her marshmallow beneath the stars at Trillium Lake...

Dad scooping me from the sand after I wipe out my skimboard at Rockaway Beach, both of us wet and laughing. Mom grabbing the board, hollering, "My turn!"

Bryan in the middle of everything...

Mom laughs with him now. Sits with him on the bleachers at Kaitlin's games. Sleeps with him down the hall from me on some nights and expects me not to mind.

What am I supposed to say to this super nice guy who maybe

wants to be my stepdad while I'm still dreaming of my real dad getting back together with my mom?

They're never getting back together.

Why can't you accept that and move on?

I swipe at my eyes—*why am I crying over this?*—and grab a halter and lead from the peg by the tack room door.

Mom's rigid about no riding when I'm home alone, but it'll only be for a few minutes, and I won't leave the paddock.

Not like she's here to know, anyway.

I'm lifting the gate latch when a car grinds over gravel on Cedar Creek Lane.

It's a narrow track, hard to find, vanishing into thick timber off steep and twisty Ten Eyck Road, and hardly anybody comes out this way unless they live here or they're visiting someone who does.

I slide through the gate and shove Tanner over to make room for me, conscious of his feet stepping away from mine. I run my hands up his neck, pull his head down into the halter, and buckle the strap along his cheek. I'm swinging the gate open when the car slows and wheels into our driveway.

The engine idles, then shuts down. A door creaks open, closes with a click.

I mop up the last of my tears and lead Tanner into the wind, Alexis padding ahead, barking at whoever's invaded our property.

"Quit it," I tell her.

She quiets and pads back to me, tail banging my thigh.

Footsteps crunch gravel across the driveway, then stop. Like whoever's making them is looking around, wondering if they're in the right place or should drive farther on.

Down they come, over the wood shavings toward the barn.

I stop and stand waiting, holding Tanner in.

The steps scrape up to me, stop again. Finally, this voice says out of the gray fog that is my world, "You do amaze me, Jenny Ryan."

I blink. I drop my jaw though I don't remember doing it.

I'm good with voices. At least ones I know or have just interacted with, especially if they're distinctive. Like this one.

Guy-voice, soft-spoken, slightly husky, classically English, naggingly familiar.

Jameson Conway.

How did he find me?

No, wait—that wouldn't be too hard. He has my address. *And* my phone number as both were required for setting up my interview.

But why would he want to?

Okay, there are the shirts he promised me. But Kyle's sick, right? He couldn't have signed anything yet, could he?

"What are you *doing* here, Mr. Conway?" My voice comes out just above a whisper.

His voice projects as pleased. "Hi, Jenny."

Pleased that I recognized him right off? That he accomplished his mission, whatever it might be? Or is he actually happy to be here?

I'm acutely aware that I'm dressed for stacking wood, mucking out stalls, or working in the yard. No makeup, of course. *Are my eyes still wet? Please, God, don't let them be red...* I've got an Arab/Quarter Horse on a lead, head hanging over my shoulder. And there's this guy interested enough in something about me to be standing in my yard on a day when rain's about to fall out of the sky.

"I read in your blog that you ride," he says. "That's brilliant."

Because I'm blind, and I do it?

No, no, take it as the compliment he intends.

"Thanks," I say.

"And this must be Tanner's Secret?"

He remembers my horse's name...

"Yes, he's my pretty boy." I slap Tanner on the shoulder. "We're going into the paddock for a bit. But you haven't answered my question, Mr. Conway. *Why* are you here?"

"It's Jamie," he says. "And I've got your shirts for you."

Already? What about Kyle?

Don't you have to be on a tour bus to Seattle/Tacoma for a show tonight?

Wait, that's tomorrow night. Seattle was the fallback plan if Morgan and I couldn't get tickets for Portland, so that date's burned into my brain.

"You could have mailed them," I say, an über lame response to this guy wanting to give me something over-the-top cool.

Morgan would kill me.

But hey, I don't know Jamie Conway. And amazing as this is, it's too weird, him standing here after driving all the way from Portland when he could have dropped a package at the nearest post office.

Or at least called in advance to make sure I was home.

"I wanted you to have them now rather than later," he says. "Besides, we've got the day off, and I felt like taking a drive. Even if your motorways *are* backward and your steering column's on the wrong side of the car."

I crack a smile.

He steps into my space, bringing the scent of apple shampoo and spicy cologne with him, his leather jacket creaking with every move he makes. "Shall I hand these to you or—"

"Um—give me a second." I tie off the lead at the hitching rail, then swipe my horsey palms over my jeans. "Okay." I reach out, and he puts a shirt, folded like the one I bought last night at the merch table, into my hands.

"This one's Leslie's. It's blue with a sketch of her on the front.

She signed the back in silver—big, round letters, classically her. *Jenny*, she says, *wishing you all the best—Leslie O'Shannon.*"

"Wow, thanks," I say.

"She's sorry she didn't get back to you last night. Somebody pulled her aside—happens all the time with her—and the next thing you know, twenty minutes had gone, and so had you."

"It's okay. Tell her thanks. And that it's all good."

"Will do." He hands me a second shirt, folded like the first. "And this is O'Shannon's black-and-bronze, breaking-down-walls design with the North American tour dates on the back. Per your request. Shall I show you where everyone signed?"

"Yes, please."

He takes the hand I offer—*why do I flinch when I know what's coming?*—and touches my fingers to the fabric where I trace both the printed design and overlying pen strokes.

"Liam went dead center on top of the dates," he says. "Long sweeping lines, very theatrical. Kyle angled his across the shoulder." He guides my hand to the right. "He's still not doing great, but he said he could hold a pen, so there you have it. And here"—he slides my fingers down the fabric—"is Sean's. Keenan's right below Liam's, Courtney on the lower left, and Declan on the shoulder above." He drops my hand—*why is it tingling?*—but doesn't step back.

Watching me, no doubt.

Waiting for my reaction?

"Wow, this is so cool," I say.

Yeah, I can pull my phone from my hip pocket, take a photo, and have VoiceOver verify what he told me. But I *felt* the pen strokes. And he's here, isn't he? He wouldn't have driven out just to chat, would he? He's a busy guy, and I'm nothing to him but a promise to keep.

"Thanks *so* much." I tuck the shirts into the crook of my elbow. "But really, you didn't have to go to all this trouble."

"I didn't mind," he says. "And here are your tickets." He slips the folded sheets into my fingers. "Signed as requested."

Less than twelve hours after I asked for this.

"Thanks," I say. "Like, a lot."

"Kyle signed your friend's *To Morgan, love Kyle.*"

"Oh, excellent! She'll eat that up."

"He thought she might." Another sheet crackles open in his hands. "And this is for you. From Liam."

My mouth goes dry. "He *wrote* me something?"

"Leslie meant him to ring her for you, and he didn't get on it like he should have. Shall I read it to you?"

"Yes, please." Because I'd way rather hear it in Jamie's real-life King's English than the recorded guy on my phone.

"'*Jenny,*'" he says, "'*so sorry we didn't connect last night. Next time we're in your area, I'll see what I can do about getting you the seats of your choice. With sincere regrets, J. Liam O'Shannon.*'"

I swallow. Gulp, even.

Liam (first name Jonathan) O'Shannon wrote to me *personally?* He's offering me seats to a future show, seats of my choice? He's going to get them for me *himself?*

I'll take front row, either side of the stage or facing the runway if he can manage it.

Wouldn't anyone?

"Wow, Jamie, I don't know what to say. This is incredible!" And then I grin.

Like the Cheshire Cat, I suppose.

"Express delivery to you," he touches the paper to my hand.

I take it from him like it's the deed to the White House. "This is super cool. Thank Liam for me, too, please?"

"Consider it done."

And then we say nothing.

Unbelievable, really, because I've got this O'Shannon Productions guy standing in front of me with time to kill, apparently, and I'm doing nothing to take advantage of it.

Meanwhile, he waits. For what, I don't know. Watching me,

perhaps. Or maybe he's taking in the trees, creek, and neighboring properties slotted into this narrow track through the timber.

Clearly, he's in no hurry to go.

"Listen, I, um—" He stops.

I wait.

"This is...really beautiful, Jenny," he says. "You have a stream?" His voice turns away. "You can fish here?"

"For trout, yes. For salmon coming up to spawn, no. You have to go to the river for that." I wave in the direction of the fish hatchery where Cedar Creek dumps into the Sandy River. "It's not far."

His voice slants back at me. "Like being on holiday year-round."

"I guess so."

What *was* he going to say before he redirected into something else?

"And this must be your guide dog?" Her tongue's slathering over his hand, paws scattering shavings, tail whapping his leg. "Alexis, right?"

"You read about her, too."

"Yes, and she suits you, I think. I had a black lab growing up. His name was Bear."

"Good name," I say.

"I'd have asked before petting her, but she basically invited herself."

"She's a people person. But when she's working, she has to stay focused."

"True of all of us, I think," says Jamie Conway. "Can I ask how you ride alone? Or did I miss that somewhere?"

"I'm not supposed to ride alone," I admit. "So I didn't write about it."

"Your secret's safe with me."

"Thanks. Anyway, the paddock's easy. Not very big, as you can see, and the dimensions are all in my head. I have a sense for how many strides it takes to get from one end to the other at the different gaits. Or to a lap if we're doing circles. I orient by sound, too—where the creek is in relation to where I am. Or the road, if a car's driving down. And by feel—where the wind's coming from. Or the sun, if it's shining. And in an arena or on trail, I use a headset."

"Brilliant," he says.

"That's how I was trained and how I ride with Morgan. We both compete in OHSET—Oregon High School Equestrian Team. Morgan or my coach uses one headset, I use the other, and they transmit whatever directions-slash-info I need to stay on course."

"I did read about that," he says. "And your injury, too. So sorry that happened. Though I'm glad you didn't let it keep you from doing what you love."

"I did for a while. My dad pushed me to ride again."

"Good for your dad."

"Yeah, he's pretty cool," I say. "He helped me buy Tanner after convincing my mom one horse accident didn't doom me to another. And he paid for my riding lessons. And part of the barn, too."

I stop.

Here I am, prattling on to this Jamie Conway like we might actually get to know each other, and yet I'm never going to see him after today. Why am I wasting my once-in-a-lifetime chance to gather some off-the-record info?

"So, um—O'Shannon." Like it's not *the* subject on my brain. "How'd you end up working for them?"

"I—" He stops, same as he did last night. "I have, um... connections in Ireland. My name's Irish though most of my family lives in the UK. I heard the band was looking for someone with communications skills to work under Richard Vaughn—their publicist—and I knew the right people. Or rather, the right people knew me."

"What's it like working for them?"

"Crazy. Hectic. Always an adventure." Shavings shift and slide beneath his feet. "They make it worth my while."

I'm sure they do.

"So what can you tell me that I'd never guess in a million years?" I ask.

"About the band or—"

"The band. If it's okay to ask."

"Of course. What would you like to know?"

"Something about Liam would be great. And I won't write it up anywhere, ever, I promise."

"Hm, let's see..." His voice warms a shade. "He speaks French, German, and Irish—called Gaeilge in its own language. It's a required subject in Irish schools, and you see it on road signs, city and business signs, just about everywhere. Along with English, of course. Most people don't speak much of it unless they're from one of the *Gaeltacht* villages."

Liam's not, I know that much. He's from Innishannon (*shannon* being Irish to the core and common as shamrocks over there), and he's fluent in Gaeilge, so obviously, he studied it elsewhere.

"It sounds really cool." At least, what he spoke on stage and sang in the band's Celtic song set did. "So, um, anything else?"

"Mm...he loves traditional Irish food. And Guinness, of course. Who doesn't over there? Italian and Mexican food, too. Anything spicy, in fact. And...what else? Likes photography and all kinds of music, not just the heavy stuff he does with the band. You know he was trained as a classical pianist?"

"He played sonatas and inventions and toccatas and such."

"You know music."

"My sister played piano for a while," I say.

"He still plays Chopin and Mozart for his mum." More scrabbling of shavings underfoot. "And, mm...he likes American action films, but also our BBC programming. Reads John Grisham, James Patterson, Tom Clancy, to name a few."

"Are his eyes really that color?"

They're this amazing, intense blue-green, says Morgan. Like the ocean in Hawaii or the Bahamas (she's not been to either one) and even more striking because his hair, layer cut and a little longish in the back, is so dark.

"Close enough," says Jamie. "He's enhanced them a bit with colored contacts."

"Does he have a best friend? Kyle, maybe? Someone else from the band? Is there a love interest somewhere?"

Just because everything trending out there says no to the last question doesn't mean something isn't brewing and yet to be leaked.

"Love interest, no, not at the moment. So you've still got a shot if that's the goal."

"Um, not likely."

"Field's wide open," he says. "As for who he hangs out with—well, Kyle and the rest of the lads, sure. But I'd say his best mate is probably Darren Richardson. Private security guy; works directly for him. And that's first-rate insider information."

"I'll keep it under wraps, I promise." Alexis pads over and bats my leg with her tail. I scrub behind her ears. She twists her neck, licks my hand. "I know Michael started the band. Why did he quit it? All I can find online is that he turned the mic over to Liam three years ago, but nobody says why."

"Michael's more of a detail guy," says Jamie. "Very talented, don't get me wrong. But better behind the scenes. And the company handling them at the time didn't have his vision, so he took over management himself. Besides, Liam's more marketable."

Harder-edged vocals.

More energetic stage presence (or so I hear).

"Definitely the right move," I say.

I mean, Michael did amazing lead on *Fire and Ice*. But nothing like the powerhouse you get with Liam fronting *Into Infinity* and *Tear at the Walls*, especially with the addition of epic choir vocals behind the band on *TatW*.

Jamie steps to one side. "So what can I do to help? Fetch your tack, perhaps?"

He knows at least something about horses.

"Um, sure. You could grab a bridle from inside the tack room next to the stall."

"Does it matter which one?"

"Not really. And would you lay these"—I hold out the shirts—"over one of the saddles, please?"

"Happy to," he says and packs them off toward the barn, Alexis padding after him.

I zip Liam's note into my jacket pocket along with the signed tickets. Like I'm taking a chance of them falling onto the barn floor or the wind kicking up and blowing them into the woods where I'll never find them.

"Oh, and would you grab me a curry comb," I holler after him, "and a hoof pick—if you know what those are."

"I do, yes," he says back at me.

"Thanks. They're in a bucket on the floor. And my helmet's hanging next to the bridles, if you don't mind."

"No problem."

Seriously, I'm asking favors of this guy?

Well, he offered, didn't he?

Jamie's back shortly, handing off my English bridle. I pull it over my shoulder, then take the helmet from him, and hang it on the end post.

"Here's the comb," he says. "And the pick, too."

"Thanks."

"Shall I fetch your English saddle?"

"Actually, I'm going bareback, an old habit I've never been cured of."

"What else can I do?"

"Nothing, thanks."

I scrub the comb over Tanner's coat, then pick his hooves clean, bracing one leg after another against my knee.

"Shall I give you a leg-up when you're done?"

"Sure, thanks," I say.

Why *is* he going so far out of his way for me?

"And then I should probably go," he adds. "Some of us want to see a bit of Portland before the bus leaves at eight."

"Check out Waterfront Park on the Willamette River," I tell him. "And Tilikum Crossing—the pedestrian bridge—over to the east side. And get some donuts at Voodoo. You might have to wait in line for an hour, but it's a classic Portland experience."

"Thanks for the heads-up."

"Thanks for the cool insider info." I find the post, snap on my helmet, leave the comb and pick in its place.

"Shall I put these back for you?" Jamie asks.

"No, I'll get 'em later."

I slide the bridle off my shoulder and ease the bit into Tanner's mouth. "So, can you give Liam a message from me?"

"Be glad to."

"Okay, um…tell him I absolutely *loved* his show. It was like, the best *ever*." I pull on the headstall, buckle the throat latch, flip the reins over the horse's head. "And tell him thanks for signing my shirt and sending me a personal message and offering me tickets to a future show and, well, for *everything*."

"Consider it done," says Jamie. "Ready for that leg up?"

"Sure." I spread my fingers across Tanner's back.

Jamie cups his hands beneath the toe of my boot, boosts me up, and I swing my leg over, take the reins in both hands as I do when I ride English.

"Thanks," I say. "We'll walk you to your car."

"Need any pointers?"

"I'm fine." I pull Tanner around, touching his flank with one heel.

The path is narrow, and Jamie lets us have it, striding off to my right. His jeans brush, ever so slightly, and his jacket creaks. His shoes, together with Tanner's hooves, fall with the faintest thud onto the wet earth. Alexis jingles her tags up the slope ahead of us. I duck under low-hanging cedar boughs that feather across my hair as Tanner clatters onto the gravel drive.

I rein him in. "Thanks again, Jamie. It was really sweet of you to drive this stuff out to me."

"Jenny—" he begins and then stops.

I wait, but my name hangs out there, nothing behind it.

"There's, um...something—" A longer pause this time. "It's just..." And then he sighs.

Must be monumental, whatever it is.

Wait—he's not thinking of asking me to *join* them, is he??? *Me* doing Portland with him and whoever else he's hanging out with?

Liam (oh my gosh!), maybe!

Not that I would go, of course. Mom would kill me. And anyway, I'd never climb into a car with some guy I know nothing about, no matter how well-connected he is to my favorite band ever.

Still.

To get asked...

"You're a pleasant change," he says, "from the story chasers and the girls with high-level security clearance we usually see backstage. I'm glad I got to meet you. Being here, seeing this place, chatting about everyday things has been, well...really nice."

Okay, just a hard-to-get-out compliment.

Consider me disappointed.

"We're even then, I guess," I say. "Learning more about O'Shannon was over the top."

"Happy to have helped," he says. "Good luck with your story and your blog, too. You're doing a great job of opening your world to those of us who know nothing of what you're capable."

"Definitely the goal."

"Nailing it, I'd say."

"Thanks."

Still, he stands here—*something more he wants to say?*—then turns and crunches over the stones. The car door creaks open, slams shut. The engine starts, idles, and he backs from the drive and crawls toward Ten Eyck Road.

I hold Tanner in, processing it all.

In my jacket pocket is a personal note to me from Liam O'Shannon, plus two concert tickets signed by every guy and the one gal in the band. Draped over one of Tanner's saddles is O'Shannon *Tear at the Walls* tour t-shirt number two, loaded with signatures, along with Leslie's tour shirt, also signed. And driving up Cedar Creek Lane is one of the most intriguing guys I've ever met.

"Working at Normal"

By Jenny Ryan

Being blind is a nuisance. It's not a tragedy.

Stuff takes longer to do, but I still get 'er done. And I don't miss out on much. Okay, sporting events kind of lose something for me, but I do go to the Sandy Pioneers home games and to the Portland Trail Blazers and Portland Winterhawks, too. And because I could see when I was younger, I can still visualize things when I make an effort. Not always clearly, but sometimes something just lights up my brain.

A memory, for instance. Like the smell of a campfire or grass after a hard rain or hearing a song from before I went blind. Or my folks talking about some kid thing I did. My now memories are non-visual, of course, but they have other elements, sometimes so intense I could swear I'm seeing what I didn't actually see.

People ask if I hear better than they do. I don't. I just listen better.

And I work at normal, at blending in.

Take my room, for example. It's all color-coordinated curtains, comforter, and pillow shams (light blue and peach). I have family photos on my desk and cutesy things on the walls. And, yes, a poster of O'Shannon sticky-tacked to the ceiling over my bed where Liam's drop-dead gorgeous eyes stare down into mine every day.

I've even got a mirror.

My besty, Morgan, was like, *wait, what?* the first time she saw it. As in, why would I have something like that when I can't possibly use it? The point is, *she* can. I want my friends to feel at home here, not like they're in this totally meh room, and oh, by the way, where's a mirror when they need one?

I could go on, but you get the point.

Being blind doesn't define me anymore than being blonde or overweight or having ADHD defines you.

We define ourselves. By who we are.

"So we were thinking..." Bryan starts in after we've finished our breadsticks and salad, and the Olive Garden waitress walks off, leaving our plates of pasta steaming in front of us.

Uh-oh, here it comes...

I put down my fork, my appetite for Tour of Italy vanishing into the rain thrumming the pavement beyond the window.

"Well, your mom and I have been seeing each other for eight months now—"

Like we can't count.

"—and we've been talking about—"

Don't say it. Please, don't, but I know you're going to...

"—something a bit more"—clearly Bryan's nervous about putting it out there—"permanent."

"Permanent, how?" Kaitlin asks from the chair beside me. She's got her social calendar realigned, and now she's on board with Family Meeting. "I mean, are you moving in? Getting married? What?"

"Married is what we had in mind," says Bryan.

"Living in Sandy, I hope."

No way would she stand for leaving friends, teammates, and her social life at Sandy High for a bigger school in Gresham. Even if she does drool over Bryan's three thousand square feet of upscale perfection near Hole One of Persimmon Country Club.

"I'd never make you give up your home," he says.

"Engaged yet?" she asks.

"No, not yet. We thought we'd discuss it first, all of us." His voice singles me out. "I know how close you girls are to your dad, and I don't want you to think I'm trying to take his place in your life."

"We don't," Kaitlin says for both of us. Her utensil, whichever it is, clinks against her plate, and the next thing she says is through whatever's in her mouth. "I mean, I'm good with it."

Of course she is.

She's totally moved on as far as Dad goes. She's realistic and logical that way, and she makes no secret of how perfectly Bryan will fit into our family.

I'm the wild card.

And my track record speaks for itself.

After settling into our new lives apart from Dad, I schemed to put him and Mom together every chance I got. Middle school graduation, birthdays, and major holidays were a given, but I also worked it for Kaitlin's games, outings, and anything else that might come up.

"Come on, Mom"—dragging out any joint event as long as possible—*"just a few more minutes?"*

"Can we go get ice cream?" Knowing Dad will be waiting at Baskin and Robbins when we get there.

"Can't we stop by Dad's"—said from wherever in Portland we might be—*"just for a bit?"*

Finally, Mom'd had enough. She declined invites and whatever else I'd concocted, so I backed off on the whole thing.

Then a little over a year ago, they started showing up for this or that on their own, sitting side by side at Kaitlin's volleyball matches or my OHSET meets. Dad would join us sometimes for pizza or mini-golf, and the two of them would laugh together like old times.

Just as my hopes were gaining momentum, Mom pulled back. Like she'd caught herself actually enjoying Dad's company the way she used to and was afraid of where it all might lead.

Shortly after that, Bryan dropped into her life, and she closed Dad down, same as before, and now here we sit in this silence I've let go on too long.

Bryan's looking at me, I can tell. Still waiting.

"Jenny?"

I find my lasagna with my fork and slice off a chunk I can manage without losing it somewhere between the plate and my mouth. At my feet, Alexis shifts and sighs, lost in her dreams.

"Do you have a time frame?" I ask.

"We were thinking"—Mom's voice slides toward Bryan—"maybe late January..."

I start.

I don't mean to, but honestly, a wedding in January? Barely three months off? Good thing I put my fork down because if I'd been holding something, I'd have dropped it.

Great.

Now they're all staring at me.

I reach for the ice water beyond my fingertips. Some of it sloshes over onto my thumb and forefinger. No chance anyone missed seeing *that*.

"Is it too soon?" Bryan's voice is low, kind. I've never heard him yell at my mom; if they've ever had a fight, it wasn't in front of Kaitlin or me. "If it is—"

I swallow and try to relax the shell shock off my face.

I've been expecting this, right? And not just after what Mom said this morning. Why didn't I work up an answer beforehand?

Because all morning and well into the afternoon, I've thought of nothing but Jamie Conway. Showing up in my yard. Talking to me in his way cool accent like he had all the time in the world. Hand delivering my autographed shirts and ticket printouts along with a personal-to-me message from Liam O'Shannon. Sharing insider details and bringing Tanner's tack out to me, boosting me up to ride, walking beside me like he'd known me forever instead of less than twelve hours. Starting to tell me one thing before derailing into another.

How could I have possibly had room in my brain for anything else?

I've told no one, not even Morgan, though she texted to say she had a bunch of stuff to do at home and couldn't come over today, but tomorrow might work.

I'll email you what I get done on my essay, she added, **if you'll look that over for me.**

"Be happy to," was all I said back.

Like I was going to share what *I* had to say in a text.

"We'll make sure it's not on an OHSET weekend," Mom's saying. "Or too close to your birthday."

I turn eighteen on January 12.

"I was just—" I swallow again, suck in a breath. "Surprised, is all."

"If you need more time—" Bryan begins.

"Um, no." I shrug, floundering.

Mom sighs, her disappointment so palpable I can almost see her sad eyes in my mind. Though honestly, I can't picture her face all that well anymore.

"Look, it's fine," I say. "It's not a blindside kind of thing." No pun intended. "You're pretty much there already. Engaged, I mean." I set my glass back onto the table. "I just thought, well...there might be more time before..."

Every word out of me bungles things that much more.

"We'd planned on waiting till April or May," Bryan says. "But since this is a second go-round for both of us"—his wife and nine-year-old daughter were killed four years ago in a car crash in the Columbia River Gorge—"we want to keep things simple. So we thought, *why wait?* But if you'd like us to—"

"I'm good with January," Kaitlin cuts in, her mouth still full.

Wonderful.

Now it's all on me.

"But if you're not, Jenny..." Bryan leaves the rest unfinished.

"No, it's okay."

Trying to make Mom and Dad happen again only drove them further apart. *They* couldn't make themselves happen. So how can I say no, I don't want her to marry again unless it's to my dad?

"We're good with holding off till spring," Bryan adds, "if that would help."

I shake my head. "No, it's fine. And you're right. You don't need to wait. Whatever you want to do is fine. Honest."

I hate lying, so I don't do it very often.

When you've been victimized as many times as I have by people who think not being able to see means you don't know what's going on, you avoid doing the same to someone else.

Besides, Mom deserves to be happy.

Bryan, too, after everything he's been through.

He'll take good care of us. He makes good money. Not the important thing, I know, but it would help Mom clear up her debts, and him being in real estate would be a total plus for her career.

Is it fair of me to wet blanket this for everyone else?

"Okay, then." Bryan lets out a breath. "We figured this engagement was pretty much a formality. It certainly won't come as a surprise, anyway. But we hope to be together the rest of our lives, and I don't see that working in the long run if we're not all on board."

I'm sure Dad hoped he and Mom would be together the rest of *their* lives, and look how that finished.

"I'm on board," says Kaitlin, clanging her fork or whatever against her plate.

"Me, too," I say, almost under my breath.

One more lie I can't take back.

"If that's settled," Bryan says, "we'll move forward. Your mom and I have been talking logistics—how to juggle our careers and blend us into a family as seamlessly as possible. I'm putting my place on the market after the first of the year. The sale of it should more than cover the mortgage on yours."

I chew my lower lip.

At one time, I'd thought he'd be iffy about having someone blind in his life. Like, maybe he'd decide Mom wasn't who he wanted after all since *I* came packaged in the deal. But no, he's always been super good with that. Respects who I am, admires what I do, and he's fine with Alexis riding in his fresh off-the-lot Explorer, which says plenty right there.

Why can't I accept the best of both worlds—a dad *and* a stepdad —and be good with that?

"And, of course," Mom says, "we want you both in the wedding."

Kaitlin's glass thunks onto the table. "Wait—you're not serious?"

Mom hesitates. "Well, it would be nice..."

"You said simple, right? Keep it to you and Bryan. It's better that way."

I'm with Kait on this.

No offense, but who wants to be a bridesmaid in their mother's wedding?

Okay, if it were her and Dad again, I'd walk the aisle with a monkey on my head if that's what they wanted. But it's not Dad, and it's never going to be, so no, I don't want to stand up there, off-the-shoulder dress and flowers in my hands, like it was Kaitlin's or Morgan's big day.

Why not fly to Las Vegas, say their vows in a chapel, and be done with it?

"We can decide later," says Mom.

"Not happening," says Kait.

"You *are* okay, Jenny?" Bryan asks.

I blink. "I'm fine."

"She's still in O'Shannon mode," Kaitlin covers for me.

"Can't blame her for that." Bryan shifts in his chair. "Thanks again for sharing your adventure, Jenn."

It was the first thing he'd asked about when we met in the parking lot an hour and a half ago. He'd given me his full attention as I detailed the show, my interview with Leslie, and Jamie walking in and offering to put the shirts she promised in the mail to me. Leaving out what happened this morning felt like a lie, too, but, I don't know, I couldn't go there.

"Thanks for listening," I say.

Seriously, could I be more of a jerk to this guy who's so considerate of me?

"Have you started your story?" he asks.

"Not yet." Though I did get my blog updated, sans photos. "Probably tomorrow."

"I'm sure it'll be great. All your others have been."

"Thanks." I poke at my plate with my fork and knife, find my parmesan chicken, and busy myself carving off a slice, hoping I don't drip marinara somewhere embarrassing and not find it till later.

Voices echo across the crowded room. Silverware clinks against plates. The little boy next to us begs somebody for more breadsticks. He talks again about the dog under our table. Ice and water splash into a glass at the next table over. Some guy laughs off to my right.

I chew my chicken and slice another bite, letting everyone's lives flow around me.

Standing in the corral with my dad, the wind on my cheek. Hooves plodding through soft dirt, the mare stopping in front of me, a sound-deadening wall.

I cringe back.

"We're just going to pet her today, Jenny," Dad says. "Nothing more."

He pries my fingers from his arm and sets them on her neck. It arcs as her head turns. She blows into my face, and I inhale the long-missed scent of horse and hay and manure. My fingers slide down her warm shoulder to the soft underside of her neck. And it's the first thing that's felt right—that's actually me—*in more than a year.*

"You could learn to ride again," Dad says. "If you want to bad enough..."

Why can't wanting something bad enough be enough now?

"Blind Trust"

By Jenny Ryan

To be blind requires a certain level of trust.

A lot of it, actually.

You have to trust your guide, be that a dog or a human. You have to trust that traffic signal, counting down the seconds till you can safely cross the street, is working correctly. Okay, you can hear the traffic, but that doesn't mean some idiot won't come squealing around the corner and not see you till the last second. You have to trust no one's dropped their stuff on the living room floor or left something in the hall or on the stairs and forgotten to pick it up (or at least warn you about it). And you have to trust that people are telling you the truth about what you can't see for yourself.

Do they really look the way they say they do? Maybe that shouldn't matter since I'm not judging you on it, but nobody likes to be lied to.

Is that cute guy across the room really cute (a subjective opinion at best), or are you pranking me? And IS he checking me out, as you say, or do you just want me to feel good about myself?

What you don't tell me matters, too.

Do I have a piece of cellophane stuck to my sleeve? A strand of toilet paper hanging from my jeans? Sauce I dripped onto my leggings and haven't brushed a hand over? A smear of mascara beneath one eye?

Be upfront, and let's laugh about it. But don't leave me to find something cringe-worthy later and wonder if someone was thinking, "Oh, well, she's blind, what do you expect?"

Tell me the truth—about everything.

It's a matter of respect.

Chapter

7

"**N**o way!" Morgan squeals when I drop the bomb Sunday afternoon. "No freakin' way!"

We're in her to-die-for bedroom with a walk-in closet, a window seat, her own mini-fridge, and a bed big enough to lose yourself in. Alexis is sacked out on the floor, and Morgan's younger brothers, Jason and Jackson, are shooting up video game bad guys in their room across the way.

"He did." I make a show of peeling off my jacket and turning my back to her.

"Oh—my—*gosh!*" she screams. "He did!"

I'd come home from the concert in a black-and-green shirt, and now I'm in a black-and-red-brown one, a bunch of names scrawled across the back, and there is absolutely no way it could have come in the mail over the weekend. Therefore, my improbable story about Jameson Conway, assistant publicist for O'Shannon Productions, showing up in my yard on Saturday morning has to be true.

"Wow." Morgan skims her fingers down my back, tracing the signatures, every one of them. "There's Kyle. There's Declan, there's Liam, Courtney, Keenan, Sean." Her voice lifts as her head comes up. "What kind of guy *is* this?"

"A super nice one."

"No, seriously." She leans around to peer at me, her hair tumbling over my shoulder. It's long and thick, streaked with purple. Or maybe dark blue this month. It's hard to keep track when all I have to go on is word of mouth. "I mean, what guy on a rock tour rents a car and drives out to somebody's house—as in, the house of somebody he's barely met—just to drop something off to her?"

"Jamie Conway, apparently." I turn so we're facing each other. "Honestly, I don't know what to make of him. I mean, he could have mailed this to me, yet he drove all the way out to hand-deliver it?"

"Sounds to me like he wanted to see you again."

"Strictly a professional visit."

"That he was in no hurry to end? We've *so* got to find this guy."

"I've tried already."

There are dozens of websites devoted to O'Shannon, including the one managed by the band, a Wiki page, and all sorts of video, lyric, and commentary pages, as well as Facebook, Twitter, and Instagram fan groups, fan pages, and the accounts of o'shannonofficial themselves. None refer to public relations people (other than Richard Vaughn) or private security, such as Darren Richardson, Liam's supposed best friend. Clearly, nobody cares about the people behind the scenes.

"I tried, too," Morgan says. "But we can look for him together."

She follows more celebs than I do, so she's better at digging them up. Not to mention her ability to skim text makes her faster at it than me listening through JAWS.

"Okay, thanks," I say.

"So did he get our tickets signed?"

I open my purse, pull hers out. "I have it on good authority you'll like what Kyle wrote to you."

She snatches the printout from my fingers, crackles it open, and then—"*Omigosh! LOVE Kyle!!!*" She sighs. Or swoons, rather, in a collapsed heap over her bed. "Yeah, love you, too, babe! So totally do!"

Of course, she says it all gooey and overblown.

"By the way..." I reach into my purse for the other folded sheet I brought along. "Jamie left me this, too."

Morgan takes and opens it, saying nothing for endless seconds. Then she breathes out in a whisper, "Liam O'Shannon *wrote* to you!

Like, actually wrote-it-*himself* to you? He's personally gonna get you tickets?"

"Ye-es," I say like it's no big deal. Like I'm suddenly in good with the lead singer of a rock band.

"Front row! Don't you dare ask for anything less! And you'd better remember who your best friend is."

"Like I'd forget."

We've been besties since that day in eighth grade when she banged her lunch tray next to mine, practically jolting me from my chair, and fired all these how-do-you-do-this and what-about-that questions at me. I could have been off-put, I suppose, but she was real about it. After that, she made sure I fit in—got friends, got invites—instead of floundering, ignored, on the outside of everything. Made sure I landed where I'm standing today, all these names on the back of my shirt.

"Ever hear of a band called O'Shannon? From Ireland?" Morgan asks at our usual cafeteria table. "They've got the most amazing guitarist ever. And their frontman is, like, to die for!"

I'm already asking Siri to bring them up. "Checking 'em out now..."

Liam-same-name-as-the-band doesn't make it through the first verse of Into Infinity *before I'm crushing on this guy with the jagged-edged vocals and gritty lyrics I totally relate to...*

"Wow, this is incredible!" Morgan says now, paper rustling as she folds and then slides it into my fingers. "I'd frame it and hang it on my wall if it was me."

"I plan to," I say as back into my purse it goes.

"So how old's this guy, Jamie, do you know?"

"No idea," I say.

Voices tell me a lot, but age is tough to estimate unless the speaker's relatively young or quite old. Given Jamie's profession and who he works for, along with the timbre of his voice, I'm guessing the younger end of the spectrum. But honestly, I don't know.

"He can't be too old, working for these guys," Morgan says like she's inside my head.

I shrug. "I've got to get my write-up done, anyway. And I want to download your pics and get your opinion on which ones look best."

"Fine," says Morgan. "We'll do pics, and you can post. Then we're going on a guy hunt."

We hunt.

But other than fangirling over a bunch of new concert shots, posted to the band's Instagram account and described to me by Morgan, nothing comes of it.

I TELL Kaitlin about Jamie dropping by when she gets in from movie night with her peeps. Show off my shirts and autographs and enjoy her overblown reaction.

I don't tell Mom.

She'll totally read something into it I don't want to hear. Like Jamie driving from Portland to bring me autographed band gear (though not actually *from* him) and hanging out for an hour while I'm home alone makes him some kind of predator.

I probably should have been concerned, but he was the same respectable guy he'd been the night before. Sometimes you get a good vibe from somebody even though you don't actually know them.

So why go into it and get called out on my lack of judgment?

I PUT off most of my Monday night homework to keep working on my story. I finish a rough draft on Tuesday. By Wednesday night, I'm polishing a second draft, sprawled across my bed with my computer, a package of peanut M&Ms at my fingertips, and Alexis flopped, unmoving, in her doggy bed.

I have a good lead-in:

A sellout crowd of seventeen-thousand-plus was over the top hyped for the first-ever appearance of Ireland-based O'Shannon in Portland's Moda Center arena...

The body is strong. But there are pockets here and there that could use serious tightening, phrases that should sparkle but don't, and a paragraph or two that lag into dullsville.

I've listened yet again to a disgustingly bad sentence when my phone bangs out the first few notes of *Tear at the Walls*. I grab it off my bed, double-tapping the screen to answer.

"Hello?"

"Hi, Jenny."

A guy.

With a British accent, soft and husky-edged.

I suck in my breath while every other thought vacates my brain. "*Jamie?*"

"Hello," he says.

My voice barely squeaks out of me. "You *called?*"

"Looks like it. Hope that's okay?"

"Um..." *Absolutely, it's okay!* "Sure, no problem. But..."

Wow, this guy is actually on the line with me!

Yes, he has my number. But just because I included every imaginable contact for setting up my interview doesn't mean I expected anyone to use it.

He's still waiting in the silence.

"But...what?" he prompts.

"Well..." I try to reorder my scattered thoughts. "I'm just... surprised"—mind blown is more like it—"to hear from you."

"I called to say thanks for your excellent sightseeing suggestions."

I breathe out.

My hands tingle, ever so stupidly.

"Glad you liked them," I say.

"Waterfront Park and the city views from the bridge were fab. Didn't have time to wait for donuts, I'm afraid, but a couple of guys from the tech crew popped over and brought some back for the rest of us. The voodoo doll with a pretzel stabbed into raspberry filling was fun."

"Yeah, but the bacon maple bar is better," I say. "Who all went along?"

"Leslie's always up for something social," he says, "so count her in. And Keenan will shoot video of anything, so him, too—plus Courtney and a couple of our sound guys."

Not Liam, apparently.

Guess I didn't miss out on him by not getting an invite I couldn't have accepted.

"Sounds great," I say.

"It was, thanks." He pauses a moment. "So, um...how're you doing?"

Why *is* this guy calling? Surely not to tell me about his adventures in Portland or ask after my health.

There can't be anything to what Morgan suggested, can there?

"I'm fine," I say. "And you?"

"Just grand."

"How was the Seattle show?"

"Seattle was great," he says. "Enough demand that we're coming back for a repeat performance in December. Not sure the exact date yet, but probably the middle of the month."

"Wow, cool." *Wonder if there's any chance Morgan and I could get up there for that?* "Hope Kyle's feeling better."

"He's fine," says Jamie. "But Sean came down with the same stuff, though he didn't eat the same food, so probably the flu."

"And Liam?"

"He, um...was iffy last night in Vancouver. Not like anyone could tell who didn't already know. They clean him up vocally in live performance if he's not quite on the mark."

"I've heard that," I say. "And Leslie?"

"She's fine, too. She talks about you."

"She does?" Super cool. "I talk about her, too. All of it good, of course." I'm finally relaxing into the conversation. "I see you're in Edmonton tonight."

"Eight P.M. show," he says. "You Yanks should use the twenty-four-hour clock. It's a lot easier."

"Seriously, I don't know why we don't."

I open the crystal on my watch—it has a Braille face for discreet time-checking and a speaker for when discreet doesn't matter—and touch the hands.

Five-fifteen.

There's one time zone, isn't there, between here and Edmonton?

"I hear Edmonton's got a ginormous mall," I say. "Like, the biggest in North America."

"It's on Leslie's to-do list for tomorrow," he says.

Of course, it is.

"Driving through the Canadian Rockies was deadly beautiful," he adds. "And fierce cold. With a powerful lot o' snow. There, some Irish speak for you."

"Thanks." I smile. "Good luck to everyone tonight."

"They'd appreciate it, I'm sure."

Silence drops on us like it did on Saturday, and I get the impression he's maybe feeling his way with this, whatever it is, and not sure where to go next.

"So, um..." he says at last, "I was thinking"—another pause —"what would you say...to doing an interview with Liam?"

I all but drop my phone. "Are you *serious*?"

"Absolutely."

"You could make that happen?"

"If you're interested, yes."

I collapse against my headboard. "Like, *yes!*"

"Good," he says. "We could arrange it for Seattle in December if that works for you?"

And here's my in for seeing O'Shannon's *Tear at the Walls* tour a second time!

"That'd be perfect." I'm actually breathing again. "Wow, this is incredible of you, Jamie. And Liam, too, of course."

"Happy to do it," he says. "So...how's your story coming?"

I'm still on the *I'm-going-to-meet-Liam-O'Shannon* page and have to drag my brain back to here and now.

"I'm on my second round of edits," I say. "Hope to be done in a day or two."

"Just read your blog on the tech you use. Care to enlighten me a bit more?"

Cool of him to ask.

"Sure." I give additional details about JAWS and how my Reader converts anything downloaded into speech, and my phone app does the same with any document I photograph.

"Brilliant," he says. "So do I get to read a copy? Of your story, I mean."

Again with almost dropping the phone.

"You *want* to?"

"I'd love to," he says. "If you don't mind."

"That'd be awesome," I say. "Wow, thanks. So do I email it to you or—"

"Email would be great. Send it to JamesonConway@oshannonproductions.com."

"I can remember that."

"I'm looking forward to reading it."

"Just so you know," I say, "I'm not a professional."

"From everything I've read so far, it'll be great."

"Thanks."

What is it with this guy that he's so interested in the littlest details of my life? Has he never met anyone blind before? Is that it? Are my every day getting-along skills so amazing he can't get over them? Or is he truly intrigued by what I have to say?

And how am I any different? Because he knows Liam O'Shannon —I don't forget *that* for one nanosecond—I find him fascinating.

"I hope Kyle's autograph met expectations," he says.

"He killed it," I say. "Morgan collapsed all over her bed in utter swoons-ville."

"I'll let him know."

"Do that. By the way"—I ease into the topic—"we tried looking you up online but couldn't find you anywhere."

"Oh...right," Jamie says. "My social media accounts aren't under my name. And public info on O'Shannon is limited to the band, Leslie, and Michael. And sometimes Richard Vaughn." His voice holds a shrug. "Fans want to read about the big names, not the people behind the scenes."

"Yeah, I get that."

Though *one* person behind the scenes might be nice...

"So...how's your family?" he asks.

Really, what *is* it with this guy?

"They're good. My sister went ballistic over Leslie's shirt. She's a huge fan."

"Wish I'd known," he says. "I'd have brought her one, too."

"You couldn't have known."

"Right. Is she older than you? Or younger?"

"Younger," I say. "She's fifteen." I tell him about Kaitlin's love of sports, clothes, and pop music."

"I like pop, too," he says.

"So does my mom. My dad's country all the way."

"They must compromise, then?"

"They used to, but...well, they're not together anymore, so no more debates about what's going up on Spotify."

"I'm sorry," he says.

"It happened a while ago, and um"—I've already blurted this much; might as well say the rest—"my mom's about to get engaged."

"Is this good news or bad news?"

"It's I'm-not-ready-for-it news."

"I see," he says.

"Don't get me wrong," I say. "Her boyfriend's great. It's just that —" And the next thing I know, I'm spilling about my dad and the divorce, which leads into ugly me after my accident, ending with Bryan McKenzie moving into our lives. Once I get started, I can't stop. Like something in Jamie's voice and his focused attention just draws it out of me.

Like I've known him all my life.

"I do try," I finish up. "I'm just not ready for someone to step into my dad's place."

"No one can step into his place," says Jamie. "This isn't about that. It's about accepting what life hands you and moving on. You lost your sight; you adjusted. Your folks got divorced; you adjusted again. Now your mum remarries, and you adjust yet again. What other choice do you have?"

"Suck into myself and be a jerk?"

"Tried that one, did you?"

"Yeah," I say. "Wasn't much fun."

"Have you talked to your dad?"

"He's out of town till Thursday. He's a sales rep, and he travels a lot. I'll call him when he gets back and see if I can spend the weekend."

"Does he know about your mum?"

"I'm not sure. I think he expects it."

"Doesn't make it easier, I know. We were all expecting my dad to die, but when the time came—" Jamie stops. Like maybe he doesn't want to go there after all.

"I'm sorry," I say. "That he died, I mean. And that I bothered you with my problems."

"It's no bother. It's just, well...sometimes a little perspective helps."

Sometimes it does.

Having him listen helps, too. It's the first I've unloaded on anyone since Mom made her announcement Saturday morning.

We talk on, and time hangs suspended.

Finally, he says, "Hey, we're about to head into the arena. Which means I have to go to work. But I've enjoyed talking to you, and I'm looking forward to reading your story."

"Thanks, Jamie. It was great talking to you, too." It's been such an uplift, hauling me out of myself, that I don't want him to go. "And I really appreciate what you said."

"Glad it helped. I'll be in touch about the interview."

Still. Cannot. Believe it.

"Thanks *so* much," I say again.

"My pleasure. Bye, Jenny."

"Bye." I hang up and check my watch again.

We've been on the phone for over an hour.

Chapter

8

My dad's waiting at the usual spot after school on Friday. I come out the north entrance, my backpack loaded with gym clothes, street clothes, overnight stuff, and my Braille-coded playing cards and *Phase 10* deck. I've got my computer case over one shoulder, Alexis's harness handle in my left fist, and Morgan striding along, talking at me.

"Text me the minute you hear anything," she says. "And I mean *anything*."

"I'll text you," I say.

I'd given her the whole load on the bus ride yesterday morning.

"*An hour!*" she screamed into my face. "You were on the phone with him for a whole *hour?*"

Who knows how many heads whipped around to eyeball us.

"Yes," I said.

And when I told her Jamie asked to read my story after I finished it *and* offered me an exclusive with Liam O'Shannon—

"*Seriously!*" she shrieked. "You're *serious?*"

"He said he could make it happen."

She grabbed me then, and yeah, I flinched, but not like I did backstage with Jamie. Morgan's always up close and pawing at me, so I expect it from her. "Wow! I mean, like, *wow!*"

"Yeah," I said, still barely believing it myself.

"Okay, I'm gonna coach you on this," she said. "We're gonna make a plan. We're gonna work it together, I'm gonna get you top ready, and, oh, by the way, you get to ask him about Kyle Finn for me

—" And on she rattled, planning out the biggest thing to hit my life since O'Shannon played the Moda Center last weekend, and I met Leslie and Jamie after the show.

She peels off now to flag down Haley Mayes about a project they're working on together for psych class.

Alexis takes me straight to the walkway, people sidestepping to let us pass. Everyone's going on about the game tonight, the date they've lined up, or where the parties are happening. Car doors slam, vehicles hum in and out of the lot, and exhaust fumes into the air.

"Hi, Jenny," Dad says when I get close enough to hear.

"Hey, Dad."

He pulls me into one of his bear hugs, and I don't care who might be looking on and thinking me uncool. Unlike some kids, I've never been ashamed to be seen with my folks.

Dad smells of musky cologne, industrial-grade cleaners from the company he works for, and his favorite guy shampoo. He's a bit shorter than Bryan with a husky-ish build that thankfully bypassed Kaitlin and me. His hair was brown when I last saw it, but Kait says it's now going gray in places.

"Let me get something for you," he says.

I hand off my computer.

"How was Chicago?" I ask.

"Wet. Cold. Windy. Nice here, though."

The day is gorgeous after a sound-deadening fog. The sun lightens my shadow world and warms my face. I'm sweltering in my hoodie, jeans, and heavy jacket. But before nightfall, the temperature will drop to that classically crisp football or warming-hands-in-front-of-a-bonfire weather that's so October in northwest Oregon.

"I'm at the far end." Dad's voice moves to the left.

"Forward," I say to Alexis while giving her the hand signal, and she takes me down the sidewalk.

Dad parked his Outback at the bottom of the lot. Alexis hops in through the hatch, and I belt myself up front while he switches his country station to a Top-Forty one.

We pull out onto the street.

"So tell me more about your concert," he says.

I texted him last Saturday, of course, but only with the highlights and a few pics, saving the best stuff for in-person. I launch into my story now, including the next-day details I skimmed over with Kaitlin and Morgan and completely avoided with Mom.

Like how Jamie Conway brought my horse tack out to me and boosted me up to ride. And how Tanner and I walked him to his rental car. How I finished my final draft last night and typed his name into the *To* line and put *Tearing Down Walls* into the *Subject* line after attaching the story, but waited till the end of study hall to send it.

Stupid, really, because I *do* want him to read this. But suddenly, the idea was turning me inside out with sick-to-my-stomach nerves.

What will he think of my amateur story? This isn't my blog, my personal life; it's what I hope will someday be my career. Will he think I have any shot at it?

Delaying the send—O'Shannon plays Calgary tonight, so he'll be out late and probably up late tomorrow—bought me time to process what I've done and work out the jitters before he answers me back.

"Sounds like quite the adventure," Dad says when I get to the end of it all.

"It was."

"A word of caution, though. I'd be careful how friendly I got with this guy. You know nothing about him, and he's touring with a band—not always the most savory environment."

"Michael doesn't allow drugs," I say. "You use, he kicks you out."

"Not what I meant."

"If Jamie wanted to hurt me, he had every chance. And didn't take it."

"Doesn't make him safe," Dad reminds me.

"I'm careful, Dad. You know that."

"I do, yes." His blinker clicks as he angles off Highway 26 onto I-205. "I *will* be curious to know what you hear back from him. Just keep in mind, he's probably very busy and won't get to your story as soon as you hope."

"I know."

"And as for free tickets and an interview with Liam O'Shannon, good intentions don't always materialize."

"I thought of that, too."

"But if it does," he adds, "I might be able to help with transportation, depending on whether or not I'm home at the time."

"That'd be cool, Dad. Thanks."

Getting myself to Tacoma?

Check that one (fingers crossed) off the list!

All I need now is for Jamie to come through with a date, tickets, and a meet-time with Liam.

And permission from Mom, of course.

Which will mean coughing up more info than I gave her on Saturday morning.

DAD and I order teriyaki burgers at Red Robin in east Portland, then go to a movie at Lloyd Cinema.

Yes, I do, in fact, go to the movies. You can follow a lot by listening, and most first-run movies have audio description. Lots of theaters have it, too. I get a headset with my ticket, and this voice tells me what's showing on the screen when nobody's talking.

Afterward, we stop at Voodoo Donuts—eastside location, not the iconic west-of-the-Willamette-River one I told Jamie about.

All the while, I'm focusing on Dad and me, father and daughter, going out on the town together, all of it great.

But now we're crossing the Fremont Bridge north of downtown. Soon, we'll be driving through the industrial river frontage bordering the Port of Portland, heading for my childhood home on the edge of Forest Park.

And just like that, everything I've held away roars back.

Mom and Bryan will be going out tonight or tomorrow night. Or maybe he'll take her to his place and pop the question there. I'll be seriously shocked if she's not wearing a ring by the time I get home Sunday afternoon.

No sense putting this off.

Better that Dad hears it from me than Mom or watch Kaitlin make a production of it.

"So, um...Mom and Bryan—" And I tell him the rest as we angle off the bridge onto Highway 30.

For the longest time, there's nothing but Katy Perry belting lyrics over the radio.

"Well..." Dad drags out a sigh. "We knew it was coming, didn't we."

"Yeah, I guess."

"I'm okay, Jenny," he says. "Really, I'll be fine."

"I know, but..."

"And you'll be fine, too."

"Yeah, but..."

"Bryan's a great fit for your mom. Better than I was, apparently."

"Don't say that, Dad. You know it's not true."

"We're not together," he says. "We were never getting back together, much as I wanted us to."

"Maybe with a little more time..."

Totally grasping at straws here.

"I know you had high hopes, and things looked promising for a while. Even if you *were* a bit obvious in helping us along."

"Yeah, well..."

Desperate times, desperate measures, and all that.

"Things have to want to change," he says. "And your mom wasn't ready for that. Because along with the good memories came the bad, and she got scared, I think."

Though her version is epically different.

"I gave it a chance. But your dad's just...your dad. Nothing changes with him."

"Bryan's a new start," he adds. "And, for her, less risk. She has to do what's best for herself. And she's made it quite clear it isn't me."

"Dad..."

"She wasn't coming back, Jenn."

Maybe not.

But how do you stop hoping for something you can never let go of?

"You're getting a great addition to the family," he says. "I hope you know that. And make the best of it."

"What happens to you, Dad?"

"Me? I'll go on loving my two best girls in the world. Nothing'll ever change that."

WE SIT in front of the fire till almost one, drinking cocoa loaded with whipping cream and listening to George Strait on his stereo system, Alexis curled on the rug at my feet. We say nothing more about Mom and Bryan. Instead, we talk about school and Tanner, Dad's job and travels, Kaitlin's games and Homecoming week, and how well the Ducks and the Blazers are doing this year.

This house I grew up in is old and smells faintly of dust and mildew no matter how thoroughly Dad cleans it. Unlike the one I live in now, all angles and jutting corners, this house is tall and square with steep, narrow stairs, a single bathroom where you can hear water draining down the pipes behind the wall, a basement, and an attic. It's a living house that creaks and groans and settles in the night, that overlooks the Willamette River with a view to Mt. St. Helens and sometimes all the way to Mt. Rainier. A house that sits on the doorstep of Forest Park.

It would sell for way more than Mom's would.

I finish my hot chocolate and go up to my room, open my window to the cold night air, and stand listening to cars on the highway below.

Breathe in hints of wood smoke from the chimney and the wet scent of the river.

Mom holding Kaitlin on the deck below, Dad's hand crushing mine. All of us bundled in jackets, breath frosting the air, as the Christmas Ships scatter colored lights across the water...

Alexis thumps upstairs, noses my hand, and flops onto the hardwood floor, tags jingling. I pull down the sash and crawl into my old bed among my childhood teddy bears and a stuffed unicorn with one floppy ear.

A mouse scurries over the attic floor.

The house settles, and the wind whispers beneath the eaves.

Everything I remember of my life before I went blind is in this house. Where seeing was more than images drawn by my hands or sound or smell. Where visual impressions are actual memories, not best guesses and assumptions. Where my family was whole and complete and, I'd once thought, happy.

Before we all changed.

And it's my fault, all of this.

I got myself thrown from a friend's horse and ruined our perfect lives.

My phone dings at me mid-morning.

An email in my inbox.

Thanks, Jenny. I'll get on this ASAP. Appreciate you sending it to me, and I look forward to reading it!

Jamie

Okay, so this guy doesn't waste time. And here I thought I might go all weekend before he got back to me.

Tearing Down Walls

From the Emerald Isle to the Rose City, O'Shannon Crosses Cultures and the Atlantic to Bring Down the House in Portland

By Jenny Ryan

A sellout crowd of seventeen-thousand-plus was over the top hyped for the first-ever appearance of Ireland-based O'Shannon in Portland's Moda Center arena. Fronted by vocalist Liam O'Shannon and powered by guitarists Kyle Finnegan and Keenan Donnelly, the band brought their blend of hardcore rock and metal-infused Celtic to the Rose City.

Kicking off their much-anticipated *Tear at the Walls* world tour in Los Angeles, O'Shannon's first three dates in the U.S. attracted sellout crowds and great shows of American enthusiasm. Along with Liam, Kyle, and Keenan, band members Sean Monagan (bass), Declan Kelsey (drums), and Courtney Galloway (keyboards) turned out a heart-stopping performance that included live video feeds, pyrotechnics, and a spectacular light and laser show.

The band opened with the explosive *Excalibur Knight*, then sizzled into a two-plus-hour set that included *Off The Grid*, *Shock and Awe*, and *Tear at the Walls*, as well as cuts from previous albums *Into Infinity* and *Fire and Ice* before cleaning up with *Beyond This Broken Night*. Balancing high-voltage pieces with occasional melt-you-to-the-floor ballads, these guys (and gal) are equally gifted with Irish harps, tin whistles, bodhrans, and uilleann pipes, and their iconic Celtic-with-a-kick transports listeners to the heart of the Emerald Isle.

Founded five years ago by Liam's older brother Michael, O'Shannon enjoyed moderate success in Ireland, the UK, and continental Europe in the wake of their debut *Fire and Ice*. Moving Liam from keyboardist to frontman was, as former lead Michael said in the UK's *Kerrang!* magazine, "in the best interest of the band." Liam's edgy vocals and stratospheric range, coupled with his stunningly theatrical stage presence at Wacken Open Air (Germany) and Graspop (Belgium), ramped up their mostly European following.

Ground-breaking *Into Infinity* rocketed the band into international stardom, and *Tear at the Walls* carved out a spot on the cutting edge of the industry. With its post-apocalyptic themes of fallen world order and ensuing chaos, *Tear at the Walls* serves as a wake-up call to rampant militarism and political power run amok.

Aspiring pop/dubstep artist Leslie O'Shannon opened the show with a forty-five-minute set from her debut album, *Dance in the Rain*. Equally versatile in the rock genre, Leslie joined her older brother on stage for *Waiting For You/Waiting For Me* and a power version of Irish folk ballad, *Siúil a Rún*.

In a one-on-one interview following the show, Leslie said she was discovered by accident, that she loves meeting people and watching them get up for her performance, and aspires to be a fashion designer with a studio in either Cork City or Dublin. Totally down to earth and amazingly easy to talk to, Leslie describes her life as an adventure and Liam as "just a regular lad who got this powerful lucky break."

Though she and Liam hail from Innishannon, a village of less than a thousand people, the band itself claims Cork City as home.

O'Shannon will be touring North America through mid-December before breaking for the holidays, then taking major cities in Europe, Australia, and Asia by storm. Check out their Facebook and Instagram accounts for concert pics and on-the-road videos. For information on which walls they'll be tearing down next (tix), visit O'Shannon.net.

I answer Jamie right away—"Hope you like it!"—and then wait, but nothing comes back.

Well, why should it?

As my dad said, he's a busy guy—stuff to arrange, people to make happy, a bus to load into, whatever.

Like he had last Saturday morning?

Okay, that was his day off. Still, he had plans, didn't he? Why complicate things by driving out to Sandy and frittering time away with *me?*

I shower and dress for the day.

Dad makes coconut-chocolate-chip-almond pancakes for brunch, and then we hike a piece of the Wildwood Trail in Forest Park. The morning is wet with fog, but by early afternoon, the sun comes sifting through the trees. We eat lunch beside Doane Creek, and I strip down to the shorts beneath my jeans and the tank under my sweatshirt. I've unbuckled Alexis from her harness, and she's diving into the creek and out again, splattering me and shaking off water in massive sprays.

Dad and I have always been the outdoorsy ones.

Kaitlin tagged along with us sometimes and Mom used to. But Kait would rather shop or hang out with friends these days, and Mom's too busy falling in love with another man to appreciate the forest she lives in and the creek at the bottom of her yard.

I finish my sandwich and find the Ziploc bag of mint Oreos. "I don't get how Mom could love you all those years and then throw everything away. Like it meant nothing."

"I wouldn't say it meant nothing," Dad says. "We just didn't know how to fix what was broken. So I understood when she had to go. Sometimes there's nothing more you can do."

"Not your fault," I say through the cookie in my mouth.

"I know you think we broke up over you," he says. "Truth is, we'd been struggling a while and failed to work through it."

"Still...my fault," I say.

"Contributing factor," he says. "It's not the same."

All I know is the fights escalated off the charts after that, and the make-ups came less often. In the end, they barely spoke to each other except when they had to deal with something.

How might things have been different if I hadn't gone riding that day? If I hadn't been thrown from Sahdjani? If I hadn't gone blind...

"You can't blame yourself, Jenny," he says into my silence. "It's a waste of time and energy."

"For you, too." I tip my water bottle back for a swallow.

Dad sighs, and the only sound is the creek clattering over rocks and Alexis being a Lab dog in the middle of it.

"Falling in love is easy," he says. "Staying in love takes work. You have to want it, have to fight for it with everything you've got."

And Mom didn't.

"It's not just about loving someone, Jenny," she'd said. "Something works or it doesn't. You can't force it."

Yeah, because Bryan dropping into her life made finding new love with him easier than resurrecting something long-dead with my dad.

"I'd just hoped..." My words trickle into silence.

"I think she did, too. In her own way." Dad sighs again. "Just not one that would work." He touches my arm, squeezes lightly. He's sitting close, and I don't startle. "Time to move on now. For both of us."

WE MAKE nachos for dinner and eat them in front of the TV.

After that, I check my inbox.

Four messages: Kaitlin, Morgan, Morgan again, and then—

Hi, Jenny,

Read your story and loved it! You're a really good writer, highly professional in your choice of words and how you balance your admiration for O'Shannon with a straightforward analysis of their performance. Would it be all right if I pass this on to the band and Leslie, too? I'm sure they'd love to read it.

Jamie

My breath goes in, and I forget to let it out, sitting very still on the coverlet of my old bed.

Jamie wants *Liam* to read my story? And Leslie and Kyle Finn and everyone else in O'Shannon?

What's happening here? How did I go from being a backstage guest at their concert to actually getting my work into their hands for personal screening?

Okay, massive kudos to Jamie Conway, of course. But still, who'd have expected things to move so far so fast?

What if Liam doesn't like it? What if Sean or Keenan or Declan or Courtney think it's too fangirl, despite what Jamie said? What if they're too busy and never get around to looking at it? Or they think I'm too amateur, or I'm—

Just say yes and don't think about it.

I answer Jamie with, "Sure, that's fine."

What else would I say?

I GO to church with Dad on Sunday morning, something I do only with him because Mom doesn't anymore, though I'm guessing she'll book one for the wedding. Afterward, we eat lunch at Rose's in west Portland. Over turkey sandwiches and a monster slice of seven-layer chocolate cake split between us, I tell him about Jamie's email.

"Okay, so I was wrong on the time frame," he says. "Looks like you could be going somewhere with this. Rather quickly, in fact."

"Yeah, maybe. Wouldn't it be cool if they asked me to write something for them? I mean, they've got their own people, of course, so why would they? But still."

"Maybe you should look into becoming a music journalist," he says. "Write about bands and concerts, that sort of thing."

Seriously, why hadn't *I* thought of that? I cover activities and events for my school paper, the *Pioneer Press*, and my love of O'Shannon and other rock artists makes writing about the music scene a natural fit.

"That'd be really cool," I say. "I'll definitely check it out."

"This guy might have some advice for you. But I wouldn't push him for it. And, like I said, be careful."

"Don't worry, Dad. I will."

After that, we walk along the Willamette River in Waterfront Park—joggers thumping past us on the cement walkway, cyclists whizzing by—before he takes me home.

Kaitlin meets us in the driveway, gravel griping beneath her feet, energy crackling off her body, and I brace myself for what I know is coming.

"It's official!" she blurts. "Mom's got the ring on her hand, and man, you won't believe the size of that rock!"

I freeze, the SUV door open between us, Dad lifting the hatch behind me.

Hello? Dad's here to see you, too. Couldn't you at least say hi first? Maybe hold off on this till after he's gone? And do you have to point out how much bigger her new diamond is than her old one?

Honestly, doesn't she think before she broadcasts to the neighborhood?

"Um, cool," I say.

As in, totally not.

Alexis bounds over, and I grab her leash. Dad closes the hatch, crunches across the gravel, then stops and touches my shoulder, hands off my pack.

"Hi, honey," he says to Kait.

They shift into each other's arms.

"Hey," she says. "Sorry I couldn't make it this weekend."

Due to bumping sets and spiking volleyballs at a tourney yesterday.

"We missed you," he says, stepping back. "But congrats on taking second."

"Thanks. I think Jenny wanted you to herself, anyway."

Yes, in fact.

Though it's equally true, Dad and I would have driven to Wilsonville to watch her play if she'd asked us to come. Of course, Bryan had said he was going, and Mom was going with him, so there's that. But it's not like Dad won't come to our events because Bryan might be there.

They've met, of course, loads of times, and things are friendly enough between them. But not comfortable. How can you be comfortable standing there, staring at the competition?

"We had a good time," Dad says.

"I...suppose Jenny told you about Mom and Bryan." Kaitlin backs her enthusiasm down a notch. Like she realizes what she's done and is trying to smooth any feathers she might have ruffled out of place.

"Yes, and it's okay. Your mom deserves to be happy."

I want to crumble to the ground. The whole thing is unimaginably uncomfortable, and I half-expect Mom to waltz into the middle of our dad-moment. But no, she's probably seen his Outback in the driveway. Or heard him pull in. She might come out to talk, but she'll give him this time with us first.

And anyway, Bryan's here.

We parked farther over than we would have if his Explorer wasn't taking up the space Dad usually slides into.

"I should go," Dad says, though there's really nothing he needs to rush off for. He pretty much spends his Sunday evenings in front of the TV.

"Can you come to my game Tuesday night?" says Kaitlin. "It's at Rex Putnun. Six o'clock?"

"Sure, honey, I'd love to." To me, he says, "Bye, Jenn. Thanks for keeping me company this weekend."

"Thanks for having me." I reach out, and he pulls me in, holds me tight.

"Always," he says and then lets me go. "It'll be fine, sweetie. You'll see."

Chapter 10

"Hey, Jenn, how was your weekend?" Bryan's voice reaches me from the sofa as Alexis and I crowd through the front door behind Kaitlin.

Mom says hi from the same spot, clearly smacked against him.

"Really great." I unbuckle Alexis from her harness, and her nails click off toward the kitchen and into the mud room. Like she's hoping I'll follow and dump something into her bowl, never mind that it's the wrong time of day.

Bryan's up now. Mom, too.

Both headed my way.

We invade each other's space somewhere between the easy chair and the piano Kaitlin rarely touches these days.

"Um, I hear congrats are in order?" I hike the harness onto the same shoulder as my backpack while Kait pounds up the stairs behind me.

"We were hoping you'd say that." Mom's voice is one huge smile.

I'm expected to hug them, so I do. Mom first, then Bryan.

I've hugged him before so that in itself is no big deal. But this time, I'm supposed to hug hard and tight, like I'm all in with this. I give it my best, but honestly, I'm not ready to embrace him like I did my dad Friday afternoon.

"And, of course, you've got to see the ring," he says.

Mom puts her hand in mine.

Bryan's is there, too, broad palm and wide fingers holding her wrist.

I find the ring right off. You couldn't *not* find it, the way that stone towers out of a four-prong setting.

"Wow, Mom, this is really beautiful," I say. "White gold? Yellow?"

"Platinum," she says.

Of course, it is.

"It's gorgeous," I say.

"Thank you."

"Have you decided on a date?"

"Not yet," she says. "We're still thinking mid-to-late January, but we need to look at schedules and see what works for everyone."

"Okay, sure," I say. "And hey, this is really cool."

I lift my words in the right places, but I'm not sure how convincing I sound.

My mom sighs, relieved, I think. And Bryan pulls me into another hug like maybe it *is* good after all.

Or will be eventually.

"So tell us what you did this weekend," he says.

We sit, them on the sofa, me in the easy chair, and I tell them everything they want to hear and leave out everything they don't, along with anything to do with Jamie Conway.

I'M SPRAWLED across my bed, working trig equations with my talking calculator, trying to forget the ring on Mom's finger and blinking hard so the tears won't fall, when my phone starts up with *Tear At The Walls*. I flap a hand over my nightstand, but no, it's not there. *Still in my purse.* Which *is* there and falls to the floor when I make the grab. By the time I've got the phone out and am double-tapping to answer, the song cuts off, and my voicemail comes on.

Hi, this is Jenny, and I'm not answering my phone for whatever reason, so would you please leave me a message?

"Yeah, hello?" I say, a bit breathless.

"Hi, Jenny."

I stop breathing.

Will I never get used to this guy's voice coming over the phone at me?

"Hi," I say softly, all thoughts of my mom and her engagement and the impending wedding blown from my mind.

I take a deep breath, hold it, let it out slowly.

Shift gears.

Relax....

"So," Jamie Conway says, "I've got some feedback from the band for you."

Already?

"Wow, that was fast."

"They've got nothing better to do aboard their tour bus between here and there," he says. "Anyway, Leslie loved it. She said to tell you she's really impressed, and you did a fine job, sure you did."

"Oh, my gosh!"

"Kyle said it was grand, like. Sean said you'll go pro, no problem. Declan's sorry he didn't get to meet you. Courtney said it rocked something fierce. And Keenan asked if he could get an autographed copy."

I snicker. "Yeah, right."

"I'm serious."

"And Liam?"

Say he liked it. Please say he liked it...

"He said you're very talented." Jamie's voice warms. "And he can't wait to see what you write after you interview him."

"He said *that*?"

"He really liked your work, Jenny."

"My gosh!" *Cannot believe this is for real!* "Thanks so much for sharing with them."

"No, thank *you*. For writing it."

Like my meager skills could have pulled this off without his key-to-it-all connections.

"To be honest," he adds, "I was expecting something a bit more fan-focused. Not this level of professionalism."

"Wow, that's serious praise," I say.

"You earned it."

"Thanks. So, um"—the idea Dad planted over lunch this afternoon has totally gone to seed—"I know you arrange interviews, and I'm guessing you read the write-ups at some point, so you're a way better judge of this than me, but..." *Why is this so hard to get out?* "Do you think I have any shot at doing this myself someday? Music journalism, I mean."

"I'd say you have a lot of potential. My advice would be to research the industry, read the leading magazines. Get into your local music scene—debut bands, whoever's solid in your area, and write about them, if only in practice."

"That's what I was thinking."

Or maybe you could pull a few strings for me? You do know some huge names...

Who've hired professional writers and photographers to do copy for them.

"You'll need a communications degree, of course," he says. "But you can do it. You seem to do everything else you set your mind to."

"Thanks, Jamie."

I have no idea why he cares about my dreams, but clearly, he does.

"It was a total pleasure," he says. "All of it."

"For me, too."

"Good."

And then, silence.

Like he's not sure where to go next.

"So"—ball in my court—"how was your weekend?"

"Excellent," he says. "Leslie got to her mall. Courtney and a few others tagged along. And some of us went to the Royal Alberta Museum."

"Into history, I take it."

"Love it," he says.

"Museums kind of lose something for me," I admit. "But I liked them as a kid."

"Something hands-on, perhaps?"

"Like OMSI, the science museum in Portland. That one's fun." I roll onto my back and tent my knees, wriggling my toes beneath a pillow. "How was the one in Alberta?"

"'Twas grand, so." He gives the words a slight Irish inflection.

I laugh, then stop. Something snags at my brain—

But he's gone all British again, telling me about the Natural History Hall, the Wild Alberta Gallery, and other highlights of his visit.

"That's really cool," I say. "Glad you got to do that."

"Me, too. So...how was your weekend with your dad?"

"It was great. We went to dinner and a movie."

"You don't visit museums, but you go to the cinema?"

"Movies are different."

I explain how audio description keeps me abreast of what's happening on screen while my mind creates the images.

"Brilliant," he says. "What kind of films do you like?"

"All kinds. I prefer lots of dialogue and audio effects—makes it easier to follow—so romcoms and action movies are a good fit."

"I can see that. I mean, sorry—"

"No, *see* is good. I use it all the time."

"Okay. Wasn't sure." He pauses. Thinking through what to say next? "If it's okay to ask, what's the hardest thing about being blind?"

"Asking is totally okay." I shove myself up and sit cross-legged on my comforter. "The hardest thing is remembering what it was like when I wasn't. Or trying something new and having it be twice as tough and take three times as long as it used to. Knowing people are staring at me. Or feeling sorry for me. Or jumping in, trying to help, and doing it all wrong.

"Like this one time when I went out for pizza with my friend Eric, and this woman in the ladies' room fell over herself, wanting to help me. And then she went on about how sweet that guy at my table was, taking me out. Like he could do better, jock that he was, but no, he chose to take *me*. Like he was just being nice to me or something."

Jamie's voice softens more than usual. "People say a lot of things without thinking, without meaning to."

"I know." I hate that I've blurted all this as if I've got some monstrous chip on my shoulder. "I don't usually make a big deal of it. It's just—well, sometimes it's kind of rough."

"Don't apologize. I asked. Most of us aren't aware of the challenges, though we mean well. Sometimes we don't know what *to* do. Or we don't think."

"I've written a blog entry on how to help someone blind, so people can learn. We're just trying to be *us* under our own power."

"I think everyone is," he says. "And I haven't gotten to that one yet, but I'll read it on the bus tonight."

"Thanks."

"Anyway,"—he brightens—"I'm glad you had a nice weekend."

"Dad and I went hiking in Forest Park in Portland. It's an actual wilderness area inside the city limits. Even bigger than Central Park, would you believe? It's where I got dumped from my friend's horse when I went blind." I shut down the memory of Tiffany and how I destroyed our friendship, too ashamed to find her on social media, apologize and reconnect. "Anyway, Dad and I had a chance to talk. He was really good about it, and he's happy for my mom, even though he still loves her."

"And that's how you know he *does* love her," Jamie says. "Because he wants her to be happy, even if it's not with him."

"I know," I say. "And she did get engaged last night."

"So now you move forward, wherever this takes you. You work at being positive. And you wish your mom well. Who knows? Maybe there's someone out there for your dad. You might find the best of both worlds."

"Maybe," I say.

Though I'm not holding my breath on that.

"Well, I've gotta get to work—we're in Salt Lake City tonight if you don't know already—so I'd better go."

"Wish everyone luck for me," I say.

"Will do."

"Thanks for calling, Jamie. And, well, for everything."

"My pleasure."

He hangs up, and I sit here, replaying it all in my mind.

Why *does* he keep calling me?

Okay, there's my story, and he wanted to tell me what everyone thought of it. But still, he could have emailed me, texted me, whatever. Why invest time he could have spent elsewhere discussing my weekend, my blindness, and the changes life's now throwing at me?

Why should any of that matter to him?

"Blind Etiquette"

By Jenny Ryan

I'm always amazed by the things people do and say around me, everything from ignoring to over-helping to being awestruck by the littlest thing I do.

I'm ignored when you don't talk to me directly. Or when you third-person me, asking Morgan or Kaitlin or my mom *Does Jenny want to go to the mall with us?* Or *What would she like off the menu?* When I can decide and answer for myself, thank you.

I'm not deaf, either, though people talk loud to me all the time. Like being blind makes me hard of hearing, too.

When it comes to offering help, don't assume I need it. I have ways of doing things, same as you do. But if I look lost or confused or uncertain, it's okay to ask the question.

Let Alexis do her job. She's highly trained, and we're an in-tune-with-each-other team. If she's in-harness, she's working, so please ask first before petting her.

If you're standing in for her, let me take your arm at the elbow. Walk at your normal pace. I don't shuffle, and I won't trip or fall. If steps or curbs are involved, stop and let me find them with my cane or foot before going on.

If you're impressed with something I do, be impressed because I do it well, not because I'm blind and manage to do it, anyway. Nobody likes backhanded praise.

Put simply, treat me as you would anyone else.
Because that's exactly who I am.

Chapter 11

organ's reaction to the latest from Jamie Conway is off the charts.

"He called you *again?*"

It's Monday morning, and we're tucked onto our bench at the back of the bus, Alexis sandwiched on the floor between us and the next seat, Kaitlin sitting where she always does with Hannah, Tyler, and Malia. There's so much talking, yelling, and laughing going on up there that no one's likely to notice Morgan's day-to-day hysterics.

"Yeah," I say, and then give her the deets—the emails, the band passing my story among themselves, Jamie asking questions about my life like he has no one more interesting in his at the moment.

"Oh, my gosh!" Morgan shrieks. "You've hooked yourself a guy!"

"Not hooked," I say. "Don't say hooked. He was just calling because of my story."

"He could have emailed because of your story," says Morgan. "He called because he wanted to talk to *you*." She sighs. "I *so* want to meet him!"

"It's not like that," I insist.

Though honestly, I've not stopped thinking about him since he hung up last night.

I mean, dropping by to visit me was way over the top, to begin with. And now, two phone calls? To say nothing of putting my story into the hands of everyone in O'Shannon.

Seriously, I don't know what to make of it all.

The bus slows for the school zone and turns into the parking lot, braking with a loud rush of air at the edge of Sandy High.

"Somehow, Jenny, we've gotta find out about this guy," Morgan's saying. "I mean, what, really, do you know about him?"

"That he works for O'Shannon," I say. "And he likes my blog."

Bodies slam from their seats, everyone talking, hollering, scraping and banging packs and whatever else they're carrying, and thunder up the aisle like a stampede of buffalo. Morgan waits with Alexis and me till the end. No sense getting taken out by some hunk of a football player.

"Not how old he is?" she's saying. "Or where he's from or what he *looks* like—"

"He's from London," I remind her. "And how would I know what he looks like?"

"You could ask him."

"Why would I want to?"

Because it doesn't matter to me. And most sighted people don't get that.

What you wear, what your makeup looks like, how you do your hair, how your body's put together—all that gets sized up about you before you've said one word. They look at me and see *blind*. But from my perspective, it's all about who you are and what you do because I can't judge you on anything else.

Morgan sighs into my face. "Well...you know..." she hedges.

"Morgs, he's gotta be way older than me," I say. "Like I'd even *think* what you're thinking about somebody that much"—*however much*—"older than me. And he's just being nice. He likes my writing, and he wants me to interview Liam because that's my dream. That's it, that's all."

Well, maybe not *all*. Jamie *has* shown incredible interest in my blindness and me in general. But that doesn't mean—

"I still think you should ask," she says. "Find out more about him. It's weird he's nowhere on the internet. And he's a publicist? For *O'Shannon*? If you didn't have autographed merch and a note from Liam as proof, I'd think you dreamed him up."

No, because I don't invent guys.

Why would I?

Though she's got a point; Jamie's cyber-invisibility probably *should* be of concern.

But what he looks like?

Why should I care when I can't see him, anyway?

I MULL it over all morning.

Texting Jamie would probably be okay at this point.

Just thought I'd ask what you look like and how old you are, too, if you don't mind...

Yeah, right.

Though *I hope your day is going great* should be acceptable.

I open my phone during study hall—*now's as good a time as any*—and check my messages.

A text from Morgan, one from Kaitlin. And this Instagram DM is from—

O'Shannonofficial!!!

Wait—*seriously?* The band is DM-ing *me?*

Well, they do know my name. But why would they—

No, it's got to be Jamie—*guess he beat me to it*—using their account, which he has access to and probably runs to some extent.

I ask for the message, keeping my voice low in case someone's closer than I think.

A few other voices murmur across the room, but otherwise, it's mostly quiet here. No shuffling, breathing, or page-turning anywhere nearby. Alexis shifts at my feet, re-shifts, and settles, her head going down, tags clinking against the floor.

Hi, Jenny, my Aussie phone voice says through the one earbud I've got in. **Jamie here. Thought it might be handy to connect on social media**.

My pulse picks up.

Why should it do that when I know this guy, and he's not in the band?

Especially, he adds, **when it comes to communicating info regarding the Seattle show and your interview with Liam.**

And there's the reason why.

"Any details on that yet?" I ask.

No, but we're hoping to solidify something soon.

"Super excited!"

Liam's looking forward to it, too.

"He is?"

Doesn't he do this kind of thing all the time? With people who have a name in the business and publish in magazines with readerships running into the millions?

Though he might be a bit intimidated by your talent, Jamie adds. **He's never been interviewed by a fan who should be a professional.**

"Haha," I say. "Hope I don't disappoint."

We've seen what you can do.

"No pressure, right?" I take a breath. Time to put it out there. "So, do you chat with everyone you make arrangements for?"

As needed, yes.

What about *not* as needed?

Is this just a business contact?

I enjoy talking to you, he adds. **You have a refreshingly different take on things which I both appreciate and find fascinating.**

My cheeks warm. "Thanks. So"—maybe now is the time; now or never, as they say—"anything you want to tell me about yourself?"

What would you like to know?

I sort through my words before voicing them. "You told me your social media accounts are private, for which I don't blame you. But I can't find you under any professional accounts, either."

My palms sweat as I wait for the answer to come back.

I'm relatively new with O'Shannon, he says. **It's my first publicist gig—I'm touring with them to gain experience—and I've had no reason to set up a website yet. Though I will certainly do so at some point.**

Unusual, perhaps, but he can't be expected to have the online presence of someone like Richard Vaughn.

"Makes sense," I say.

What else?

"How about a description?" *There, Morgan, I asked.* "Just for a point of reference."

What I look like, you mean?

"Yeah, if you don't mind."

Not at all, he sends back. **Blonde hair. Blue eyes. Five-ten, American height, and about one-sixty, American weight.**

Pounds? Oh, right, they use that in Britain, too.

"Okay, that helps. And"—seriously, I don't want to ask, but at this point, I should probably find out—"would you mind telling me how old you are?"

I'm twenty-one, he says.

I breathe out, and I don't know if I'm relieved or...something else.

He's too old.

He's not *that* much too old.

It totally doesn't matter, so why am I even thinking this?

"Wow, you landed a great first publicist job young," I say.

Never mind that he's out of my league in every other way.

An incredible stroke of luck for which I'm grateful every day, he says. **What else can I tell you?"**

"Something most people don't know?"

I'm an introvert in an extrovert job.

"No, wait, you're not. You're—" I break off my voice text.

Then again, maybe he is. Would that be why he goes all quiet on me at times? He doesn't do that with professional clients, does he?

"—good at what you do," I finish before sending.

I work at putting myself out there, he says. **Every day.**

"So I'm helping you practice, then."

And doing a fab job of it, too.

"Glad to hear it," I say. "Where in London are you from?"

In my fruitless search to find his name, I learned the city has multiple boroughs, same as New York.

Chelsea, he says. **In the West End.**

"Nice." I'll be sure to look it up. "London sounds so cool. Ireland sounds cool. Europe sounds cool."

You know what they say about home—no place like it and all that.

"Yeah." Dad's house on the edge of Forest Park rears in my memory. "Maybe I'll go to the UK someday."

Maybe I'll show you around.

Maybe I'm getting too friendly with this guy.

"So"—moving things along—"how's your day?"

Excellent. And yours?

"Great."

And on it goes to the end of the period, and I don't get one trig equation, one Frost sonnet, or one biology question worked out, read/listened to, or answered the whole time.

"Wow, he sounds gorgeous!"

It's the first—no, second—thing out of Morgan after I tell her what happened while she was doing stretches in yoga class. The first was projected at attention-grabbing decibels about Jamie and I exchanging messages through O'Shannon's Instagram account.

"I knew he'd be blonde. And blue eyes?" She sighs. "Heaven!"

We're back on the bus now, and no matter how she begs, I am *not* showing her my chat window with him.

I'd never hear the end.

"Now, if only he's available..." An even bigger sigh.

"I didn't ask," I say. "And being blonde doesn't make him gorgeous."

"Kyle's blonde." A long, metal boy mop she adores almost as much as his studly tatted arms. "Blue eyes, too. Trust me, he's gorgeous."

"Whatever," I say.

"No, seriously," she says.

"Like it matters." I thump Alexis with the foot I've uncrossed. "Like I'm looking for a relationship with some older guy on tour with a rock band. I'm not jumping into anything with anyone else."

"Forget anyone else. We're talking cool Britisher here. And at those body specs, yeah, he's hot. With amazing connections and obvious interest in *you*."

"It wouldn't work," I tell her. "Besides, I'm not interested in him that way. He's just this really nice guy who's I-don't-know-why interested in how I am and what I'm doing."

"The key word here is *interested*," says Morgan. "Though being scorchingly hot doesn't hurt."

"Thought you were concerned about his lack of online presence."

"I said it's weird he doesn't have any. Not that it would stand in *my* way. Anyone who matches that description—he *did* send you a pic, I hope—*and* works for O'Shannon can be as invisible as he likes."

"And what would *I* do with a pic?"

"Not you. *Me*," Morgan says. "And I'd salivate over it."

Two days later, I get another DM from O'Shannonofficial.

Hey, girl, it's me, Leslie.

Now the whole thing really *is* getting out of hand.

"**H**i, Leslie," I say back.

Imagine getting Liam in the chat feed with me...

Grand to talk to you, she says.

Like I'm doing *her* a favor.

"You, too," I say. "So cool of you to contact me."

I owe you, girl. We never finished your interview, and I'm sorry I didn't get you your shirt like I promised.

"It's all good. Jamie brought it out."

He said he enjoyed seeing your place and talking to you about your horse and your dog.

"It was nice of him to deliver."

He likes doing things to brighten someone's day, she sends back. **And we loved your suggestions of where to go and what to see in Portland. All of it grand.**

"Awesome," I say. "So, how do you like it here in the States?"

Love it! I've been to the East Coast before, but this is my first time in the west. Vancouver is savage gorgeous. San Francisco, Portland, and Seattle, too. Some of us went shopping at Pike Place Market and down onto the waterfront and rode up the Space Needle to have lunch in the restaurant there. Deadly cool!

"My dad took us to the observation deck once." Back when I

could see the view. "And my grandma lives in Seattle, so we go there a lot."

Brilliant.

By now, I'm settling into this, the way I did when I interviewed her at the Moda Center. Like I'm chatting with Morgan or another friend from school. Nagging at me is the notion of asking more about Jamie—what he's into besides history and museums and something about his family, too. But no, those are questions for Jamie himself—that I could have asked the day he contacted me through Instagram instead of derailing into O'Shannon's performance of the night before. Besides, I don't want to look interested in a way I'm not.

Leslie signs off, and I go back to U. S. Government, Chapter 8, playing off my Reader at warp speed. Not ten minutes later, *Tear At The Walls* bangs out of my phone.

I stop my Reader and voice-check the name. *Jameson Conway* comes back in my Aussie guy accent.

I let the song play on, my heart hammering in my throat.

Why should it do that?

I've phone-talked to him twice now, not to mention chatted with him online. You'd think the adrenaline rush wouldn't kick in so hard and fast.

I pick up before the song cuts off. "Hi, Jamie."

"Set my name with the number, I see," he says.

"Figured I might as well."

Seeing how this is becoming a habit.

"Good idea," he says. "So, how's everything?"

"Everything's great. How about with you?"

"Just grand."

"You're in Denver tonight?" I say.

"You follow us pretty closely, don't you."

"You—well, *they*—are all over social media with their tour."

"Publicity and all that," he says. "Yeah, we're in Denver. Where it's snowing."

"Raining here. Which it does a lot," I say. "So I just talked with Leslie on Instagram."

"She said she was going to contact you. She likes you a lot. And I happen to know she'd love to interview with you again. If you ever want to write more about her."

Are you kidding?

"I'd love to!" I did, after all, give her just two paragraphs; everything else focused on the band, as intended. "We can do it through Insta or FaceTime, if she's okay with that, and go from there. Like a personal profile or something?"

"That'd be perfect," he says. "And a good starting point for you if only to do her a favor. It can take years to break into this business, so any contacts you make along the way will certainly help. You've definitely got talent. And determination, too, it seems. And"—he pauses—"I happen to know some people."

Yes, yes, yes!

"But I wouldn't expect too much at this stage. You'll have to work hard for it. Get knocked down and tell yourself newspaper reporting looks good after all, then fight for your dream, anyway. Even if it never plays out like you hope."

"Thanks, Jamie."

It's more—really, everything with this guy has been more—than I would ever have expected.

"No promises," he says. "Though a little optimism never hurts."

"Of course." I pause, waiting, but he doesn't go on. Time, I guess, for those other questions still brewing in my mind. "So what can you tell me about your family? Do you have brothers, sisters? What does your mom do?"

"Mum's...a nurse." He spaces out the words like he's thinking them through. "I have an older brother in the Royal Navy...and a younger sister studying archeology in Egypt."

"Archeology sounds super cool," I say. "And in Egypt, too."

"Yeah, pretty fascinating."

"And your dad? What'd he do?"

"He was...a solicitor. An attorney, you say here."

"Criminal law?"

"Business."

"Okay." I'm curious how he died and when, but I'm not sure I should ask. "So, what kind of schooling did you do to become a publicist?"

"Um...two years at Leeds in Yorkshire." He stops—*why is he struggling with this?*—then starts again. "Communications major. I haven't finished yet because I got the chance to work for O'Shannon —great pay, great benefits, and the on-the-job training is brilliant. I'm taking a couple of classes online."

"And what do you do for fun? Besides visit museums when you're on tour."

"I visit them at home, too. Got some great ones in South Kensington, just north of Chelsea. As for other stuff, I like films—all kinds, but especially drama, action, and documentaries. And watching sports. Love fishing, traveling, photography. Riding horses when I get the chance. And spending time with my mates. I play mahjong and chess, too."

"My dad tried to teach me chess," I say. "I guess he did teach me, but I've never been very good at it. I always lose my queen right off."

"Maybe you should hold her back a bit," says Jamie. "I could show you some time—" He stops, like that slipped out of nowhere.

"Um...sure," I say. "When you're back in the area."

"We can do it online. But we're definitely coming back. We're in the process of lining up Seattle along with a second show in Chicago."

"Do you have a date for Seattle?"

"Not confirmed," he says. "We're negotiating with the Tacoma Dome for some time between the twelfth and the sixteenth of December. Any chance you can come up to do the interview then?"

"My dad might be able to drive me. If not, I'll get there somehow."

Like I'd miss this for anything.

"I'll let you know, then."

"Great."

"So, what do *you* do," he says, "besides go to school and write your blog and compete in horse sports? Do you have a part-time job?"

"I babysit for my neighbor sometimes," I say. "And tutor a couple of middle school kids on English subjects." Morgan, too (though I never charge her), because she sucks at that even worse than she does math. "Sometimes, I clean stalls and feed horses for my OHSET coach."

"And for fun?"

"I hang out with friends. Go shopping, hiking, camping, fishing, anything outdoors. I want to learn rock climbing. I've done indoor walls, but I want to get on some actual rock. Like Smith Rock in central Oregon. And ski season just opened on Mt. Hood, so some of us are putting a trip together for the weekend."

"You don't sit still, do you," he says.

"Sitting still would be boring."

"Do you use the headsets for skiing?"

"Most of the time. Though, I've skied with a guide calling instructions back to me. Left turn, right turn, stuff like that."

"And climbing?"

"With a partner. It's all about hands and feet, anyway. And it's not like I'm scared of heights or get vertigo or anything."

"No, I guess not."

"Ice skating's fun, too. It was something I did before I went blind and, like everything else I thought was lost forever, I found if I tweaked things a bit, I could do it again."

"Your determination amazes me," he says.

"I had none after my accident," I say. "I was all *why me* and raging at God because it *was* me, and there was nothing anybody could do about it."

"Me, too. After my dad died," Jamie says. "Blaming myself, blaming God, blaming my dad. It's called grieving. And it takes time to heal, to pick yourself up again and go on."

"I know."

"So, what changed your outlook?" he asks.

"Someone showed me where I was headed if I didn't turn things around. It was super hard making the change. But better than sitting in my room, crying all day. Or throwing my lunch at the wall."

"You did that?"

"Twice. The first time my mom cleaned it up. The second time my dad made me clean it up. Not fun when you can't see what you're doing, and you have no idea if you got it all, and then you step in something later and find out, no, you didn't. Never did that again."

"Wise choice."

"Only choice." I inhale, blow out a breath. *Maybe it's okay to get real with this guy.* "No matter what it looks like, Jamie, I don't have it all together, not always. Sometimes I'm scared. Some days I want to scream. Some days I want to hide in the closet and just...not be blind. But I don't have that choice. I have to work at being the me I show the world because if I don't, here come the do-gooders and feel-sorry-for-me people, and that's so much worse."

"Everyone puts on a front of some kind." He goes quiet again and a bit troubled. Like when we talked about me being patronized because I'm blind. "But no one can live it twenty-four-seven. You have to find the balance between who you need to be and who you are when no one's looking."

"I know."

"That said"—and his voice lightens—"what do you want to do that you haven't already?"

"Besides meet Liam O'Shannon? Hm, I don't know. Travel somewhere, I guess. I've been to Victoria and Vancouver, Seattle, San Francisco, and Disneyland. But I want to see other places, too. Like New York City. And Hawaii. Australia, maybe? And Ireland, definitely."

"Forgive me for asking," says Jamie, "but what's that like for you? Seeing someplace you can't actually *see.*"

"It's"—I stop, think for a minute—"everything else, I guess. What a place feels like, smells like, what you eat and do, the people, the culture, all of it. Just because you can't see something doesn't make you any less there."

"No, of course not. It's just...one more thing I've never thought of."

"And you?" I ask. "What do you want to do that you're not doing now?"

"Mm...enjoy some downtime. Not much of that happening these days. Beyond that, find a girl, make a life together, have a couple of kids. The posh, suburban dream."

"I'm sure you'll get there."

A guy like him can't *not* find someone, nice as he is. And I'm sure they'll have a great life together in London or wherever they choose to live, and he'll be a great dad, too, and work himself into a lead publicist job with some other band. Or maybe Richard Vaughn will step aside, and he can take over that slot with O'Shannon.

"Hope so, anyway," Jamie says. "If anyone can inspire that, it's you, Jenny. From where you've been to where you are now. You're going places, I can tell."

"Thanks," I say. "And you'll find your dreams, too, I'm sure."

We talk until he has to go. No agenda. Just talking, discovering, getting to know each other, working out our friendship.

For surely that's what it's becoming.

Chapter
13

"Now, this dress here"—Mom taps the computer screen—"What would you girls think of this?" To me, she adds, "Fitted bodice with a flared skirt. Two panels, front and back, a panel on each side, uneven hemline."

We're not talking bridesmaids here, never mind what she'd hoped for back on Family Meeting Night. Now she's settled for us as guest-book-and-program hand-out people. She's cool with it, and we've got roles we can live with.

Plus new dresses, apparently.

"More like a jagged-y hemline," Kaitlin says. "The longest points are maybe, three, four inches below the knee."

"Scalloped neckline"—Mom keeps going—"fitted sleeves, v-point over the back of the hands, gauzy fabric. Lined, of course."

"Color?" I ask.

"Several options," she says. "But I was thinking burgundy. I'm looking at a mauve dress, so burgundy would set it off nicely, don't you think?"

"Not like we're going to be up front with you," says Kaitlin.

"For the pictures, I mean," says Mom.

"Okay, sure," says Kait.

"Burgundy's fine," I say.

"And the dress itself?" Mom's nail ticks against the screen.

"Maybe," says Kaitlin.

"Jenny?"

"I'd like to see it." Figuratively, of course. "But it sounds fine."

Fine has become my standard answer for everything these days. The date is fine, the cake is fine, the music is fine, and the dress, too. Though I do, in fact, like uneven hemlines.

"So, where's this dress you're looking at?" asks Kaitlin.

"David's Bridal. Similar style, very flattering lines."

Mom has a great figure for being forty-two. Even so, she complains about what we girls did to her waistline all those years ago. So she goes for clothes that are slimming about the middle and keeps her hair highlighted blonde for a younger-than-she-actually-is look.

"Colors would be mauve and burgundy, then," says Kaitlin.

"And white," Mom adds. "Pink and white roses would be nice against something wine-colored, I think."

"Is Alexis going to wear a big, burgundy bow?" asks Kait.

"I hadn't thought of Alexis." Mom aims her voice at me. "I'm not sure you'll need her. We're looking at Dover Church"—it's relatively small—"and we can walk through everything as much as you like. But if you want her there, of course, she's welcome."

I haven't thought that far, either.

The whole thing is unreal as it is.

Whenever I've envisioned myself as part of someone's wedding, it's always been Morgan's, Kaitlin's, or somebody I'll meet at U of O, perhaps. Not my mother's. It's so utterly embarrassing that I've told no one but Morgan, and her reaction was an over-hyped, *you're kidding*, implying an endless stream of exclamation marks flying behind the words.

Okay, that was back when Mom was talking about bridesmaid duty. But still. We'll be on display. Not what I want for a wedding I wish wasn't happening.

"We'll see," I say about Alexis.

"Who's on the guest list?" asks Kaitlin.

"Family, of course," Mom says. "And a few friends. Your Uncle Trevor said he'd bring Grams down from Seattle. And your cousin Jared's driving the family up from Grants Pass."

"What about Dad?" says Kait.

Silence falls like shards of glass.

I've already banged that question around in my head.

It's not like Dad would actually show, of course. Okay, maybe if he was happily in a relationship instead of sucking up his loss and sticking himself with all the blame. But no, he doesn't want to be here for this. Why would he?

But not sending him an invite when everyone else is getting one feels like total snubs-ville.

What do you do when part of the family isn't always family anymore?

"Invite him," I say.

"Yes, please," Kaitlin agrees. "He won't come, but at least he won't feel shunned."

Mom hesitates. "Very well," she says.

But I can tell she's less than thrilled.

Not like he's going to stand and raise an objection, like in Taylor Swift's *Speak Now*.

But imagining him sitting in that pew, wishing he could, makes me rethink what I just suggested.

THE TEXT I've been waiting for hits my phone a few days later.

December 14th at the Tacoma Dome. Does that work for you?

"Yes," I send back, scrambling about my brain for what day of the week the fourteenth might be.

It's a Saturday, adds the Aussie version of Jamie Conway.

"Perfect," I say. "I'll be there."

TWO DAYS LATER, this one comes in:

Everything's set with Liam. Interview before the show, if that's okay?

"Totally okay," I say back. "Can't wait!"

Front row work for you? VIP package, of course.

"Wow, that'd be killer! Thanks!" And then, because I need to be sure, "There's a ticket for Morgan, isn't there?"

Tickets are included with your backstage passes, which you'll get when you arrive at the venue. And yes, for both of you. If you need pick up from somewhere, I can arrange it.

"If my dad can drive us, we're good. But if anything changes, I'll let you know."

Sounds grand.

THEN THIS DINGS into my phone as I walk to the bus zone after school, Alexis weaving me among the bodies, stopping to let this one pass, angling right to skirt a jam up ahead, ducking left to avoid a bunch of rowdy, hollering boys.

Enjoying my view of the St. Louis Arch. Hope your day is great!

"My day is perfect," I say. "And your view sounds amazing."

I wait, but he says nothing more.

"Who was that?" Morgan pesters, striding along beside me.

I consider blowing her off. Then again, what's the point? She's going to know sooner or later, the way she knows everything else going on in my life.

"Jamie Conway," I say.

"Oh, my gosh, he's *texting* you now!"

"Lots of people text me."

"Not hot publicist guys who work for European rock bands." She sighs, over-dramatic. "When did this start?"

"The day after I talked to him through O'Shannon's Insta account."

"That was more than a week ago! And you didn't tell me?"

I shrug. "It was just chitchat stuff. Mostly about the Seattle show and my interview with Liam." We're standing now in the bus zone, waiting. "And our seats. They're front row."

Morgan screams and launches herself at me (not entirely unexpected), then rocks me hard, like I scored a winning goal or something. "Oh, my gosh! Seriously?"

I laugh with her. "Yes, seriously."

"Amazing!" She sighs again. Or drools, perhaps. "I'm going to stand there and just inhale Kyle Finn; he'll be so close!" She crushes me again, then disentangles herself. "*That's* what Jamie was texting you about?"

"That was yesterday. Today he was just saying hi."

"*Yes!*" Her voice falls and swings away like she's dropped into a little victory dance. "That's a *just because* message. As in, *just because I'm thinking of you, I text you.* Which you don't get with a this-is-strictly-a-business-deal kind of relationship."

I groan. "He's a friend, Morgan. Friends chat. Friends text. Friends call each other."

"Yeah, but he's a *guy*"—like that needs pointing out—"who doesn't live anywhere around here and has no reason to keep such close contact, *if* you don't mind my saying so, with everything you do unless he's interested in more than just friendship. *If* you know what I mean."

With Morgan, it's impossible not to.

"Yeah, and he lives in *London*," I stress, "a whole continent and an ocean away. And it's not like he'll be around once he goes home. Or like we could see each other on a regular basis. At best, he's a social media friend. Anything more would be stupid and pointless."

"Well, if *I* had some guy chasing after me like that"—Morgan doesn't at the moment, so she's always on the lookout for possibilities —"I wouldn't waste time worrying about where he lives."

I'm doing food prep in the kitchen when I throw out the question, phrased as a statement. "Mom, I want to go to Seattle on December fourteenth, if that's okay."

Like I'm asking to go to the movies or a sleepover at Morgan's.

"What's happening in Seattle on December fourteenth?"

Ground beef and taco seasoning flavor the air as she scrapes it around the skillet. Water runs in the upstairs bathroom; Kaitlin's in from volleyball practice, homesteading in the shower.

"Tacoma, actually." I'm cutting tomatoes on the breadboard, my palm flat on the knife, slicing straight down, then repositioning the blade for the next cut. "O'Shannon is doing a second show in the Tacoma Dome, and I've been invited to go."

"You just went to see O'Shannon," she says.

"Yeah, but this is different."

"Who invited you?"

"Okay, um"—this part gets a little tricky—"remember the publicist guy I met at the Moda Center?" I've told her that much, at least. "The one who got me backstage after the concert and set me up to interview Leslie O'Shannon?"

"Ye-es." Mom sounds faintly puzzled. Like that part of the conversation had gone over her head.

"Well, now he's set me up"—really, this is harder than I thought it would be—"to interview Liam. In Tacoma."

Mom says nothing for a moment, just scratches some more at the skillet, the ground beef popping and splattering into the silence between us.

"Dad said he might be able to drive me," I add, like that might help. "He should be home that weekend and—"

"How was this arrangement made?"

"With Dad or—"

"With this guy who's setting it up."

"He, um—his name's Jamie Conway, and he talked to Liam about—"

"With you, I mean."

"Okay, um—"

I start with my article.

How Jamie wanted to read it, and I emailed it to him, and he got back to me and said the whole band liked it and that Liam had agreed to meet with me before the Tacoma show and give me a one-on-one interview. Okay, the events are slightly out of order, but I let them stand. I say nothing about Jamie showing up in our yard the day after the Portland concert or that we've talked on the phone several times as well as on O'Shannon's Instagram account. Or that we've been texting each other for over a week and not always about anything connected with me going to Tacoma or interviewing Liam O'Shannon.

Mom slides the skillet from the burner to the stovetop. "Backup plan if your dad can't drive you?"

Looking promising...

"We could take Amtrak, maybe." I scrape my pile of tomatoes from the board into a waiting bowl. "Or the bus."

"*We* means Morgan's going with you?"

"Yes. And our seats"—I pause for emphasis—"are front row."

I eventually told Mom about my autographed shirts and Liam's note promising me seats of my choice. Morgan was over for dinner that night and said she'd ordered the same shirt I got from the band —"the one that's autographed"—so I jumped in to explain, making it sound like an oversight on my part.

Mom just doesn't know Jamie handed them to me outside by the barn.

"Where would you stay for the night?" she asks.

"With Grams, probably."

Grandma Ryan lives on Queen Anne Hill, just north of the Space Needle, and she's always up for company no matter how last minute it might be.

"And if you take the bus or the train," Mom says, "how would you get to Seattle from Tacoma?"

Grams doesn't drive much after dark, so delete her from the equation. And navigating the light rail into Seattle and the bus system after that isn't something I want to deal with late at night.

"We'd probably stay with Jordanne instead." Morgan's older sister lives in Fife, five miles out of Tacoma. "But Dad thinks he can drive us. He just wants to make sure his travel schedule's clear."

"Would you take Alexis?"

"I'd like to, but then I'd be leaving her with Grams or Jordanne for the show. Might be more hassle than it's worth."

"I can watch her if you like." Mom pads across the room. The faucet handle squeaks. Water rushes into the sink. "Food money?"

"Got that already. Spending money, too."

I might need yet another O'Shannon shirt or band poster, or maybe, if I scrimp and save enough, their amazing tour jacket Morgan said was priced off the planet.

Imagine Liam's name scrawled across the back of that!

Mom crosses the room again. The refrigerator door opens behind me. "Have you priced out alternate transportation?"

"Not yet, but I will."

She closes the door, strides toward the table.

"So we can go?" I ask.

"Get me the information," she says back, "and we'll come up with a plan."

Yes, yes, yes!

"Thanks, Mom!" I set my knife down and make my way around the island to hug her—something I don't do so often anymore.

Not that we don't have our good moments. It's just the fewer boats I rock, the better.

For both of us.

"So my dad said yes, he can drive Morgan and me to Tacoma on the fourteenth," I text Jamie two days later.

Perfect, he answers back. **I'll confirm the time with Liam when I know what works. Gotta be a flexible one, just so you know.**

"If it works for him, it works for me."

Will you need lodging somewhere?

"We're staying with my Grams in Seattle."

Sounds like a plan, he says. **I'll email the logistics when I have them.**

"Thanks *so* much!"

One more piece falling into place, everything shaping up for the night of my life!

October slides toward November with a major temperature drop and an epic downpour of rain. Halloween is wet and windy, soggy leaves plastered to the walk as Kaitlin, Morgan, Alexis, and I scramble from the Townsend minivan and make for Haley Mayes's front door.

We arrive at her party as pirates—stockings and wide-legged pants, bandanas, eye patches, and stubble beards (courtesy of Morgan's eyeliner). Alexis was no-go on the eye patch, but she does have a skull-and-crossbones bandana around her neck. The music's loud, the cider's hot, the cookies, cupcakes, and snack-size candy bars prolific, and the neighborhood kids punch the bell and bang on the door every other minute.

My house is too far off the grid for trick-or-treaters, so Mom never stocks up on handouts. She and Bryan made plans to go out for the night. And Dad will do what he always does; sit home in front of the TV with a Marie Callender dinner and maybe a bowl of candy corn. I always hurt for him, and this year is worse than ever.

At home, it's nothing but flower talk, dress talk, cake talk, photographer talk, and catering talk (*catering* for a simple wedding?) from when I turn up for breakfast until I shove out the door for the bus. And then again at night till I go upstairs to study, sleep, or escape the endlessness of it all.

Like my cousin Taylor's wedding all over again. Only Taylor was a twenty-two-year-old, first-time-arounder, so wedding-itis was the order of the day. Mom's case is more like a mid-life crisis trying to relive her bride-to-be days.

I text Dad several photos of Alexis and me from the party, then call the next morning from Morgan's house. We don't talk about his home-alone night. Instead, we remind each other of years past when Halloween was a family event, laughing over costumes and escapades and parties with too much candy and apple cider.

Moments captured in time.

Remember when we stopped doing Halloween, Thanksgiving, Christmas, Easter, and every other holiday together unless I schemed it to happen?

Thankfully, I have Jamie in my life, texting me almost every day, showing up on social media, and, yes, calling me, too.

"Hey," he says a few days later after I answer on the second ring. "How's it going?"

"I'm okay." I swallow and try to reorder my midterm-scrambled brain. "I'm fine, actually." Not entirely true, but close enough. "How about you?"

"Doing great. Got a few minutes of downtime, so I thought I'd ring you."

"Thanks."

I'm getting used to this now—him calling (I leave that to him because it works best, he says, with his schedule), me looking forward to it, me missing him on the days he doesn't. "You're in Detroit tonight, aren't you?"

"Yes. And Cleveland tomorrow night."

"I watched the vlog Keenan made in Chicago a couple of days ago," I say. "He was talking about how the city dyes the river green for St. Paddy's Day, and Sean said they should come back for that and a pint of Guinness, and Liam said there should be a song in there somewhere."

"Probably about Guinness," Jamie says. "And I love how you say *watched.*"

"Because saying listened when everyone else says watched would be stupid."

"Right. And I haven't *watched* it yet, but I will." He pauses half a beat. "So, how's everyone in your life?"

"Busy," I say. "At least, at my house. The wedding and all."

"Ah," he says. "The wedding."

"Last Saturday of January," I say.

"Date set, I see."

"Yeah." I sigh. "A bit overwhelming at the moment. And midterms coming up on top of everything."

"Sorry if I caught you at a bad time."

"No, it's fine. I could use a break, anyway."

"Happy to give you one," he says. "So, as we say in Ireland, what's the craic? Anything fun?"

"Halloween was great."

"What'd you do?"

I tell him about Haley's party, and he laughs over our costumes. It's the first time I've heard him laugh, and it's the warm, all-in kind that makes you want to laugh with him.

"It was really fun," I add.

"Was Alexis a pirate, too?"

"She wore a bandana. And she twisted herself up in these streamers Haley had hung from the windows, then yanked them down and dragged them across the room. Everyone was roaring, and I couldn't figure out why till Becca goes, 'Your dog looks like a bunch of walking crepe paper.'"

Jamie laughs again. "Sounds like a grand night. Halloween's huge in Ireland, you know. Even bigger than here, I think, so I appreciate your American take on it."

"What'd you do that night?" I ask. "Other than be in Chicago for a show."

"That *was* my night."

"I'd love it."

"We'll give you a taste of being on tour in Tacoma," he says.

"Can't wait!"

"So, I've got this for you." His voice holds a smile. "I've been in touch with a couple of music journalists who were very interested in what I had to say about your work. One of them asked to see a sample."

My heart climbs into my throat. "My gosh, are you serious?"

"Just to get a feel for where you are now. Though I wouldn't get your hopes up too high just yet."

"No, of course not," I say as they launch to the moon.

"Shall I pass your story on, then?"

"Yes, please."

"Consider it done," he says.

"Wow, thanks so much."

"I'm looking forward to reading your new write-up on Leslie. She loved doing the FaceTime interview with you."

That was four days ago, and we've not talked since, but she follows me now on Instagram and sometimes clicks *like* on my status or whatever photos I post.

"I haven't started it yet," I add, "but I hope to soon. My journalism teacher said she might squeeze it into the next issue if I slant it more on Leslie as a teen girl rather than a rising pop star."

"That'd be good," Jamie says. "And she'll be happy no matter what you do."

"When is she not? Hyper happy, I mean."

As if the dark side of life rolls off her like the rain she dances in.

"More often than you think," he says. "She thrives on attention, sure, but when the bottom falls out, she falls with it."

"Like, when her dad died?"

That was a little over three years ago while the band was realigning itself with a new manager and new frontman. Before I started following them. Before anyone had heard of yet another O'Shannon who could sing. The publicity was mostly European, and I read about it after the fact.

"It was very rough on her," Jamie says. "She'll tell you she sings for fun, but singing helped her heal."

"What about Liam?"

"Listen to him much?"

I grin into my phone. "Once in a while."

"He wrote it into the music. That's how *he* deals."

In minor keys. With grit and loss, with fire and anguish, and the will to crush the odds. Heavy music, power themes.

> *The ground shakes, the sky falls*
> *It's the shock, it's the awe*
> *And I'm fallen, still fallen*
> *Scraped bleeding and raw*
> *Resurrect, let it go*
> *Hold the truth that you know*
> *Don't let it go…*

Everything I fought through all those years ago.

His stuff would have been the soundtrack to my life had he been rock-starring back then.

"You can't listen to him," I say, "and not feel everything he wants you to."

"Everyone handles these things differently," says Jamie. "Leslie and I have talked a lot about it. My dad also passed of cancer"—and there's my answer—"so we have that in common. It helped her, I think."

"Glad to hear it."

"The key to surviving the curves, as you well know, is having someone walk through them with you. Someone you trust."

"For me, that's my dad," I say. "Or Morgan. They're best at pulling me out of whatever funk I've landed in. Mom never gets me like Dad does, so she's not my go-to for that."

"Your dad sounds like a great guy."

"He is."

"I was always closer to my mum," he says. "I worry about her because she's alone, though she does fine. I ring her a lot."

"I call my dad a lot, too."

"So, Jenny..." He hesitates. "If I'm ringing you too often or keeping you from something, you can say so."

"You're not keeping me from anything." *That can't wait, that is.* "And...I like it that you call." My voice softens. "Talking to you is always uplifting."

"You, too." His words are quiet, warm. "This is a high-pressure business, full of demanding people. I don't mean the lads and Courtney in the band. They're a good lot. The crew and the production people, too. But at the end of the day, it's still a business with bills to pay and higher-ups to keep happy. It's refreshing to talk to somebody on the outside about everyday life and remember the world's not all one giant, money-grabbing music machine."

"Am I finally hearing frustration from take-it-all-in-stride you?"

"Maybe a bit," he says. "It's exhausting being on the road, dealing with event managers, promotional people, and anyone with inside connections who wants favors. Kyle's always on about this or that. Leslie runs late to everything. And Liam sucks into himself and his music every time he has a row with his brother."

Wait—did he just drop something super personal he probably shouldn't have?

Not that I'll pass it along.

Except maybe to Morgan.

"Does that happen much?" I ask.

"More of late than usual. Michael can be tough to work under, especially over the long haul. And he's been riding everyone extra hard these days. He wants Liam to get more screen time in Keenan's vlogs, more visibility when the band's out in public rather than keeping to himself off-stage. And whilst the publicist in me gets that, why should it matter how any of them spend their downtime so long as they do their jobs where it counts?"

"Considering how freaking amazing they are, it shouldn't."

"Because Michael keeps them tight, on target. Especially on the road."

Dad pushing me to get out into the world, get back on the horse, keep crafting my writing, put on those skis, grab the next handhold on the rock wall...

"I get it," I say. "And that it's hard, too."

"Shattering, we say. And we've still got the whole Euro/Asian/Australian tour slated for the first of the year—" Jamie breaks off, sighs. "I don't hate this, Jenny. I'm just a bit knackered these days. Anyway, you bring a sense of normal to my often chaotic world. And that helps. A lot."

"I'm glad. Though for me, it goes the other way. You've opened a world I could only dream about."

"Then we're even," he says. "So, um...casual question for you. And don't take this as anything more because really, that's all it is, but..." He stops, tries again. "Do you have someone else in your life—not family, not Morgan—but, you know...someone special?"

Like boyfriend-special?

My heart rate kicks into high gear.

Is *this* how he sees me?

No, no, he just said not to read anything into it. And anyway, we hardly know each other well enough for that, to say nothing of the impossibility of it all.

"Several of them, actually." Best to keep things light. "How 'bout you?"

"So many to choose from, you know." His voice softens, turns wistful. "There was a girl in London a while back. But that's dropped off since I'm not around anymore. Guess it wasn't much, to begin with."

"I'm sorry," I say.

"I'd rather know now than later."

"Yeah," I agree, though not from experience. "I mostly go out with friends. Somebody here, somebody there, nothing steady. We usually go as a group."

"Social's good," he says. "Plenty of time later for finding someone."

"Maybe in college," I say. "Or after that. I want to go slow, though. A guy's got to be ready for what it means to have me in his life."

"A handful, are you?"

"Blind," I remind him.

"I'm sure you'll be worth somebody's while."

My pulse picks up speed.

It's a compliment. Don't take it as anything more.

"I hope so," I say. "It's just—well, I worry about getting close to somebody only to have him decide I'm too much hassle—"

Did I just say that? To this guy who told me someone decided he was too much hassle?

"Anyone who thinks that," Jamie says, "isn't worth having."

"Yeah, I know. So I want to be dead sure before I get involved with anyone."

"*Deadly* sure," he teases me. "And there's nothing wrong with that."

I laugh, and then he says, "I've got to go, but I'll be in touch. And hey, I'm sorry we haven't gotten to that chess game yet. I keep meaning to, but there's always so much going on."

"No worries. And Jamie... Thanks for caring about me. You don't have to, but you do. And that means a lot."

"I could say the same," he says. "I'm really glad I met you."

"Glad I met you, too," I say.

IF THERE'S a flipside to the endless wedding planning and impending D-Day (as I'm calling the official date), it's counting down the days till I get to meet Liam O'Shannon. And not just a shove through the line meet-and-greet, but actually sitting down and talking to him, getting to know, even a little, the guy behind the image and hearing what he has to say about himself and his career, not just what some internet jockey put up on a website.

I've done my homework, rereading everything available online. I'm already solid on his background.

A classical pianist turned synthesist who does most of the band's synth programming and studio keyboard work (along with Leslie's dubstep tracks). Guitarist, bassist, writer, arranger, vocalist. And an actor whose talented performances in secondary school musicals and dramas—before he went on the road with his brother—account for his highly theatrical stage presence.

I've Googled Ireland in general, Cork City in particular, and whatever I can find on the village of Innishannon. All I know is it has a main street and a pub, two churches, a castle and a river nearby, and a wooded area with a nature trail.

And a rock star, if he's at home.

I've written out my questions, crunching them to six from the original ten. If I get the chance, I'll squeeze in another one or two, but really, I don't want to intrude on him more than I already am.

Just meeting him will be enough.

Interview Questions

for Liam O'Shannon

1. What first attracted you to music, and when did you know you wanted to pursue it as a career? How did you decide between music and acting?
2. What was it like playing keys in an internationally touring band at age 16, and how did you handle the demands of the road while being tutored for school? In what ways have things changed now that you're frontman?
3. As a lyricist, you tend toward darkly epic themes. What inspires this? And which do you write first, music or lyrics?
4. Is being a recording/stage artist your ultimate dream? Or is there something more you want to do beyond this?
5. What do you love most about what you do and why?
6. If there's one thing you would love to get across to your fans, what would that be?

EXTRA QUESTIONS (JUST IN CASE)

1. What was it like launching Leslie's career?
2. Which venue/location have you most enjoyed playing?

Chapter
15

November brings the usual stream of teacher in-service days, Veteran's Day, and mid-semester exams. I study, finish papers and projects, and crack out five pages of extra credit write-up for English Lit. Polish my article on the school production of *Our Town*, try on the dress Mom picked out, help her fine-tune the guest list, sample this cake, that filling, this frosting. Go to OHSET practice, shop in Portland with Morgan, and spend a weekend with my dad and Kaitlin in Astoria. Email my everyday-pop-girl story to Leslie for fact-checking—*will I be doing this with Liam when I finish his story?*—and she loves it so much she FaceTimes me.

Just for a few minutes.

But still.

Maybe I *can* do this music journalism thing—going to concerts, interviewing the big names, getting to know them on a personal level.

When I'm not doing all the above, I'm talking to Jamie Conway in one form or another.

We text each other.

Him: **My music journalism contact says you've got a lot of skill for your age and encourages you to seriously consider pursuing this.**

Oh, my gosh, yes!!!

We email.

Me: **Here's a copy of my story on Leslie. And my questions for Liam, too, if you wouldn't mind taking a look?**

Him (next day): **Spot on, Jenny. Excellent story! Great questions, too!**

And he calls, well, a lot. By mid-month, we're talking every day, and I'm fully expecting an adrenaline rush every time VoiceOver announces his name. Not once does he fall silent as he did that day in my yard or those first few times on the phone. Like he's totally at ease with sharing my life and his, too, so there's no more tangling himself up in where to go next.

I Google Chelsea.

The district sits on the Thames and is best known for its upscale shops, annual RHS Chelsea Flower Show, and close proximity to West End destinations, such as Kensington Palace, Hyde Park, and the Natural History Museum. Plenty of culture here to keep Jamie happily occupied when he's at home.

I study London and all those world-class sites everyone wants to see—Buckingham Palace and the Tower of London, Big Ben and Piccadilly Square, and the giant London Eye. I bone up on English history and culture, binge-watch BBC programming for nights on end, and switch out my Aussie phone voice for a British one.

And when Jamie calls, I ask questions.

"Do you have Thanksgiving in England?"

"We don't," he says. "But we're familiar with the custom."

"Any special plans for that day?"

O'Shannon has the night off, so maybe they'll get to do something fun while in Charlotte.

"We're hoping to order your traditional dinner from somewhere," he says. "Wouldn't want to miss the experience."

"It's heavy on the calories," I say. "And absolutely amazing. Make sure you try the cranberry sauce. And leave room for the pumpkin pie."

He chuckles. "Will do."

"So, do you have goose for Christmas like in *A Christmas Carol*?"

"Sometimes," he says. "But Mum makes turkey sometimes, too."

"When are you flying home?"

The North American tour wraps up on December 16th, the date of the added Chicago concert. And for the first time, I think of Jamie actually *being* in London, on the far side of the world.

Will he call me then? Text me? Message me through the band's Instagram account? Or am I just an on-the-road distraction? And why does the thought slam me with such loss?

"December seventeenth," he says. "We get three weeks at home before opening the European tour on January fifth."

"I'm sure you're anxious to see your mum," I say.

"Looking forward to it," he says. "Though I have to admit, I'll miss being here in the States."

Care to elaborate on that?"

"Guess you'll have to come back," I say.

"Definitely doing that. So what are your holiday plans?"

"Dad gets the evenings, Thanksgiving and Christmas Eve," I say. "Mom gets the days."

"Celebrating twice, then."

"I guess."

Not that it makes up for Thanksgivings and Christmases past, all of us together in the same house. But better than one of us not being here at all...

THE NEXT TIME JAMIE CALLS, we talk about firsts.

First days at school—

Him: "I was scared, so my brother walked me to class."

Aw, too cute. And what a sweet brother!

Me: "I met a girl named Tiffany. Later we became best friends."

Till I cut her off like we never happened.

First adventures—

Him: "My uncle took me up in a Cessna when I was ten. I think my mouth hung open the whole time."

Me: "Whitewater rafting the Deschutes in central Oregon. I was seven. Biggest adrenaline-rush-ride ever!"

Fave first—

"Hmm..." he says. "The first time my mum and dad let me go to the Continent on my own. I was fourteen, and I visited a friend in Munich. We took the train to Austria, then Switzerland and France. His parents came, too, of course. The point is, mine didn't."

"That'd be really hard for me to do," I say. "Alone, I mean. I'd have to ask for help. I know some Spanish and a few words in French. But that's it."

"Most northern Europeans speak English, so you're covered. Though"—he draws out the word—"it would be nice to go with a friend. Or visit a friend."

"I don't know anyone in Europe."

"Don't you?"

My cheeks warm. "Well...okay, yes, I do."

Maybe our friendship won't *end when he flies home in a couple of weeks...*

"There you have it," he says. "Okay, your turn."

"My first hike after I went blind. Dad and I did Punchbowl Falls in the Columbia River Gorge. The trail climbs a ledge with a handrail attached to the cliff wall and a huge drop on the open side. We took it slow, and when we got to the falls, he helped me over the rocks to the swimming hole. And it was the coolest thing, doing something I thought was lost forever."

"I love that you don't let anything stop you," Jamie says.

"Lots of things stop me," I admit. "If I can't find a workaround, I move on to something else."

"I've learned so much from you."

"Me, too," I say. "From you, I mean. Stuff about touring—well, the whole music industry, actually. And London and Ireland and other places in Europe from the perspective of someone who isn't an American. Which is important, I think."

"Glad to hear it."

"If I ever do get over there, I'll be sure to connect with somebody from wherever I visit so I can have the best experience."

"Make it Ireland—" He stops. "Well, England, first, of course. *Then* Ireland."

"Absolutely."

"Though we should probably throw in a music festival to make it the ultimate experience."

We?

He's suggesting I do this with *him?*

Well, he offered before in a for-fun way. And he's all upbeat now, so...*playing along...*

"Which do you recommend?" I ask.

"Probably Wacken Open Air. O'Shannon will be headlining there next summer. And I happen to have a few connections, so we should be able to snag some meet-and-greets, photo ops, autographs, you name it."

"That'd be super cool."

"Think about it."

Wait—he's serious???

Like I can just hop over to England and then Germany with some guy I know only over the phone and in Cyberspace.

"Well, it would be *fun*..." I hedge. "But it's not like I've got the money to go to Europe for a month. Or even a week."

"We can work on that," he says.

Doesn't sound like *he's* just imagining this.

What *would* that be like? Seeing each other outside of O'Shannon's tour. Talking and laughing along the banks of the Thames. Eating fish and chips in a Chelsea pub and visiting Castle Cor in Innishannon. Screaming on the grass field at Wacken while my favorite band tears up the night.

Falling for each other beneath a star-studded sky...

No, no, not that...

"Right." Practical me reasserts itself. "And we'll grab a ride on the tour bus to wherever they're playing next."

"See what I can do."

I laugh, lightening the moment, and we go from there—Graspop, Roskilde, and every other festival on O'Shannon's summer schedule, along with whatever else we can explore on Jamie's side of the world.

Not that it's ever going to happen.

⊞ ▮

THE BOX ARRIVES two days later.

Kaitlin doesn't have practice today, and neither do I, so we ride home together, walking down Cedar Creek Lane from the bus stop on Ten Eyck Road. We've just clumped onto the front deck when she says,

"Look. There's another one."

I don't actually look, of course, but I know what she means.

UPS and postal deliveries are multi-weekly these days, with Mom ordering online for the wedding. The arrival of one more box is hardly a noteworthy event. We haven't even got to the Amazon pre-Black Friday or Cyber Monday orders. To say nothing of basic online Christmas shopping.

Whatever's inside shifts and slides when Kaitlin picks it up.

"Hey," she says, "it's for you."

Alexis stops me behind her. "Me?"

"Says *Jenny Ryan.*"

"I didn't order anything."

"Has your name on it." The door creaks as she shoves it inward.

I squeeze through after her, unbuckle the harness, and let Alexis go free, pull off my backpack, and unload it (and the harness, too) onto the dining room table.

Kaitlin puts the box into my hands. It's maybe two feet by eighteen inches by four inches, roughly the size of a J.C. Penney or a Gap box and heavier than a pair of jeans or a sweatshirt, but not by much.

"Who's it from?" I ask.

"Doesn't say. No company name or anything."

"Postmark?"

"Washington," Kaitlin says. "As in D.C."

"D.C.? You're sure it's not the state just north of us?"

"Says *Washington D.C.*"

We have no relatives in the national capital or anywhere else on the East Coast and no friends there, either.

Of course, someone passing through?

That's a strong possibility.

I head for the kitchen, set the box on the table, and go to the counter for the knife block, pulling out the first handle my fingers touch. Back at the table, I feel for the wrapped edges and insert the knife, carefully sawing through the packing tape on both ends and beneath the center flap.

Kaitlin hovers beside me. "Any guesses?"

"Maybe."

"So guess first and then open."

"About who sent it, I mean." I fold back one flap, then the other.

Her breath sucks in. "Oh, my gosh, Jenny!"

I reach into the box and touch nylon fabric tucked back on itself. A jacket? I pull it out and—yes, it *is* a jacket, a nicely made one with a thick, glossy feel, fully lined and—

And then I know.

"It's their tour jacket," Kaitlin says, ultra-reverent. Like she's staring at the Gutenberg Bible or the ceiling of the Sistine Chapel. "The one they're all wearing in the promo shot on their webpage."

The one available at the official O'Shannon gear vendors in the Moda Center that Morgan said was styled like the shirt (black with metallic green) I bought and has the band's name embossed on the back in their shamrock-for-an-apostrophe logo.

I hand it to Kaitlin, shrug out of the one I'm wearing, and trade with her.

The fit is a little big, but that's a given. Half the time, I buy kid sizes because I can't find the adult size zero or two that fits me.

"Looks amazing on you, Jenn," she says. "It's got your name on it, too."

I touch the fabric above my barely-an-A-cup breast and feel the contours of my name, stitched in the flowing style of everyone who wears this jacket on tour. Maybe I'll buy a silver pen and get it autographed to match my shirt.

I reach back into the box, fingering the crepe paper, looking for the card.

"It fell out when you grabbed the jacket." Kaitlin scrapes it from the envelope. "'Jenny,'" she reads, "'thought you might like to wear this to your interview next month. It's the smallest size we have available, so I hope it fits okay. See you soon. *Jamie*,'" she finishes, extra stress on his name.

My stomach flutters.

A shiver touches my arms.

This guy's giving me the ultimate night, making sure I look the part when I live out my dream, wanting everything to be as perfect as he can make it.

What is *going on between us???*

Kaitlin stuffs the card back into the envelope. "Yeah, he's into you."

Is he?

"Not like that." I pull my phone from my hip pocket, snap off a selfie, bring up Dictation, and shoot the photo to Jamie.

Hey, I got the jacket today, I send with the pic. **Wow, thank you *so* much! Fits great, too. See you soon!**

"And you're into him," says Kaitlin.

"*Friend*, Kait," I remind her. "He's a friend, nothing more."

"Trust me," she says, not buying one word, "he's way more."

Morgan goes ballistic when the same shot, along with my text —"Look what showed up at my house today!"—lands in her phone.

"Omigosh!" she screams the minute I answer my ringtone. "Seriously???"

"Total wardrobe makeover."

I'd planned to go casual-dressy—black slacks, purple blouse, the silver herringbone chain Dad gave me last year for my birthday. The totally professional look. But now I'll go concert-style—skinny jeans and my autographed shirt and the tour jacket over that—and hope I look like I'm with the crew.

"Just wow, Jenn!"

"Awesome fit, too."

"I don't mean the jacket," she says. "Though, yeah, that's super cool, and I'm so jealous I could scream. I'm talking about *Jamie*. How much more obvious does he have to be?"

"Morgan, it's not—"

"Hello? Pricey tour jacket. With your name on it?"

"He's just doing something nice for me," I say. "Because it'll look amazing for my interview. Like I'm a serious enough fan I got their jacket?"

"They know you're a serious fan," she says. "This is Jamie giving you a gift he knows you'll love. Think about it."

I *am* thinking about it.

Ever since he suggested—teasing or otherwise—that we go to Wacken together.

And now *this*.

"It's a gift," I insist. "That's all."

"It's more than—"

"How's the essay coming?"

"Don't deflect."

"Due on Monday," I remind her.

"Got enough done to keep Mom off my back." She sighs. "Wish I could write about rock stars like you do."

"Extra credit," I say. "Between the meet-and-greet and Kyle practically guitaring in your face, you ought to get *some* inspiration."

"You know I suck at this, right?"

"You know I'm here to help."

"You should be," she says, "since you're halfway to going pro already, thanks to some guy using every inside contact he's got. For *way* too obvious reasons."

JAMIE'S TEXT dings in after I finish with Morgan.

Looks fab on you, Jenny! YOU look fab!

My breath catches.

Is he saying *I* look good? Or just that I look good in O'Shannon gear?

"Thank you, thank you, thank you!!!!!" I send back.

Happy you like it.

"LOVE IT!!!!!"

You're gonna rock your interview, no worries, he says.

"I hope so."

And I'm smiling. Because he's making me believe I can do this, all of it.

No matter how *un*believable it is.

Chapter
16

Mom catches on the week before Thanksgiving.

The tour jacket sends up a big, screaming red flag. Though I could explain that easily enough. With me being a guest of the band in Tacoma, it's entirely possible they arranged for Jamie to gift it to me as he did Leslie's shirts and Liam's note. But the constant onslaught of phone calls is getting harder to keep under her radar.

So on this drippy Thursday, after I've double-tapped my screen, ending Jamie's call, she walks into my room, leaving me wondering how long she's been out in the hallway, listening in on my end of the conversation.

"So, who were you talking to?"

Excuse me?

How about a little privacy and respect here?

Not that I can keep this from her forever with logistics for Tacoma to be worked out.

Still.

Shouldn't it be my business when and how much I tell her?

"Um..." *What* do *I tell her?* "Jamie Conway."

"This is the guy you met in Portland?" Clearly, she's scrambled some pieces together over the last few days. "Who's arranging things with the band?"

"Yes."

"I thought that was all taken care of."

"It is, but—" I stop, and silence hangs like a thick, wet fog. "Okay, I'm thinking of becoming a music journalist, and he's helping with that—giving me advice, I mean. He arranges interviews for the band, and he had someone look at my story, so we've been talking and—"

"How often?"

"What?"

"—do you talk," she finishes.

I'm not sure that's any of her business, either, but I've pretty much hung myself, so—

"Um...a bit."

"How much is 'a bit?'"

Is this The Inquisition or what?

"Um..." I tug at the frayed hem of my scrappy jeans. "A few times a week."

Mom says nothing for a moment, but her stare burns a hole through me. I can almost see the wheels spinning through her head.

"*Why* is this guy calling you?" she says. "And don't blow me off with interview arrangements or career advice. That doesn't require multiple phone calls a week."

"Okay, um...he's interested in—" I stop again. *Interested* is the wrong word, but it's too late to unsay it. "Well, in me. But not *that* kind of interested." Like I would tell her if he was. "More like I'm *interesting.* Because I'm blind, I guess, and it's all new to him. And I'm a fan of O'Shannon, and I listen to what's going on with him, and he listens to what's going on with me, and he tells me about England and Ireland, and we've just, I don't know, become friends."

"How old is this guy?" she says.

"Mom—"

"It's a question, Jennifer." And there's my real name, so she's serious about this. "How old is he?"

"He's"—I take a breath—"twenty-one."

"He's *twenty-one?*" Her voice climbs an octave. "You're seventeen!"

"Eighteen in January," I remind her. "Only three years difference."

"This isn't January. And you're still in school. He's *too* old."

"He's a friend, Mom. That's it, that's all."

Why do the words fall empty as I say them?

"Did *he* send you the jacket?"

I hesitate too long.

"You told me it was from the band," she says.

"It...might have been their idea."

We both know it wasn't.

"You met this guy one time," she says, "and he keeps calling you, and now he sends you an expensive jacket? That you lied to me about?"

I say nothing for the longest while.

"Twice," I admit. "We met...twice." And I tell her then that Jamie showed up in our yard the day after the concert with my autographed shirts and a hand-written note to me from Liam O'Shannon.

"He was here when you were alone?" She's getting louder now. "And you said nothing about it?"

"The alone part was no big deal. We stood outside and talked, and he brought my tack out for Tanner and boosted me up—"

Oops, didn't mean for that to slip out.

"You went riding alone, too?"

"Just a couple laps around the paddock."

Like I could focus on side passes or forehand turns with Jamie having just driven off the property. Too muddy for fancy footwork, anyway.

"We had an agreement on that, Jenny."

"I know, and I'm sorry," I say again. "But Jamie was here part of the time." Okay, not when I was in the paddock, but I *did* ride beside him to his rental car. "And he was entirely respectable the *whole* time. He's always been respectable and super sweet and—"

"The point is, you didn't tell us. You let us think he sent you the shirts in the mail."

"I never actually *said* that."

Oh, the guilt!

"Not saying it is still a lie."

I fidget with my phone. "You were all caught up in getting engaged. And I wanted this to be my special something for a while. I didn't expect him to call me, but he did, and then he kept calling, and I figured you'd read something into it that isn't there."

"Are you sure of that?"

"That you'd read something into it?"

"That there's nothing there." Her voice drops back to normal, but it's cold and stiff now. Like her point is better made by freezing the truth from me rather than yelling it out.

"Mom, we hardly know each other—"

"You talk several times a week, you said. And you were on the phone for over an hour. Don't tell me you hardly know each other."

How much *did* she overhear? And what was she doing, hovering out there, mouse quiet, all that time?

"Look, I'm sorry I never told you," I say again. "But you don't have to worry about Jamie. He's this really nice guy who's setting me up to do an interview—two, actually, because I did a FaceTime follow up with Leslie—and he's giving me music journalism advice, and"—I shrug—"he likes to chat with me, I guess."

"Sounds to me like he's stalking you."

"He is *not* stalking me."

He had me alone that day in the yard if that was the goal. And he's got easy access to girls every day on tour—prettier, sexier, sighted ones—so why prowl after me via phone and Instagram?

"How much do you know about him?" she asks.

"He's from Chelsea district in London, and—" I give her what I know of Jamie's background and his family, his job, and what he likes to do when he's not traveling with the band. I leave out the online chess game we finally tried—a few moves here and there; enough for me to see how much better he is than me—and his suggestion we meet in London next summer before going to Wacken Open Air.

Like I'd ever drop *that*.

"We talk about stuff that matters," I finish up, "not just Liam and the band. He's never asked me for anything."

"I'm guessing he will."

"Mom—"

Her feet shift on the carpet, slacks whispering together. "This won't stay a friendship," she says, "and it won't work as a relationship if that's where it's headed, and you'll be picking up the pieces when it all falls through."

"You're making huge assumptions here. I'm *not*—"

"Older guy, underage girl," she goes on. "If he's not stalking you, then you're a diversion. Not a relationship."

Am I a diversion?

I kick the question to the curb.

"We can't go anywhere with this," I say, "even if we wanted to, so—"

"You're seeing him next month."

"For a couple of hours. Then O'Shannon will wrap up their U.S. tour and go back to Ireland, and Jamie will go home to the UK, and they won't be around till next tour."

Mom goes silent again, processing it all. "You'll do what you want with this, of course. But I hope you'll think long and hard about the potential ramifications with this guy and use some wisdom." She sighs. "And remember the next time you decide to hold out on the truth that honesty is what holds a relationship together."

Is that why things fell apart with you and dad?

I stop myself short of saying it, sitting on my bed, stung into silence as she walks out, leaving the door open behind her.

She's right.

Completely.

Jamie should never have been a secret. At least, not for so long.

Why did I make him one?

Blindsight

"Love and Why I'm not on the Market Just Yet"

By Jenny Ryan

No, I don't have a boyfriend.

I have guy friends, and we go out with my girl friends, and there's one or two guys I sometimes hang out alone with (strictly as friends). But not often.

I'm not ready for the expectations, whatever they may be, and I'm not ready for the commitment, either. I don't want to get my heart broken—happening to friends everywhere I (figuratively) look. And I don't want to lose my goals and dreams, trying to make someone else happy who might not be here beyond graduation day. Hey, *I* won't be here. And by the way, I come with a bunch of extra challenges not every guy is willing to take on.

Or at least, not for the long haul.

Like, at what point will he get tired of describing whatever's on my plate (if I didn't dish it up myself) or what's going on in the movie (if no audio description is available) or who just walked into the room and didn't announce themselves? Will he get tired of being the driver wherever we go? At what point will I embarrass him when I spill something somewhere and then step in it, sit in it, whatever or spit something out because it's, say, a glob of butter and not a chunk of cheese ball? When will he decide a girl who can see is much easier to be with than one who can't? Will he love the me that I am after the novelty of the me I project wears off?

And he'd better like dogs because Alexis and I are a package deal.

Advice to self? Crush on the guy, but don't let it show. Keep it friendly. Say goodbye as friends after Grad Night and move on. And when the time comes to explore something long-term—at college, perhaps, or after I finish my degree—I want to go for a slow burn. Be super sure. Give him time to be sure. Because losing my heart to someone I can't have in the end, whether by my choice or his, is somewhere I never want to land.

Mom puts on the works for Thanksgiving.

Bryan stayed over, so he's here when I drag myself awake at eight-forty-five. His voice drifts up the stairs, and when I go down to the kitchen, he and Mom are clanging pans and scraping bowls and whatever else they're doing together. The result turns out to be sour cream blueberry waffles smothered in blueberry sauce. Roasting turkey scents the room from one direction, and the sweetness of candied yams (or pumpkin pie?) assaults me from another.

"Just in time, Jenn," Bryan says from across the island. "Got one coming up, soon as you're ready."

"Give me five minutes," I say.

I take Alexis out and am barely back inside when he hands off a plate, warm and steamy, oozing berry smell.

"Kaitlin up?" Mom asks from over by the fridge.

"Not yet," I say.

The Macy's Thanksgiving Day Parade is on in the front room, and a cinnamon and nutmeg candle spices the air, everything holiday normal like it was all those years ago.

Mom and Dad in the kitchen together, the turkey in the roaster, pies in the oven. Kaitlin and I underfoot, pestering them for a snack...

Only it's not Dad in the kitchen.

It's Bryan McKenzie. And soon, Mom's name will be McKenzie, different from mine and Kaitlin's. And Dad will never live with us, carve the turkey, say grace, or cuddle with Mom on the sofa during the football games.

Dad will have his dinner alone at Red Lobster or Applebees. He'll pick Kaitlin and me up in the late afternoon, and we'll stay over at his place, then go Black Friday shopping tomorrow morning and come home on Saturday or Sunday. And it will be this way next year and the year after that, and Christmas will always be in two different places—

"Something wrong?" Bryan asks me.

"Um, no, nothing." I shake the thought away. "I'm fine."

"Sauce is on the island. Twelve o'clock, about eight inches away."

Like fighter pilots, we, the blind, use the face of the clock for direction and location.

"Got it," I say and paste on a Thanksgiving Day smile.

Dinner is ready at two. The turkey cooked to perfection, the dressing melt-in-your-mouth moist, the cranberry sauce fresh made with just the right amount of tang, the crescent rolls utterly flaky, and the pumpkin pie smothered in whipping cream like it came straight from Martha Stewart's kitchen.

I take pics of my plate, the table, and me in my diamond-patterned sweater and post them to Instagram. O'shannonofficial (yes, they follow me!) hits *like* on every one, adds comments, and Jamie and I text each other during the Cowboys and Patriots game.

He calls at halftime to wish me a Happy Thanksgiving, and I talk to him from the sofa, letting the listeners-in think what they like.

Mom's gone silent on the subject, no matter how much we're obviously on the phone together. But she's not happy. Bryan voices his concerns like I'm old enough to accept them, but he's the middleman here, so how much, really, can he say? Dad reminds me to be careful. Beyond that, he lets it go. He knows I *am* careful and that saying anything more would be a waste of breath.

"Good," I say when Jamie asks how I'm doing, but in a tone that implies it's not an easy kind of good.

"For what it's worth," he says, "it was really hard that first year after my dad died. And the year after that, too. But it gets better, I promise."

"Thanks," I say.

"We'll get you through this."

Something warms inside.

We, he said, like he's not planning to vacate my life any time soon.

My voice softens. "Thanks for being here, Jamie."

"Always," he says.

Clearly, this guy cares about me.

Does he care for *me, too?*

The way I'm starting to care—

No, no, it's nothing like that, can never be like that no matter where we seem to be heading.

Okay, maybe if he lived in the States, I could bring him to the house and say, *Hey, Mom, I'd like you to meet this really cool guy* or *Dad, this is Jamie I've been telling you about.* If he was planning to go to U of O or some other West Coast school, then yeah, I might give it more thought.

But he's none of those things, and I can't let myself fall into a relationship doomed to fail in the end.

DAD COMES for Kaitlin and me in the late afternoon. We go for a cold walk along the Sandy River in Oxbow Park, then cozy up at his place with hot cider and homemade donuts. In the blackness before dawn, we brave the mobs at Walmart and Lloyd Center for the official opening of the Christmas season, followed by brunch at Denny's and a Winterhawks game in Memorial Coliseum. On Saturday, we pick out Dad's tree and decorate it to the music of Mannheim Steamroller and Trans-Siberian Orchestra.

The whole time I'm comparing Mom's Thanksgiving with his, both of them great in their own way and better than I'd expected.

And I'm thankful; really, I am. But neither are quite right—Mom totally happy, trying to make it the family event it was before, and Dad doing his level best, yet again, to make up for her not being here.

The front room is fragrant with noble fir sap, wood smoke, and molasses from the cookies Kaitlin and I made, everything so Christmassy, helped along by TSO's *The Lost Christmas Eve* playing on Dad's stereo system.

"How's the wedding coming?" he asks as we finish the tree.

"Coming," I say.

"Like crazy," Kaitlin adds. "Mom's so over-focused it's like she hardly remembers Christmas gets here first. I'm afraid she'll forget to go shopping."

Dad's quiet for a moment, then he laughs and hugs us both. "Not likely," he says. "And I'll make sure you get plenty of Christmas."

You are what we want for Christmas.

"Don't worry," says Kaitlin. "We'll get lots."

Come on, Kait, think before you open your mouth.

"Good," Dad says. "And don't worry about me. As long as I have you two, I'll be totally fine."

December gears up with all things Christmas—Mom's noble fir (fourteen feet of it) hauled in, set up, and trimmed, the house fully decorated, shopping underway, Winter Break looming in less than two weeks, Bryan ordering tickets for *The Nutcracker* on December twentieth, and Mom planning a party at his place for New Year's Eve. I've bought all my gifts, frosted cookies, and made fudge with Morgan. There's nothing major on my agenda between now and the fourteenth.

Coming so incredibly fast!

Should I buy something for Jamie?

Wait—where'd that come from?

Well, it's logical, isn't it?

Christmas is almost here, and we'll see each other in a little more than a week. What if he gets something for me?

Honestly, meeting Liam O'Shannon is more gift than I could ever want. Even so, do I want to be standing there empty-handed while he hands me a box of chocolates—no, not chocolates. More likely some other piece of O'Shannon gear or an autographed band poster, whatever.

What on earth can I get him?

Something from *Made in Oregon,* perhaps?

Too generic.

Something more personal?

But not *too* personal.

Not yet, anyway...

A photo of Alexis and me, matted and framed?

Maybe. But what would I be saying with that? That I don't want him to forget me ever? Besides, he can see all the pics he wants on my Instagram page.

Maybe I'll bake him cookies or something and give him a card, thanking him for everything he's done for me. Though a card is way too insignificant for how much his friendship means in my life.

MORGAN all but shoots me down.

"Cookies or biscuits or whatever they call them in England are something he'd get from his grandma. Or his mum, maybe. Is that the statement you want to make?"

We're standing in the stall aisle at Coach Kelly's arena, blanketing Tanner and Morgan's paint mare Cocoa, stabled here for OHSET season.

"I don't know." I twist the metal latches along Tanner's flank, holding his blanket in place. "What statement would you have me make?"

"Something that sets you apart from Mum and Grandmum."

"I'm not *dating* him, Morgan."

"You don't have to be dating him to show proper decency." Her riding boots thud around Cocoa's back end as she invades my space. "How 'bout a gift card? Does he read? Download music? Play video games? Stream movies? Find out, if you don't know by now—which I'm guessing you do—and give him something to buy it with."

"That's barely a step above money." Though honestly, it's not a bad idea. "Besides, I don't want to give anything too personal."

"What's personal about an Apple gift card? Or an Amazon one? That's pretty much all I do for Christmas. Why make it hard?"

Yeah, I know all about Morgan's Christmas gift-giving. And birthday gifting, Valentine's gifting, and every other special event gifting. Last year it was H&M for my birthday and Hollister at Christmas. The year before, Amazon and Forever 21.

"It just needs to be *right*," I say.

"Trust me, it's perfect."

"Okay, I'll think about it." I twist the final latch into place. "But I don't think cookies would hurt anything. They're a personal touch without being too personal, if you know what I mean."

"Sadly," she says, "I do."

I shoot Morgan a text that night after getting off the phone with my dad. "So we're doing brunch at Gram's next Sunday and then going to the waterfront before driving home."

Sounds good, she says. **Can't wait!**

"Me, either," I say.

Truth be told, now that we're in a dead march for December 14, I'm half in a sweat over meeting Liam O'Shannon. I mean, dreaming him up in some corner of my mind is one thing. Actually sitting down and interviewing him, having him see me as *me* and not whatever image Jamie and Leslie might have painted for him is something else entirely.

Will I come across as professional? Competent? Confident? Or will I fumble around like the newbie journalist I am? Or, worse yet, come off as star-struck?

I practice my questions. I practice my poise—sitting gracefully (hopefully I don't knock over something I don't know is there), standing just as gracefully at the end, extending my hand to meet his—

How hard can it be?

He's Liam O'Shannon, I remind myself.

And I'm...nobody.

"WHAT TIME SHOULD we be there on Saturday?" I ask when Jamie calls Monday night.

"One, one-thirty would be great. That should give us time for the interview and get you into the soundcheck."

"We get to go to the soundcheck?"

"In addition to the VIP Q and A and music set, yes."

"Wow, that's so cool of you! Thanks!" I say. "Any chance Morgan can meet Kyle Finn?"

"I'll see what I can do," says Jamie. "Maybe we can set it up for the same time as your interview."

"She's gonna go ballistic."

"No promises, but I'll do my best. And I should have the logistics for you in a day or two."

"Sounds great, Jamie."

Cannot believe this is happening...

"See you soon," he says.

"You, too."

"I'm really looking forward to it."

"Me, too."

"Good," he says. "Because I can't wait to see you."

Whoa, what'd he just say?

No, not what he said so much, but *how* he said it. Like there's way more behind those words than what's on the surface.

And for the barest second, panic almost doubles me over.

No, Jamie, no! You can't move this ahead so fast...

But in the next moment, I'm massively flattered. Because, in all honesty, I do want to move ahead, if a bit more cautiously. And I want to spend time—like, a lot of it—with him. And not just so he can introduce me to Liam O'Shannon.

When *did* I start feeling more than friendship for this guy?

Before the jacket.

Before we quipped back and forth about going to Wacken together.

Before he asked if he called too often or if I had anyone special in my life.

When he listened to me pour out my soul and showed more than professional courtesy to a girl who should have been nothing more than a professional contact.

"We could do FaceTime," I suggest, not for the first time.

"Unfair advantage, me," he says, probably not for the last time.

"I'm afraid you'll always have that," I say. "Even in person."

"In-person feels more...equal somehow. I'm making myself wait."

I swallow hard, a bunch of stupid tears gathering in my eyes.

Why *not* Jamie? He's the kindest, sweetest guy I've ever met.

And he lives in London.

So wherever you think this might be going, no matter what you've imagined doing together, it's not going very far. You'll be lucky to see him once a year.

And really, do I want that? A long-distance relationship? Getting together occasionally at best? I mean, when am I—like, *ever*—going to the UK? And how often does he get here, outside of O'Shannon on tour?

"My mom thinks you're too old," I say.

"My mum thinks you're too young," he says back.

"You live on the other side of the world."

"Not at the moment."

"But you're going back. And besides, I'm a lot to take on."

His voice falls quiet. "So am I."

"You don't *know* me, Jamie, not in real life."

"I want to. But if you're uncomfortable with whatever you think I'm offering, think of it as a phone conversation...without a phone."

I giggle—laugh, actually—and nix whatever mood has worked up between us. "I'm not uncomfortable. I've never been uncomfortable with you"—okay, maybe a tad at the beginning, but that hardly counts now—"and, well, whatever you're offering, I'd like to look at that. Just...slowly, okay?"

"Of course," he says. "And if you ever think I'm out of line in any way, let me know."

"You've never been out of line," I say. "You've always been over-the-top nice, and I super appreciate it, but, well, you're not here and—"

"I'm always here, Jenny. Just not always in person."

"I know. And thanks for that."

Because he *is* here—he's *been* here—no matter the distance between us. And in this moment, he's closer to me than anyone in my life.

Chapter 18

A cold front pushes down from Canada on Tuesday night. Temperatures drop from the mid-forties to the low thirties, and the forecast calls for clear skies with a chance of precipitation over the weekend. No word yet on what form that precipitation might take, but I'm hoping whatever it is holds off till I get back Sunday afternoon.

Because no way are we driving to Seattle if any amount of snow is falling and slicking the roads. We are, after all, total rain county around here, and a mere two inches on the ground is enough to close schools, cancel community events, and keep everybody at home who doesn't own a 4x4 or have chains or studded tires.

Dad's got all three, but he's not going to do something people this side of the Cascades consider stupid. He didn't grow up learning to drive in near whiteout conditions as Bryan did in Minnesota or my grandparents in Montana. And with me sitting at the bottom of Ten Eyck Road, five hundred feet down the ridge from Sandy city limits, I'll be crawling out the back way (if I get out at all) where the roads are less likely to be plowed and sanded.

"If it snows," I tell Jamie that night, "I'm not sure we can get to Tacoma on Saturday. It's a three-hour drive, and if the roads are bad—"

"Do they expect snow?" he asks.

"They're saying there's a good chance and that it'll probably stick around a few days."

"Shall we make a contingency plan, then?"

"Meaning the train?"

"Or a flight."

Ticket prices will be ridiculous this close to departure. But then, how do you put a price on getting together with Jamie after all these weeks of phone talking, texting, and finally admitting we want to explore the possibility of *us*? Not to mention meeting, greeting, and interviewing my favorite rock star ever.

"Okay, I'll talk to my mom," I say.

After that, I get to deal with Morgan, all over-the-top panicked.

"If it snows, Jenny," she wails over her phone at me, "I'm so gonna hate my life!"

"You're not going to hate your life. You're going to buy an air ticket, same as me, and we'll fly up together."

"Where am I supposed to get the money for that?"

It *is* Christmas, after all, and she hasn't finished her gift card shopping (how hard can it be?). Though she did invest a boodle in getting her hair salon-streaked (green this time) and her nails acrylic-tipped and painted white with shamrocks on her index fingers.

"You're talking air ticket," she says, "Über fare—how else do we get to the Tacoma Dome?—food, and, well, we can probably stay with Jordanne instead of your Grams if it's a snowy mess all the way to Seattle, but still—"

"Airport shuttle," I say. "It's free, and there's a Best Western across the parking lot from the arena. We take the shuttle to the hotel and walk over. And we ask Jordanne—you said she's got four-wheel drive—to drop us back in the morning to catch the shuttle to Sea-Tac."

"There's still the cost," Morgan points out. "I can afford gas money and a Burger King stop on the way, but an air ticket?"

"Maybe it won't snow," I say, not the least bit hopeful.

"If you fly up," she says, "you don't need me. There are airline people to help you and flight attendants on board and staff people at Sea-Tac to connect you with your driver, and Jamie meeting you at the other end. It's you he wants, anyway. He doesn't even know me."

"You're my best friend," I say, "and I'm asking you to come. I need you for moral support, not just getting me from Point A to Point B. Besides, hello? Kyle Finn's going to be there, and you're dying to meet him, remember?"

Jamie hasn't solidified a meet and greet with Kyle Finn, but he sounds optimistic, and that's good enough to go with for now.

"I've never forgotten for one minute," she whines. "I just don't know if my folks will pay for it, make me a loan, whatever."

Dad will fund me, I'm sure. I've told him enough about Jamie—not the recent shift in our relationship, but almost everything else—to satisfy his concerns, and he trusts Morgan and me to act responsibly.

Bryan's a solid backup plan. He'll be good for an overnight at his place on Friday if needed and a ride to the airport in the morning, too.

"Don't give up, okay?" I tell Morgan. "Something *has* to work out."

COME WEDNESDAY NIGHT, forecasters are still predicting weekend snow. Only now, they're more aggressive about it. They've posted a winter storm warning, zeroing in on Saturday as the most likely dropping-from-the-sky date. They're using phrases like *snow to the valley floor* (lower than where I live) and *accumulations of up to six inches*.

"How 'bout I just fly you up?" Jamie says from Atlanta, where it's past midnight his time.

Clearly, O'Shannon's not canceling their show on account of projected weather.

"I was looking at that." I'm sprawled across my bed, my computer open in front of me. I'm not web surfing at the moment because listening to Jamie *and* JAWS takes too much effort, and I'd rather listen to him. "Buying an air ticket, I mean."

"I can get you on an eleven ten AM flight on Alaska," he says.

"Puts you at Sea-Tac around noon, about fifty minutes after we get in."

Band and crew members are chartering a plane from Miami and will overnight in Tacoma before flying to Chicago, then hopping over the Pole to Ireland. As for their gear and staging, one trucking convoy is already en route from Charleston to the Northwest; the other leaves Miami tomorrow night for Chicago.

"Yeah, I saw that one," I say. "Pretty spendy for a jump from here to there."

"Don't worry about it," he says. "Does it work for you?"

"Well, yeah, but—"

"I know it's earlier than I suggested two days ago, but with the weather—"

"No, that's fine."

"Shall I book it, then?"

"My dad said he'd pay."

"*I* want to pay," says Jamie. "I should have booked you a flight straight away."

Wait, *he's* offering to buy my air ticket?

Like I could accept that.

"You don't need to," I say.

"I'd like to."

"Thanks, but...my mom would *not* be on board with that."

"Right, then," he says.

Mom talked to him once on the phone. Even conceded he sounded nice. But she's still plenty edgy about him—the age thing, the living in London thing, the working for a rock band part of the equation. She's letting me go to Tacoma because if she doesn't, she'll have to live with miserable me for who knows how long, and she's not forgotten how horrible that was all those years ago. Besides, she's counting on Morgan being present every possible second.

Not that Morgan will be.

"Super appreciate it, though," I say. "I'll send the link to my dad."

"What time are you looking to fly back?"

"When do you fly out for Chicago?"

"Nine-twenty," Jamie says.

"Something not quite so early would be nice," I say. "Noon-to-one range, maybe?"

"One-ten sound good?"

"Where do you see that?"

"About halfway down the page."

I bring the audio up on JAWS and check it out.

"Okay, perfect."

"Morgan's still coming, I hope?" he asks.

"Yes," I say. "She doesn't know Dad's buying her a ticket on loan, but she'll be all over that when she finds out."

No matter how long it'll take her to scrape the funds together after the fact.

"Great," he says. "Got Kyle all lined up for her."

"She'll love you for life," I say, and he laughs on the other end.

"Confirm your flight info when you have it," he says, "and I'll have a pickup person waiting at the airport when you get in. Sorry it can't be me."

"No worries. And we *can* catch a shuttle to the Tacoma Dome parking lot."

"Our people have to get there, too. You might as well snag a ride with somebody."

Okay, cancel that shuttle.

"Sounds great, thanks. Texting this to my dad." I mute Jamie, so I can send it from my phone. "I'll let you know as soon as I hear something," I add when I'm back.

"Perfect."

"Can't believe I'm actually doing this."

"Can't believe you'll actually be here—or there, rather. We'll have a full evening with everything going on, but maybe"—he lets the word hang—"we could do something together when I'm free?"

"Yes," I say.

Too quickly, perhaps, but I don't take it back.

"Good." He pauses again. "I'm okay with sitting up all night talking if you want. Find someplace open, have tea—coffee, if you prefer—or breakfast. Walk a bit, if the weather's not too bad. Whatever."

"Yes," I say. "All of it."

I can sleep on the plane coming home.

"Good," he says again.

I don't tell him I'm a bit nervous.

I remember going out for pizza with Eric and the lady who patronized me in the bathroom. And me stumbling up the bleachers at the Pioneers home game, tripping over somebody's backpack and spilling somebody else's drink. It was a long time ago, and I didn't have Alexis then. Still, I can't imagine doing something like that with Jamie sitting, standing, whatever, looking on.

Okay, he saw me on the floor in the Moda Center, trying to find my Reader. But that was then, and we do everything long distance now, so if I drop or spill something or go hunting with my hands, he's not watching me, not getting off-put by a girl who really *is* blind. And if we spend enough in-person time together, I'm going to screw something up somewhere, and he's going to see what he's in for with me, and maybe—

No, I can't think about it.

Not when I'm falling so hard for this guy.

If falling for him means I can't imagine my life without him.

Blindsight

"The Power of Music"

By Jenny Ryan

Music is huge for me. And not just because I'm blind. That's a stereotype, anyway. We don't all sing (I can carry a tune, but don't expect me to get up and do karaoke) or play an instrument (I have zero talent that way), and some of us (not me, of course) prefer silence. I can't even say I'm more focused as a blind person when I run my playlist because I'm often listening to my homework at the same time.

I loved music when I *could* see, growing up on my dad's country tunes and crushing on pop stars and boy bands when I was barely in middle school. That's shifted a bit these days. Because however hot that guy might be, strapped behind his guitar, is simply lost on me.

But his voice? And the shreds he can do on those strings? The drive of drums and keys—or a whole orchestra —behind him?

That's what attracts me!

Puts me in touch with who I am. Spikes my energy levels, raises my mood or bleeds with my wounded heart, and fills me with hope and inspiration. Shows me a world I can no longer see.

I owe my love of the heavy and hardcore to my bestie, Morgan. She got me connected, acclimated to, and involved at Cedar Ridge Middle School, and she opened her world of

European power and symphonic metal bands—stuff I'd never listened to but soaked in like thirsty ground. Lyrics based on philosophies and social issues, what's wrong and right in this world, and the rawness of the human condition. Like these artists understood the darkness I'd fought through in getting my blind game on and showed me I wasn't in this alone.

And when O'Shannon roared onto the American scene with *Into Infinity*, I found my fandom. It's not just about the band as musicians or Liam as a vocalist (though yeah, that's huge with me). It's about the people who follow them—the fan groups I've joined and the connections we've made over a shared love of five guys and one gal from Ireland; that sense of belonging to something bigger than ourselves. It's getting responses—generally from Keenan because he handles most band-to-fandom correspondence—to comments I've made on anything posted by o'shannonofficial. Buying downloads, O'Shannon gear, and tickets to see them live. Dreaming of someday meeting them for a handshake—or a hug, if I'm lucky!—and a photo, too. Of telling Liam just how much his music means in my life.

When I listen to music—whether his or anyone else's—the darkness recedes, and light cracks through.

The weather hangs out, clear and cold, through Thursday night. But in the morning, the clouds come in. Slowly. Like they're dragging their heels across the sky.

Not that I see them, of course, but Morgan and Kaitlin keep me posted. The air has warmed a few degrees, and now it's damp and heavy. As though something up there is plotting to dump on us. By the time school's out, the temperature is dropping, and the latest forecast calls for six to eight inches on Saturday with overnight freezing and icy road conditions.

"I can't believe I'm doing this," Mom grouses as Morgan, Alexis, and I pile into her Sentra after OHSET practice.

Dad came through with air tickets, and Morgan's folks okayed her going, so we're off to Bryan's place for the night and an airport run in the morning while Kaitlin spends the weekend with Hannah.

"You have every chance of getting stuck up there," Mom goes on, "and I'm just...making sure of it."

"We'll be fine, Mrs. Ryan," says Morgan, though it's me Mom is focused on. "Jordanne says we can stay longer if we need to. It's supposed to warm up and rain by Monday, anyway."

And Dad said he'll change our tickets if we can't make the sixteen-mile drive from Fife to Sea-Tac on Sunday or our flight gets canceled.

Mom's less than happy with him for not flying with us. Like he'd go to a concert he'd totally hate to monitor our every move. Besides, he trusts us. And I've promised Mom—cross my heart, pinkie swear, whatever—that nothing objectionable, however she defines that, is going to happen in Tacoma. It's a quick up and back with a show, an interview, IRL time with Jamie thrown in, and staying over at Jordanne's.

Okay, I left out a huge chunk.

Like, I'd get out the door tomorrow morning (with or without any snow storming from the sky) if Mom knew Jamie and I plan to go out tomorrow night.

"Half the time, the weather doesn't do what they predict, anyway," I say.

And the other half, it does worse.

WE GET to Bryan's just as he's pulling a u-bake pizza from the oven. He and Mom are all lovey-dovey with each other, but there's this tension between them because she's so not on board with this, and he promised to make it happen.

We eat in front of an audio descriptioned movie, but I've seen it enough times, and my brain's too disengaged to track what's happening. Jamie's done for the evening, so we run a texting chat from the opening credits till I crawl into the queen bed I'm sharing with Morgan.

"That's like, three hours," she says when I finally sign off for the night. "No way can you tell me he doesn't feel something for you."

"Maybe a little," I admit.

"Maybe a lot," she says. "And you feel something for him, too. Say it, already."

"We're taking it slow, okay? Seeing what happens."

I don't tell her Jamie and I are going out after the show. Even if we're just talking and having breakfast somewhere, she'll absolutely go where I don't want her to. Not something I want to deal with yet.

"You do know," Morgan says, "he's leaving—like, the country—in a few days and not coming back any time soon?"

Yes, and I don't want to think about it.

"He's been hurt before," I say. "And I'm a lot to take on. I don't want to lose my heart and then find out he can't handle everything that goes with *me*."

"If you ask me," she says, "it's lost already."

I sigh and roll over. But I don't go to sleep, lying here, my brain on overload.

When I finally drop off, I'm sitting at a sidewalk café somewhere in Europe with an English guy who's making me smile, making me laugh, making me never want to wake up...

BRYAN SHAKES me out of a dead sleep.

"It's snowing," he says quietly. "We need to get on the road ASAP."

"Okay," I mumble.

Morgan snores raggedly beside me, dead to the world. Alexis, scootched on the bed between us, raises her head. She's breathing on my arm, and her tags clink when she looks away.

I fumble for my watch on the nightstand and press the voice button.

Five-thirty-three, says my digital Brit guy. (All my techie devices use British accents these days).

"Morgan." I find her PJ-ed arm and give it a shake. "Get up."

She groans at me.

"They're talking eight to ten inches," Bryan's saying, "and there's three down already. You girls need to hurry."

"Okay." I thump Morgan again. "Get up, already."

We set a record time for showering, throwing on jeans and O'Shannon gear, and grabbing jackets and overnight bags. Alexis whines at me when I close her inside the house, but I tell her it's for her own good, that she doesn't want to be scrunched into my foot space on the plane or get her ears blown out at a rock concert. Mom stays behind, exhausted from her work week and not the least interested in crawling to the airport over slicked-up roads.

Or maybe she doesn't want to go head to head with Bryan on the drive back.

Morgan and I climb into his Explorer, already chained up in the driveway. My hair's wet, I'm gobbling a muffin on the way, and everything I need (brush, travel dryer, makeup case) is at the top of my bag for an easy grab when I get to a ladies' room at PDX.

Morgan's all hyped for the night of her life, starting with meeting Kyle Finn (yeah, she launched into the stratosphere over that) and ending, she hopes, in her connecting with him the way I connected with Jamie Conway. Never mind that Kyle's got a girl, broadcast all over the tabloids, and a trail of broken, European hearts a mile long behind him.

I let her talk—it's pointless interrupting when she's going full bore, anyway—while trading texts with Jamie, who's already in the air. Snow grinds beneath the chains, wiper blades slap the windshield, and Bryan's talk radio drones at a low volume.

When we get there, Portland International is early-morning/holiday-season/bad-weather-moving-in busy—mobs of people and rolling luggage, voices oozing stress everywhere.

We've already checked in online and printed our boarding passes, and we're keeping our bags with us, so Bryan takes us straight to screening.

"I don't need to tell you girls to have a good time," he says. "You're plenty capable of that. Just take care. Be safe. Call if you need anything, and I'll do what I can."

"Okay," says Morgan.

"Thanks, Bryan." I'm only too aware of how much I owe him. "I can't possibly tell you what this means to me."

"You don't need to," he says. "Just go have the best time ever."

"We will."

I reach out to hug him—this time, I want to—and as he holds me, something warm and tentative passes between us.

"Thanks, Jenny," he says and lets me go. "See you tomorrow."

"Bye, Bryan. Thanks," says Morgan.

And then he's gone, swallowed into all those voices, footfalls, and mish-mashed clatter around us.

"Right, then." Morgan pulls my arm through hers and hauls me into line. "We're off to see the wizard. Or, in this case, a whole band full of 'em."

The wait at screening is endless. I do everything for myself, but Morgan hovers close by just in case. Once through, we hunt up a Starbucks, then duck into the nearest ladies' room to make ourselves presentable.

"You didn't forget his gift, I hope," she says.

Like I could go back and grab it if I had.

"It's in my bag."

I put a package together—two dozen of my homemade chocolate chip, salted caramel cookies, a photo book of Oregon from Powells, an Amazon gift card, and two Christmas cards, one from Hallmark and one I made myself.

Not overly personal, but personal enough.

"Solid on your questions?"

"Got 'em nailed."

"I can't wait," she sighs. "This whole night's so gonna rock!"

Literally, in fact.

We arrive at our gate so early *Seattle* hasn't been posted to the reader board.

Morgan finds us seats. I'm pulling out my phone when a text chimes.

Just landed, says Jamie.

"Still in Portland," I send back. "They've posted a delay, so we won't get in now till twelve thirty. How's the weather up there?"

Snowing. I'll rearrange the time with your pickup

person. She'll be waiting when you get through security. She's got your number, just in case.

"Sounds great. Thanks."

We chat a bit longer, and finally, the call comes for pre-boarding.

One of the perks of traveling with me is getting to board early (along with anyone needing assistance or flying with young kids). Being blind qualifies me even though I don't need much help.

Morgan's already on her feet, scraping her bag off the chair. I grab mine from the floor, and she guides me across the crowded waiting area to the line already forming at the gate.

It's a fifty-minute puddle jump to Sea-Tac. She gets the window (like it would do me any good), and I'm sandwiched between her and a man who says hi to us and goes back to whatever he was doing before he stepped out so we could squeeze in. Morgan keeps up a running monologue the whole way, and while I'm glad she's here, part of me wishes she'd leave off long enough for me to practice my opening lines with Mr. Rock Star.

Not that it would work.

Jamie keeps jumping into it.

How soon will I see him? What happens when I do? Will he hug me? *Kiss* me? Tell me what he feels for me?

What will I tell him?

It's where all this is leading, isn't it? To see if there *is* an us.

I text him once we're on the ground.

I'm at the arena, he sends back. **See you as soon as I can.**

"Sounds great."

I follow Morgan up the narrow aisle, one hand on her elbow, the other steadying my bag so it won't bang into the seats. Once off the plane and out of the jetway, she strides me down the concourse, speculating about who's waiting at the other end.

"Seriously," she says, "I'd kill for it to be Kyle Finn."

"It's a *she*. So I'm guessing not."

"Never hurts to dream."

We hit the security checkpoint. Trays slide over tables and along rollers. People yabber, machines bleep, bodies shove past me for the gates. We've not gone far when somebody calls my name. I whip around, trying to isolate one voice from all the rest.

"Jenny?"

I recognize it now, all musical and classically Cork Irish.

"Omigosh!" Morgan squeals beside me. "It's Leslie O'Shannon!" She drags me over while I process what she said.

Leslie's our pickup person? Mega busy as she must be with a show to do in a few hours and a soundcheck on top of that, she has time for this? Jamie got *her* to wait?"

Unbelievable!

We're in each other's space now, hugs all around, and I breathe in her scent of roses and herbal shampoo along with something faintly strawberry, like the lip gloss Morgan wears.

""Tis grand to see you, girl," she says. "So happy you made it."

"You, too," I say. "I can't believe Jamie got *you* to stay behind for us."

"I volunteered, like." She angles her voice to my right. "And you must be Morgan?"

"Yes." Morgan's all breathless. "Wow, it's amazing to meet you!"

"You, too, girl. Glad you could come."

"Any chance you can sign a shirt for me?"

"I'd love to." To me, she says, "You wouldn't believe what a mess it is out there. We drove through the Canadian Rockies and 'twas grand, to be sure. We fly here, and things are touch and go. The arena's set, of course, but not everything's up and runnin', and everyone's helping out, even the band and the behind-the-scenes people."

Jamie included, I take it.

"And you waited for us?" I say.

"I'm needed here."

"This is super cool of you.

"Happy to do it," she says. "Shall I carry your bag, so?"

"I'm good. But thanks." I reach for Morgan's arm.

Leslie catches my hand before I latch on and slides it through her elbow, like she knows what to do, and then we're off through the jammed terminal together. I'm waiting for someone to stop us and ask her for an autograph or something, but nobody does, and it takes me a moment to realize why.

She's still up and coming, not so on the spot recognizable as she will be later on. Even Liam's not always picked out of a crowd. Being part of a band blends you in rather than stands you out, the way being a solo artist does. Besides, everyone slamming past us apparently has more on their minds than scrutinizing one face from the mob.

Then again, maybe not.

"Hey," some guy's voice booms out of the foot traffic, "you wouldn't be Leslie O'Shannon, would you?"

"I am, boy," she says, and we stop because this guy is gushing about her music and asking her to sign something. A crowd presses in, and Leslie's signing, laughing, answering questions, and throwing out thank yous, thriving in the spotlight she loves.

"Have to go, like," she says after a bit. "Hope to see you at the show tonight." And she hustles us away. "Sorry about that. Doesn't happen every time, but, well, it goes with the territory, as they say."

We finally make it outside, and the air snatches my breath away. Definitely colder here than in Portland. Steady snow is falling, sticking to my hair, several inches already down, whispering underfoot.

Leslie steps me from the curb and slides me into a waiting taxi, then belts herself beside me while Morgan takes the seat up front.

"Tacoma Dome," Leslie tells the driver, and we're off at a chained crawl.

I text Jamie with my ETA, but the response I get isn't reassuring. **Technical issues**, he sends back. **Hope to see you soon.**

Sucksville, but it's not like I can do anything about it.

He *is* working, after all.

It's just that we have so little time together and so much ground to cover. *Do* we feel what we think we feel for each other? How can we possibly know in so short a time? Will it all be pointless in the end?

Chapter 20

Morgan's got Leslie locked down for the forty minutes it takes, given road conditions, to drive south from Sea-Tac to the Tacoma Dome, and she's making the most of her once-in-a-lifetime opportunity. Leslie fields her questions (when she's not taking calls from her peeps at the arena), even the ones that run to the bolder end of the spectrum. Such as:

"What's it like to be eighteen and famous?"

"Not *that* famous," says Leslie.

Or—

"Are you seeing anyone at the moment?"

"I never kiss and tell, girl," Leslie teases.

I love how she comes across as so relaxed like she's totally one of us. Being a rising pop star hasn't gone to her head. Not yet, anyway. I'm so hoping Liam is like her because it'll make interviewing him that much easier. Though I can't imagine forgetting for one moment who he is the way I'm starting to do with her.

Our speed drops as we exit I-5 and ease down to the street below where the twenty-three-thousand-seat Tacoma Dome sits beside the freeway. Tonight's event is sold out, but given weather conditions, I don't expect everyone who bought a ticket will show up.

"Made it," I text Jamie as we crawl into the parking lot. "See you soon?"

I don't get an answer.

I haven't heard from him in fifteen, twenty minutes, and who knows where he is now or what he's doing or when *soon* for us might actually be.

I touch my watch face.

One thirty.

Soundcheck for O'Shannon is at four. Leslie's is at four-thirty, the VIP Q and A is at six, and the show starts at eight. The delay in our arrival means less time with Jamie before things gear up. And given the technical issues, I might not interview Liam till late tonight—which hopefully works out to having more time with him than, say, between rehearsal and the VIP set.

The driver parks, idling the car, and we climb out. Leslie guides me through snow that spills into my low-rise boots and freezes through my layered socks. Morgan's carrying our bags, and she keeps banging me with one of them.

I've clipped the pass Leslie handed off in the taxi to the front pocket of my jeans, and it takes no effort to imagine Morgan flashing hers at the guy who greets us inside the secured entrance.

We go into a corridor, beyond echoing doorways, then turn into a wider passage. Some guy walks by and says hi to Leslie. American accent, same as the woman up ahead, so probably not with O'Shannon Productions. Something metallic bangs and clatters beyond. Somebody hollers farther off.

Leslie stops and opens a door on the right. "Welcome to my home on the road," she says, pulling me into a bigger room than the one we interviewed in at the Moda Center.

Less empty, too.

Bread and something sweet and other foods I've not yet identified snag my attention. Obviously, there's a table. Chairs, most likely. A clothes rack, for sure. And a mirror, too—some intense lighting white-outs my shadows and radiates heat across the room.

Our bags hit the cement floor not far from my feet.

"This is it?" Morgan says.

"Sure, why not?" says Leslie. "It's got everything I need, like."

"Not even a star on your door?"

"This is the road, girl." She laughs. "It's not Hollywood. Anyway, make yourselves at home. I've got minerals—Coke, Diet Coke, Sprite—on the table and some sandwiches if you're hungry."

"I'm fine." My nerves are ramping up, so no, I don't want anything in my stomach just yet.

Morgan brushes past me, clatters a can from the ice, and hisses it open. "Thanks."

I text Jamie again—"In Leslie's room"—but he doesn't respond this time, either.

"So when do we get to meet everyone?" asks Morgan. "Like Kyle, for instance?"

He's the only "instance" she's thinking of.

"They're fierce busy at the moment," says Leslie. "But we can go into the arena if you like. Someone might spare us a minute."

"I am so taking a selfie with him," says Morgan.

Yeah, I want some of those, too.

Me and Jamie.

Me and Liam O'Shannon.

Me with the whole band.

Imagine putting *those* up on Instagram!

"Kyle'll be happy to pose with you," says Leslie. "He loves being the center of attention, that one does."

I peel off my ski jacket and stuff my gloves into the outer pockets, my cane folded inside where no one will see *blind* written all over me.

Leslie takes everything from my hands and rattles hangers on her rack.

"And *that* looks deadly on you, girl." Meaning the nylon jacket I'm still wearing, the one with *O'Shannon Tear at the Walls Tour* stitched on the back.

"Thanks." I flash her a grin.

I've got my autographed t-shirt on beneath it, and I'm wearing black jeans, slightly snug, but not too snug. As for makeup, I tried to keep everything a bit understated to look professional but not overdone.

"Anything need touching up?" I ask.

"You look perfect, sure you do," says Leslie.

"Yeah, you rock the rock fan look," says Morgan.

"Thanks."

I shoot off another text. "Going into the arena. Are you there now?"

Just got a break, Jamie sends back. **Coming to you shortly, if that's all right?**

"Staying put, then."

I want to see him before anyone else, and I'm good with doing that here, just the two of us, where it will be less awkward if the moment isn't quite what we hope. And if it is, I don't want to share it with Morgan, Leslie, and an arena full of roadies, tech crew, and Irish rock stars.

"Go on," I tell Morgan (in case she missed some of those words blitzing by). "He's coming here. Meet up with you later."

"We'll take our time, so," Leslie teases.

Morgan's already opening the door. "Don't do anything I wouldn't do," she throws back at me.

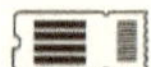

I'M ALONE, but I don't wait long.

On my way, Jamie texts me. **Sorry for the delay.**

"No worries," I send back.

My palms are sweating. My stomach's a jittery mess.

I'm standing where Leslie left me because I don't know where the chairs are exactly (though I worked out the table location easily enough), and I'm not about to go exploring for them. And anyway, sitting would feel too much like...*waiting*. Not what I want Jamie to see when he walks through that door, and we're together after all this time.

Voices and footsteps come and go, passing through the corridor beyond.

Not him, not him...not him, either—

Someone clips up and stops outside the door, knocks lightly. "Jenny?"

I close the distance—a straight shot—and swing the door open.

"Hi," he says.

My face splits into the hugest grin ever. And everything I've stressed over—what if I can't get here and how will I handle my interview and what happens when we see each other—collapses into the reality of him standing in front of me, right here, right now.

"Hey," I say back.

Jamie comes in and closes the door—sound deadens, but not completely, so not quite all the way. And he doesn't hesitate.

He gathers me up, his scent of cologne, apple shampoo, and fresh-laundered shirt resurrecting everything I remember from that day in my yard. And it's so right, so perfect, the most natural thing in the world.

A phone call without a phone.

No, it's way better than that!

He lets me go and eases back like maybe he overstepped his bounds. "Hope that was okay."

Absolutely, it was okay!

"Not very British," I say.

He laughs in his easy way. "We're not all that stuffy, you know."

"I can't imagine you being stuffy, ever."

He hugs me again, and this time, when he steps back, he takes my hands. And I sense his gaze like he's very much wanting something more from me, but he's not going there without my invitation.

It's okay. You can go there...

"It's so good to see you," he says. "You look great!"

"You, too," I say, and we both laugh.

"The jacket's perfect on you."

"So sweet of you to send it." I'm hyper-aware of his fingertips, warm on mine. "Makes me feel like I belong."

"You do belong," he says. "It's so *you*, you know."

"Yeah," I say. "The diehard O'Shannon fan."

"You're the perfect fan." He pulls my hand through his elbow, folding my fingers over his arm. "Let's see if I can do this right."

"Doing great so far."

"Good. Shall we check out the food?" He's already leading me across the room, and I'm more than okay with being snugged this close, my fingers registering every shift of his body. He stops at the table. "Plenty to eat here, I see. Hope you're hungry."

"Yeah, I could go for something." Just like that, I'm famished. I can't remember when I ate last. Breakfast, maybe. And some pretzels and coffee on the plane. "Leslie said there were sandwiches and drinks."

"Veggies and dips, crisps and pastries, too," he adds.

"Sounds great."

I put my hands down, find the table with one, the edge of a plate with the other, and everything I smelled when I first walked in waters my mouth. My stomach growls, and I fold my arms over my waist, embarrassed.

"Sorry," I say. "Breakfast was ages ago."

"Just in time, then," he says. "What would you like?"

"A sandwich, I guess. And crisps are—"

"Potatoes. Like Lays?"

"You mean chips," I say.

"Chips go with fish," he says.

"You mean fries," I say, and we both laugh.

"Okay." He takes my hand again. "We've got ham and Swiss, beef and cheddar, turkey and provolone." He points here and there down the table as he gives me my options. "Veggies and *chips* and minerals —soda, I mean—and some pastries, too."

"Sounds great," I say, entirely focused on his hand holding mine. "All of it."

"All of it, then."

I'm still waiting for him to turn and hold me, not just hug me. Kiss me, too, maybe. The moment is right, and I think he wants to.

Or is it me that wants him to?

He drops my hand and starts down the table, filling my plate.

I tag along after him. "I *can* do this, you know."

He stops again, and I bump into him. "Do you want to? I should have asked first."

"No, you're fine. It's just, well, I shouldn't make you do all the work."

"What work?" he says. "This isn't about you needing help because clearly, you don't."

"It's a small space," I say. "I can probably handle it okay. Turn me loose in a mall—no cane, no guide dog, no GPS app—and you'll see how blind I can be."

"I'd never turn you loose in a mall," Jamie says, moving down the table again. "I'd take you there myself. Anywhere you wanted to go."

To the mall, to a park, to a café in Tacoma.

All of it...

"I'd be good, then," I say.

We've come to the end of the table, and he shifts about, his voice hitting me straight on. "So if I do something wrong, you'll say so?"

"If you want me to."

"How else will I do it right?"

Seriously, this guy's amazing. I'd be stupid not to take a chance on him, however impractical the logistics might be.

"Thanks, Jamie."

He takes my hand again and tucks it through his elbow, guiding me back to the chair. "Here you go." He waits while I seat myself, then hands off my plate. "What would you like to drink?"

"Coke." I find two half sandwiches, a pile of chips, a cinnamon roll, carrot sticks, and broccoli before smearing my hand through the dip. "And a napkin, too, please? Maybe a bunch of 'em?"

"Here," he says. "Oh, I'm sorry, Jenny."

"No worries." I'm already cleaning up after myself. "You're eating with me, I hope?"

"Not yet, I'm afraid." He's back with more napkins, then takes them from me when I've finished.

"Welcome to my life." I've already started on one sandwich, I'm so hungry.

He hands off my drink, ice-cold and dripping water, then scrapes a chair into place. "I love your life." He sits close in front of me, his knees touching mine. He's wearing jeans, the same as last time, and the scent of his cologne makes me want to lean closer. "What I've seen of it, anyway. I love everything you tell me—your school days, your horse rides, your Halloween party, your American Thanksgiving, all of it."

"It's just...everyday life."

"I miss everyday life. Yours sounds amazing."

I laugh, then cover my mouth, remembering it's full of food. "Right." I swallow. "My mom getting married to somebody who's not my dad and me doing homework I can't see and always going to the same places and doing the same things, and you traveling the world and seeing, well...the world."

"Still sounds amazing."

"If you like boring, I guess. I mean, it's not *boring* boring. It's just not...exciting."

"Exciting is overrated," says Jamie.

"Trade you."

"Done." He chuckles, and I laugh with him.

"So, how go the technical issues?" I ask.

"Almost resolved. We've got audio now, so we're go for soundcheck in an hour."

"Can't wait."

Though honestly, I'm in no rush to end this.

I reach for the unopened Coke I set near the leg of my chair. "I know you do this stuff all the time, but *I* can't imagine it. Going to the soundcheck, sitting front row at the show, meeting these guys afterward. It's like, I don't know, a dream, maybe." I pop the tab on my can and tip it back for a swallow, set it again on the floor.

"And this?" Jamie's voice turns serious. "Here and now?"

"This is really nice." I stop chewing and swallow the wad of bread and meat at the back of my throat. And just like that, I'm not hungry anymore.

"Good."

"Would you believe I was nervous?" *If you are, too, it's okay.* "Stupid of me, perhaps, but we've only met twice in real life—"

"Three times now," he says.

"Yes, but the others were two months ago, and everything's been long distance since then. And I was okay with that because I'm not blind over the phone or on Instagram. But here, in the real world, with you actually looking at me, I *am* blind, and I do blind things, like drag my fingers through the dip and—"

"Jenny." He says it so gently. "You think that matters to me?"

"It might. It matters to some people. Even though they think it won't."

"Does it matter to Morgan?"

"She's used to me."

"Then I'm working on that. Getting used to you. You getting used to me."

"Like I said—stupid."

"Not stupid," he says. "It just takes time. For both of us."

He's so good, so kind.

"Thanks. And everything today"—I set my plate on the floor—"has been perfect."

"Happy to hear it. Because being here with you...is a dream for *me.* And, um...I'm scared, too."

"Why *me*, Jamie? I'm just—" I don't know how to finish it.

Ordinary.

Damaged.

Too young, too inexperienced.

What can he possibly see in me?

"You're *real*," he says. "Your life is real. It's what I want and don't have these days, not on the road. Out here, real can be hard to find."

He's talking, I think, about the girls with inside connections and backstage privileges. The ones he told me about that day in my yard. Who he obviously meets and maybe gets to know on some level.

The ones I don't want to think about.

"I look at you," he's saying, "and I see a girl who's not afraid of life—"

"Yeah, well, remember those days I told you about?"

"The ones where you got up again and kept going? That's the girl *I* see. Who dreams big and wants to do big things no matter how hard she has to work at them. Who smiles and laughs and dresses her guide dog like a pirate and hikes to waterfalls she can't see, and rides in horse competitions when a horse took her sight. Who's on the phone to me when she could be skiing or eating pizza with somebody her age, someone who's actually *with* her, who she doesn't have to get on a plane to go see."

"Like I wouldn't be here," I say. "And not just because you arranged an interview for me. And gave me front row seats to see my favorite band."

"Liam did that," he says.

"I didn't come just for Liam."

"Good." His voice smiles, then goes serious again. "I think about you every day, every night, Jenny. And when I'm not talking to you or texting you, I'm wishing I was, wishing I could be *with* you. Like I am now. And hoping you might...want to be with me, too..."

My breath catches.

I do, Jamie...

"And seeing you here," he adds, "having you with me, makes me want it all the more..."

Now he's going to kiss me.

He leans forward, his cologne-and-shampoo scent drawing closer, and no matter how ready I think I am, I flinch when his fingers graze my cheek.

"Sorry." He pulls back.

"Don't be. It's just—I can't see it coming."

"Trying again, then. If that's okay..."

I nod.

Take a breath.

Close my eyes.

His fingertips skim my jawline, then lift my chin, and I'm trembling but in a good, I-want-this-to-happen-with-you-Jamie kind of way.

It won't be my first kiss, but it'll be the one that counts. A *real* kiss. Not a goodnight peck on the lips or something somebody tries to get away with because they think I don't know it's coming or they're hoping to push me for more than I want to give. It's the kiss I've been waiting for with the guy I could never have imagined sharing it.

He leans in again.

I ease forward.

His lips touch mine, breath hinting of mint, and his kiss is soft and gentle, nothing demanding. I press into it, kiss him back, and it's so perfect—everything I want.

He kisses me again, deeper this time, then draws away.

"Was that okay?" he says.

"Yes," I say, still tasting mint.

Way more than okay...

"I was going to wait till later. But then"—his voice comes closer again—"everything just seemed right..."

I lean forward, then close my eyes as his breath meets mine.

Chapter

21

His ringtone goes off.

Are you kidding me?

Jamie sighs and eases back in his chair, grabbing his phone from wherever on his person he keeps it. "Yeah, hi." His voice is husky, strained, his accent less clipped.

Wait—where have I heard—

"No, you've got me." Voice back to normal. "I'll be right there."

My breath slides out, heart banging every which way. I was just moments from slipping my arms around his neck and—

"Sorry, but I gotta go," he says after hanging up on whoever called at the worst moment ever. "Something's come up, and I'm wanted straight away."

"Seriously?"

"I'm afraid so," he says. "Leslie's sending Morgan to fetch you. Soundcheck's been moved to three-thirty, and I know you want to be down close for that."

I *do* want to be down close. Just not at this exact moment. I want him to kiss me again and say whatever else he might come out with, never mind that it's all happening too fast or that I'm marching like a lemming for the nearest ledge.

You're a diversion, not a relationship flashes through my brain, but I squelch the words. I'm not losing these few moments we've snatched in the middle of everything going on to Mom's unfounded fears or my growing dread of saying goodbye.

"It's okay," I tell him. Why make him feel worse than he already does? "And yes, I want to be there." *So totally do.* "Any idea how long you'll be?"

"Not sure exactly. Hopefully, no more than an hour." He takes my hands and squeezes them, then kisses me, short and sweet. "I'd much rather stay here with you." Another sigh, and he lets my fingers go; stands and shoves his chair back. "Text you when I'm done."

I nod, saying okay again.

And he's out the door, closing it behind him, leaving me here alone, every thought zeroed in on his lips pressed into mine.

I sigh and reach down, find my plate, and grab my other sandwich. I'm not remotely hungry, but I might as well finish while I've got the chance. I'm swallowing the last bite when Morgan bangs through the door.

"Jenny, it was incredible!" she gushes at me. "They are *so* cool, all of them!"

They being O'Shannon, I presume.

"And their accents..." Her sigh makes me think of a glob of butter melting all over who-knows-what.

"I want to hear it all," I say. "But first"—I tip back the last of my soda and then stand, my plate in hand—"where's the garbage?"

She snatches everything away and dumps it for me so as not to hold up her story.

"Anyway, Kyle's even hotter up close, if you can imagine it. I talked to him for like, fifteen minutes, and it was like talking to anybody. And Declan and Keenan, they're great, too. Declan's pretty funny—he likes to tease. And Keenan has the most adorable smile. We were standing around on stage and—"

"You were *on stage?*" Now I *am* a bit jealous, never mind how amazing it was with Jamie before some stupid phone call ended it all.

"Yeah, and it's ginormous," she says. "I was looking out into all those seats, and I can't imagine being up there when that place is full and everybody's screaming at you—"

"Did you see Liam?"

"He walked by at one point. But I was with Kyle then, and I

didn't want to lose the moment, if you know what I mean, so no, I didn't chase him down."

Of course, she didn't.

"Anyway," she says, "they were testing gear and stuff, and Leslie took me up with her. They all came over, and we started talking like we'd known each other forever, and then we took selfies together"—she comes up for air—"and well, everyone's just *so* ordinary you'd never guess they're rock stars if you didn't know already, and they acted like I was one of them. They gave me a shirt and signed it for me. Okay, I've still got to get Liam's name on it, but—"

"They had one with them?" I ask.

"Courtney went and grabbed me one. It's black and silver, a different design than yours, and I'm wearing it now, just so you know. I've already put some pics on Instagram." She heaves another monster sigh. "It was so unbelievable, all of it."

"Can't wait to meet them," I say.

"Kyle and Keenan asked about you."

"They did?"

"And Sean, too. They all want to meet you."

"Wow, cool."

Though not entirely surprising. They've read my article; they know I'm interviewing Liam, so that factors in, I'm sure. But I totally want to meet them, and that alone will enhance the background and perspective of my story.

"They said we could talk more later, me and them," Morgan's saying. "After the soundcheck, maybe. Like, while you're off doing your interview."

"Jamie didn't say, but I'd guess that's being rescheduled for after the show."

"So, how'd it go with him?"

"It was really nice—being together in real life instead of talking over the phone—"

"I don't mean that," says Morgan. "Okay, maybe some. But tell me something I *do* want to hear. Like, did he kiss you?"

"Mmm...maybe a little."

She squeals and—I'm braced for it—crushes me up close. "Yes, yes, *yes!*" She sighs again. "Wow, Jenny. You're not wasting time, I see."

"We don't have time to waste," I say.

"So, when can I meet him?"

"After the soundcheck? Or the VIP set, maybe." I disentangle myself, step back. "He said he'd text me when he's done with whatever he's handling now."

"He'd better be taking you out later tonight."

"We talked about it. I'll have to come up with a plan for getting to Jordanne's, though. And you can *never* say anything to Mom. Like, ever."

"Wouldn't dream of it," she says, all gleeful. "I'm sure *he'll* get you to Jordanne's, no problem." Her voice turns sly. "I won't wait up for you."

I ignore that, finger-reading the face of my watch. "Soundcheck's in ten minutes, so we ought to go in there, don't you think?"

"I do think," she says.

I take her arm, and she pulls me out the door, striding fast as Alexis does, already back on her schmooze with Kyle and the rest of the band.

I'm only half listening.

What are the chances Jamie might get done early and find me in the arena? Take me on stage after the soundcheck? Introduce me to Liam there instead of somewhere behind the scenes?

The band's already gearing up, guitars grinding, drums slamming, keyboards scorching hot. I recognize the underlines of *Cataclysm* even without Liam's signature vocals in the mix.

Morgan hustles me forward. We swing a right and enter the arena at floor level and stage end. Like, where *else* would we go? The sound, throbbing from all those massive speakers, is absolutely mind-numbing. Stripped of my echolocation skills, I am utterly disoriented, and only because I'm latched onto her arm do I have any idea where I am or should go.

The band is roaring into *Ignite the Stars*—that's Kyle's guitar shredding riff from the bridge before they storm back into the chorus —and Morgan's hauling me over the floor like we'll miss the moment if we're not in the best spot ever. She steers me around whoever's in the way—staging crew, technicians, who knows, who cares—and then stops so abruptly I nearly overstride her.

She leans in close, her hair falling over my shoulder, breath brushing my cheek. She's shouting, I think, but I can't understand a word, so I nod and mouth *okay*. She turns me slightly to the left and puts my hands on the barricade between us and the stage.

They're at right angles, my hands. We're standing at the junction with the runway, so we won't be hard to find if someone up there wants to come over and sing (or play) down at us.

I'm so hoping they do. I hope Liam drops to the floor and opens the barrier for me, takes me up on stage with him like Leslie took Morgan.

Okay, probably not.

But still, that would be the ultimate, if only for the soundcheck.

The staging, Morgan told me at the Portland show, is this post-apocalyptic, *Walking Dead* sort of thing, built up of broken walls and scattered rubble backdropped by a burned-out city skyline. Multi-level platforms and catwalks everywhere, hydraulic risers, giant video screens, and machine-generated fog so thick she didn't know the band had come on stage until Liam's voice shattered into the opening bars of *Excalibur Knight*.

They're in a full-on jam. They've switched to *Tear at the Walls*, and he's in with them now, his razor-edged vocals frying through the sound system and fracturing down from the walls and the ceiling overhead.

> *"Imprisoned by your own design*
> *Walls closing in, shatter dreams in your mind*

> *Shadows of the night track you into the day*
> *Where the things you fear won't chase away*
> *Gotta fight back, no matter what you find*
> *Behind the walls you've built, still there in your*
>   *mind."*

His voice is everywhere—in me, around me, undoing me—till there's nothing *but* him, and me being consumed by it all.

> *"Tear at the walls till they all come down*
> *Till the whole place reels with the shock and the sound*
> *Till there's nothing to say, and you've killed all doubt*
> *Somebody help me, please, somebody get me out..."*

Seriously, I'm going to meet this guy? Do an interview and a write-up on him?

Right now, I can't think of a single question I've practiced the last however many weeks or imagine talking to him about anything or even saying hello without falling all over myself.

Second verse and he spits out every line. Courtney brings up the keys behind him, Keenan backing her with his heavy guitar work, Declan power drumming over the top, and Sean driving bass underneath. Kyle's lead wails in on the chorus, his voice blending with Liam's, and now the rest of them are in vocally, all tight harmonies and monster sound.

Flash pots roar up, searing my face with intense heat.

How *do* they stand on stage with those things and not get fried?

Liam drops out halfway through the bridge, and the music and backup vocals stumble and scatter off into near silence.

My head rings, and then everything goes muffled. Like someone wrapped it in a cocoon or stuffed a whole cotton plant down my ears.

"Wow!" Morgan's shouting, I think.

I pull the earplugs I shoved in to protect my vital-to-life hearing.

"They're so incredible this close-up," she says. "I mean, if they sweat, I can see it, we're *that* close."

"Wish *I* could see it."

"Kyle was looking dead at me like he could see me through the lights and—"

"Wanna bring Declan up in my monitors, like?" Liam's Cork lilt staggers into the arena and hangs over the place. He's a bit more jagged-voiced than usual. Like maybe he's not totally on top of his game, though you wouldn't know it from his vocal work two seconds ago. "And back Kyle off a wee bit, would'ya?"

He sounds *so* Irish-gorgeous.

I mean, seriously.

Somebody answers him, from the mixing board station, no doubt.

"He's at the end of the runway," Morgan says, "but he's looking back at us."

"He doesn't know it's *us*," I say.

This place has to be full of video and sound techs, road crew, people with early access passes (same as we do), and Tacoma Dome personnel. To say nothing of all those lights searing into his eyes.

"If Leslie showed him an Instagram pic," says Morgan, "he might know it's *you*."

Okay, yeah, possible.

In fact, she probably did. I mean, if it were me, I'd want to check out someone *I* was interviewing with. And if my sister had photos and inside info, so much the better.

The band's gearing up again. They're working *Adrift in Time* now, the song Liam wrote after his dad passed that no one knew existed when he took over Michael's slot, and the band recorded *Into Infinity*, the album before *Tear at the Walls*. They break off after the first verse, and he's asking for more audio adjustments from the sound crew.

Morgan nudges me.

I pull my earplugs again. "What?"

"He's still watching us," she says. "Okay, he's talking to these guys and working on presentation and whatever. But he keeps looking this way."

"Doesn't mean anything." But I'm hoping it does. I'm hoping he knows it's me and comes over to talk the minute he gets done. I'm hoping—

"And bring up Courtney on this one, too, would'ya?" he says, quiet voiced yet mega-powered.

Something jars. A memory from somewhere. Something about his voice, though I'm not sure what exactly. Or where I remember it from. But this isn't the first time I've heard him talk. And not just from the Moda Center stage two months ago or a YouTube video in my room.

The band is up and running again, and Liam's testing the vocals on the second verse, the use of delay effect echoing his words over themselves at the end of every line.

> *"Whisper across the untamed sea*
> *Where darkness meets the dawn*
> *Perhaps somewhere between the two*
> *Lies the reason to go on*
> *While the tides and trade winds know*
> *The seasons and the signs*
> *I'm left without a shore in sight*
> *Sometimes...*
> *Adrift in time..."*

It's a softer song, but his voice is just as raw and breathy and—

Cold gathers in the pit of my stomach. Pain hits my head, pulsing behind one eye, and picks up speed. From all that sound—music in, music out, everything so close, so brutal, then falling off again.

"A wee more of Courtney, please?" he says.

Whatever's jarring me is still there.

I'm picking up patterns and nuances and timbres I should know, that I *do* know, that I've heard before, and not just at the Portland show. I hear them now, and I heard them forty-five minutes ago and yesterday, too, and the day before that. Not exactly the same. The accent is different, the pitch not as low, but the pieces are all there.

What I'm hearing. What Morgan's telling me. What didn't happen earlier as it should have.

Not able to wait for me at the airport...

Not getting away from whatever was tying him up...

Not finishing with me before getting yanked out here.

And where is he now?

Something shifts and changes, like the kaleidoscope I looked at when I was a kid, back when I could see. A bunch of fractured pieces turning and clicking, locking into place.

No social media presence...

No ready answers when I pressed for them...

I stand very still, everything frozen in my brain, my heart hammering in my chest.

I *know* where he is.

And I'm not breathing.

The music's up again, devastating loud. It's *Adrift in Time* and then *Into Infinity*, I think, but really, I'm not sure. All I hear now is *him*. Not even the words, just *him*—under me, over me, through me, ripping my soul from me.

I grab the barricade, my head falling onto my fists. Morgan nudges me, she pounds at me, she screams at me. She pulls me away and turns me into her, and I bury my face in her shoulder.

"Jenny?" She's still screaming, but I'm barely hearing her. "Jenny?"

> *"From this chaos to calm*
> *Into infinity, you've gone*
> *And I'm still here, asking why—"*

Liam breaks off again, and the band drives on without him, splintering into silence. And for the space of forever, there's nothing but layers of echo and my heart rocketing into the endlessness of it all.

I'm shaking.

I'm already crying.

And he's sprinting up the runway, feet pounding the stage floor above us. Someone power boosts his name into the arena, someone else gets on a mic, and then it's all voices and questions and mindless noise that smears into the background and means absolutely nothing.

His feet hit the cement behind the barricade. *"Jenny—"*

Morgan inhales. She gasps.

My legs go to gel beneath me.

He vaults over the structure between us. "Can-I-have-her-Morgan-please?"

Her grip goes slack, and he takes me. Right from her arms, he takes me, and he's not hugging me this time. He's holding me. "Oh, Jenny—"

I'm breathing shallow; I'm breathing fast.

And he's holding me, right here, right now.

"I'm sorry, I'm sorry." His voice is in my hair, softly jagged and lilting, all desperate and panicked and unplugged, his heart pounding beneath my cheek.

I'm hyperventilating, trying to breathe.

"I'm so sorry..."

I hear him, and yet I don't. Like he's talking to someone else, and I'm off in the distance, only half listening.

"I am, Jenny."

I'm dragging in air, still fighting to breathe. I'm hanging onto him like I'll collapse to the floor if I don't. He's slimmer than I remember from those moments backstage—*before we started laughing and teasing each other*—and he's wearing a battery pack, the one that powers his in-ear monitors, clipped to the waistband of his jeans.

"Sittin' you down, okay?" He pivots me from the stage and puts me into a chair, drops to his knees in front of me, his breath coming hard and heat radiating off him.

My eyes are streaming.

"Oh, Jenny..." He gathers me up again, presses my head into his shoulder, holding me tight. His shirt is wet, the hair on the back of his neck is wet, and he smells of cologne and apple shampoo and sweat soaking through the fabric beneath my cheek. "It wasn't supposed to be like this, no." His voice breaks, shatters into my hair. "And I'm so fierce sorry."

I'm shaking so badly.

Where I am.

Who I'm with.

What's been going on the last two months, two hours, two minutes. None of it possible, none of it making sense, and yet it's all so brutally real.

"I tried to tell you," he's saying, "so many times, and I just—I never could. But I was going to today. I swear I was going to tell you."

I'm sobbing, and he's holding me, he's cradling me, he's whispering words I don't always understand.

"It's my fault, *mo chuisle,* it's all my fault. And I'm so, so sorry."

"Please..." It's the only thing I can choke out.

"I mean that, Jenny." His voice is in shards, and his tears run down my forehead, over my eyelid, onto my cheek. His fingers are in my hair, and everything he says to me now is in that language I've heard him use on stage and in video footage and the band's Celtic metal songs.

The old Gaeilge language of Ireland.

"Please..." I try again. "Just leave. Please, just...leave me..."

"I can't leave you. I don't ever want to leave you." He drops his head onto mine, holds me hard against him, fingers still tangled in my hair. "I love you, Jenny."

Chapter

22

When I was ten, my folks bought me one of those glass floats you see in all the gift shops on the Oregon Coast, replicas of what used to be found on the beaches after drifting across the Pacific from Japanese fishing nets. We'd barely gotten back to our Cannon Beach hotel when it slipped from my hands—I don't even know why I was holding it—and shattered into a zillion glittering pieces, sparking blue, green, and purple fire all over the sidewalk.

And that is me now, so fractured and splintered, I can barely process anything. Except I am here, in a chair below the stage, and Liam O'Shannon is on his knees with me in his arms, where we've been since he sat me down a lifetime ago.

He's crying into my hair.

He's killing Jamie Conway with everything he's saying in Jamie's speech patterns filtered through his beautiful Irish accent.

"I know you don't believe that now. Why should you ever believe that, ever want that, ever want anything from me? But Jenny, I do. I love you."

This isn't happening...

This is SO *not happening...*

"And I'll do anything, anything a'tall, anything you ask of me, I will."

"Please..." My words fall into nothing.

"Whatever you need to sort this, however long it takes you—a day, a week, a month, a year, forever, if it takes that long, if you need that much time, it doesn't matter—I'll wait."

"Liam..." My voice breaks on the only name that was ever truly his.

"I won't ask you for promises, for anything." His brogue is coming through thicker than it did on stage, and it's breaking me down, everything I'd thought solid collapsing beneath me. "Only that you hear me out before you tell me this can never work."

"How—how could—how could you"—I can't stop the tears soaking into his shirt—"do this...to me?"

"I just—I did it. And I could never get myself out. I was so afraid of how you'd take it—take *me*—once you knew..."

How am I supposed to take it?

"You"—I swallow, choke on the words—"you lied to me..."

"I'm so very sorry."

"You *lied* to me?"

How could you stand in my yard, making promises you could have kept right then and there, and lie to me about it? How could you call me and text me and keep lying the whole time? How could you talk about an interview—seriously, Liam??!!—and not just give it to me? We had an hour backstage, and you didn't come out with it then? Instead, you kissed me as someone else? Just when were you going to let me in on this? When changing your voice range and your accent can't disguise who you are anymore?

"*You're* Jamie." Morgan blurts, dropping into the chair beside me.

Liam lifts his head to look at her. "I am."

For once, she has nothing to say.

Leslie's voice registers out of the commotion around, above, behind me. She scrapes up another chair, and now she's massaging my arm as if that might soothe me somehow.

"Jenny..." she says and then nothing more.

What exactly *is* she going to say?

You knew all along, and you said nothing...

Liam fingers my hair and kisses the top of my head, then eases me back, thumbs the tears from beneath my eyes. "I don't know where I stand with you just now," he says, all ragged-edged like he did from the stage five minutes ago, like he did in my yard two months ago, like he always sounds over the phone. "But I can't imagine it's very good." My tears are running over his fingertips. "And you deserve so much better than I've given you. It's just"—his voice washes out on him—"I don't want a life...where you're not in it."

My breath is coming in heaves. "I can't—I can't do this..."

Not with you...

"Even if you can't. No matter what you do, what you decide about me, I love you, *mo chuisle, grá mo chroí.* And I'll always be waitin'."

"Please..." My voice cracks. "I just—I want—"

"Anything you ask," he says. "Just tell me, so."

"—to go." My nose is running, my eyes are swelling, and I've got to get myself out of here, away from him, and I can't do that, either. Can't stop crying, can't stop bleeding out in front of this guy I thought I knew so well and so totally don't.

"All right. Okay."

"—go now."

"It's okay. You don't have to stay here." He fingers a strip of wet hair from my face and slides it behind my ear, smudges the tears across my cheeks. "But I do. For a wee bit longer. And then I'm done for now, and I'll come to you straight away." His hands fall from my cheekbones. "*If*...you'll see me, Jenny?"

"I—" My mouth closes.

What do I say in this moment?

"Here, girl." Leslie leans over me, her hair falling onto my shoulder, and shoves a wad of tissues into my hands. "You need this"—her voice shifts—"both of you. And I can take you out. I've got a few minutes."

Not you.

You lied to me, too.

I scrub at my eyes, blow my nose, crumple the tissues into my fist. Only now do I remember who's here in my space, where she's always been.

"Morgan's...taking me out," I say.

"Of course I am." She slides an arm around my shoulder and squeezes me up close. "You'd better have a killer explanation for this," she levels at Liam.

"I wish I did," he says. "I wish I could make this go away for you"—he's not talking to her anymore—"if that's what you want." And he's sniffling like he needs those tissues his sister handed off. "Because I don't want the best thing that ever happened to me...to be one of the worst that happened to you."

I pull myself from Morgan—*a bit late for that, isn't it?*—and swipe at my eyes. I'm dragging in one hard breath after another, my tears falling in wet splotches onto my jeans, and I can't imagine getting up from this chair and going on to—what, I don't know—because right now, there's no beyond *this*.

"I meant it, Jenny," he says. "All of it. What I said to you."

"I want to go," I say to Morgan. "Now." I shove myself up, legs shaking beneath me.

"We're going now," she says.

Liam picks himself up from the floor. "Ring you when I'm done... if that's okay?" He's standing at my shoulder, his arm brushing the sleeve of the jacket he gave me—*the one with his name on the back.* "And you can say yes or no? If you'll see me or not."

Twenty minutes ago, I wouldn't have turned this down for the world.

And now...

"*Liam!*" an Irish voice storms out of nowhere. "We gotta get Leslie up in ten minutes, and you're all AWOL with some fangirl!"

I cringe into Morgan.

Not a fangirl.

So not a fangirl!

"*Girlfriend*," Leslie corrects him.

I dig my fingers into Morgan's arm.

Not THAT, either...

"She's Jenny," Liam says back. "You know—*Jenny?*"

Like my name should mean something to this guy.

"Yeah, she looks happy with you," Irish Guy growls.

"Leave off, Michael!" Leslie fires at him. "Give 'em a bit, so."

Michael?

As in *O'Shannon? That* Michael?

"We've got a schedule to keep," he snaps. "And this girl's been nothing but a distraction for weeks on end!"

I swallow, my fingers digging deeper into Morgan's arm. "Now, *please!*"

"Yeah, he's totally in the doghouse over you," she says, still standing here, like she's grown roots.

Liam's not moving, either.

Was it for me *you were keeping too much to yourself? Hiding out backstage or in your corner of the tour bus, texting and phone talking to* me *instead of whatever your brother wanted you to do?*

Leslie's into it now with Michael. He's snarking back. Liam's stepping in to defend her. And I want to throw myself down a hole somewhere.

"Go, already!" I hiss at Morgan.

"Jenny—" Liam starts.

"Stage!" Michael snaps him off. "Now!"

"Doin' it, so," he grouses in his razory *Tear at the Walls* voice.

Clearly, being Liam O'Shannon doesn't make this his band.

Or put him in charge of anything.

Morgan's already hauling me off.

I keep my head down, tissues pressed to my face. It won't take half a brain to know whatever my just-now-discovered relationship with O'Shannon's frontman is—*how is it we even* have *a relationship?* —it's not going very well at the moment.

He's already back on stage, apologizing to the band and his tech people in this power-boosted mix of Irishisms and Jamie-speech patterns, and I'm losing it all over again.

Get me out, get me out, get me out...

Chapter 23

Someone falls in step beside us, guy shoes thudding on cement, the smell of coffee and leather in our space. "Come with me," he says in a cut-glass (and probably authentic) British accent.

"Who are *you?*" Morgan shoots at him.

"Darren," he says. "Richardson."

The name means something, but in the chaos of the moment, I can't place it.

"Again with the same question," says Morgan.

"I'm Liam's bodyguard," he says.

I stumble over my feet, catching myself on Morgan's elbow.

Bodyguard?

As in, Liam's best friend and security guy, the one he told me about that day in my yard?

So I need security now?

"We're fine, thanks," Morgan says back.

"I can shortcut you out of here," says Darren Richardson. "You might want that considering the attention you're attracting from people with *work* to do but mobiles in hand."

Yeah, apparently I do.

Wait—I'm being *photographed?*

Going up on Instagram and YouTube with my arms around Liam's neck and my head on his shoulder, both of us breaking down over each other in full view of who knows how many opportunists with their phones out for the photo op of a lifetime?

You went public with me??!!

"Passageway under the stage drops you close to Leslie's dressing room," Darren's saying.

"Did *he* put you up to this?" Morgan throws at him.

"Escorting you out," says Darren, "was *my* call."

The arena explodes then in a blitz of overdriven guitar and the massive synth orchestral lines opening into *Shattered Ground*.

Get. Me. Out.

We're ducking into the passageway beneath the stage, the flooring shuddering above me, cement vibrating under my feet when Liam fries the house with his hardcore vocals, his voice scorching straight through me.

> *"In a world breaking down*
> *Hope is lost, hope is found*
> *All the cost, all the pain*
> *In the end's not worth the gain*
> *It all remains*
> *When darkness falls*
> *Beyond the walls*
> *On shattered ground..."*

My head is roaring, pounding, my nose streaming into my tissues, and this passage is, like, the longest walk ever.

We come out the far side, and Darren takes us through a curtained exit and down a short hall, the decibel levels falling slightly behind us. We hang a right, and now we're in a backstage corridor, all echo-y with footsteps and the rhythm of passing voices, a woman's inflection changing as she turns to look at me.

Crying into my fist while being escorted through a private exit by Darren Richardson has got to mean something, especially if the word's hit back here already.

"How far to a ladies' room?" Morgan asks.

"Straight ahead, on your left," says Darren.

"Thanks. And we're good from here."

"Going that direction myself," he says.

Three or four other people pass by, soft-soled shoes and thudding heels, stale cigarette scent trailing behind them. I put one foot in front of the other, face turned away, my head throbbing with all that sound pulsing beyond the walls.

Morgan stops and pulls me through another door. It sighs behind us, closing Darren out. "Sinks on your right," she tells me, "stalls on your left."

I reach out and slap my hand into the nearest sink. Shove the faucet on full force and plunge my hands into the water, letting it splatter.

Jamie's gone.

He's dead.

He never was.

I swallow hard. Drench my face, again and again, rinsing away my tears and Liam's, too, and then stand here, still heaving, the water roaring into the sink.

I'm going to be sick.

I'm going to lose my ham and provolone in this sink.

I'm going to—

"Deep breaths," Morgan says beside me. "In and out, slow it down."

While Liam's nailing it out there on stage.

So *not* the guy on the phone or texting with me. Not the guy teaching me online chess or laughing over my Halloween getup or asking how I do Christmas or why I want to see a place I can't actually see. Not the guy kissing me backstage or holding me on the arena floor, soaking his tears into my scalp.

What am I supposed to do with you?

I twist the faucet handle.

Morgan hands off a bunch of paper towels, and I scrub my face dry.

"You've got mascara here." She touches the corner of my right eye, then traces my left cheek. "And here. And a bit here, too." She smudges one side of my nose. "I'm guessing the rest ended up on Liam's shirt."

I drag in another hard breath. "I want to go home."

"It's a mess out there, Jenn. And our flight's not till tomorrow afternoon."

"I can't stay here."

She goes quiet for a moment, then finally says, "Should I call Jordanne? Ask her to come for us now?"

I shake my head. "I don't want you to miss the show."

"I've seen their show. And I've met Kyle. Talked to him and got his autograph. I'm good."

"You don't have Liam's."

"I'm okay with that."

"Front row seats," I remind her.

"I don't think you should go alone," she says.

I don't want to go alone. I've met Jordanne twice, and I don't think we talked for more than ten minutes either time. So the prospect of going to her place, caved-in mess that I am, does *not* appeal.

But I also know this is a one-time shot for Morgan.

How can I take that from her?

"I'm going straight to bed," I say, "and sleeping the whole night. Don't give this up for nothing."

"It won't be for nothing. You'll have someone to talk to—cry on if you need to—till you fall asleep."

I blow my nose into my soggy tissues. "Stay here. I'll be fine."

"You won't be fine," she says. "And you shouldn't be alone."

"Morgs—"

"Let's go."

I toss my towels into the bin, take her arm, and we shove through the door to find Darren loitering where we left him.

"Seriously?" Morgan says.

"Nothing better to do," he says back.

She huffs at him, but he sticks to my side all the way to Leslie's room, opens the door for us, and then says, "If there's anything more I can do for you, Jenny..."

I shake my head.

Just go, already...

Morgan tugs me inside. "We're good," she says at Darren, then bangs the door behind us.

Leslie's perfume hangs in the air along with the cedar scent of my bag and hints of bread and fruit and whatever else I noticed earlier and couldn't care less about now.

Morgan pulls me in, hugs me hard. Like she did last summer when I got word my cousin Raelyn drowned rafting the Rogue River out of Grants Pass.

"I'm so sorry, Jenny..."

I'm going shaky again, inhaling air, my fingers fisted into her shirt. I'm hoping I'll wake up any minute now, and this will be nothing but a bad dream—the kind that leaves you half-wishing it *was* true, but mostly you're glad it's not.

Only I'm not waking up.

And this *is* real.

"I'm so scared," I whisper into her shoulder.

"You don't have to see him again if you don't want to," she says. "But I think you do."

I pull away, sniffling, and wipe my eyes with the tissues I stuffed into my jacket pocket. "I don't know..."

"He was crying, Jenny. I think he means it."

I swallow, and his voice lilts through my head—what he said that I wasn't expecting, even from Jamie. Not so soon, anyway.

Morgan steps aside, grabs something from the ice bucket on the table. "Here." She comes back and puts a frigid bottle into my hands. "You need this."

"Thanks." I unscrew the cap with shaky fingers, tip the bottle back and inhale water, letting it freeze my raw throat going down.

"That guy on stage in there?" she's saying. "The whole place knows who he is. But the one kneeling on the floor, giving you his heart? I'm guessing *that's* Jamie Conway. Like, when he takes off his rock star hat and kicks back on the tour bus, phone-talking to you, he turns into the guy you thought he was. With a different name. And an Irish accent."

"It wouldn't—" I drag in a hard breath. "It would never work."

"Do you want to spend the rest of your life wondering what if?"

I take another long pull from my water bottle. "What part of him epically lying to me did you miss?"

She sighs again. "Okay, it's really huge. I get that. And you don't know what to do with it. I get that, too. And what he did to you? Yeah, I want to kill him.

"Then again, he is who he *is*. In case that still matters. And he wants *you*. I'd at least hear him out, no matter what I did with him in the end."

"I don't know," I say again.

But I *do* know.

I want this over, want it done. I want Jamie to be Jamie still, and Liam O'Shannon to be who he's supposed to be, even if that's less overwhelming in real life than I'd always imagined.

"What am I going to do, Morgan?"

"Do you love him?"

I open my mouth, then close it again.

Do I?

If I loved Jamie—*I did, didn't I?* I thought I did—does that mean I love Liam, too?

Like I even *know* Liam, whoever he might actually be under his media-hyped persona.

"He used me." I close my eyes, and in the silence beyond the walls, I hear the thud of my heart, blood pulsing in my ears. "And he lied."

"Not what I asked," she says.

I shrug and stand here, waiting for everything to roar up again.

It doesn't.

So they're done, then.

He's done.

And now his voice is belting at me from the phone in my hip pocket.

"Show time," Morgan says.

Do I let it go to voicemail and buy myself a few more minutes? Tell him no, we're finished, we're over, and I never want to see him again? Say fine, okay, but only for so long, and Morgan stays with me the whole time? Give him a blank check because I want to know *why*, no matter where that wrecks me in the end?

My leave-a-message spiel is microseconds from clicking on.

"Gonna answer that?" asks Morgan.

I reach for my pocket. "Hi..." I'm all cloggy-nosed like I'm sick with a cold.

"I'm done, so." His voice, softly ragged sans power boost, sounds as it did in my hair not thirty minutes ago.

How can you sing like that and talk like this?

Is it because *you sing like that?*

"Will you see me, Jenny?"

"I—" My throat closes.

What *am* I going to say?

Do I want to see him?

"Do it for closure," Morgan says. "So you can live with yourself, whatever you decide."

"Um, okay..." slides out of me.

"Thank you. Comin' straight away."

I end the call, stuff my phone back into my pocket.

"Good," Morgan says. "Should I wait till he gets here?"

I shake my head. "No, it's fine."

"You're sure?"

I shrug.

How can I be sure of anything right now?

"Make him answer for what he did. Then do what's best for you."

She pulls me into a quick hug—"I'm a phone call away if you need me"—then crosses the room and opens the door.

Footsteps clip up the corridor, steady strides coming fast.

"Guess he called you on the way," she says, and out she goes.

And now he's here.

"Jenny?"

Chapter 24

My eyes flood, and I fold my arms over my waist, the only protection I have left.

His steps fall on the cement as they did—was it only two hours ago?—when Jamie walked into this room and swept me into the best hug ever. And I was so sure, in that moment, he was exactly what I wanted; that some way, somehow, we'd make this impossible thing work between us.

And now it's Liam O'Shannon walking in.

But not like I'd dreamed all these years.

He doesn't hug me like he did as Jamie or hold me as he did out front. Just closes the door enough to deaden sound, but not so far that it clicks, and says from across the room, "I don't even know where to start..."

Like he's doomed already.

My arms tighten over my waist. My eyes are a watery mess—*how did I think I was going to handle this?*—and I want him to go back out and leave me be. Or come over and hold me, anyway. Kiss me. Make me believe this is some nightmarish mistake, that I haven't been epically played by the performance of a lifetime.

I blink, and the tears run down. "Is he even"—I swallow—"a real person?"

"He's, em...a name," Liam says, "I sometimes use in emails. When I want to write to someone as a rep of O'Shannon Productions. Not as myself."

So not the guy tearing down walls in the arena five minutes ago.

"So you were going to lie to me from the start."

And here I thought you cared about me and my blindness and everything that goes with that!

"I wasn't, no. I've never actually tried to *be* Jamie. But when I walked in on you backstage in Portland and saw you on the floor, I—" He stops, blows out a breath. "'Twas a fierce night, to be sure, with Kyle ill and Michael on about everything he thought I could have done better. And in the moment, I just wanted *not* to be me—or at least, not my name—for a wee bit." He sighs. "And there you were."

"So you used me." I sniffle too loud. "Because I'm blind."

"I'm so sorry, Jenny."

I turn away.

How can you say you're sorry and expect it to be enough? How can you lie to me and tell me you love me and expect me to believe it? How can I believe anything you say to me ever again?

He crosses the floor and stops behind me, his breath going in and out, and I catch the mix of cologne and sweat from the shirt he was wearing out front. "I want to hold you more than anything right now," he says. "But I'm guessin' that wouldn't...be okay."

"It was okay *out front*." My voice is raw, tight, tears close to the surface. "Part of the show, was it?"

"I would never do that to you."

"You *did* do it to me! And now everyone's got the photos to prove it!"

"You were collapsed in Morgan's arms," he says, "and you weren't pullin' away from her. I knew you knew. And I had to be with you when you did. But I'd *never*—"

"You think you can"—I swallow again—"can lie to me and then—then pour out your heart to me, and"—I gulp in air—"because you—you're—Liam O'Shannon, I'm supposed to—to what? Say it's all good? That I forgive you, just like that?"

"We're not good," he says. "I'm not good. I know you're not. And I don't know what it will take to make us good. It's just"—his voice catches—"please, Jenny..."

I whirl to face him. "You *used* me! Broke my heart, my trust, my dream!" I reach out and connect, slam my hands into his chest. "You *lied!*" I shove him back, shove hard, and he stumbles and collides with the table. "And I believed you. I believed it all!"

"Jenny, please..."

"*You lied!* You walked through that door"—well, not this one, but one like it—"and you knew it was me and why I was there, and you just...switched up your accent and your voice range and told me you were somebody else!"

"I did it, so," he says, still standing where I slammed him, not moving at all.

"And now you want to change it up and be *you?* And I'm supposed to just roll with it? Like it doesn't flip my whole world upside down?"

"I know it does. I know it's gonna be powerful hard—"

"You *think?* I can't even—even process *you* right now. And what you did—"

"I hate what I did," Liam says. "And if I could go back and undo it, I would. Even though that'd have meant never knowing you. Because I'd have signed your shirt. Done a selfie with you and moved on. And I can't imagine that"—his accent thickens as it did in the arena—"never knowing you. But then you wouldn't be here like this because of me. And you'd be okay. Because none of this would have happened."

Yeah, that would have been easier.

Me going into Christmas like everyone else and remembering, every now and then, that I did meet Liam O'Shannon after the Portland show, and he made my whole life by saying hi and signing my shirt, and then I got on with my real life, and that was the end of it.

Because in what world would I ever want *this?*

"You should have," I say.

"'Twas only to be for a few minutes, so," he says. "And then I'd tell you. Sign your shirt, your tickets, whatever you wanted."

"You didn't."

"No. So I came to your house the next day. To tell you. Because I couldn't live with what I'd done."

Liam O'Shannon standing in my yard, bringing my horse tack out to me, giving me a boost up to ride...

"Didn't do it then, either." I sniffle again, wipe my nose. My tissues have fallen, and I have nothing but the back of my hand. "You handed off a note while you stood right in front of me. Didn't tell me on paper, didn't tell me in person. You just. Kept. Lying!"

Liam steps away and then back again, puts fresh tissues into my hand. "Here, now."

"Thank you."

"There was no one around to know it was me," he says. "To force me to say it. But I did try."

And I remember.

Him starting to say something, then redirecting.

Me thinking he was going to ask me to join the group in Portland only to have some complimentary line tumble out instead.

Was that a lie, too?

"All you had to do was switch up your accent," I say.

"And I meant to. But it was so easy to keep bein' Jamie. And the more we talked, and I didn't tell you, the more I couldn't. Because I could be *me* with you in a way I can't with most everyone else. And I was ashamed that I'd lied."

"Not like you stopped."

"I was going to tell you over the phone," he says. "But that wouldn't have been fair. You deserved it from me in person. And I wouldn't have gone through with it, anyway. So I set up the interview. So I'd *have* to tell you."

"And you didn't do that, either. You just kept lying and lying to me, over and over and over again!"

"I knew where it would all end."

"So you, what? Be Jamie forever? How exactly does that work? Oh, right—it doesn't!" I step back, sensing the wall behind me, then hip-slam into the table on my right. Like my radar isn't working, everything skewing on me.

I throw out a hand to steady myself, and Liam shifts into my space, his fingers brushing the sleeve of my jacket. I twist away, club my foot into something I didn't know was there and grab at a chair to keep from going down.

He catches my arm before I hit the floor. "Jenny—"

I get my feet under me and yank myself free. "Yeah, I'm blind! And this is what I look like blind, what my whole life looks like! This is *me*, okay? It's always going to be me, and you"—I swipe again at my eyes—"you think you want *this?*"

"I want all of it," Liam says. "I love you."

I wrap my arms about myself, hanging on tight. Like I did all those months after going blind, rocking to and fro in the gray nothingness, as though that would keep me from flying off in pieces everywhere.

"And I'm supposed to—to believe you now"—I gulp—"when everything you told me before was a lie?"

"Not everything."

I shiver.

Step back.

Do it now.

Instead, I stand waiting for his fingers to fall onto my shoulder or graze my cheek, both of us breathing in the silence. And beyond the walls, Leslie's band gears up with the techno rhythms and dubstep undertones of *Never Walk Away*.

Liam steps back, giving me my space. "Will you, em...sit and talk with me?"

Where I won't smack him into a wall, he means?

I suck in air, let it out slowly, then reach for the chair that almost toppled me to the floor, turn it about and sit, my hands in my lap.

He pulls up another and slides in opposite me like he did earlier, but farther back this time. His knees don't touch mine as they did before.

"About Jamie..." he begins.

"Was he—was all of him—a lie?"

"Not all. His da—*my* da—dyin' of bone cancer at fifty-one? That's me. But you know that already."

The story was all over the fan pages, magazines, and online write-ups when the band dropped their summer festival dates to accommodate a new manager and new frontman in a family crisis. Morgan and I read about it after the fact, having not discovered them till *Into Infinity* snagged U.S. attention. But still. Common fandom knowledge.

Though his dad was a business consultant, if I remember right, not a lawyer.

"And flying with your uncle?" I ask. "And going to Germany for Christmas holiday? And getting dumped by the London girl for someone who wasn't going to spend his life being somewhere else?"

"That's me."

She was an aspiring artist; I've put the pieces together now. Somebody no-name like me, and it didn't last long.

Did he love her?

Am I jealous if he did?

"And playing mahjong?" I sniffle again. "And shooting photography? And the rest of it?"

"Me, Jenny." He's leaning forward, his voice hitting me close in. "All of it."

"And the whole Wacken thing? How was *that* supposed to work?" My voice ratchets up a bit. "Me on the grass and you on stage?"

"For another band, maybe? Though we, em...generally drive in, set up and play, tear down, and drive on."

"So that was a lie, too."

"I'd have made it work. If you had wanted me to."

Like it was anything more than a fantasy to begin with.

"And my interview?" I ask.

"It's still yours. Any time you want it."

What would I do with that now?

"And *kissing* me as someone else?" My jaw's so tight it aches. "Seriously, how *could* you?"

"I'm sorry I did that. I was going to wait till after I'd told you—if there was any chance you might still want that from me. But then I, em...gave in to the moment."

"Because it's always been about *you*, hasn't it? Whatever you want, whenever you want it."

"No, Jenny, I—"

"So not doing FaceTime *wasn't* about you getting seen by whoever might walk by or be in the room with me?"

"Okay, that, yes," he says. "But I wanted to, so much. I just—I couldn't."

"So you fed me a feel-good lie instead."

"How could I say this and not be with you?"

"What part of us in here two hours ago wasn't 'being with me?'"

"I had to do a soundcheck, so. How could I tell you and then leave you?"

"You're leaving me now." I slash a hand over my eyes. "You'll always be leaving me. You'll always be somewhere else, and I'll be—"

"With me," Liam says. "You'll be with me. If...you could ever want to be."

"And why would I?"

"Because you made me believe you feel something for me, too."

"For Jamie," I say. "Not for—"

"I *am* Jamie," he says. "Just...not by that name."

"Jamie wasn't a rock star."

He sighs and shifts back in his chair, and the truth hangs in the silence between us.

You may be Jamie in your *mind, but not in mine.*

And from the arena beyond, Leslie's band jams into *Cause and Effect,* driving the point home.

Finally, he says, "I've been agonizing over this for weeks. What to say and how to say it, how to make it right, if I even could. And all the while, I was fallin' so hard for you, and nothing I could say or do would ever be enough. And still, I couldn't tell you, and I couldn't walk away. Because I've never felt for anyone...what I feel for you."

I shiver. "And how many have you said *this* to?"

"To you," he says.

"Not London girl?"

"Only you."

My eyes close, open again. "If I can't trust you with the truth, how do I trust you with my heart?"

"Because you have mine," Liam says. "You have my life; you have it all."

I shake my head.

"Everything, Jenny."

I fist my hands in my lap, the tissues crushed between them.

Even if I could forgive you, if I could believe you mean this—

"I never—never said"—I swallow—"I loved you."

"Said it, no." His voice is so quiet. "But that's not the question, is it, now?"

I swallow again, harder this time.

Do I love him?

You used me.

Do I love him, anyway?

"You—you'd get tired of me," I say.

"Why would I, now?"

"You have no idea what my life's like, not really. I'm not blind on the phone or in an email or sitting in a chair. If you spent just one day with me, you'd see how blind I really am. I'm totally inconvenient sometimes, and you're—"

"—*more* inconvenient," he says. "All the time."

"You can have anyone."

"I can't, no," he says. "And I don't want anyone. I want *you*. Because you're the one I'm in love with."

I open my fists, the tissues light and wet on my palms and close them again.

Where do we go when there's no hope for something ill-fated from the start? When we don't fit into each other's worlds, not even close, and everything lies ruined between us, yet we still feel something for each other, anyway.

Liam slides from his chair, scooting it behind him, kneeling in front of me as he did in the arena. "I've made such a mess of us, Jenny. And you have no reason to want me ever again. But I'd do anything, so I would, for another chance with you."

My resolve cracks.

He's so close. And I'm so raw. And he's saying everything I want to hear, talking me down from this ledge I'm teetering on, and I'm believing him without meaning to, without wanting to, just falling so hard where I've already fallen.

"It won't be what it was, I promise," he says. "I'll only, always tell you the truth. About everything. Never take advantage of you in any way, ever again. I'll do anything you ask of me, whatever it takes, to make this right, to make us work if there's any chance at all. Because the only life I want...is with you."

His eyes are looking through mine; I know they are, and I'm drowning in them, in him, in everything I've said I can't do, can't have, can't want. And in this moment, when it's just me and him and whatever comes after this isn't something I'm thinking about right now, I go with the one thing I am. Because I'm never getting this chance again.

I take a breath.

Lean forward.

Reach out—

And he hauls me in.

"Oh, Jenny..." His voice breaks over me, breathes into my hair, and I close my eyes against his shoulder, bleeding my tears into his stage-wet shirt. "*Tá grá agam duit, mo chuisle, grá mo chroí.* So much, I do..."

I sob while he holds me and whispers into my hair, and we're so broken now I can't imagine what it would take to piece us—*how can there even* be *an us?*—back together. I only know I want this, if only for here and now; I want everything he's saying to me in those words I don't need translated to understand.

I turn my face to his—*make me believe this, Liam, even if it can never work in the end*—and I'm opening my mouth when his crushes onto mine. And this time, it's like fire; an all-in, I-didn't-know-I-had-it-in-me kind of kiss that's everything I wanted earlier when he was Jamie, and I was dreaming this up, him and me together like this.

I kiss him.

And I don't see the rock star.

I see the guy who stood in my yard and carried my horse tack out from the barn before boosting me up to ride. I see the guy who called me on the phone, day after day and asked about my everyday, ordinary life, who wanted to know what the world looks like to a girl who hasn't seen it in five years. Who texted me and asked about my family and my guide dog and my homework assignments, who listened to my frustrations and showed me the good in everything. Who laughed with me in Leslie's dressing room while I ate my sandwich and dragged my fingers through the ranch dip. Who arranged for me to be here tonight to live out my dream. Who is my dream, and who destroyed my dream. Who is still the guy I can never have.

His lashes are wet on his cheekbones, and his eyes, closed beneath my fingertips, are beautiful, like the feel of his skin and the smell of him so close to me, and I want him like I've never wanted anything. I kiss him hard with the tears on my cheeks and my heart shattering like the glass ball I dropped onto the cement all those years ago. I kiss him, and I don't stop. I don't ever want to stop.

He grabs a breath—"I love you, *mo chuisle, grá mo chroí*"—and he's kissing me again, whispering to me in Irish, and I'm drowning with no one to pull me out. I don't want to be saved, not from him, not from myself, not from where we're headed at breakneck speed. But something is pounding at me, screaming at me, telling me what I don't want to hear, but I *am* hearing, what we both already know.

This can never work.

And I've just made the stupidest mistake ever.

I break it off and turn my face away. "Liam—"

"Anything," he says, all husky, kissing the back of my head. "I'll do anything, so I will. I'm so much in love with you…"

I shift and shove myself from his arms, catching my breath, my palm pressed to my mouth.

What was I *thinking?*

How could I have done this?

Because nothing has changed, and we're still where we were forty-five minutes ago, where we are now, hopeless and damaged beyond repair.

"Jenny? Did I do something wrong?"

I'm breathing hard, my heart slamming in my chest. "I'm sorry, I can't—" I close my eyes. *What have I done??!!!* "I shouldn't have…"

"I loved it, to be sure." His fingers skim my cheek, slide into my hair, then fall away. "But it's okay. We can go slow with this. With us." His voice is so gentle. "I didn't mean to push you."

"You—you didn't." *That one's on me.* "It's just"—I swipe at the hair falling in my face—"it was a mistake."

All of it.

"Not to me." Liam takes my hand, the one in my lap, and laces his fingers through mine.

They're small and fragile in his, yet they fit perfectly. Like they belong there.

Like *we* belong.

"You have every right to hate me," he says, "and every right to be afraid. *I* hate myself right now. And *I'm* afraid." His thumb strokes my palm. "I'm afraid I won't be everything you want me to be, that I can't live up to what you think I am or should be, no matter how hard I try. That I can never be enough for you…"

"No, it's not—I mean, it's just—it's this, all of it." *What you did to me.* "And nothing can change it, no matter how much you try or want to or whatever. We can never go back like you're still Jamie, and none of this happened."

"I don't want to go back. I want to be *me* with you, not somebody who doesn't exist."

I pull my hand from his. I'm trying not to cry anymore, but everything I have yet to say is breaking me all over again. "It's too"—I snuffle back the tears—"too late for that."

For us.

"*Mo chuisle…*" He sighs, ragged, breathless. Hurt. Confused.

And that's on me, too.

"Because I can never"—down they come, anyway—"never live with what you did to me."

Or who you are.

"Jenny, please…"

His phone goes off then, and the ringtone is the same classical something I heard earlier. Mozart, maybe, though really, I don't know.

He sighs again and scrabbles it out from wherever he keeps it. "This means I have to go," he says, and I hear the silence beyond the walls.

Leslie's done, so they're setting up for the VIP Q and A and music set, scheduled for six.

"Yeah," Liam says into his phone. "No, I'm okay. Comin', like." He shoves it back where it came from and says, "What can I do, Jenny? Anything a'tall?"

I shake my head.

It's over. We're done. And the sooner we end this and walk away, the sooner I can gather the shards of my heart and move on.

"You need to go," I say.

"Come with me."

"No, I—" Just. No. "I can't."

I can't see anyone, not these guys I've fan followed for the last three years, not their support crew, and certainly nobody looking to score the story of the night. I don't need any more shots of Liam and me going up on social media. Or in *People Magazine*. And no way can I sit out there while he does what he's so killer good at doing.

Because I totally can't deal with the rock star part of him right now.

"Then wait for me," he says. "See me one more time? Before I go out tonight? Or after I'm done?" He's still on the floor, and his voice is more jagged-edged than ever. "Anything, Jenny."

I close my eyes, my hands in my lap.

"If only to say goodbye?" His fingers touch my cheek, catching my tears.

I nod before I realize I'm doing it. "Okay."

It's what he wants to hear.

"Thank you." He lifts my chin, skims his thumb over my lips, leans in, and kisses me. But it's a simple kiss this time, not like before. "I'll ring you when I'm done, so. And you can say when."

"Okay." My voice is soft, choked with the lie.

He gets to his feet, then crosses the room, stops, and says back at me, "If I could undo this, I would. For your sake. Not mine."

I don't answer him.

He goes out, and the door closes between us.

And it's done.

I had my dream with Liam O'Shannon, and it's over.

Blindsight

"Broken Trust"

By Jenny Ryan

Trust misplaced is not trust broken. Sometimes you're gullible, like a trout in a stream, snapping at the first wiggly worm you see. Stupid of you, but you were enticed and should have taken a second look or maybe thought things through before grabbing a bite.

Broken trust goes beyond that.

Everybody gets lied to—accidental lies, feel-good lies, get-me-out-of-trouble lies, and vicious ones, too. Half the time, you don't know it *was* a lie. And if you do, you get over it, move on.

Betrayal is deeper, uglier, *more*.

It's trust built over time, then shattered for a selfish purpose—faith destroyed, self-worth damaged, confidence depleted—leaving you scrambling to gather the pieces.

Being blind requires levels of trust from me that may not be required of you. Because I might literally be putting my life into *your* hands. To take advantage of or betray that trust would be unthinkably cruel, and our relationship, whatever that may be, isn't likely to survive. Because trust, once broken, is one of the hardest things in the world to repair.

Chapter 25

I'm tucked over my knees on the floor, scootched against the wall beyond my chair, where I've been since Liam left me to go be a rock star again.

How could I have been so stupid?

Kissing him. Like I meant business.

Lying to him after he lied to me. Leading him on, like I actually *want* something with him. Like it could even happen. Like anything could work between us, *ever*.

How could I have not recognized him, even a little?

Okay, the accent and altered voice range was huge, and no, he doesn't sound exactly like he does on my playlists or in online interviews, being unplugged and unpolished in real life. But still, I'm *good* with voices, and I listen to his stuff every day of my life.

Why didn't I pick up on how gloomy he'd get over Michael's micro-management of his career? *What happened to the big brother who walked Little Brother to class that first day at school?* Or how easily he got music journalists—surely Michael has no lack of connections—to look at my work and arranged interviews for me with himself and his sister?

To say nothing of the total lack of traceable Jamie Conway info. Nothing out there to show this guy actually existed.

And when I asked about it, he lied.

Which makes me stupid *and* gullible.

My phone dings at me.

I ignore it, my face mashed into my knees.

Now it's ringing, Liam's voice stabbing me all over again.

I pull it from my hip pocket. "Yeah, hi," I say, all nasally, my voice scratchy.

"You sound awful," says Morgan.

How am I supposed to sound?

"It's a mess," I say. "All of it."

She sighs. "I'm on my way."

I hang up and fold back over my knees. Never mind what Morgan said about getting closure; I'm *not* closed. More like laid open and bleeding and wanting, more than anything, to throw all logic to the wind and make things epically worse than they already are.

Text him.

See him.

Let him hold me, kiss me breathless, make me believe the impossible. No matter how ruined I am when it's over.

The doorknob jiggles, and in she stalks, Doc Martens slapping the cement, her vaguely Morgan-ish scent on the air. "Hey," she says and then slides down beside me like she's not the least surprised to find me parked on the floor of the Tacoma Dome. "So, how bad is it?"

"It's over," I say into my jeans. "If that's what you mean."

"You're sure about that?"

I nod.

"Well, you failed to make it clear to him."

I raise my head. "Wait—you *talked* to him? Like, when?"

"Two minutes ago." Said like she hangs with rock stars every day of the week. "I don't think *he* knows where he stands. Like, maybe he has a chance with you, and maybe he doesn't, and he thinks you love him, but he's afraid you'll say no in the end, that you'll never be able to forgive him."

Pretty much sums it up.

I sigh, resting my chin on my wrists. "I kissed him again. Like, a lot."

"That'd do it," she says. "My gosh, Jenny!"

"It was such a mistake."

"Not to him, apparently."

"I never should have. Now it's a massive disaster."

"Or not. I mean, he did ask what it would take to convince you."

"It's not about being convinced." I scrub the heel of one hand over my eyes. "It's what he *did*. And I'm supposed to want him now? After he lied to me and used my blindness against me?"

"Yeah, even *I'd* have to think about that," she says. "And that's saying a lot because I want *somebody* to notice me. And if it's an Irish rock star who's hotter than hot, and I don't take him up on the offer, how un-Morgan would that be?" She shifts on the floor, her arm thumping mine. "But that's not you, I know. Because I don't think you were making out with him for the bragging rights."

I lean my head back on the wall. "Do *you* see this working? Like, ever?"

"Realistically?" she says. "No. I mean, you'd have to go to Ireland if you actually want to be together, and what's the point if you don't? And get blown up in the tabloids and on social media with him. Oh, wait—happening as we speak."

"Don't, Morgan."

"And live with everything that goes with him being *him*. Which means his career will always come first, and your identity as a writer and a blind advocate or whatever else you might want gets crushed behind who he is."

Exactly.

Because Jamie—if he'd been a real person—might have worked into my life plans. I'd go to college. He'd get a lead publicist job, maybe in the U.S., or I'd go to London (that could have been fun), and I'd write concert and musician reviews, and we'd have a normal-ish life together.

If we'd wanted it bad enough.

Liam O'Shannon isn't leaving Ireland. He's not leaving the band. And he surely knew I adored him when he squatted beside me backstage in the Moda Center—why am I always on the floor in these places?—and told me he was Jameson Conway, which makes his being wretchedly sorry for it now worth less than nothing.

"Then again," Morgan says like she missed me checking out however many sentences ago, "how much do you love him? And what are you willing to give up for that?"

Ten minutes ago, I'd have traded my soul.

Now I know I never will.

"Nothing." I close my eyes, my head still pounding. "I'll always remember he lied to me and wonder if he's telling me the truth or just feeding me another story."

"This guy loves you, Jenny," she says. "He's not lying about that. I can see it in his eyes when I talk to him, and he's totally telling *me* the truth."

Wish he'd told me.

"It's done," I say. "*I'm* done."

"Then you need to be super clear on that. Because he's still hoping to make this work with you."

"Yeah, well, I, um...told him I'd see him one more time. To say goodbye or whatever." I shake my head. "And I can't do it, Morgan."

Because I won't walk away a second time.

She grunts at me. "You two deserve each other."

I blink back the tears. "Like I said. It's a mess."

Steps clip up the corridor. Not the ones passing by now and again —soft-soled shoes, casual strides—but clickety heels on a mission. They stop at the door. Knuckles tap on wood.

"It's me, girl. Leslie," she says. "Will I come in, so?"

Like I'm denying her access to her own dressing room.

Morgan scrambles to her feet. "Yeah, sure," she says.

I'm clawing myself up the wall, backhanding tears from my cheeks, when the door opens and Leslie walks in.

"Jenny, are you okay?" She pulls me into a hug, her spiral curls falling down my back, and I inhale the scent of roses and whatever salon products are definably her. "I've been after worryin' about you, so I have."

"Not okay." I shove myself from her arms. "And you lied to me, too."

"I'm sorry, but it wasn't my place to say anything." She sounds so much like Liam I can't believe I didn't pick up on that earlier. "He did hear about it, to be sure. And not just from me." Bracelets clink on her arm. "It was really stupid, what he did. And, well, for somebody who can get up on stage in front of twenty thousand people, you'd think he could tell one person what an eejit he's been."

I don't answer that. I stand holding myself against the world like I've been doing since Morgan and Darren walked me out of the arena.

"I know you're havin' a brutal time with this," Leslie goes on. "And that it's gonna take a while to sort it and get used to him as, well, Liam. I can't believe he waited so long to tell you."

"He *didn't* tell me," I say.

"Sure, but he meant to. It's just—he knew it wasn't going to go well—how could it?—and he stalls off stuff like that, especially when it's his own fault. But he does love you; I swear he does."

"I want to go home," I say.

"It's fierce out there tonight. Morning'd be better, don'tcha think?"

"I can't stay here." Never mind what I promised. "I'm...going to Morgan's sister's place as soon as I can."

"No one expects you to go to the show," says Leslie. "You can wait in my room. See Liam when he's done? He wants that more than anything."

So he can convince me to stay?

My throat constricts. "I—I can't."

"I'm going with her," Morgan says.

"You are *not* going," I say. "You're staying for the concert and more hang time with Kyle and the rest of the guys. I'll call a taxi, so Jordanne won't have to drive here twice."

"She'll come, no problem."

"Not happening. And I'll be fine."

She grunts at me. "You're sure this is what you want?"

"I'm sure." One more lie tripping off my tongue.

"Text me when you get in, so I know you made it."

"Okay."

"What do you want me to tell Liam?"

"Nothing," I say. "I've said it already."

"I'm so sorry for this, Jenny," Leslie says beside me. "I wish there was something I could do, and there's nothing, I know." She sighs, and her accent thickens the way his does at times. "I only hope someday you can forgive us. Because I still want to be your friend. And Liam doesn't want anyone but you."

I don't comment on that, either.

"I gotta go." She steps away, rattling something off the rack across the room. "I only came to ask about you and grab a change of clothes for the Q and A."

"You can have your room," Morgan says. "I mean, it *is* yours."

"I don't need it, so." Her heels cross the floor.

"What does it mean?" I say after her. "He keeps saying something, calling me something, starts with an *m*, I think, not English."

She stops, and her voice turns back to me. "*Mo chuisle?*"

I nod.

"We use it to mean *my darlin'*," she says. "Literally, it's *my pulse* and comes from *a chuisle mo chroí*—meaning *pulse of my heart*. It's much prettier in Irish, don'tcha think?"

Morgan nudges me. "Told you he's got it bad."

"*Grá mo chroí* means *love of my heart*," Leslie adds. "Which he said to you, too." She opens the door. "He means it, Jenny. He'll do right by you from here on if you give him a chance." And then out she goes, the door closing behind her.

Chapter 26

I'm going to run.

I didn't know it five minutes ago, but I do now. Everything's so perfectly set in motion I won't have to tweak much to make it happen.

I line up a taxi after Leslie goes out. The guy on the other end says it'll be half an hour before someone gets here, so I send Morgan to the arena to catch the Q and A she's dying not to miss (no matter how she insists on staying with me). She promises to leave early enough to take me to my ride, but I'm confident Kyle will suck her in with his answers, and she'll lose all sense of time. Especially since she's gotta have the most epic view imaginable, considering *who* arranged this night for us.

The minute she's out the door, I go to Alaska.com and buy an air ticket.

Flights between Portland and Sea-Tac run more or less on the hour. I pick the first available for the time frame, putting it on my credit card. Mom won't be happy (she ultimately pays the bill), but this is an emergency as far as I'm concerned, and she'll be less happy with everything else that goes with it. Starting with what I have to say the minute I show up alone in Portland, fifteen hours before I'm supposed to.

I can't even lie about it. Or say Jamie and I decided it was all a mistake, that we'd never work out together. Because we've got to be uploaded to every site imaginable by now. The world will be seeing what I can't, and it will be screaming obvious who I'm with and that we're not shaking hands or taking selfies together.

Do I want to be in a relationship with a rock star?

No, I don't.

Seriously, I don't.

I want to be gone already, but I'm stuck in this room with nothing but a wall or two between me and what I'm so desperate to outrun.

I press the speaker button on my watch.

Six-twenty.

The Q and A in progress runs close to an hour, including questions texted from the VIP audience and a three-song set. The walls mute band member responses, so I have no idea who's talking, but they're at least fifteen minutes into it, best I can tell.

Liam's struggling with his answers, zings into my phone. **So not like him.**

Getting dumped by the girl no one—including the girl herself—knew he was seeing would probably do that, no matter how slickly polished he comes across in every interview I've heard him do.

"Does he know I'm going?" I send back.

Not from me, says Morgan. **Leslie, maybe.**

Will I message him before I leave? Text him after I get on the road when it's too late to change my mind? When am I telling Morgan I'm not going to Jordanne's?

Shouldn't that taxi be here by now?

"I just want out of here," I say into my phone.

Best I can tell, she replies, **so does he. If you're going to text him, you'd better do it soon.**

I should.

But I don't.

I slouch in the chair I sat in earlier, replaying everything from that night two months ago with this one, overlaying the guy who knelt holding me and crying into my hair with the one who's two-plus hours from storming into the smoke and the lights. And I'm putting me into the mix, and no, I don't fit anywhere, not with any of it.

Which means we can't make this work no matter what we feel for each other.

What I feel for him is already tearing me to shreds, so no way am I putting myself into a situation I won't walk away from.

The Q and A segment wraps up, the VIP song set is about to begin, and I'm still waiting in this chair. No text from my driver—he's officially late—and no sign of Morgan, either.

"So, where *are* you?" I shoot at her.

Coming now, she says.

"Hurry, already."

Music swells beyond the walls—layers of digitalized keys and the sizzle of overdriven guitar, Kyle's lead keening over the top. The drums slam in, everything segueing into the opening bars of *Fire and Ice*. And when Liam sears into it, he is so on the mark, so incredibly good. Like he hadn't broken down in my arms at the foot of the stage or sat here gutted while I took back everything I'd made him believe I wanted.

Get me out of here...

The door swings in, and Morgan strides through without bothering to knock. A man's step falls onto the floor behind hers, and I catch the leather and coffee essence of this guy who walked me out during the soundcheck and refuses to let us be.

"Couldn't get rid of him," she grumbles.

"You're my responsibility as long as you're here," Darren Richardson says. "Besides, I'm good at getting people from Point A to Point B."

"Not much to brag about, is it," Morgan says back.

I'm already out of my chair and into my jacket, reaching for my bag.

Darren snaps it up ahead of me.

"I can take that myself—"

"Got it already." He steps toward the table. "Here. A gift from Leslie." He's back in one stride, putting a pair of glasses—sunglasses? —into my hand. "Your eyes are pretty swollen."

"Thanks." I slide them on, the plastic frames too big for my face. "I'll make sure she gets them back."

"Don't bother. She's got dozens."

So now I have sunglasses. I couldn't look more blind if I tried.

Yeah, I could.

I could pull out my cane.

My phone goes off as the band launches into a metal version of the Celtic *Oró Sé do Bheath Abhaile* duet Liam does with his sister. My driver says he's waiting outside the entrance (the one I did my best to describe to the dispatcher), but who knows if I got it right or where he's actually parked.

"Ready, then?" Darren asks as I double-tap the screen.

I nod and shut down my phone.

I'm not taking any more calls till I'm decently beyond reach.

"Let's get you out." His voice is kind, full of regret, and I hate the choice I'm making.

"*I'm* getting her out." Morgan steps in close, and I hook my fingers below her elbow. "Tag along if you must."

She leads me across the room and into the corridor, Darren striding beside us. I hide my face behind one hand, but the only other footsteps out here are receding into the distance.

"Is he—" I begin. "How is he?"

"He's going to have a rough night," says Darren. "But he's pulling it off okay, as you can tell. He always does."

"And you think I should stay."

"I think you should do what's best for you," he says. "Liam knew what he was getting into when he chose to do this, idiot that he is. If it doesn't work for you—either of you—it doesn't work. Not your fault." We turn into the side corridor Leslie brought Morgan and me through earlier. "Though I wouldn't write him off yet."

The band is now razing the night with *Off the Grid,* performed in the show itself in Portland. Morgan said Liam goes onto one of the catwalks for this one, and Kyle and Sean do this cool lead/bass faceoff amid a frenzy of blue and green lasers.

Get me out, get me out...

Footsteps clip up ahead, followed by "Wait—is that *her*?" as a girl passes by, her voice flipping around.

"Is she okay?" some guy asks.

Darren hustles me on. "Not feeling well." To me, he adds, "You get used to it."

I don't plan on getting used to it.

I'm leaving Liam to his rock star world and going back to my safe and quiet one where the biggest issue is my mom and dad getting on with their separate lives and Bryan moving full-time into mine.

We reach the exit and go out into the frigid night. Snow is still falling, and the air snatches my breath away. A car idles to my left.

Morgan walks me through the seven or eight inches already crusting on the ground. "Text me when you get in," she reminds me.

I drop my hand from her elbow. "I will."

Darren hands my bag to the driver, opens my door, and eases me inside. "I know you have Liam's private number," he says. "Call him when you're ready to talk."

I shrug, say nothing.

The driver closes my bag into the trunk, then climbs up front.

Darren reaches across my space. "Run my card," he says.

"No," I say back. "I'm the one going. *I'm* paying."

"Run it," Darren says again.

"I have my own card," I insist. "And some money, besides."

I'm the one, after all, who's sneaking to Sea-Tac, a way bigger expense than Darren thinks he's in for. Assuming, of course, he knows where Fife is. Or at least that it's close by. On the other hand, working privately for Liam O'Shannon must make him incredible amounts of money. He won't miss whatever's racking up on the meter.

"Done already," he says. "Anything more I can do for you, Jenny?"

I shake my head. "I'm good, thanks."

"I'll come in quietly when I get there," says Morgan.

"Make Liam sign your shirt," I tell her.

"Oh, he's gonna hear loads from me." Her voice eases back. "I still wish you'd stay."

"You know I can't."

"Hope to see you soon, Jenny." Darren closes me in.

I pull on my seatbelt and click it into place.

The driver's voice turns to me, rattling off the address I gave over the phone, a question mark lifting on the end.

"Make it Sea-Tac," I say. "I changed my mind."

"All right." He swings around, and we grind over the lot, turn onto a side street, then climb the onramp to I-5.

The headache that eased up as I sat alone backstage roars again to life. My throat burns, and I want to curl under a thick comforter somewhere—my dad's place would be perfect—and shut out the world.

The driver is talking to me. "So what event's up here tonight?"

"O'Shannon. From Ireland," I say. "They're a band."

"Are you okay?" He's hearing my sniffles, the catch in my voice.

"I have a cold," I tell him.

"Bad night for it," he says.

We're clanking north along I-5. He says nothing more, and I turn my face to the window, the cold breathing through the glass though the heater's blasting on high.

I pulled it together in Leslie's dressing room, held it together the whole time I was grabbing my gear and walking through corridors and out a secured entrance with Darren and Morgan. But now I'm in the dark where no one can see me cry.

Because I'm here, and Liam is back there, and every mile I make away from him is one mile further we'll be apart.

He should be done with the VIP set by now, so he's got to know I'm gone already. Probably trying to reach me, and I've made sure he can't. I *will* text him. But not till I'm sitting on the plane.

The car is slowing down. We ease off the exit ramp and crawl along endless streets to the airport, finally circling around and pulling up to the drop-off zone for departures.

"Which airline?" the driver asks me.

"Alaska."

"Do you need help to the door?"

"If you would, please."

It'll cost Darren more than he's already paying, but I don't have anyone to get me there, and Alexis isn't here to say *find the door* and have her do it.

"Be glad to," he says.

I dig my wallet from my purse—I can at least add a tip—and open the cash slot at the back.

My money, like everything else in my life, is precisely organized. The ones lie flat, the fives are folded lengthwise, the tens in half, the twenties in quarters. I grab a ten and stuff it into my jeans pocket.

The driver opens my door, gives me a hand, then retrieves my bag from the trunk while I pull out my cane and flick it open. He takes my arm and starts me forward. I use the cane as a walking stick till the snow thins out beneath an obvious overhang. Now I skim it over the ground—left, right, left again—finding cracks in the cement, the curve of a trash can over there, the automatic door pad up here.

We go inside, and the sudden warmth slams me. The driver takes me to the ticket counter and hands off my bag.

I offer him the ten from my pocket.

"Take care of that cold," he says.

"I will. Thanks."

He vanishes into the commotion flowing around me.

The agent at the counter pairs me with the assist person I arranged for after buying my ticket.

"Hi," she says in a mildly Hispanic accent. "I'm Lucia."

"Jenny."

"This way." She tucks my hand beneath her arm and guides me to the kiosk at the ticket counter where she punches in my flight info and prints my boarding pass. She then takes me to screening, loading my bag onto the belt, and stays with me all the way to the gate, checking in with the guy at that counter before finding me a seat.

"They'll get you an assist onto the plane," she says.

"Thank you," I say, and then she's gone.

I check my watch.

Eight-forty.

My flight boards at nine. Leslie comes offstage from her opening act at eight-forty-five. And O'Shannon goes on as the headliner at nine-fifteen. By the time Liam's done fronting his brother's band, I should be at my dad's place.

Because that's where I'm going.

Mom can crucify me tomorrow.

I pull my phone from my hip pocket. I know what's waiting the minute I power up, but I've stalled off too long already.

I check for messages, finding a voicemail and a text.

And yes, both are from Liam.

"Any chance I can see you tomorrow before you fly home?" Quietly resigned. Like he knows I'm done, that it's over. "Just to say goodbye?"

Should not have listened to this.

I cue up his text.

Love you always, Jenny, no matter what.

Like my heart isn't shattered enough as it is.

I power down, biting my lip, trying hard not to cry, and shove my phone back into my pocket.

What am I to do with you? We can't change what you did. And I can't risk my heart on someone I can't trust. We could never make this work, anyway. Not me in Oregon and you in Ireland. Not me being me and you being you. So what difference does any of this make?

The call comes for pre-boarding. Someone shows up to take me into the jetway and onto the plane, puts my bag in the overhead bin (though I can do that myself), and seats me on the aisle. It's a pretty open plane, best as I can tell—not many people flying south this dreadful night.

I pull my phone out again, power it back up, and call my dad.

He answers on the first ring. "Jenny?"

Clearly, he wasn't expecting to hear from me tonight.

"Can you, um"—I swallow—"pick me up at the airport? Like, in an hour or so?"

"What *happened?*" explodes out of him.

For the space of forever, I say nothing.

"Jenny?"

"Um..."

"What'd this guy *do* to you?"

"Not what you're thinking, Dad," I say. "He wouldn't—"

"Then why are you on a plane?"

I drag in a hard breath. "Because Jamie's real name"—my voice cracks—"is Liam O'Shannon."

Stone silence on his end.

"And I want to come home."

He exhales into his phone. "Are you sure of this?"

"That I want—"

"Of who he is."

"I'm sure," I say. "I gotta get off the phone. We're pushing back from the gate."

And I don't want to add WiFi for a fifty minute flight to my credit card bill.

"Is Morgan with you?"

"She's at the show."

He sighs heavily. "All right. I'll see what I can do."

"Thanks, Dad."

"Call me when you get in."

"Okay."

I hang up, ask next for Morgan.

"I took the taxi to the airport instead," I text her. "I have a flight home. Don't be mad. It's what I have to do."

Two down, one to go...

My chest squeezes. My eyes fill.

I bring up the name I set with this number.

Jameson Conway.

"I know I said I'd see you one more time—" My voice is shaky, the words running together, garbled. I delete them, then start over with the same first line. "But I've already said my goodbyes, and I can't say them again." I'm half a second from trashing this one, too, but I keep going. "I changed my mind about spending the night with Morgan's sister. I'm flying home. Even if I could work through what you did, I can't be what you want me to be, and I can't tell you what you want to hear, so it's best if I go." I haul in more air. "What I felt for Jamie, I can never feel for you. Because you're not Jamie, no matter how much you want me to believe you are."

I hit *send.*

And then I delete his number from my contact list.

Me Without You

In the spaces between
Where all is unseen
And the ghosts shadow through
It's my life without you
Can't undo, can't forget
All that's shattered and yet—
It's regret
It's choices we've made
Can we somehow be saved?

Me without you
Is the best I can do
All that's lost, unregained
Strands me here, still unchanged
And what remains
Is the worst I can do
Left alone, unreclaimed
Without you.

~J. Liam O'Shannon

Chapter

27

The plane roars down the runway and lifts off into the night. I lean back on the headrest and close my eyes. I'm trying not to cry in front of whoever's sitting across the aisle, but holding it together is unbelievably hard. And I am so exhausted. I didn't sleep well last night, what with stressing over the weather and getting here today, and then the last five hours have been, well, more gut-wrenching than anything since a) I went blind and b) my mom walked out on my dad and took Kaitlin and me with her. All I want now is to fall into a dead-to-the-world kind of sleep, if only for a few minutes...

I slam awake when the wheels hit the runway in Portland. The plane is roaring, bouncing, dropping back to the asphalt, shuddering as it comes in. I shove myself up, groggy and disoriented, my eyelids so thick I can barely open them.

Then I remember, and my breath scrapes out in a ragged gasp.

Don't cry, don't cry...

I'm crying, anyway.

We reach the end of the runway and roll over the tarmac, finally angling left and parking at the gate. People crowd off the plane, but I wait till the last, till the flight attendant comes to help me into the jetway. I've pulled my bag down from the overhead bin and dashed away my tears, but I'm still sniffling like I've got the worst cold ever.

"Are you okay, sweetie?" she asks me.

I nod and say yes. It's barely a lie because I'm so obviously *not* okay I can't imagine anyone believing otherwise.

"Do you have someone here to pick you up?"

"My dad."

Though I haven't checked for his message yet.

She tucks my arm through hers, slides me ahead into the narrow aisle, then passes me off to some airline guy just inside the jetway.

"Take care," she says and squeezes my hand.

"Where am I taking you?" The guy's voice is big, and his body seems to match.

"Um"—I haven't thought it through yet—"to the, um, entrance at Arrivals. My dad'll pick me up there."

"Okay."

He walks me through the jetway and into the gate where the air smells of water, of Portland, of coming home.

I *am* home.

And Liam's so far away now he might as well be back in Ireland.

Don't cry, don't cry...

The guy asks about my flight and if I live here or am just visiting. I say enough to pass for answering, and he says nothing more. We go onto the concourse where it's all big space and endless echoes, then past screening—way fewer voices and footfalls than when I came through this morning—and to the ticket counters beyond.

He leaves me in a chair near one of the revolving doors constantly whirling cold air in from outside. I shiver but don't ask him to move me, and I don't bother relocating myself. Just thank him and open my phone as he strides off.

A voicemail dings in, then another.

I check the time.

Ten-fifteen.

Liam is still on stage, so this won't be him. And Morgan—well, I don't know where she is exactly, but I can't imagine she's not slammed against the barricade, screaming at his feet.

Or at *him*, maybe.

I cue up the first message.

"Jenny"—Dad's voice—**"there's been an accident at**

the bottom of the hill, and they've blocked that whole section of the highway. I'm sorry, but I'm not going to be able to get to the airport, so—"

Wait—he's not *coming?*

"—I've called Bryan—he's a better snow driver, anyway—and asked him—"

No, what???

He called *Bryan* instead?

Did he talk to *Mom,* too?

"—to pick you up. He said he'd do that and leave you a voicemail."

No, no, totally the worst!

"I'm really sorry," the message runs on. **Call me when you land—**

I voice activate his number.

"Can't you take Skyline?" I blurt when he picks up on the other end.

It's the long way around and switchbacks up and down the ridge of Forest Park, but it *would* get him here.

"There's a lot of snow up there, Jenn," he says. "All crusted to ice, I'm sure. I don't feel good about trying it, even with chains."

"Dad—"

"You had a place close by. And Morgan there with you. And a ticket home tomorrow. We could have talked on the phone."

Okay, I didn't expect him to be happy.

But this?

Not like I can go back and undo it.

"I need *you* to come get me!" My voice is rising, attracting attention, no doubt. "I've got to talk to *you.* And I need someplace that's...home." I could have gone to Jordanne's if I'd wanted someplace *not* home. "It's why I didn't stay—"

"Jenny, I get that you're upset," Dad says. "*I'm* upset. But there's nothing I can do at the moment. And Bryan's already on his way."

So much for throwing myself into the arms of the one person I figured would best understand.

Dad's voice softens. "It's not that I don't want to be there, honey. I just *can't*. But you can call me later. Or we'll talk tomorrow. Right now, though, you need to connect with Bryan and not keep him waiting."

"Fine," I say, all grouse-y. "Whatever."

I hang up and check Bryan's message. He's on his way and asks me to meet him at the curb at ten-thirty.

It's ten-thirty-five now, so I'm officially late.

The revolving door flaps open, swirling in a batch of icy air. Mom's voice cuts across the space between us.

"Jenny—"

I am so *dead.*

I stuff my phone into my jacket pocket and grab my bag off the seat beside me. "Yeah, I'm ready."

Alexis jingles her tags over and slams into my legs, all tail wags and wiggles. *At least someone's happy to see me.* I give her a quick hug —"So sorry, I had to leave you, girl"—then take the leash Mom hands off and curl my fingers around the harness handle.

"Bryan's *waiting*," she says, tight-voiced, stress rolling off her in shock waves. "He left you a voicemail, which you didn't bother answering, and we've been trying to reach you—"

"I was talking to Dad."

"You might show *some* consideration. Bryan's been up since four-thirty on your account, the roads are an icy mess, and you had *no* business making a decision like this without talking to us first."

"Sorry, already." I cue Alexis forward, and we slide through the revolving door and into the freezing night.

"I'm expecting a full explanation when we get to the car," she adds.

Of course, you are.

Worst. Night. Ever.

A vehicle idles in the wait zone just ahead. Mom opens the rear door, and I scramble in behind Alexis, belt myself onto the seat as another vehicle grumbles past, chains clanking over pavement kept clear beneath the overhead ramp.

"Sorry to keep you waiting," I say to Bryan. "I was on the phone with my dad, so I hadn't got your voicemail yet."

"No worries," he says.

"Thanks for coming. I know this was a huge hassle."

"I don't care about that," he says. "Only that you're safe."

"I *was* safe." Just maybe not from myself. "I couldn't stay." I pull off the sunglasses and lean my head on the window, close my eyes. It's throbbing fiercely now, my head. My throat is raw, and my stomach heaves like I might lose the sandwiches I ate all those hours ago.

Bryan puts the rig in gear, pulls out into the street. "Where'd you get the glasses?"

"They're Leslie's. I hear I look bad."

"Nice of her to give them to you."

Nice would have been her telling me the truth.

His Explorer eases from under the ramp, chains grabbing the snow, and swings around toward the exit. The heater is roaring, and the stereo's so low I can barely make out a man's voice crooning I-don't-know-what.

"We've seen the photos," Mom says.

My eyes snap open.

What?

"You—with *him*."

Already?

I shove myself up in my seat, then slouch back, my brain hammering at my skull. "I can't believe this. I mean, it was just—"

How long ago? Six, seven hours?

Long enough, apparently.

"You didn't think you'd get photoshot in an arena full of people?" she says.

It wasn't full. It was the soundcheck and—

"I'd just figured out who he is," I say. "He came offstage and—"

"That doesn't tell me *why* he's holding you."

"Because it's a relationship," says Bryan. "He wasn't a secret anymore, and he needed to be with her in the moment. Or he would have no shot at being heard."

Exactly.

"I never wanted this, okay?" I say. "I only wanted to meet him. Do an interview. Spend time with Jamie. Only there *isn't* any Jamie. And Liam—"

"You are *not* seeing him again." Mom's voice is scary cold, so beyond mad there's no chance of coming through this unscathed.

"I left, okay? I didn't stay for the show or the interview, any of it. Just left him and flew home."

"I told you this guy wasn't what you thought he was. That sending you gifts and offering you perks should have warned you something was off. That he was stalking you or—"

"He *wasn't* stalking me. That's *not* him. And I didn't know he was Liam till right before those photos were taken, I swear it."

"What else have you sworn to that's a lie?" Mom fires back.

"Karen," Bryan says softly.

"Nothing," I say. "I made a stupid choice, okay? I didn't think things through. And I'm sorry." *For all of it.* "I'll pay you back for the air ticket and whatever else I owe you."

"And the part where you lied to me?"

"I didn't *know*."

Honestly, how many times can I say it?

"I don't think he'd have put himself in that position," says Bryan, "if she had."

"When you told me this was just a friendship," Mom corrects us both.

"It *was* just a friendship." My voice tightens. "And then it was... more. And now it's nothing."

Satisfied?

"I asked you before," she says, "and I'm asking you again—*why* was he contacting you?"

I take a breath and fumble about my brain for a place to begin. "Because he was sorry he lied to me. At least, that's what he said. He *did* keep doing it, after all."

I go into the rest from there, keeping my answers short, skimping on details, and avoiding anything I'd rather she didn't know about.

"I warned you about this guy," Mom says again. "I told you—"

"Liam's not"—my jaw tightens—"whatever you're saying he is."

"You're an underage minor. He's an adult. Have you even considered the implications of *that* while you're all over social media with a rock star?"

"It's all I can do to process *him*," I say back. "I can't deal with the rest of it right now."

"Nobody's going to buy into this as an innocent relationship. And if you think he cares for you—"

"And if I say he does?"

"This isn't love," Mom snaps. "It's an older guy with a big name and a lot of money taking advantage of a teen girl with a crush—"

"I *left* him. I broke it off."

"You think the publicity's going away just because you did? This is only the beginning!"

My ringtone goes off.

Morgan, VoiceOver tells me.

I let the song play, let it ring on and on—this will *not* be a pleasant convo—before double-tapping the screen.

"Yeah, hi..." I mumble.

"How could you do this??!!" she lights into me.

"I'm sorry. But I couldn't stay."

"So you *abandoned* me? What kind of friend does *that*?"

"The worst kind." My voice is so raw it hurts to talk.

"You seriously couldn't wait till tomorrow? Already paid-for tickets in hand?"

"You would have tried to stop me. It was better just to go."

"For you, maybe," she says. "Not for *me*. Definitely not for Liam. Now I'm going to Jordanne's *without you* and flying home tomorrow *without you* and trying to clean up the mess you made of your boyfriend's heart—again, *without you*—and I'm failing miserably at that!"

"He's not"—I gulp down the lump in my throat—"my boyfriend."

"Tell that to the guy who didn't get to say goodbye to the girl he's in love with."

"Did you talk to him?"

"And say what? That I'd talk to you? What good would that do? That you'll come around, given enough time? I don't know that, and neither do you. That I'm sorry you're too lame to keep a promise? Like that changes anything. That you're totally in love with him and won't admit it? You *left!* Pretty much says it all."

"So, how'd he do?" I ask.

"He's Liam O'Shannon," she says. "He crushed it. But you could see in the close-up screenshots that it was brutal on him. Like something was going on inside he couldn't peel off his face no matter how killer he was on stage. And *Me Without You?*"

"Written for his dad after he passed."

"No one thinks of his dad when he sings it. Seriously, I don't know how he pulled that off tonight. And then he gets backstage and finds out you ditched him? With a Dear John text?"

Could I have been any more cruel?

"We don't work, Morgan," I say. "We're never going to work." *Happy with that?* "Some things are over, they're done, and there's nothing anybody can do about them. I've got a ferocious headache, okay? I just want to go to bed and forget this miserable night ever happened."

"Call me when you're ready to talk."

And she hangs up.

I pull my phone from my ear, stuff it back into my jacket.

"I take it she didn't know you had gone." Clearly, Mom didn't miss Morgan's voice blaring out the phone at me.

"I texted her from the plane."

"We had an agreement on this, Jenny. You could go to Tacoma so long as you and Morgan stayed together—not every second, of course, but reasonably so—and by implication, came home together. And yet here you are. Alone."

"I didn't want to stay with someone I barely know," I say. "And I'll fix things with Morgan tomorrow."

No idea yet what that'll look like, but we've been besties since eighth grade. We always fix it.

"Some things don't just fix—"

A text hits my phone.

My fingers freeze on the Otterbox case.

Mom rattles on, but I've stopped listening.

I lower the volume, cue up the message—yes, it's from him—put the phone to my ear.

You have nothing to be sorry for, Jenny. That's on me, all of it—everything I screwed up with you. And it's absolutely *everything*. I'm sorry I can't be Jamie for you like you want me to be. Or that who I am isn't enough. But I love you no matter what. And I'll always be waiting.

> *In the spaces that grew*
> *Between me and you*
> *From the price we both paid*
> *For the choice that I made*
> *Can't let go, can't forfeit*
> *All that's remembered and yet—*
> *It's unpaid debt*
> *When the shadows pass through*
> *It's your ghost; it's not you...*

It's twelve-fifteen when I close myself and Alexis into the room I shared last night with Morgan. I am beyond exhausted, yet here I stand amid the ruins of my dream, twenty-six hours after we went to bed in this place, all wired for the adventure of a lifetime.

Me texting with Jamie long after I should have fallen asleep...

Him: **Any thoughts on where you want to eat afterward?**

Me: "Anyplace. I don't care."

Him: **How does a walk in the snow sound?**

Me: "Perfect!"

Him: **Coffee after that?**

Me: "Yes! All of it!"

And now this.

My phone dings at me.

Kaitlin.

Only one reason she'd be texting me on an overnight with her best friend.

WHAT IS THIS, JENNY? YOU AND LIAM O'SHANNON TOGETHER???!!!! (Followed by a row of hearts and gasping emojis.)

Of course, she's seen pics. *Mom's* seen them. And neither of them follows the band. Imagine what's happening among those who do, especially if they know me. How long before my name gets leaked, and the world as I know it completely upends?

"How bad is it?" I send back.

A bunch of photos. Some video. I thought at first he'd come down to hug you, but—no.

"That's me finding out he's Jamie Conway."

OH MY GOSH!!! Are you SERIOUS????

"He's Jamie," I say.

Are you with him *now*???

"I'm at Bryan's place."

Oh, Jenny. I'm so sorry. (Mobs of wailing emojis.)

"Me, too."

If you want to talk, I'm here to listen.

"Thanks, but I'm going straight to bed. Mega headache, super rough night."

I don't brush my teeth, don't pull on my PJs, just shrug out of my heavy coat and toss the band jacket—*why didn't I give* that *back to him?*—down with it. I crash onto the bed, Alexis hopping up beside me, and haul the comforter over my head. Grab the spare pillow and crush it to my chest, my eyes too heavy to keep open, and my head pounding more furiously than Declan's intro into *Excalibur Knight.*

Why did I think if I could just get home (which I'm *not*) and crawl into my old bed at my old house, surrounded by all my memories of everything that once was and shut down everything that now is, things would somehow be better?

"Sometimes you need a refuge"—Dad's voice falling between us as we sit on the back deck, overlooking the Willamette River—"and sometimes you need to refuel. Either way, the real fight's out there. You can't live your life behind walls, Jenny."

Tear at the walls till they all come down...

Liam on the phone with me, always so fascinated by everything and genuinely interested in my life and how I do things blind. Laughing in his kicked-back way about Alexis winding herself up in streamers at Haley's party or the time I stepped in the Jello Morgan's brother Jackson flopped onto the floor. Pep-talking me when I got overwhelmed by school deadlines and tutoring commitments. Telling me I had a serious shot at being a music journalist. Pointing out the upside of having a stepdad because he knows the downside of no dad at all.

Or is he just that good of an actor?

Was he acting when he held me on the arena floor, both of us shaking, and bled his tears into my hair? When he told me he loves me and wants to make this work between us when we both know it never can.

Am I supposed to forgive you now because you said you're sorry, and you want to take it all back?

Cold breathes through the window glass, mingling with heat rising from the vents. A clock ticks across the room and wind soughs beneath the eaves. I tuck my knees into my chest and leak my tears into the pillow.

Why couldn't you have just told me the truth?

DAYLIGHT FLICKERS SHADOWS across my non-vision, and for a half-second, I can't remember why I'm in this bed with the super cushy mattress in a room that smells of laundered sheets, air fresheners, and dog-in-need-of-a-bath. I roll over, my headache kicking up out of nowhere, and everything I'd forgotten in the night slams me all over again.

I groan—*back to sleep, back to sleep*—and curl deeper into the nest I made of my blankets and the extra pillow after Alexis moved to the floor. My eyelids are swollen, my brain already cycling on endless Tacoma repeat.

Why couldn't I wake up back in October, and I'm going to the concert, but there's no interview set up, so the rest of this never happens? Or I *am* meeting someone, but it's Leslie only, no one else. Or it *is* Liam, but he's upfront about it. Says hi and signs my shirt, takes a selfie with me, and maybe answers a few questions. But that's it, that's all.

Not this.

What am I supposed to do with this?

Ding! goes a text.

I bring up Dad's message.

I'm thinking of taking the MAX to Gresham to see you today if that's all right?

"Actually, I'm going with Bryan to pick Morgan up from the airport," I send back. "She gets in at two."

How about I meet you there, then? Maybe half an hour early? If Bryan's okay with that.

"I'll ask."

Let me know.

"Okay."

I don't fall back asleep. Instead, I open my social media accounts —can't avoid them forever, can I?—and listen through my messages, one after the other.

The count is already off the charts—notices and shares, tweets and retweets, texts, DMs, and voicemails. From friends at school and kids who don't know me well but follow me on Facebook, Instagram, and Twitter. From readers who enjoy my blog and people I chat with on the O'Shannon fan pages. From extended family in Grants Pass, Kalispell, and Seattle (even my Grams!). Who all know I've fangirled over Liam for years and can see enough in those photos, multiplying like rabbits—or weeds—on every platform out there to recognize him holding me.

Against my better judgment, I Google *Liam O'Shannon Tacoma*. Call it morbid curiosity, but I have to know what's out there, what I'm up against and can do nothing about. Up comes link after link, photos, and YouTube videos, views already trending into the millions, captions screaming—

Love Interest? O'Shannon Frontman Liam O'Shannon With Unidentified Girl in the Tacoma Dome Arena.

Liam O'Shannon With Girlfriend (?) Prior to Second
Tear at the Walls Tour Performance in Tacoma.

O'Shannon's Liam O'Shannon in a Relationship?

Viewer comments number in the thousands, all asking the same
question—*who* is *she?*
Like Cinderella without a slipper.
Or a prince.

By the time I get out of the shower, my name's been leaked.
Now there's a shocker.
Active as I am on social media and my fan pages, it's a wonder it
took this long. Enlarge my profile pic, and you've got *me*.

*The girl photographed with Liam O'Shannon, frontman for Irish
hard rock band O'Shannon, has been identified as seventeen-year-
old Jennifer Ryan of Sandy, Oregon. O'Shannon and Ryan have
apparently been seeing each other via social media for some time
and finally met in person at the Tacoma Dome for the band's repeat
Tear at the Walls tour performance on December 14. Sources say
that Ryan, a visually impaired senior at Sandy High School, has
been an avid fan since the band first gained popularity in the U.S.
three years ago...*

Not strictly accurate, of course, but the key points are all there.
Along with Liam-and-me pics come others only someone from Sandy
High could have taken—me at a Pioneers home game, me waiting
with Alexis outside the school, me posing with friends at the
homecoming dance, the senior photo I submitted to the yearbook
staff.

Though, to be fair, I posted these myself on all my platforms, so pretty much anybody could have leaked them.

Whatever.

They know who I am.

MOM STARTS in on me the moment I show up in the kitchen.

"You don't talk to anyone about this, you don't give out *any* information, and you don't make further contact with him. Is *that* understood?"

I scrub at my eyes, the Tylenol I've taken barely making a dent in my headache.

Didn't we go through this last night?

"And if we need to hire someone to protect you at school, we can look into that."

Shall I see if Darren Richardson's available?

"He's in a band, Karen." Butter scrapes over toast on Bryan's side of the table. "From Europe. Not like he's British royalty. And he's not *here*. I doubt Jenny will get mobbed."

"I've got family members and neighbors down the road—people in my office, even—asking if that's *my* daughter they're seeing on their screens. At this rate, I expect to find reporters staked out on the deck by the time we get home."

I re-hang the mug I grabbed from the holder on the counter and stalk from the room.

Guess I don't need coffee after all.

"Jenny—" Bryan calls after me.

I keep going.

Apparently, it's okay for people to know who I am through my blog site. Or my byline in the *Pioneer Press*. Or my involvement in the Oregon Chapter of the American Federation of the Blind.

Just not as the love interest of Liam O'Shannon.

BRYAN and I are on the road by eleven.

The day is cold and sunless, and I'm shivering in the passenger seat, even with the heater roaring. My headache has backed down to a dull thud, and my eyes are sore, scratchy, my brain begging for sleep.

"I'm so very sorry, Jenny," he says, and there's this broken glass edge to his voice I've not heard before. "I know how important last night was to you. And how much it hurts to lose something you care about. Or some*one* you care for."

His wife and daughter, driving through the Columbia River Gorge toward The Dalles. Freezing temps, and their car hitting a patch of ice in the passing lane, skewing into the concrete barrier before flipping back over two lanes of interstate...

I swallow and turn my face to the window while Liam's words —*the* words—rise and fall in Irish rhythms in my head. And I remember every second of us together and us falling apart, and now there's this huge gap between us, and I'm the one who put it there.

"If there's anything I can do," Bryan says, "any way I can help..."

"You drove to Portland twice for me yesterday. And again today. That's more than enough."

"I know mistakes were made on all sides and concerns are valid. But from what you've told us and what I've observed these last few weeks, I believe this was a bad decision spiraled out of control, not him playing cheap games with you or deliberately being cruel."

"What difference does it make?"

"One is probably easier to forgive than the other."

I scrunch down in my seat while Mick Jagger belts *No Satisfaction* from a classic rock station.

"Does *not* excuse his actions," Bryan goes on. "Or make anything work between you. But if you feel for him what I think you do, you'll need to find closure. Because whatever happened in Tacoma and apparently went back and forth in messages afterward doesn't look like that to me. And walking away like it didn't happen or wasn't real, on whatever level, won't be enough."

"One message." I close my eyes, the thrum of wheels and the rush of oncoming traffic lulling me into drowsiness. "And I didn't answer him back."

"I know what your mom said, and I understand where she's coming from. But if you decide it's necessary to make contact so you can move on, I'll back you on that."

"Not...making contact..." slurs out of me.

"Your mom's talked about what closure looked like after your dad, and we've tried to work through what was left unresolved. She knows it didn't finish well for you, that you've never forgiven her, and she wants to reconcile that. She just doesn't know how."

She could have gotten back together with Dad...

"This isn't about staying in a relationship you don't want or can't have," Bryan's voice recedes into the distance. "It's about freeing yourself to move on. Because you can't, not completely, with a ghost unburied..."

And I'm back at that sidewalk café in Paris or Florence or wherever, Jamie looking at me out of intensely blue-green eyes, his fingers laced with mine. I glance aside at the pigeons on the stones, and when I turn back, he's gone. And my fingers are empty...

Chapter 29

I jolt awake, breath catching in my throat, my hands shaky, and fragments of images—I can't remember the last time I dreamed visually—still burned in my mind.

The pigeons on the stone wall...

The silverware beside my plate...

Liam across the table from me, looking more or less the way I've imagined him—dark hair and the planes of his face, those incredible eyes...

"Jenny?" Bryan says beside me.

"I'm...okay," I breathe.

"We're here."

Only now do I realize we've stopped, the engine idling, the heater blowing full bore, and the SUV too warm.

"Thanks." I rub my eyes, blink them open.

"I'll be back in an hour."

"Okay."

I stumble onto the pavement, still seeing that café suck into the distance and me sitting there alone.

Without you...

I open the back door for Alexis, grab her leash and the harness handle as she hops down, then step up when she pauses at the curb.

Bryan pulls away.

And Dad's already here.

"Jenny? Are you all right?"

The harness handle slips from my fingers. I reach out, and he crushes me close.

Skinned knees and failed tests, falling-off-the-horse-and-getting-back-on-again times, learning to navigate my darkness, and he's always been here for me...

"Oh, honey..."

I hang onto him and soak my tears into his canvas jacket, not caring who's looking or what they might be thinking.

"Should I want to kill this guy?"

I shake my head against his chest. "No."

I've done it already, I think.

"I am so sorry, sweetheart." Dad lets go with one arm, grabs something from his pocket, and stuffs a handkerchief into my fingers. "Here."

"Thanks." I pull myself away and hold the hanky to my face beneath the sunglasses I'm wearing again today.

"New look?" he asks.

"Messy eyes."

"Let's find someplace to talk, shall we? Do you want coffee? Tea? Cocoa, maybe?"

"No, I'm good."

"Get you something, anyway."

We slide through the revolving door—was it only fifteen hours ago I walked out with Mom?—and go through ticketing to the Blue Star cart on the main concourse. Dad orders two coffees and two lemon-and-key-lime-curd donuts. We sit at a table tucked back from foot traffic, Alexis settling at my feet.

"I would have called last night," he says," but I figured you'd go straight to bed. And I didn't want to interfere with Mom and Bryan."

"It was awful," I say. "Bryan was fine. But Mom was so mad."

"She's had a lot of concerns over this and no idea you and *Jamie* were as involved as you were."

"We weren't—until we were. And I didn't tell her because I was afraid she wouldn't let me go to Tacoma, and everything was already arranged with Liam and—" I stop. "Well...with *himself.*"

Because that took no effort.

"As your dad, I totally want to go after this guy," he says. "Not that I could, of course. But he's got a lot to answer for as far as I'm concerned—starting with the whole cyber-stalking-my-daughter-under-a-fake-identity thing—and I wouldn't go easy on him, I don't care who he is."

"He wasn't stalking me, Dad."

"What *would* you call it?"

I shrug.

"His actions—over the past two months *and* yesterday—were completely unacceptable. And unprofessional. He should have cared enough about his image to have used *some* discretion."

"He told me he reacted in the moment. And there we were."

"With witnesses on hand to document the event." Dad shifts in his chair, the table creaking beneath his arms. "So what *did* he have to say for himself? Not only for that bit of theatrics in the public eye, but for everything else he's done these last several weeks?"

"Um..." I go into it then, best as I can remember, the details hazing into uncertainty after some of the worst hours of my life.

"You knew it could never work, or you wouldn't have flown home," Dad says after I've spilled everything I'm going to. "But to make that decision without consulting anyone was irresponsible, unfair, and put family members at risk."

"I know."

"And to set him up with expectations, either because you're off kissing him—I'm guessing that's where this ended up—or offering false hope or making a promise you have no intention of keeping was as much a lie as what he told you as Jamie."

I say nothing to that, sitting here with my untouched donut and my barely sipped coffee gone cold.

"And what you did to Morgan was equally unacceptable."

"I know," I say again. "And I feel awful about it."

"We trusted you on this. We had misgivings about Jamie, but it was just for a few hours, you'd have Morgan along, and you've both proven yourselves responsible and mature. And then you pull this."

"I was afraid," I say. "And overwhelmed. And I couldn't...see him again."

Dad's voice hardens. "Did he push you for anything?"

"No."

"That's where these things generally go. And you're underage."

"It wasn't about that."

"*What*, then?"

"He's in love with me." I have no doubt about that. "He wants us to be together."

"You're seventeen," Dad says. "He lives in Ireland."

Like the elephant in the room, the blockbuster piece of this—the words *rock star*—go unsaid by both of us.

"Not now," I say. "But someday, eventually." I massage my temple with my fingertips, my headache revving up again. "He talked about it sometimes, in a fun way, as Jamie. Like, us going to a metal festival together or him showing me places in London if I ever came to visit. But this...he was serious. Like he was offering me some kind of...future." I fight off the tears. "Like that's even possible? Like I could ever trust him again. It could never work anyway, even if I wanted it to, and I just—I just—"

"You wouldn't last with him," Dad says. "Even if he'd told you the truth from the beginning."

"I know."

Every tabloid screams out the latest loves and cheatings, breakups, hookups, marriages and divorces, and kids caught in the middle, broken lives piled on broken lives.

Look at Kyle Finn. He's been linked to at least three long(ish)-term relationships and a score of fly-by-nighters in the last eight years. And the girl he has now is a high-profile model with a long history of exes, so I don't expect it to last into next year, let alone the rest of his life.

I don't want to be part of Liam's past, along with whoever (besides London Girl) is back there. He's always kept his private life, well, *private*. But I'm not stupid. He's been around, he has a past, and he can do so much better, so *way* better than me.

So why wouldn't he?

"Doesn't mean you don't love the guy, anyway," Dad says like he's reading every thought in my head.

"I don't know what I feel right now."

"I think you do."

I swallow, blink hard, then cue up the text Liam left me last night and hand my phone across the table. "This is what I sent him from the plane. And what he sent back after he got off stage."

Dad sits in silence while feet click-clack this way and that through the concourse. Finally, he sets my phone down in front of me.

"I don't know what to say, Jenny. We both know where this lands in the end."

"I know."

"That said, I don't believe he's lying about what he feels for you. What would be the point? He invested a lot in building this relationship, even if his reasons at the outset were only to right a wrong. And the photos I've seen of you together say everything."

I pick at one edge of my donut.

"Running away and telling him, from a distance, that whatever happened backstage meant nothing to you was neither fair nor the truth. He deserved an honest reason for why you broke off with him."

"I'm not getting in touch with him again," I say.

"I'm not saying you should. Only that you need to take ownership of the choices you've made and what you've done to everyone around you in the process."

My finger smooshes into the gooey center. I break off a piece, push it around the napkin in front of me, lick the tangy curd from my nail.

"I'll help you work through this anyway I can," Dad adds. "But

I'm not going to excuse irresponsible behavior. If something needs to be made right, you need to woman up and do it."

"Yeah, I know," I say.

Just *not* opening a can of worms I've already hammered shut.

PICKING Morgan up doesn't go like I'd hoped.

I don't get a hug.

No   how-are-you-doing-in-the-wake-of-dumping-your-favorite-rock-star?

Not even a mumbled hi.

"I can't believe you abandoned me," she starts up the minute she clears the checkpoint. "Like you literally didn't care what happened to me so long as *you* were out of the equation."

"I'm sorry, okay?"

"You should be," Morgan says. "Besides having to explain to Jordanne *and* fly home by myself, I had to fend off questions about what's going on between you and Liam after you deserted him in the arena."

We're striding down the concourse, my fingers latched onto the harness handle, and Leslie's glasses slid over my eyes where no one will think anything of them on a girl with a guide dog.

"What'd you say?" I ask.

"Glad you care about *something*."

"Morgs—"

"Nothing, of course. I'm not getting quoted in any tabloids. And I wouldn't do that to you, anyway."

No, because she's a better friend than I am.

"You're trending fine as it is without my help," she adds.

"Wonderful."

"If getting back at Liam was the goal, congratulations. You nailed it."

"What was I to do, Morgan? I couldn't stay, and I didn't want to go to Jordanne's by myself."

"I didn't want to go to a concert by myself," she says. "Which sucked, I hope you know."

"Look, I—"

"I said I'd go with you. Skip the Q and A and the show and more schmooze time with Kyle, all of it. *You* told me to stay. And then you ditched me. And Liam, too. How are we supposed to feel?"

So she's siding with *him* now.

"I said I'm sorry."

"I don't suppose you called and told *him* that."

"I texted him from the runway."

"Yeah, that went over well."

I blink so the tears won't fall. My head throbs and I'm desperately thirsty. Besides a few sips of cold coffee, I've had nothing since that Coke and a bottle of water yesterday afternoon in Leslie's room.

When Liam was still Jamie.

Before he kissed me as someone else.

Now he's on a plane out of the Northwest. And I threw away my one chance to say goodbye.

Chapter 30

om drives Morgan and me home from Bryan's place behind a wall of silence. Whether it's the stress of road conditions— yes, she chained her car, and yes, Highway 26 has been plowed and sanded—or her epic displeasure with me and an Irish rock star she's never met, I don't know. But nobody talks. And Mom rarely drives with music on, so there's only the endless grind of chains and the whoosh of vehicles passing in the opposite direction.

"Call you tomorrow," Morgan says when we pull into her driveway. She leans over and hugs me, like the drive and the silence have mellowed her mood, and nothing's changed between us. "Hope you can sleep okay."

"I'm so sorry, Morgs."

"Forget it, already."

We pick Kaitlin up from Hannah's. She scrambles inside and throws her arms around me, sighing into my hair.

"I cried when I saw your text. Oh, Jenny, you *had* him."

"We're not encouraging this, Kaitlin," Mom warns from upfront.

"So comforting her is off-limits, too?"

Mom huffs and the drive finishes as it started.

In silence.

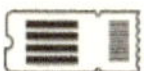

ONCE HOME, I hike up to my room and collapse onto my bed, so exhausted I can barely function. Whatever I'd imagined this weekend might have been, walking into *this*—what I feel in the aftermath of last night—was never part of it.

I don't fall straight asleep. I lie with my empty eyes aimed at the poster overhead, tears trickling back into my hair. Alexis heaves herself from her bed, whines, and noses at my cheek, then jumps up beside me, licks my face.

Someone taps at my door. It opens with a sigh, and Kaitlin's voice falls into the space between us.

"Jenny?"

I swallow and say nothing.

She slips into the room, a wash of Redkin and Chanel #5 on the air, then closes the door behind her. Comes over and climbs in with me, opposite Alexis, the mattress shifting and sighing beneath her weight.

I snuffle and wipe my nose with the sheet.

"Breakups suck so hard," she says.

Not that she's broken up with anybody. But she suffered through Malia's drama-riddled relationship and stormy blow apart with running back Mark Hessman, which I heard about for weeks on end.

Exactly why I didn't want to get involved with someone till after high school.

"Want me to stay?" she asks. "Like back when we were kids?"

When she was afraid of the dark. Or the monster under her bed. Or the lie she'd told and knew Mom would find out. Back when all we had was each other in the middle of a messy divorce, hauled off from everything we'd known and moved to this town we'd only driven through on our way to Mt. Hood. Before she started climbing the popularity ladder, lettering in three sports a year, while I leveled out several rungs below her with the nerds and the brainiacs.

Before we got too busy to be sisters to each other.

"I don't care," I mumble.

Kaitlin crawls under the comforter, wraps me in her arms, and holds on. "I'm here, Jenn. If you need me."

"Thank you," I whisper.

"I really *am* sorry."

"How could I have been so—so stupid?"

"You weren't stupid," she says. "That's on him. Though if it means anything, he looks wretched in those photos. Like he hates what he did, and that, in being Jamie, he fell in love with you."

Was leaving him what I needed to do?

Or one more bad call in a night loaded with them?

"I never—never even"—I swallow—"said goodbye..."

And there's been nothing from him beyond that one text, all resignation and promises to wait.

How long can he be expected *to* wait?

"It's not too late," Kaitlin says. "For saying goodbye. Or trying to work things out." Her voice softens against my shoulder. "Maybe it's not too broken to fix."

I sniffle, wipe my nose again.

What difference does it make when there's no hope of anything lasting beyond the rush and passion of the moment?

What do you do when loving someone isn't enough?

THE MORNING IS all dull shadows and frigid temps. I sleep in till noon (no school, of course), waking up once to find Kaitlin still in my bed and again after she'd gone out and taken Alexis with her.

Now I'm lying here, dull as the morning itself, my tears cried out, and this gaping hole in my chest where Jamie used to be.

He's not calling my phone. Not dropping something cutesy into my inbox or sending me a hey-thinking-of-you text from wherever he might be.

He's just gone.

But my social media feeds are happily blowing up, messages and tweets and DMs racking up by the minute, none of which I open.

Until this one comes in from Leslie:

Forgive me for contacting you if this is not acceptable. I just want you to know how sorry I am for how things played out on Saturday and for my involvement in Liam's deception. To say nothing of all the publicity, I'm sure you never wanted, and we never meant to put you through. Even if things can never work out between you and Liam, I still want to be your friend.

I close my phone, set it back on the nightstand.

Almost forty-eight hours since my world blew up and *now* she messages me?

Too busy being a pop diva on the last show of the North American tour? Or giving me time and space to sort through this without interfering?

Whatever, I don't answer her back.

One more Tiffany, severed into the past...

NOT HALF AN HOUR LATER, something chimes into my Gmail account.

The name attached is Michael O'Shannon.

My breath catches, and I hold myself still, my heart thudding in my chest.

Seriously???

He emailed me? What's he got to say that he didn't make abundantly clear in that dreadful round of the O'Shannon Family Feud? Like I don't know already how totally wrong I am for Liam's life and his career and need it pointed out!

Delete now! screams through my brain.

I hesitate—do I want to wonder forever what might be in this? —then open it instead.

Dear Jenny Ryan,

Apologies for my rudeness in Tacoma. It wasn't about you, and

I had no business making it that. Events were ill-timed, to say the least, and I've minced no words in telling my brother how unacceptable his actions were in not disclosing his identity to you. That said, I would never object to whoever he chooses to spend time with in his personal life, and I am truly sorry if my actions influenced your decision. I would love to have met you under other circumstances.

With sincere regrets,
Michael O'Shannon
O'Shannon Productions

I sag into the pillows plumped against my headboard.
Did not *see this coming.*
Michael writing to *me.*
What do I do with this?

I had no business making it that. Events were ill-timed, to say the

BRYAN SHOWS up after work with a bucket of KFC and a cold vase scented with roses and carnations that he puts into my hands.

"Not sure this is the right thing," he says, "and I know it's nowhere near enough, but I wanted to do something."

I have no words.

The only flowers I've ever received were from my dad on my sixteenth birthday. Well, and the wrist corsage Eric gave me for Prom last year.

Now I'm holding a vase full of them.

I set it on the dining room table, then hug him for the second time in three days. "Thank you."

"I want to help, Jenny. Any way I can."

"You already have."

How could I have missed who this guy is, who he's always been? Have I never really *seen* him?

MOM BLOWS through the door fifteen minutes later, all worked up over my escalating view count and how that's going to disrupt—yes, she uses that exact word—our lives. She says nothing about the flowers sitting in plain sight; just herds us into the kitchen before the KFC gets any colder, then launches into her agenda.

Have I talked to anybody? *Does Kaitlin count?* Has anyone come prowling about for a story? *Not yet.* Just so I understand, I am *not* to contact Liam via text, email, FaceTime, or any other method. *Didn't I say I wasn't?* And might it be better if I sat out the week at home, Kaitlin bringing in my assignments, till after Winter Break when this thing will hopefully have blown over?

"I can't miss class," I say.

I'm not hiding out like I did the year after my accident. And I'm not falling further behind, due to a total lack of studying this weekend, than I already am. I can't bail on OHSET practice, either. Meets start in January, and we're missing hunt seat over fences tonight because of the weather.

"I think it should be up to Jenny." Bryan's voice shifts in my direction. "I'm happy to drop you off at school if you'd rather not take the bus."

One hour less each way enduring an onslaught of questions.

"Maybe." I turn to Mom. "I've got most of the money to pay you back for the air ticket. And I should have the rest by the first of the year."

"And the taxi fare?"

"Liam's bodyguard paid it. Though I feel bad he got charged for Sea-Tac instead of Fife."

Kaitlin's utensil—spoon for mashed potatoes?—clangs against her plate. "I wouldn't worry over what someone working for Liam O'Shannon might have to pay."

"Anyone who comes packaged with a bodyguard," Mom says, "is *not* someone I want you seeing."

"It's a *breakup*, Mom," says Kaitlin. "That Jenny made happen. Give her a chance to work through it, okay?"

Thanks, Kait.

"Might I voice an opinion?" Bryan asks.

Mom sighs and thumps her chicken onto her plate. "Yes, of course."

"I think we need to work this through together. Accept where we are and make a plan for handling the publicity and getting Jenny back on her feet. Because she has to live with the decision she made— or possibly remakes. And if at some point that involves Liam, then yes, him, too."

"We are not—" Mom starts.

"We don't have to be comfortable with it," he says. "But we do need to be open-minded. It's not just about us—what we want, what we like or don't like. It's about what's best for Jenny and what she wants to do. Because she *is* going to make the final choice if she hasn't already. And regardless of how you feel about this, Liam is part of that, and he should get some say in his relationship with her. *If* Jenny chooses to give him that."

"I told him I'm done," I say. "And I haven't heard from him since the text he sent me coming home. We're *over*." I shove myself from the table, my Extra Crispy barely touched, and cross the kitchen floor, Alexis bounding up to join me.

"Jenny—" Bryan says.

I stop at the mud room doorway and turn to face him. "Thanks for the flowers. That was really sweet of you." My voice is tight, tears close to the surface.

I'm so done with crying, with being analyzed and criticized, publicized all over social media, and now abandoned by the guy who threw me there in the first place.

If you love me, convince me. Don't leave me to work through this alone.

"I'm always here," Bryan says, "if you need me."

"Thanks."

I grab my horsey jacket from its peg, pull on my boots, and go out with Alexis in-harness. The air has warmed slightly, snow already softening underfoot. We take the path below the barn, the creek rattling in the stillness, everything smelling of water and cedar trees and encroaching winter night.

Almost Christmas.

And I never gave Liam his gift.

For which I'm unspeakably grateful. Because cookies and a homemade card, great, no problem. He'd love them, I'm sure. But a *gift card*? Like, *seriously???*

It lies on my desk along with the Oregon photo book I bought and the Christmas cards I signed to Jamie. I've already thrown out the stale cookies. The gift card goes to Morgan, never mind that she'll know where it came from.

Won't stop her from spending it.

As for Jamie handing me something as I'd once thought he might, I never really cared about that. Only being with him. And anyway, he'd already sent me the tour jacket, arranged airport pickup, front row seats, and backstage passes—more than gift enough—and an interview with...himself.

Liam standing here in my yard...

Did he come alone? Was Darren waiting in the rental car the whole time?

Handing me the note he'd written out, talking about himself in the third person...

How hard could it have been to say, "Hi, Jenny, this is from me... *I'm* Liam?" Why stick to the lie when I'd asked question after question about *him*, opening every door imaginable that he could so easily have walked through?

Him starting to tell me something—his real name?—more than once, and then changing it up. Cupping his hands beneath my muddy boot, shoving me up to ride...

My arms around his neck, my mouth opening to meet his...

Almost on cue, a text dings in from Morgan.

You might want to look at this, she says.

I'm not sure I do, but I open the link, anyway.

"In a statement released this afternoon," VoiceOver reads back, *"frontman Liam O'Shannon of Irish rock/metal band O'Shannon said, 'The girl and I were long-distance friends who developed an interest in each other and have since parted ways. My deepest and most sincere apologies to her and her family for the storm of publicity they should never have had to endure.' Band founder and manager, Michael O'Shannon, could not be reached for comment on his brother's statement."*

I shove my phone back into my pocket.

It's a decent response.

More than decent, actually.

And standing in the softening snow, Alexis bounding up from the creek to nose at my hand, I mop up the last of my tears and accept what I've known since I crashed in bed last night and found nothing from Liam on my phone.

We are *over*.

He's on a plane now, back to his homeland. I knew exactly when he was scheduled to roar out of O'Hare, and in letting that moment pass, I said goodbye to him forever. And in the morning, he'll be back in Innishannon, on the far side of the world.

By Wednesday, the roads have cleared enough to put school back on my agenda.

I take Bryan up on his offer and arrange for Morgan to meet me at the curb near the north entrance. While not exactly bodyguard material, she does have a few inches and more than a few pounds on me, so that's something, at least. And Alexis, striding along like being in-harness is a delight after loafing about for days on end, speeds us for the doors.

Somebody falls in step beside me.

"Jenny Ryan?" A man's voice I don't recognize. "I'm Peter Hodgkins with—"

"Not talking to you," I say over the name of his publication.

"—and I want to ask you—"

"No."

"—a quick question—"

I push Alexis into a faster-than-her-normal-speed-walk.

Reporter Guy stretches his legs and keeps up. "How long have you been seeing Liam O'Shannon? And how do your parents feel about—"

"What part of her not talking to you don't you get?" Morgan snarks at him.

"—your relationship with him?" Peter Hodgkins finishes.

I steel myself, putting one foot in front of the other.

My relationship with him or anyone else is none of your freaking business!

A crowd is gathering. Like I can go unnoticed attached to a guide dog. Voices pound me from all directions, bodies press in, and I'm breathing hard, my focus zeroed in on the next step, on getting myself inside the building.

"That's *two* questions," Morgan shoots at Hodgkins. "And *you've* run out of ground."

She hustles me through the entrance, letting the door fall behind us, closing him—and all unauthorized visitors—outside.

"Jerk," she growls under her breath.

I'm shaking, my fingers slick on the harness handle, my heart pounding on overdrive while my growing entourage crushes in on me.

Sierra Hanover's voice cuts across the crowd, ragging on me for avoiding her DMs. Metalhead Damien Johnson begs insider details (fandom over O'Shannon is the only thing we have in common). And queen bee Lyssa James invites me to her lunch table for the first time in history.

I say nothing to any of them.

I wouldn't get two words out, anyway, and they'll believe their own truth no matter what, so why waste breath?

I make it to period one Shakespeare and drop into my second-row seat, ignoring shoulder taps from Seth Norton and voices honing in, trying to suck me into a convo.

"You were *seeing* Liam O'Shannon??? Like, in a relationship seeing him? And now you're *not*?"

"How'd you even *meet* him? Or did this happen when you did that backstage interview with his sister?"

"Is *this* the guy you've been on your phone to all this time, and we didn't *know*?"

I didn't know.

"Of course, they were seeing each other. It's all over Twitter. But now they're not. Because I read his statement online and—"

I suck in a breath, letting it all flow past me, and try to focus on what I listened to yesterday evening from Act II of *Twelfth Night*.

Like that's even possible.

And every period afterward, every walk through this corridor to get to that class is more of the same.

I tell Ms. Perkins from the *Pioneer Press* I won't be able to write the story I promised, but I'll get her an alternate by the first of the year. At lunch, Morgan and I avoid the cafeteria crowd, hiding in Mr. Sunderson's Spanish II room with our sandwiches and Pepsis.

By the time school lets out, I am utterly raw. I so want to go home, but I've got OHSET practice. Thankfully the eight girls on the team already know I'm not talking, so I'm left to focus on running barrels instead of getting hammered with questions. Even so, I'm off my stride (literally), colliding Tanner with the left barrel on the first pass and nearly unseating myself on the second.

Coach Kelly calls me out. Being blind—or broken up with your rock star—is no excuse with her, and I work at getting my game on. But the whole thing exhausts me. And when I finally make it home, my study load keeps me at my computer and plugged into my Reader till way after midnight.

BRYAN TAKES us to *The Nutcracker* in Portland on Friday night. The music is gorgeous (orchestra seats, of course), and I spend the whole evening saying nothing unless spoken to while on stage some girl falls in love with a nutcracker turned prince in a Christmas dream.

All along, I'd planned to send Jamie photos of me dressed to the nines in a black skirt and teal blouse, the stage backdropped behind me.

Now there's no Jamie to send them to.

The photos go straight to social media, and I wonder if he'll see them on Instagram or if o'shannonofficial even follows me anymore.

I've unfollowed all my fan accounts and cleared three O'Shannon albums (and Leslie's, too) from my phone. Changed my ringtone. Buried my band t-shirts beneath the scrappy jeans in my bottom drawer. Slid their tour jacket to the far end of my clothes rack. Peeled their poster from the ceiling over my bed, rolled and stuffed it into a corner of my closet. And deleted "Jamie's" number (again) from my contacts after it resurfaced with his final text.

If he does see what I post, I'll never know.

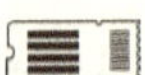

"So, have you decided about the wedding?"

I'm walking with my dad around Hug Point, between Arch Cape and Cannon Beach, Alexis steering me among the tide pools in basalt dips and crevices, surf cracking against the rock wall below, throwing up an icy spray.

"Whether you're coming or not?" I add.

Not a question I'd imagined asking, but in this moment, where nothing is as it used to be, I need to know.

Dad doesn't answer right off, and a feathery rain falls around us, wetting my hair and jacket, gulls mewing on the wind.

"I want to be supportive of you and Kaitlin," he says at last. "But I won't deny it would be awkward. Especially with people who used to be family and aren't anymore."

"It's okay if you don't," I say.

"If it's important to you, I'll do my best."

"I don't want you to suffer through something you'll hate."

"How could I hate being with my girls?"

We round the point where the ledge—an old road used by wagons and Model Ts a century ago—angles down to the sand. The tide's rolling in, and we need to get onto the beach before rising surf levels cut us off.

"How are *you* doing with it?" he asks.

"Okay, I guess. I mean, I've accepted it. And Bryan's been really supportive of me. Especially after...Tacoma. So that helps some."

"And how are you doing with *that?*"

I shrug, and we walk on without words.

Finally, he says, "I've been giving this a lot of thought. I've not said anything because I needed time to come to terms with it and stop being the angry dad."

A chill hits my shoulders that has nothing to do with the wind and the spray.

"This guy has *his* story, Jenny. And you've not heard it all."

I say nothing; just keep putting one foot in front of the other, the harness handle tugging in my hand, the sea sucking back from the rocks below.

"You're clearly not moving on from this. And from what Kaitlin's told me after talking to Morgan, I'm guessing he's not, either."

"Dad, I—"

"You need to be very sure of the choice you're making. Because letting go of someone you love—if you *do* love this guy, Jenny—will haunt you forever."

"And hanging on to something doomed to fail?" I ask.

You already know what that looks like.

"*I* was the one who gave you permission to go riding the day of your accident," Dad says. "Your mother never let me forget it, and she never forgave me. And we couldn't survive. So if you decide this *is* something you want, you'll have to forgive him. No matter what you feel, no matter how ugly it is. Because you'll never make it work any other way."

"Dad, we can't—"

"And then you let it go. You can't bring it up, can't remind him of it, can't throw it in his face every time you have a fight, or you'll kill the relationship. Trust me, I know."

I remember only too well.

My mom badgering, my dad begging, the blow-up fights, and then finally, he didn't argue, didn't beg her anymore. He caved in, gave up. And she walked out for good.

I don't want to be her, tearing a family apart when it comes time to go.

And I don't want to get walked out on.

So we leave this where it lies and save ourselves the endless misery down the road.

Because that's the only way it can end.

ON CHRISTMAS EVE, Kaitlin and I go to a candlelight service with Dad, then open gifts at his place, and in the morning, we do a late unwrapping at home. Between him and Mom and Bryan, we make a haul—clothes and gift cards, a new iPad for Kaitlin, new ski gear for me, and a ski getaway at Sunriver this coming weekend.

After spiral ham with all the fixings and pumpkin pie slathered in whipping cream, I walk Alexis down Cedar Creek Lane to where it cul-de-sacs among the trees. A bone-chilling fog wets my face and seeps through my jeans and jacket.

Christmas is almost over.

A new year's on its way.

And I've been doing okay; kind of. Keeping things together; sort of. Getting on with my life, focusing on the holidays, on upcoming OHSET competition, on Dad time, and prepping for the Big Day with Mom and Bryan. Shutting down every memory of Tacoma and all those days and weeks going into it.

I don't let myself wonder what Liam's up to over his holidays back home—if it's all about Christmas and family or just catching his breath before storming the European stages after the first of the year.

But now...

It's Christmas Night, and all I can think about is you over there and me standing here, wondering what your Christmas was like, and if you're as lost and empty inside as I am. Are you staring at the stars, wondering how I'm doing? Did you see any of the pics I posted with Kaitlin and Dad, Mom and Bryan? Or have you totally moved on the way you sounded in your statement?

Never mind what he promised about always waiting.

What might this day have looked like had I tried to work things out instead of throwing away what was left of us? Would we have talked across the miles as we did at Thanksgiving? FaceTimed (now that it's okay for him to be seen on my phone) with each other's families? Made plans for doing Christmas together next year?

Me going to Ireland...

Him coming here...

Alexis and I reach the turnaround and head back home, my bare fingers freezing—*why didn't I wear gloves?*—on the harness handle. She picks up the pace, skirting the puddles that always collect here, while the mist soaks strands of my hair peeking from my hood, and the creek chatters into the night.

Me Without You plays through my head, never mind that I haven't listened to it in weeks.

> *When the shadows pass through*
> *It's your ghost; it's not you...*

And I'm ruined for anyone else.

WITH THE HOLIDAYS WRAPPED UP, the wedding roars into the foreground.

Dresses hanging in our closets. Catering scheduled and paid for. Programs printed. Bryan's house on the market, already attracting attention. His jet skis and ski boat tarped outside our garage, his furniture mostly sold, and what he's keeping moved in already. A honeymoon cruise booked to St. Kitts, St Maarten, and St. Lucia for the week after Vow Saying Day.

As if that's not enough, I'm loaded with classes and practice, meets on some weekends, homework, and whatever it takes to keep my head in the game.

At least the publicity has died off.

Hodgkins did get something printed, sketchy on details, in his rag. And *People* ran a short in their *Star Tracks* section along with one of those over-circulated photos of Liam and me on the Tacoma Dome floor. Other tabloids published snippets while my blog readership skyrocketed (okay, that was a plus). But with nothing more to build on, I've fallen off the celebrity watch list. And my friends have finally stopped trying to wrangle what they're never getting from me.

Life pauses, takes a long breath, and eases back toward normal.

And then the email comes in.

Chapter 32

It's from a Rachel Meyers with *Kerrang!* magazine.

I freeze, my breath catching. Then it slides out in a rush.

Kerrang! is the UK's big rock/metal music publication. Yeah, I've read it online—O'Shannon album and tour reviews, write-ups on band members, interviews with Michael and Liam—but I've never written to the magazine or commented on any of their stories. Why would one of their people be contacting *me?*

I sit unmoving, willing my heart rate to back down, then ask VoiceOver to read what's on the screen.

Dear Jenny Ryan,

I have again been approached by Liam O'Shannon, asking if I would contact you directly with further advice on a career in music journalism. I was very much impressed with the stories he passed on to me a few weeks ago, and I think you have incredible potential. I've attached a list of universities, including several outside your own country, which I highly recommend for your consideration. Having interviewed Liam myself and spoken to him on multiple occasions, I trust his perception in this matter. He has great faith in your abilities and wishes you to succeed in what he believes to be the field of your choice.

Please, feel free to contact me if you have questions or simply wish to chat.

Looking forward to hearing from you,
Rachel Meyers

Associate Editor
Kerrang!

My hands are trembling.

Not because the editor of a big-name music publication contacted me, but she did so at Liam's request. That he's doing this regardless of how thoroughly I rejected him. And everything she says about him fits, no matter how I've told myself his whole Jamie-esque personality was a sham.

What if faking his identity *was* just a one-time thing?

I mean, how many girls does he meet who would offer the kind of opportunity I did?

What if he *did* have a suckish night as he said—Michael riding him extra hard and criticizing what writers for the *Oregonian* would describe as a stellar performance? Like Michael was anywhere near the rock star his brother is! Could this have all been what Liam said it was? Something he jumped into in a bad moment, then didn't have the courage to dig himself out of?

What if he *does* mean everything he said?

What if it's not too late?

I DON'T ANSWER Ms. Meyers's email.

My motivation for writing about music and the people who make it is dead to me now. Why would I want this?

I couldn't even cough up a simple interview story, one I didn't need to ask questions for in light of what I already knew. I haven't blogged in weeks. Haven't checked in with the #WritingCommunity on Twitter. And that less than sparkly OHSET story I subbed to Ms. Perkins came back with comments and corrections blasting at me from Google Docs.

I told her it was writer's block.

She knows better. But she let it go. Said inspiration would return in time.

Probably.

For now, I don't know what I want beyond getting myself through the next day, the next hour, the next few minutes.

"Everything okay, Jenny?"

Bryan and I are driving back from Kaitlin's basketball game at Hood River (Mom had to work late tonight), and I've barely said two words the whole way.

"Stuff on my mind," I tell him.

"Anything I can help with?"

"I don't know," I say.

He snaps the Blazer game off the radio. "I'm willing to try."

I sigh and shift in my seat.

"I know it's been a hard few weeks," he says. "And I haven't always known what to say, if anything, or whether I should keep quiet and not move in where I might not be wanted."

"You've always been the best," I say. "I'm sorry I haven't been more...welcoming at times. You deserved better than that. It was never about *you* exactly. Only about...losing my dad."

"I showed up unexpectedly," he says. "And now I'm marrying your mother. That's a lot to ask of a girl still dreaming of her folks getting back together."

Guess I didn't hide much from him.

"Yeah," I say.

"If I'd thought there was any chance of that happening, I would have bowed out long ago."

"I know." Because that's the kind of guy he is, and I never gave him credit for it. "I kept thinking I could change her mind. That maybe she and Dad could be happy again, and everything would go back to the way it was...before I went blind."

For the first time, I tell him how I blamed myself for destroying their relationship, never mind that it was floundering long before, and that if I could have turned *my* attitude around, I could have fixed them, too.

"You were only twelve," he says. "How could it have all been your fault?"

"My dad says that, too. And I probably remember things differently than they actually were."

"Things tend to adjust themselves, either better or worse, in our minds."

"I know."

"I don't want your dad's place in your heart," he says. "Only a place of my own someday. Even a small one?"

My eyes sting.

And it's not just Bryan I'm thinking of.

"It's not a small one," I say. "And I'm sorry it's taken me so long... to make you feel wanted."

"You put too much on yourself," he says. "There's no right or wrong time frame for these things."

"I tried so hard. I did what I thought was right, what I had to do." My voice catches, stumbles over the words. "And everything just... hurts so much."

"Are we still talking about your parents? About you and me?" His voice softens. "Or you and Liam O'Shannon?"

I sniffle, and the tears fall, wet stains on my jeans. "I thought I could kill what I feel for him. Go back to being who I was before like none of this ever happened. But I'm just so"—I swallow —"lost... without him."

"I've known all along you love this guy. And it's not about him being who he is or who you thought he was as Jamie Conway. And you need to resolve this. Because pretending to move on when you haven't won't heal what's broken."

I swipe at my eyes, tears running through my fingers.

"And you have to weigh the consequences of giving him up when you still have a choice in the matter. Because I *don't* have that choice. And there are so many things I'd do differently if I did."

He wouldn't be marrying my mom, for one.

So he wouldn't be in my life.

What would this—where I am now—look like if he *wasn't* here to share it with me or help me work through it like he's doing in the moment?

"I haven't heard from him in almost four weeks," I say.

My eighteenth birthday came and went, and there was nothing. Why should there have been?

"I'm guessing he doesn't think you want to," says Bryan. "He made a PC statement—yes, I saw it—honoring what he believes to be your wishes. It has nothing to do with what he actually feels for you. Because a guy who feels what I saw in those photos won't be moving on anytime soon."

I fold my arms over my waist, sniffling in the silence between us, my head roaring with everything that happened and everything I walked away from.

"Love is a choice, Jenny," he says. "Not so much falling into it. That doesn't seem to need much help. But staying in it? That's a commitment you make every day. It requires sacrifice. And forgiveness. And seeing beyond faults and failures to what matters most. And wanting each other more than what you'll give up. Anything less, and you'll kill what you love and carry that the rest of your life."

Like my folks did.

"Liam used me," I remind him. "Because I'm blind."

"Yes," he says. "And Tracy cheated on me."

My head swivels toward him. "What?"

"Eight months before she died, she met an old friend at the mall. They talked a while, then went to have a drink together and ended up at his place. She came home hours later, a mess of tears. Confessed everything. Said she hated what she'd done, that it meant *nothing* to her, and she didn't want to lose me. I had a choice to make.

Forgive her and help her work through this. Or throw away fourteen years of marriage to the woman I loved."

Clearly, he chose well.

"Did you ever trust her again?"

"I did," he says. "But it was a conscious decision. I would never bring up the incident again. And I would treat her as though it never happened. At some point, Jenny, you just *trust*, period, and accept no alternative. Because playing watchdog and suspecting every move she made would have destroyed us. She never broke faith with me again."

And they spent the last eight months of her life together, making things work.

How would that have looked to him now, in light of what happened, had he divorced her instead?

"And the whole rock star thing?" I say. "How does *that* work?"

"I don't know that it does," he says. "But that's a separate issue. First, you forgive and make peace, regardless of how that finishes. Because it's the right thing to do. God forgives us when we ask, even though we don't deserve it. Why shouldn't we do the same for others? And because forgiveness is the only way to free yourself to move on. Then you decide what matters most. If it's a normal life, however you define that, this probably isn't the best fit. But if it's Liam, at all costs, then you make *that* the priority and go from there, whatever it takes."

"Does Mom know how you feel?"

"She does, yes," he says. "We're not on the same page, but I'm trying to help her see the long-term damage of leaving things unresolved. That this has to be your decision because you *will* make it in the end, no matter how she pressures you into what she wants. That if you pursue this, you'll need support and guidance, not polarization from us. And Liam will need our forgiveness. And acceptance."

"What'd she say?"

"It's a work in progress," he says.

"Thanks."

Not that I know what to do with this, even if he could swing her perspective. Which I'm not holding my breath on. Yes, I'm of legal age, but I'm still in school, under her roof, and until I graduate in June, I'm still under her rules.

But what I've been doing isn't working. And what Bryan says makes sense in a way nothing else has.

"So, um," I start, "when I said I hadn't heard from Liam, I meant not directly. But I did get this email a few days ago..." I go into the rest of it from there—what Rachel Meyers offered me and what she said about Liam as someone she knows personally. And that I haven't answered her back.

"You should at least thank her," Bryan says, "whether or not you choose to pursue her offer. You might want it later even if you don't at the moment."

"I thought about that."

"And I would give serious thought to thanking him, too. In a text, perhaps?"

How can I say thank you and nothing more? Do I want to open everything up after all this time? Then again, do I want to keep slogging through like I have been, hoping things get better on their own?

"I'll think about it," I say.

"Every day you wait," he says, "reduces your chance of closure. Or reconciliation. You can't expect him—or anyone, for that matter—to wait forever."

"I know," I say.

Chapter 33

"So've you seen this?" Morgan asks on our way into Coach Kelly's barn for OHSET practice. "Okay, probably not since you don't follow them anymore, but—"

"No," I cut her off. "I don't follow them."

She reads off her phone, "'Irish band O'Shannon to offer complimentary VIP tickets for people with visual impairment.'"

I stop, turn to face her. "*What?*"

"'Available for all European, Australian, and Asian tour dates to the first ten applicants per show and includes staff assistance to seats, concessions, and other public venue areas as needed. Apply at O'Shannon.net and let us know how we can assist you.'"

I'm still standing here, unmoving.

Why is *he doing this?*

Okay, I know *why*. But still.

Is it *because* of me? Is he sending a message, hoping maybe I'll notice and get in touch? Thank him? *Take him back?*

Morgan's still reading. "'According to O'Shannon lead vocalist Liam O'Shannon, the idea was born of his short-lived relationship with Jenny Ryan of Sandy, Oregon, who was blinded at age twelve in a horse riding accident. In a brief press release yesterday, O'Shannon said, '*She is the most incredible person I've ever met, opening my eyes, as it were, to both the challenges and skills of people with visual impairment. I've been looking for a means of giving back to this community ever since.*' O'Shannon emphasized that tickets will be free of charge and will include all supports needed at the venue.'"

Something surges inside me, a kind of lost hope, perhaps.

It *is* because of me.

"'Band manager Michael O'Shannon clarified that his younger brother is personally underwriting all costs, putting no obligation on the five other members of the Ireland-based rock group. Which says a lot about this energetic, young vocalist now tearing down walls in the name of accessibility.'"

Morgan finishes reading, and we stand here together, each of us waiting for the other to say something.

Boots clop past us for the barn, Samantha Ryerson and Gretchen Walsh going on about the pricey Tennessee Walker Sam's rich parents are taking her to see.

Because one OHSET horse isn't enough for some people, apparently.

"Well?" Morgan says.

I shrug, keeping my voice low-key. "It's cool and all. I mean, I appreciate him doing this for the blind. But...if it's all about scoring points with *me*—"

"I'm guessing that's part of it," she says. "Since he doesn't feel he can contact you directly."

"I never told him not to."

"You might as well have."

"Morgs—"

"This might interest you, too." She taps at her phone and then reads, "'Liam O'Shannon, frontman for Irish hard rock/Celtic metal band O'Shannon, has made sizable donations to Guide Dogs for the Blind and the American Federation for the Blind in the wake of his recent breakup with a seventeen-year-old blind student from Oregon.'"

Do they have to call it a breakup? Why do they always give my age—inaccurate, by the way—and point up the fact that I'm blind? Wait—he *what*? What was that about contributions and guide dogs?

"Still convinced he doesn't love you?" she says.

WHEN I GET HOME, I go online and look at the O'Shannon homepage for the first time in weeks. Google *O'Shannon Visual Impairment Ticket Giveaway* and *Liam O'Shannon Guide Dogs for the Blind* and *Liam O'Shannon National Federation for the Blind.*

The stories are there, exactly as Morgan read them to me, along with links to others she didn't mention. Like this quote, included in an online magazine article dated less than a week ago, *"I am forever grateful to a girl who opened my eyes to the blind community and the abilities of those who've lost their sight, but not their courage, who strive to make the world a better place for us all."*

Hashtagged with it are links to the American Federation of the Blind, Guide Dogs for the Blind, and various assisted technology sites.

Not long after, Morgan sends me the URL for a YouTube video.

Liam lost it two nights ago in Stockholm, she says. **Keys only version of *Me Without You,* and he completely drops vocals at one point and has trouble getting through the ending. Song was cut from the setlist for Helsinki and replaced with *Nightscape.* Some comment makers wonder if there's a connection between this and the girl he was seeing but now isn't. Need I say more???**

I don't open the link.

Just sit back, my phone in hand.

What *am* I going to do with this? Shrug it off and keep going like I don't know it's out there? Keep telling myself he doesn't care when he so clearly does?

In the end, I cave and cue up the video. The music, minus the heavy drums and metallic guitars, is way more gut-wrenching than the original. And the words, *his* voice, especially when he stumbles, make a mess of me.

Left alone, my world ends

Without you...
What are we going to do with this, Liam?
I'm not over you.
You're not over me.
Is there any chance for us at all?

THE HOUSE IS quiet when I pad downstairs with Alexis. I don't give myself time to think through what I'm going to say beyond my opening lines. Just walk into the dining room, where Mom sits shuffling whatever's in her hands.

Bills, I suppose.

She stops, papers whispering onto the table, her stare seeping into me from across the room. She says nothing; waits, not moving.

I take a breath, then let it out slowly. "I know I held stuff back I should have told you. Not always intentionally"—because I *am* getting that point in—"but still... It's what I did. And I'm sorry." I close my eyes—just my mom, after all, but I'm on sketchy ground here—open them again. "So this is me being upfront." Another pause, a deeper breath. *And here goes...* "I'm going to contact Liam."

It's a statement.

I'm not asking her permission.

"Jenny—" she starts and then stops.

"I know you think what happened between us was all famous-guy-taking-advantage-of-a-blind-fangirl. But it wasn't like that. Not all of it. He was always sweet and sensitive and super interested in everything about me. And that didn't change when his name did. All this time, I've been telling myself that leaving him was the right thing to do. That we could never work, that he didn't mean it when he told me he loved me, that the statement he released, saying we'd parted ways, meant he was done, too. Because he's never contacted me again, not directly. But now...I'm not so sure."

I tell her then about the email from Rachel Meyers and how

everything she said about Liam aligns with what I knew of him as Jamie Conway. About the causes for the blind he is currently supporting and the comment he made about me positively impacting his life. That he's underwriting tickets for the blind on O'Shannon's European, Australian, and Asian tour stops. That he's probably doing for the blind community what he can no longer do for me.

Hoping I'll notice, perhaps.

Because he has no other way of reaching out to me after what I told him the night I destroyed what was left of us.

Mom sighs. Like she doesn't know what to do with this, but maybe she sees some validity in what I'm saying.

"I know you adored this guy, Jenny, but—"

"I *loved* him." Tears crowd my eyes. "And no matter how I've tried to kill what I feel"—what I told him I *didn't* feel—"it just. Keeps. Hurting."

She sighs again, and her voice comes out softer, laced with sadness. "Just because you love someone doesn't mean you can make it work."

"You think I don't know that?"

"If you pursue this, it's only going to hurt that much worse when it's over."

You mean, worse than it does now?

How is that possible? Do I seriously care in this moment?

"Do you still love Dad? Even a little?"

She doesn't answer right off, and I stand waiting, arms folded over my waist while Alexis clicks her nails into the kitchen. Finally, she says, quiet and resigned, "Leaving him was the hardest thing I've ever done."

"Then *why'd* you do it?"

"Because we couldn't make *us* work, and I knew we'd only keep destroying each other. And I couldn't put myself through that anymore. I saw what it was doing to you and Kaitlin, and I thought we'd all be better off if your dad and I went our separate ways."

"All these years," I say, "I've told myself it was *my* fault—for going blind, for acting out, for making the rest of you so miserable. I know that's not exactly true, but getting ripped away from Dad did not make things better for *me*. And Kait used to cry herself to sleep in my room, night after night because she couldn't understand why you didn't want him anymore."

Another silence.

"It wasn't that I didn't want him," she says at last. "And I probably could have handled things better. Kait and I *have* talked. But I could never get you to see any side but your own."

"Because I *hated* what you did. And I hated what I had to go through because of it."

"Jenn—"

"And Kaitlin hated it." I swipe tears from my face. "And all I've seen over the years is Dad stuffing his pain down where he hopes it doesn't show and trying to move on past his endlessly breaking heart and never quite getting there."

Her voice spikes into a higher register. "You think I didn't hate it, too? You have *no* idea how much! But some things are just too broken to fix. So you give up what you want for what you know will someday be better for everyone."

"I miss Liam every second of my life. He's not on the phone with me. He's not DM-ing me on Instagram or sending me text messages. He's nowhere in my life. I can't tell him what great or awful thing happened today or ask how he's doing, none of it. Like my heart's been ripped out, and the bleeding will never stop."

"Jenny..." she says, more softly. "I told you..."

"And I didn't listen."

"It wasn't just the publicity. Or the deceptions, yours and his. Or the age difference, though that concerns me, too. It's that you can't possibly *know* each other, not really. How can you when you've never spent more than a few minutes in each other's worlds? When you don't know how you'll respond under pressure or what you can live with and what you can't?"

"I've already thought about it."

"And the world he lives in? You can't begin to comprehend it. *I* can't comprehend it. The thought of you getting thrown into that—following him to Europe, because you'll want to—and dealing with the pressures of his career and everything that goes with him being who he *is*—" Another sigh. "Do you seriously think this will last any length of time? A year? Two at most? Then he's off with someone else. Or you decide the lifestyle is just too difficult to live with? It *will* happen, Jenny. Because beneath all the glam is a guy who's *just a guy*, and you'll know that better than anyone while you're living with the star machinery that makes him who the world thinks he is. And I can't bear to see what that will do to you in the end."

I backhand more tears from my cheeks.

It's everything I've told myself all these weeks, staring me in the face yet again. That even if I *could* forgive Liam, work through what he did, risk my heart and my trust all over again, his life isn't what I want, not really.

Living in Ireland.

Okay, that wouldn't be so bad, maybe. A lot like Oregon, I hear. But so far from my family, my friends, and from everything I've ever known...

And all that grueling on-the-road stuff?

O'Shannon plays the big European rock/metal festivals every summer, releases an album every other year with Liam writing most of their music, and tours aggressively. How does that work if I'm in school? Or I get tired (hard to imagine) of seeing them night after night? Or I stay behind because I've got things, whatever they might be, I can't do aboard a tour bus? Or I don't want to live that lifestyle anymore?

Like, when *do* Liam and I ever get a life together, if that's where this ends up?

Or are we doomed no matter what?

Then again, how do I go on, torn up on the inside while pretending I've got it together on the outside? Wondering what might have been had I followed through on what I promised him that night.

If we'd gone off and talked somewhere like he offered.

How would that have even worked, sitting in some coffee shop with a rock star? Would we have dragged Darren along? Because *that* would have been romantic. Or just hoped nobody in that particular Starbucks was a hardcore O'Shannon fan?

I haul in a ragged breath. "So tell me, *is* Bryan your first choice? Or do you still wish it could be Dad?"

"I'm not sure I can answer that."

"Because if it's not Bryan, I need to know what it looks like to settle for second best."

For an endless moment, there's only silence between us.

"I wouldn't call it second best," Mom says. "Things *do* change, including what you feel for somebody, no matter how much you loved them at one time."

"Bryan says you can choose that."

"I'm not sure it works in every situation."

"And if I don't try?" I ask. "Do I wonder forever what might have been? If maybe I walked away from the one person I was meant to be with, and anyone else is Plan B?"

"I'm not sure there *is* one person any of us are meant to be with," she says. "Even if there is, in some cases—this one, most likely—the cost may just be too high."

"Then it's my cost to pay," I say. "Because what I've been doing isn't working. And I can't live with this unresolved anymore."

Blindsight

"Out of the Darkness"

By Jenny Ryan

You don't have to be blind not to see. Sight isn't only what you take in with your eyes, and blindness is more than the lack of visual input.

It's a mindset.

Thinking you've got the total picture when maybe it's just a slice. Misinterpreting something. Or someone. What they did, what they said. *Who* they are. Slapping them with labels, with prejudices, and preconceived notions. Or misconceptions. Or judgments about what you don't fully understand.

Which is what I've done to my almost stepdad—this super fun, really cool, kind, and caring guy who showed up while I was still hoping my folks would get back together. So hello, resentment, resistance, and holding myself away while going through the motions of being on board. And it wasn't just about someone taking my dad's place. It was me not wanting to love him—or anyone else—as a dad, even if that love was different.

But I'm working on that now. And as my heart opens, I see what I've missed all along—this guy who loves me as a daughter and accepts me as his own, who's not out to replace my dad, but only wants a relationship with me.

And my mom's no different. We've butt heads over the

years, especially since the divorce. But I've accepted she was never going back to my dad, no matter how hard I pushed for it. And she's been alone long enough. Time for her to move into a new life, a happier one, and for me to stop holding her back.

And that childhood friend I dumped in the process of tearing down my own world? I've always wanted to fix things with her but never knew how. Or maybe I never tried. But I know where she lives—the same place she did when we were kids—and how to find her on social media. So I'll definitely be reaching out. I'm hoping she can forgive the blind eye I turned to her when she only wanted to help. That we can rebuild what I so foolishly destroyed.

So now I'm re-evaluating this whole not-seeing thing. Not the one I've been living with the past six years and will for the rest of my life. But the one I can do something about. I'm opening my eyes to what's around me and taking what steps I can—building up what I failed to before, rebuilding what I've torn down, repairing what can yet be mended.

To quote my favorite band.

> *Resurrect, let it go*
> *Hold the truth that you know*
> *Don't let go...*

> (from *Fallen* by O'Shannon)

In the end, perhaps blindness is simply a failure to see the truth.

And sight is doing something about it.

Chapter 34

I hike upstairs, pulling my phone from my hip pocket, my heart fluttering like the parakeets Grams keeps caged in her kitchen.

I am doing this now.

I've waited such a stupidly long time, and it'll be exactly what I deserve if it's too late for what I've known all along I want.

What I'm hoping and praying and believing he still wants.

Recovering his number from iCloud means losing every update and contact I've added over the last four weeks. Like I care. And when I'm done, my phone is restored as it was the night I flew home from Tacoma.

Before I sent that horrible text and deleted him from my life.

I Google O'Shannon.net and am instantly slammed by everything I've missed so much about this band. Following and fangirling. Talking about their music with online peeps and the hard rock/heavy metal crowd at school. Listening to their albums, from *Fire and Ice* through Leslie's *Dance in the Rain*. Getting blown away by them on stage. No matter how I've tried moving on to other artists and music styles, no one and nothing even comes close. Like O'Shannon defines me, and Liam is my lodestone.

Being without him—the Jamie him and the rock star him—is this dull and constant ache that never goes away.

I check their European tour schedule.

Vienna last night.

Well, for *them*, it was last night. It's eight p.m. here, so four-ish a.m. wherever their bus is between Austria and the Czech Republic.

One more reminder of how far apart—in more than the eight time zones between us—we are.

I set his real name with his number, then ask Siri to send him a message, my palms slick with sweat, blood pulsing in my ears. Speak the words I've already framed in my mind.

"If there's any chance you still want to talk, I'd really like that."

For half a second, I consider adding a broken heart emoji. And a crying one. But no, too soon.

I send it off—*please, Liam, one more time*—then slouch into my pillows, the tension draining out, a measure of relief trickling in.

If all I get from this is closure and (hopefully) the ability to heal and move on, it'll be enough. It's been so long since I've been happy, even everyday, nothing-special-going-on kind of happy; I can't imagine what that feels like anymore. To wake up and see what the day holds, nothing planned, nothing dreaded—

A message dings in.

Seriously?

No, it's gotta be Morgan. She texted earlier with questions about our U.S. Government assignment, and I'm yet to get back to her on it.

I open my phone. Ask for the name.

Liam O'Shannon.

I close my eyes. Forget to breathe.

He answered me *already?*

Okay, these guys keep crazy hours on tour. But still. After doing a twenty-song set last night—*his* night—and having to do it again this night, shouldn't he be dead asleep by now?

I ask for the message, my heart in my throat.

It's all I've wanted. Is it okay if I ring you?

I breathe out.

Thank you, thank you...

"Yes," I send back, and this time, the emojis go with it.

My phone's already vibrating in my hand. Now the ringtone's going off. It's not *Tear at the Walls*—that didn't transfer over—and I wish it were. I wish everything was different—what he did, what I did, what we put each other through.

"Hi." My voice is barely above a whisper.

"Hi, Jenny." All Irish-inflected and softly jagged, exactly like I heard from the stage that afternoon. And in my hair when he held me below it. Like it was yesterday. Or forever ago. "How're you doin', so?"

My eyes flood. Everything I've tried to stuff down and shove away all this time roars back from those hours in Tacoma, from all those weeks of phone talking together, from everything still shattered and unfinished between us.

"I'm...okay." I suck in a breath. *Can't believe you're on the line with me...* "Better than okay, actually. Because you answered me back, and I wasn't sure"—my voice thickens—"you would."

"All this time," he says, "I've waited and hoped and dreamed I might hear something, *anything*, from you, even if it couldn't be what I wanted. And then I looked at my phone...and there you were."

My tears fall.

Not too late...

"I'm sorry it took me so long."

"Don't be sorry for what you needed to do. You contacted me. Nothing else matters."

Yes, it does.

Everything I did and can never make up for, everything I have yet to tell him...

"You answered me so fast," I say. "I didn't expect that."

"I don't sleep good these days," he says. "We have a lounge at the back of the bus, and I like to sit here when I can't sleep and watch the stars if they're out, and the sunlight coming up on the road behind us, the snow on the mountains..."

My eyes close, and I see it in the vague-ish way I image anything when I make the effort.

"I like the back of the bus, too."

A breath of silence between us.

"Wish you were sharin' it with me, so," Liam says, a bit hopeful.

More tears hit my cheeks. "Me, too."

"Jenny?" Seriously hopeful.

"I'm sorry I left you…without saying goodbye." I swallow, swipe at my eyes. "That I left you at all. It was wrong of me, I know. But I couldn't see anything coming of it"—*of us*—"but more pain. And I just…couldn't take that."

"I never blamed you for going," he says. "That was on me. All of it."

Not all.

I made a promise I didn't keep. Said things I didn't mean. Crushed him so badly, focused on my hurt, my rage, my fears, shoving my guilt to the back of my brain and telling myself he didn't mean what he'd said, that this was all some twisted game he'd played. While he waited, so Jamie—no, *Liam*—polite. Like he's always been. Never presuming what I might want, never forcing himself back into my life.

Have I judged him too harshly, then?

Would he have done what he's been doing, all this time from a distance, if he doesn't care for me deeply, even now?

"It was such a mistake," I say. "And I've been wanting some kind of…*something* to make me believe everything you told me. Because I *did* in the moment. I was just so devastated and out of my depth, and I couldn't see this working long-term. I know what short term looks like"—another swallow—"and how much it hurts"—more swipes at my eyes—"and I don't want any part of it."

"Me, either," he says. "I've had enough already."

Whoever he's been with before me that I still don't want to know about and he so clearly regrets.

"And anyway," I add, "I suck at forgiveness."

My mom.

Tiffany Whitman.

Liam O'Shannon.

"I gave you a lot to forgive," he says.

No more than I've given him.

"I already have." Because in the end, what was at stake mattered so much more than the emptiness I was hanging onto. "And I knew why you didn't get in touch. That it was *my* fault, not yours. But then all the publicity hit, and everything heaped up on me. And your statement—I *did* read it, and it *was* nice—sounded like you were done, too, so I just"—my voice catches—"wrote you off."

"It's what I had to say," Liam says. "Because I didn't want to give the media anything more to work with. They do fine, sure they do, on their own."

"I do know. And I appreciate you doing that."

No matter how thankless I sounded two minutes ago.

"Michael was on me to say nothing a'tall. That any statement I made would look bad on me—because of your age—and on the band, too. But I hated that you were going through this without support from me"—his accent thickens as it did in Tacoma when emotion kicked in—"because *I'm* the one who put you there. But I was afraid gettin' involved directly would only make it worse, that you didn't want to hear from me."

"Not your fault," I say.

"I'm sorry I misunderstood what you wanted."

"You didn't. And I probably wouldn't have responded."

He says nothing to that, waiting in the silence like he did as Jamie. And as himself backstage in Tacoma.

Sorting out where I am with him now?

"But then you gave me what I was looking for," I go on. "And I saw *you*. Your statement was part of that. Even if I took it the way I wanted rather than how I knew you meant it. And then I got this email from Rachel Meyers—about schooling for a music journalism career? And you had everything to do with that, I know. And everything she said about you was, well—*you*. No matter what I'd told myself. Or you."

"You shouldn't lose your dream because of me."

"I'm not sure it *is* my dream anymore." *Because what's the point if you're not in it?* "But now...I don't want to lose an opportunity you made happen, that I wanted so much. And maybe still want."

"You'll be good at it," he says.

Because you believed in me...

"Thank you. And not just for that."

"I figured fillin' your room with roses wouldn't be an acceptable move. But maybe...I could do something that would be?"

"What you did was perfect," I say.

And roses would be, too...

"Good," he says.

"Morgan told me you were giving away tickets to the blind community and making contributions to blind causes, and when I checked online, I found write-ups, quotes, everything, so I knew it was true."

"I asked you what I could do," Liam says. "If there was anything a'tall. And if not for you directly, then I'd do it for what matters most to you. Because if it matters to you, it matters to me. And now I look at people, in any community, so much differently. Because you opened my eyes to that."

If nothing else, I've impacted his life, shifted his focus.

And that's no small thing.

"Thank you for what you're doing. Seriously." My fingers trace formless patterns over the comforter beneath me. "Morgan said you were reaching out to me the only way you could. And from what I'd heard and read—and the letter from Rachel Meyers—I figured she was probably right."

"I was hopin' you'd notice, like," he says. "Though I'd have done it even if you didn't."

"Super appreciate it." *All of it.* "Not everybody has the money to buy a ticket or the ability to get to an arena on their own. Or a friend like Morgan"—how truly great a friend she is and how badly I treated her that night isn't lost on me—"to help them get where they need to."

"That's generally left to the venues," he says, "whatever they provide in terms of disability access. Michael and our road manager handle most contact with them. But now, because of you, I'm wantin' a wee more say in that. And it's not about selling more tickets. We'd sell 'em, anyway."

Because they're O'Shannon.

Selling out arenas and grass fields at European metal festivals is what they do.

"I know you're paying for it," I say.

"It's not that much," says Liam.

No, it's *everything*.

It's why we're talking right now.

"And that awful thing I texted you from the plane?" Every word is still burned into my brain. "I only said that to make it easier to go. But it wasn't the truth. You were *never*"—the tears seep again, spill over—"my second choice..."

He sighs again, and his voice goes softer. *"Mo chuisle..."*

"I thought I could walk away, that what you did was reason enough. But it doesn't change what I feel"—I swallow—"for you..."

"Jenny..."

"And I'm so tired of being broken and empty"—*without you*—"and pretending I'm not."

"I don't even try," he says.

Because...Stockholm.

"And all I could see was me never getting over what you did or being able to trust you again." I fumble a tissue from my nightstand, soak the tears from my cheeks. "I know what you promised. But I know how that goes—how it went with my folks—so why take a chance on something destined to fail from the start? Because in what world would *you* ever want *me*?"

"The world in which I'm forever in love with you," says Liam.

"And you'll still want me...when the fire and the novelty wear off, and I'm just the girl who can't see, who has nothing to offer that you can't get"—*so easily*—"somewhere else? When we're just us, you and me?"

"Till I die, Jenny."

His words are all I've needed to go where I've wanted to all this time, the reason I contacted him in the first place.

And yet I sit here, waiting...

"But if you need somethin' more," he says, "I wrote you a letter on the plane home to Ireland. It's everything I wanted to say that didn't come out right when I tried to say it, and I—"

"Wait—you *wrote* to me?"

"I don't think I did very well when we were together that night, and I'm better at writing out what I want to say than gatherin' words on the spot. I thought if you could hear this from me, one time, maybe we could talk again."

"But I never got anything from you."

"I never sent it," he says. "I was afraid I'd be oversteppin' my bounds, sure y'know. That it wouldn't be respectful of what you wanted. That you needed time, like. But the more I waited and didn't hear back, the more I couldn't send it. I knew it was already too late."

Oh, Liam...

Would this, whatever he wrote, have made the difference had he sent it, anyway?

Maybe not in the moment. But later, when I'd had time to process? Because no matter how hot a mess I was, I wanted to be convinced, to believe everything he'd said to me was for real.

"I'm *so* sorry," I whisper. "I had no idea—"

Because of what I'd made so brutally clear.

How could I have missed, even then, seeing Jamie behind the image all this time?

"How could'ya, now?" he says.

"Do you have it with you?"

In his lounge at the back of the bus, looking out at the road running away into the distance.

Starlight through the windows...

Shadowed moonlight on the snow...

"It's on my phone, so," he says.

"Read it to me?"

The Letter

Jenny, Mo Chuisle,

You were on your knees when I first saw you, and your dream was mine to give. But in that moment, I chose what would one day capture my heart and shatter yours. So now I'm on my knees, begging for one more chance and asking what's left for me to do when nothing can ever be enough. For you deserve so much better than this lad who lied to his own advantage, then crushed you with the truth.

And if you still choose to walk away, I'll understand; open my hands and let you go. But I'll always wish it could have been me you chose. Because you're everything I've ever wanted, and I can't imagine my life without you.

You're real, not trapped behind an image you have to maintain. You're honest; at least, for the most part. And you care about the people in your life, even if they don't all fit together the way you wish they did. You're smart and talented —have I told you enough times? You take on tough challenges and do them blind; dream big dreams, and make them happen.

And you're so achingly beautiful...

Every conversation we had opened your world and re-imagined mine. We talked, and I saw without using my eyes. You laughed, and I smiled and laughed with you. You cried, and I was losing my da all over again and walking through secondary school apart from the crowd because I'm not

Michael, who did everything right in Da's eyes, or Leslie, who makes friends without trying. You listened, and in the silence, I heard a girl who appreciated me as me and not what she could gain from the relationship.

Every day I waited for you to get home so we could talk, not just trade messages back and forth, and I wondered what you were up to. How was school? What was happening with your family? With Tanner and Alexis? Were you warming up to Bryan? Did you think of me—the me you knew—when I wasn't on the phone with you?

Day after day, more and more, I was becoming consumed with you. I'd think of you when I should have been focused on other things, and every night on stage, I'd wish you were there so I could do this for you. Because it is for you, every night I do it.

Do you know that beyond being introverted, I'm naturally shy? That getting up in front of 20,000 people terrifies me, no matter how many times I do this? That I have to work up the image you adore and think I am?

Have I told you I like nature and quiet places? Walking in a soft, Irish rain and watching fish in the hollows of a stream? Sitting in front of a fire while shadows dance over the walls? That crowds make me claustrophobic, and peaches with cream are my favourite dessert, that an angry ocean steals my breath and a sky alight with stars is the most spectacular thing I've ever seen? That I want to write a song for you, but I can't find the words because you're so far beyond them—and the stars, too.

And I dreaded what I had to say. I knew it would devastate you no matter how much I dreamed it'd be everything you wanted. I'm not Jamie like you want me to be. And I'm not your idol, either. I'm wrong for you in every way —wrong image, wrong age, wrong side of the world, and clearly, no sense of honor. So, in the end, would you hate me for what I'd done and walk away when I was already so hopelessly in love with you?

There's so much I have yet to learn, so much I want you to teach me. I want to see your world, Jenny—your blind world, your Oregon world, your everyday life with your family and school and friends. I want to meet your mam and your da, meet Bryan and Kaitlin. Walk beside you as you work Alexis. Watch you compete with Tanner. Go skiing with you on Mt. Hood. It's so beyond what I can imagine, how you do what you do and the courage you've found to become who you are.

If we could have one day together, I don't know what I'd choose—a long walk in your gorgeous nature or sitting and watching a film with you in my arms. Could we ever make this work, you and me? Could you ever want me, now that you know what I've done?

Not my name on your O'Shannon t-shirt or your Tear at the Walls ticket. Not my face in your selfie or my voice on your Reader, doing an interview I still owe you. Not being your rock star on stage.

Just...the me that I am.

It's all I'll ever want from the girl who sees in ways I can't begin to, who renews and inspires me, who still holds my broken heart in her beautifully capable hands.

Till the stars fall and the oceans run dry, I love you.

Liam

Chapter

35

I am wrecked, and so is he. I'm crying so hard, and all I can think of is what I did to this guy who writes so beautifully and wants me so badly, who held on all this time, waiting and hoping against his own odds for me to see what's been right in front of me all along.

How could I have rejected the one person I wanted most in this world, who I knew loved me even then, and asked only for my forgiveness and the chance to rebuild what he'd destroyed?

I only know I'm not walking away, ever again, from this lad sitting aboard his tour bus five thousand miles away with his heart in his hands.

Reaching for mine.

"Liam..." I swipe back wet strands of hair sticking to my face. "Oh, my gosh, Liam, this is *so* beautiful... I can't even, can't even—" I swallow, blink down more tears, my voice washing into a whisper. "I don't have any words..."

"I'll wait while you find 'em, like," he says.

The ones I've owed him for so long.

"I love you."

And he sighs through the messiness that was his voice the whole time he read to me, fighting to get through his own words. "*Yes,* Jenny. It's all I've wanted to hear, all this time."

"I did in Tacoma, too."

"I knew it, so."

And you waited for me...

"I love you," I say again.

And I mean it in the all-in, whatever-this-entails sense. Of him being who and what he is and everything that goes with that; beyond the lies and the regrets and the price I'll have to pay to fit myself into his world. What I could never say under less commitment than the one he's already made to me.

Till I die...

"And I love you, *a chuisle mo chroí*," he says, all husky and ragged-edged, like the time he first told me. "So much, *so* much..."

My eyes close.

And this is not how this moment should be—me alone in my room and him on a bus under the stars, and the whole world between us. We should be in the same space, losing ourselves over each other the way we did in Tacoma, not just saying words that fall short from a distance.

"I need you to hold me, Liam. And you're just"—my voice falls to a whisper—"so far away."

"I'd give *anything* for that, so I would."

"I had no idea when I left you that night how hard it would be. Or how much it would hurt. And I don't"—more swallowing—"want to be me...without you...anymore."

"I'm going to book a flight, so," Liam says. "'Twill be over and back, but—"

"Wait—you can *do* that?"

Drop your tour and come?

"We get a few days here and there. Might not be for a couple of weeks, and I'll have to fly back straight away. Maybe in twenty-four hours?"

"Michael'd let you do that?"

"Michael doesn't get a say in what I do in my downtime, so long as I'm where I need to be to do my job."

Because for him, rock star *is* a job.

"Okay, yes," I say. "Anything. Just. Yes!"

I'll take him exhausted—because he will be. And us having to do the whole goodbye thing at the end. We've never had more than an hour or two together at most, so if twenty-four is all we get, I'll consider it a bonus. No matter how much it'll kill me to let him go when it's over.

"Let me know your schedule," he says, "so I know what works on your end."

"Anything works on my end." Mom and Bryan's wedding, OHSET meets, Valentine's Day (yes, please!), whatever. "Just come!"

I'm not at all sure my folks (all three of them) will let me go to Australia over Spring Break for the Down Under leg of the tour. And anyway, I want this first time together after the wreckage we were in Tacoma to be about us. Not the band. And no security, no media, no stardom glitz. I want it to be in my everyday world with my everyday family. Where I get to know him as Liam, and he gets a break from his own image.

"And if nothing works," he says, "I've got two weeks open in March before we fly to Sydney."

"Okay."

"All right." He falls silent again, for longer this time. "So, em... somethin' for you to consider. And I'm totally open to this if it would help." Another pause. "If what I am and everything that goes with that isn't something you can live with...I'll submit my resignation to Michael and never look back."

My breath strangles, my phone all but falling from my fingers.

"It couldn't take effect for at least a year. But I told you I'd do anything to make us work, and I meant it."

I've stopped breathing.

Like, completely.

Once upon a not-so-long-ago time, I might have wanted this.

Convince me I matter more to you than anything else in your world.

But now...

"And I'm okay with it," he finishes. "If you decide it's something you want."

"Don't you *dare!*" explodes from me. "I'm serious, Liam! This is *not* up for discussion, not with me!"

"'Twas only a suggestion, so it was. Because I know you're concerned. And I've already lost you once to my eegit choices. I don't want to lose you again over something negotiable."

"It's *not* negotiable." I'm breathing hard. "You don't get to stop being *you!*"

"I don't have to be in a band to be me."

"Yes, you do! Because *you* want to be. And you're so killer good at it." *You're Liam O'Shannon, for heaven's sake!* "And when I said I wanted to be with you, I meant *all* of you"—*the you that lied to me, the you that's offering to trade your career for loving me, the you that's still my rock star*—"not just the parts you think I want."

"I'm good with that," he says. "But the offer still stands."

"*Never* going to be an option," I close him down. "Unless *you* choose it for yourself. And then you'd better discuss it with me first."

"Good with that, too."

"Because it's not like you get an option with me. I can't resign from being blind to make things easier for you."

"I love you blind," he says.

"I love you in a band," I say back. "So when the sun comes up, you'd better still be my rock star, knocking 'em dead in Prague."

"See what I can do," says Liam.

You'll do amazing.

Maybe they'll bring back *Me Without You*. Because I'm guessing now he can pull that one off, no problem.

"With live video streams, I hope?" I ask.

They do for some shows.

"If not in Prague," he says, "Budapest, to be sure."

"Good. Because I threw away my chance to see you in Tacoma, and I can't be in Prague or anywhere else you're going in Europe. And I want to feel like I'm there, even if I'm not."

"I'll see it's done, so," he says.

"Thanks."

"And the roses, too."

"I love roses."

"Might be a lot of 'em."

"I love you."

"More than anything, *mo chuisle*."

My voice goes quiet, my tears all dried up, and this endless ache —the one I'll live with every second we're apart—hollows me out inside. "Look at the stars for me, Liam. I'll be looking at you."

"Will you, now."

"Your band poster's going back up on my ceiling."

How I SLEPT at all is beyond me.

We talked for hours. Ended up on FaceTime, having fallen into who we were before Tacoma—me being me, and him being...Jamie. Different accent, slightly higher voice range, and no more hesitations as we talk.

But still. Jamie.

Who he's been all along.

And I was too blind—in the stupid, head-in-the-sand way—to see it.

In the morning, I have a copy of his letter on my computer and a Braille copy (yes, he's having one transcribed!) coming by post, as he calls it, so I can actually *read* it. And the DMs chiming in from his personal Insta account are loaded with described-for-me gifs— dancing cats throwing flowers and the words *thank you* and a teddy bear, heart in its paws with *I love you* flashing over its head, along with photos I can't see, but want, anyway. Of Liam (bleary-eyed, he said) on the Charles Bridge over the Vltava in Prague and outside his tour bus with his last name in Irish green above his head.

I put up the bridge shot as my lock screen and the bus shot as my home screen.

Load O'Shannon's music back into my phone.

Restore *Tear at the Walls* as my ringtone.

Sticky tape my poster to the ceiling where it belongs.

And when I come down to the kitchen for my before-I-catch-the-bus cereal, Mom doesn't need me to break it to her. Or maybe it's the black-and-metallic-green O'Shannon t-shirt I pulled from my bottom drawer and hauled over my head this morning.

"It's done, I take it," she says across the room at me.

"Yes." I stride over and hug her.

She holds me tighter than I'd expected.

"Looks like you got what you wanted."

"I did. Thank you," I say into her shoulder. "Liam says thanks, too."

"I had nothing to do with it."

"You didn't say I couldn't." I pull away, go to one cupboard for a bowl and grab the Braille-labeled All-Bran from another.

"It was a bit late for that," she says. "But there *will* be some ground rules on this, just so you know."

"We're good with that." I'm hauling milk from the fridge when Kaitlin shambles in from the dining room. "So he wants to schedule a Zoom chat with you and Bryan—you, too, Kait—if that's okay."

"Him, who?" She stops. "Wait—*Liam?!!* You *talked* to him?"

I *am* wearing O'Shannon gear, after all.

"Last night—"

She flies over, and I've barely slid the milk onto the table before she engulfs me in a massive hug. "I knew you wanted this. And that he did, too. Super happy for you both!" She lets me go and throws her words at the ceiling, "My gosh, we've got a rock star in the family!"

"Not so fast, Kait—" Mom starts.

"He wants to be Liam with us," I say, "not who he is to the rest of the world. Anyway"—I grab a spoon from the silverware drawer —"he's got a lot to apologize for, he says. But he wants to meet you, too. And he's looking for a time to fly over, just for a day or two—his tour schedule's pretty tight—so we can see each other, and you can meet him in real life."

"Wedding on deck, in case you've forgotten," Mom reminds me. Like I could.

"It'll be after that," I say.

"My concerns haven't changed," she adds.

"Give him a chance, Mom. He's not scary. Just an Irish lad who sings in a band and is in love with your daughter."

I OPEN my phone where Morgan can't miss seeing the screen.

Wait for it…

"You've got Liam on your lock screen??!!" she screeches at me. "And your home screen, too???"

Okay, maybe I shouldn't have done this on the bus. Heads have gotta be whipping our way, though I don't expect anyone to chase down the press with something so insubstantial.

"As of this morning, yes," I say.

"You *talked* to him???"

"For about four hours—"

She grabs me in a hug that rocks me hard and is full of screams and other attention-grabbing non-syllables. No matter how braced I thought I was, it's still a bit overwhelming.

All of it.

"Yes, *yes*, YES!"

"I didn't say how it turned out—"

"You've got his photo for your lock screen!"

"He sent it to me." I pull myself free and make a show of unzipping my jacket.

"And you're wearing his band gear! You're like happiness on steroids! Need you say more?"

Damien Johnson's voice hangs over the seat ahead of me. "So now you *are* seeing Liam O'Shannon? Like, officially?"

"Looks like it," Morgan answers for me. "You are, aren't you?"

"Yes—" The word's barely out before she hauls me in again.

"Do we get the story now?" Sierra Hanover pipes up beside Damien.

Morgan shoves me away. "You mean the one about Jamie Conway on the phone to her day and night with his fake accent and fake name and her not finding out who he really is till he's on stage at the Tacoma Dome and she figures it all out? Someone oughta make a movie!"

Epilogue

Dad texts me the night before the wedding.

Can we meet for coffee in the morning? Six-thirty, maybe?

Ghastly hour, but okay, sure.

He's my dad. And this won't be an easy day for him.

I'm on the front deck at six-twenty in black leggings and the diamond-patterned sweater I wore on Thanksgiving Day, my Columbia jacket zipped over the top, and Alexis harnessed and on leash. The January cold seeps through every layer I've got on, and the creek, swollen with winter rain, roars through its channel at the bottom of the yard.

Dad's Outback crunches in over the gravel. Alexis rises from her haunches, tail whapping my leg. I grab the harness handle.

The passenger door clicks open, then slams shut. My name reaches me across the wind.

"Jenny!"

I freeze in the endless silence that follows, my breath sucking in and staying there, my brain screaming *not real, not real, oh, my gosh, this IS real!!!*

"Liam!"

I drop the harness handle and bolt for the edge of the deck, knowing where I'll land and where he's likely to be. He catches me before my feet hit the ground. My arms go around his neck. I wrap my legs around his waist, find his mouth in nothing flat, and have at it.

You're here???

You're here!!!!

"Love you, *mo chuisle, grá mo chroí*," he says, all breathless, and kisses me again.

I surface for air—"Love *you!*"—and go back to kissing him hard.

In full view of my dad. And Mom and Bryan, no doubt still taking their morning coffee by the kitchen window.

Whatever.

"How are you even *here?*" I grab a breath. Kiss him again, my eyes spilling the happiest tears ever.

Praise be for not bothering with makeup this morning!

"I've got eighteen hours," he says. "Don't wantcha goin' to a weddin' without me, like."

He's in jeans and a heavy jacket. He's wearing glasses (contacts taken out on a red-eye flight?), and he smells of cologne and apple-scented shampoo and, well, everything that's *him*.

"Thank you, thank you, *thank you!*" I slide to the ground, my arms going around his waist, his hands on my face, his mouth still on mine.

Behind us, Dad clears his throat. "Coffee?" he says.

THE DAY GOES FROM HERE, in so many ways I would never have imagined.

Spending it with Liam O'Shannon.

In *my* world.

How he even got here, three weeks earlier than the scheduled February date, takes me all the way to the nearest Starbucks to fully understand.

Morgan was a huge piece of that, laying the groundwork for him with Mom and Bryan, and then my dad shortly after we got back together. And you'd better believe I'm going to be on that late-night run to PDX in seventeen-and-a-half hours!

But for now, I'm walking into Starbucks with my dad and Alexis and a rock star flown in from Barcelona.

All of it surreal.

A line to the counter, voices murmuring from all corners of an overflowing room. My fingers locked in Liam's—that perfect fit I remember backstage in Tacoma—waiting for someone to get a clue and hammer him with the obvious.

Nobody does.

The barista takes orders and names.

"Jonathan," Liam gives her in a flawless, American accent.

Recognition: none.

We take a table in the farthest corner we can find, and I'm struck with how right this is and how much we belong together—me and Dad with this guy who gets up on stage for a living, having macchiatos in a coffee shop and talking about trolling for steelhead on the Columbia River.

It sets the tone for the rest of the day.

Because who would have expected Liam O'Shannon to carry stuff from Bryan's Ranger into Dover Community Church and help set up tables and chairs for the reception? Or to suck in his breath when I walk out of the ladies' room in heels and my burgundy dress with the uneven hemline? Followed by both of us getting called out by Mom for too much PDA in the hallway. Or banter with Morgan (of course, she's here early) like they're old friends? Or Kaitlin like she's a sister? Or sit with me at the guest book table in a sweater and slacks, contacts in and his Irish on, disguising nothing?

He does get recognized, but not by everyone, and he rolls with it, chatting with whoever wants to and signing wedding programs and anything else they shove at him. We're so obviously a couple *that* doesn't miss getting commented on, either.

I'm wearing the Christmas gift—a heart-shaped pendant crusted with stones—he gave me beside the creek at my house. I'm told it's stunning. And my birthday gift—a gold bracelet with joined hearts and more stones—gets noticed, too.

"I wasn't sure what you'd like," Liam says as I open the box and explore the contents with my fingers. *"So I went with diamonds. Hope that's okay?"*

Okay???

Till ten seconds ago, I'd never had a diamond in my life. And this is like lots of them. Like full stones, not the little chips Morgan has in the monogram necklace her folks gave her last Christmas.

Like what you get when you've got a rock star boyfriend.

AND THE WEDDING ITSELF?

Short, simple, and exactly what it should be.

Even the parts that are bittersweet.

To his credit, Dad shows up for the ceremony, his game face on, and soldiers through it all, sitting with Liam and me, Kaitlin and Alexis (in her burgundy bow), Morgan, and my Grams from Seattle (who scolds Liam for taking three years to notice me before asking him to autograph her program). Even Tiffany, who swept me back into her life without hesitation, is here at my invite. I've hooked my fingers (the ones not laced with Liam's) around Dad's elbow, and I tighten my grip when Mom and Bryan go into their vows.

Her making the promise to him she failed to keep to Dad...

But much as I wish it could be Dad, I'd miss Bryan in my life should he suddenly drop out of it. We're getting along amazingly well these days. And I'm super grateful to him for giving me the courage to believe in second chances. Maybe he and Mom *do* belong together at this time in their lives.

Mom and I are working on making *us* better. She's still sketchy about the whole me-in-a-relationship-with-a-rock-star thing, but her barriers are coming down. FaceTiming with Liam has helped, and despite her ongoing concerns, she clearly likes him.

And Dad's finally ready (so he says) to look for someone to share *his* life with. I wish him the best, hoping for somebody who'll complement him the way Bryan does Mom, who'll fill the hole she left behind.

And Liam?

He's done nothing but prove himself to me since that moment he fell to his knees on the Tacoma Dome floor and told me he loves me. Beyond the money he pours into blind causes and getting the visually impaired into European, Australian, and Asian venues, he's immersing himself in my life (from a distance), with my family, and everything that goes with that.

And I'm getting to know his.

Leslie graciously accepted my apology for ending our friendship, and now treats me as though it never happened. We talk almost every day. And their mom (met via FaceTime) is super sweet and totally welcoming. As is Michael, who brushed off my non-response to his email as of no consequence.

I'm beginning, I hope, to fit in with them, closing the gap (a bit, anyway) between my world and Liam's.

Or maybe they're not so far apart, after all.

AND WHEN THE day is over, we go out into the deepening cold, walking the forest's edge, walled behind the church, hanging onto the moments running out from beneath us.

"Next diamonds I give you," Liam says, holding me under the stars, "go on your hand, just so you know."

"A bit soon for that, don't you think?"

"Not for me," he says. "But I'm okay with waitin', like. I'm deadly good at it."

"Thank you," I say, "for not giving up on me."

"Never." He tips my chin, and his eyes—those gorgeous teal ones I'm never going to see—are looking into mine, I know they are.

"I love you," I whisper.

"*Tá grá agam duit, mo chuisle,*" he says, just as softly. "Till I die."

He kisses me then, kisses me hard, and I'm kissing him back with my eyes closed and the blood pounding in my ears. And it's everything I remember from that night in Tacoma, but in a good way, an I'm-all-in-with-you way that goes beyond the moment and reaches down somewhere to the rest of our lives.

> *Waiting for you, waiting for me*
> *Is this the way we're always to be?*
> *Open the skies when I look through your eyes*
> *And see you waiting, still waiting, see me...*

~J. Liam O'Shannon

Acknowledgments

To my editors Julia King and Holli Anderson, acquisitions editor Staci Olsen, and proofreader Jared Lindsay along with Jason King and all the wonderful staff at Immortal Works Press—thanks so much for seeing the potential in this story and for putting *See Me As I Am* out into the world!

To my developmental editor Katie McCoach Lynch of KM Editorial—where would this book be without you? Thanks for choosing *See Me As I Am* as your RevPit 2019 winner and for all the hard work you put into making this story the best it could be!

To my beta readers Larissa Lopes, Cate Townsend, and Janet Wright—wow, what can I say? For all your ideas, encouragements, and pointing out the error of my ways, thank you beyond words!

To my family betas: husband Ed, daughter Jennifer, and son Kevin—you guys rock! Amazing job helping me sort through the mess of what this story once was and helping grow it into what it is now. Love you all more than words!

To my nieces Bridget Botts, Angie Fife, and Brittany Murray—thanks for reading earlier drafts and providing comments and suggestions.

Thanks also to my sister Pam Neumann and my nephew Ryan Weller for answering coffee/Starbucks related questions for this non-coffee drinker.

Special thanks to Tracy McGee for showing me her assistive technology and for taking me walking with her guide dog. Thanks also to Amy Flores for sensitivity reading this book.

To the amazing #WritingCommunity on Twitter, thanks for support, encouragement, and enabling *See Me As I Am* to be discovered. You've made all the difference in my writing career.

To my dear friend Julie DeForrest—thank you for years of support and your many prayers for this book to find a home.

To my Lord and Savior Jesus Christ—it's all Yours!

All locations in *See Me As I Am* are real. Author's license has been taken with backstage areas of Portland's Moda Center and the Tacoma Dome along with some tour scheduling details that better accommodate the plot line.

I'd love to hear from my readers! Contact me at www.cherylwanner.com.

A portion of my proceeds from the sale of this book will be donated to Guide Dogs for the Blind. Direct contributions can be made through their website at www.guidedogs.com.

About the Author

Cheryl Wanner is a YA author and long-time contributor to *Oregon Coast Magazine* whose passion for telling stories stretches back to her childhood. Besides crafting words into images and creating characters that won't let you go, she loves photography, music, and, of course, the Oregon Coast. She's a former host mom of exchange students from all over Europe and Asia. She and her husband have two grown children and live in the forests of northwest Oregon. *See Me As I Am* is her debut.

This has been an
Immortal Production